COMING IN
HOT

Other Books by Josie Juniper

Double Apex

COMING IN HOT

JOSIE JUNIPER

FOREVER

NEW YORK BOSTON

This book is a work of fiction. Names, characters, places, and incidents are the product of the author's imagination or are used fictitiously. Any resemblance to actual events, locales, or persons, living or dead, is coincidental.

Copyright © 2025 by Josie Juniper

Cover design and illustration © 2025 by Fernanda Suarez
Cover copyright © 2025 by Hachette Book Group, Inc.

Hachette Book Group supports the right to free expression and the value of copyright. The purpose of copyright is to encourage writers and artists to produce the creative works that enrich our culture.

The scanning, uploading, and distribution of this book without permission is a theft of the author's intellectual property. If you would like permission to use material from the book (other than for review purposes), please contact permissions@hbgusa.com. Thank you for your support of the author's rights.

Forever
Hachette Book Group
1290 Avenue of the Americas, New York, NY 10104
read-forever.com
@readforeverpub

First Edition: June 2025

Forever is an imprint of Grand Central Publishing. The Forever name and logo are registered trademarks of Hachette Book Group, Inc.

The publisher is not responsible for websites (or their content) that are not owned by the publisher.

The Hachette Speakers Bureau provides a wide range of authors for speaking events. To find out more, go to hachettespeakersbureau.com or email HachetteSpeakers@hbgusa.com.

Forever books may be purchased in bulk for business, educational, or promotional use. For information, please contact your local bookseller or the Hachette Book Group Special Markets Department at special.markets@hbgusa.com.

Library of Congress Control Number: 2025930322

ISBN: 9781538768990 (trade paperback), 9781538769003 (ebook)

Printed in the United States of America

CCR

10 9 8 7 6 5 4 3 2 1

For my mother. My first and best friend, first and best writing critique partner. You're my sunshine too—always an inspiration, always hilarious. "Bummer Sisters forever!"

1

ABU DHABI

DECEMBER

NATALIA

New York to London, London to Athens, Athens to Abu Dhabi. Nineteen hours in the air, and I'm exhausted. There are very few people in the hotel lounge, but maybe that's normal for nine p.m. on a Wednesday.

I pause in the archway, taking it all in. French pop plays too loudly over the speakers. The Sputnik-sphere lamps cast an intimate speckled glow. Bartenders glide back and forth, all agile charm. The air smells like toasted sesame and pricey booze.

I cross the room and lean against the bar, shooting another text to Phaedra.

> **Me:** Phae! Omg why aren't you answering??? This place is booked solid during grand prix week, so if you don't LET ME IN I'm going to have to sleep in the lobby.

2 **JOSIE JUNIPER**

I darken my phone and stuff it into my purse before signaling the bartender. He strolls over and leans opposite me with a gleaming white smile and an unsubtle once-over.

"How can I...*help you?*"

Oh my. He really put everything he could into that pause. "Bless his heart," as Aunt Minnie would say.

I point at the ice water he's just set down. "Thank you for this, but I might be here awhile. May I get some juice?"

He rubs a knuckle against his jaw, following the precise line of dark beard scruff. "Sure, beautiful. What kind?"

I offer a friendly shrug as my purse vibrates with a text. "Surprise me."

Of course the message isn't from Phae.

I can't get a break...

It's Josh, my (former) editor at the arts and culture magazine where I've been a staff writer for three years, before resigning via an email on Monday night.

> **Josh:** Did you seriously jump ship without notice and take a job with Auto Racing Journal? Or was it the thing about Shelby? You have to believe me, doll—we are NOT back together. I just need to move in again because it's less confusing for the kids.

My nostrils flare and I jab out a reply.

> **Me:** ARJ is a better salary, plus free travel. And I have an "in" with F1 because my best friend works for

Emerald. Shelby is welcome to have you—I don't need another married liar. Have a nice life, Josh.

A glass of magenta sludge is set before me. The bartender's lips curl in a flirty smirk as he drags a wrapped drinking straw suggestively between two fingers.

"Beetroot," he informs me. "You said to surprise you."

I flash jazz hands. "Surprise!"

"Beetroot is good for stamina. I drink it every day...so I can go all night."

I'm now apparently being seduced by the Dwight Schrute of the United Arab Emirates. What's next, karate moves?

Mercifully, someone at the other end of the bar catches his attention and he walks away.

Me: RESCUE ME, Phae. It's like a tank of piranhas down here.

Seconds later, he's back.

I'm about to snap at the Drakkar Noir–soaked Romeo mixologist when he sets a tumbler of fragrant bourbon down and tips a grudging nod toward the end of the bar.

"From the gentleman." He walks off without awaiting my response.

"Good lord," I mutter, prepared to send a crisp *No, thank you* to some lonely businessman who'll surely look like the Rich Uncle Pennybags Monopoly mascot.

Mercy.

4   **JOSIE JUNIPER**

At the far corner sits a complete smokeshow in a charcoal suit.

Tall as heck. Hair mostly pepper with just enough salt; wavy, with a widow's peak that makes him look like a classic film star.

Maybe midforties? I think. *Probably has a decade on me...*

His bone structure is angular, complexion outdoor-tan, and he has firm-but-tender lips that seem to say, *I'll tell you what to do, then reward you for doing it.*

He also isn't looking at me.

Huh.

I pick up the bourbon and bring it to my nose.

I like to say I know my bourbon because I grew up in Kentucky. But Auntie Min is a strict nondrinker, and I left for North Carolina at eighteen, so there goes that theory.

Glass near my lips, I look up. Gray Suit Smokeshow moves his aloof gaze in my direction. He raises his own glass—eyes smiling, mouth impassive—then looks away.

Who does he think is in charge here? What a smug jerk.

I set the glass down, ignoring him.

A minute later, charcoal gray drifts in like a storm cloud on my periphery. I can smell him, and if that isn't Neroli Portofino cologne, I'll eat my hat.

Please let his voice sound like it does in my head...

His right hand—oh God, what a gorgeous pair of hands—opens toward the liquor. "Would you prefer something else?"

His voice is heavenly—a deep, smoothly accented incantation. I feel it down to my toes.

"Bourbon served neat," I reply, not looking at him. "Good choice. Not chardonnay or something silly with an umbrella."

COMING IN HOT

He gives a rumbly chuckle, and I peek to see his smile. Boyishly asymmetric, single dimple on the left.

"What are you drinking?" I ask, picking up his glass and tipping it toward my face. The scent blooms into my nostrils, warm. "Ooh, cognac?"

"Mmm-hmm. Courvoisier—help yourself."

"Ah, we're sharing?"

He offers that whisper-light Mona Lisa smile. "I will certainly order you an untouched glass...if you're shy."

His eyes are dark as puddles of ink, and oh the things he's writing with them...

"Are you shy, kleine Hexe?"

I know only a smattering of German but am pretty sure this deliciously bad man just called me a little witch.

Without breaking our gaze, I take a sip of his cognac.

"Nope. Not shy."

｡ﾟﾟﾟﾟﾟﾟﾟ｡

As we take the elevator to his room, I'm surprised he doesn't try to kiss me. He leans in the corner, fingertips resting on the handle of my suitcase, eyeing me speculatively.

He looks vaguely familiar. Have I seen him before? Maybe just in my fantasies. Because he is exactly...my...type. Wow.

"Thank you for inviting me up for a drink," I tell him, my gaze angling away. I'm both excited and unnerved by his coy smile, and the challenge flashing in those dark eyes. "That loud music in the lounge was too much. I'm sure my friend'll text soon."

"Thank *you*," he counters, "for treating me to your company."

6   **JOSIE JUNIPER**

The accent is lovely—clipped and neat, with a soft, cool texture like a layer of fresh snow.

"You're German?" I ask.

The elevator eases to a stop and chimes.

"Austrian." He opens a hand to invite me to precede him into the hallway.

"What line of work are you in?"

We haven't exchanged names; the window closed on that halfway through a flirty glass of bourbon. It's clearly a game at this point.

"Management. And you?"

We walk to the end of the hall—double doors leading to the floor's biggest suite. He takes his phone out and taps it to unlock the door, then slides a finger along the screen to bring the lights up before ushering me in.

"Oh, I'm a writer," I say, keeping it as vague as he is.

He pauses in the doorway and gives me a guarded look. "What do you write?"

Ah. So he's cautious about journalists? Best to go with a little truth-stretching...

"I'm researching a novel." My mind scrambles to think of what I might be doing in the city if not attending the grand prix. "It's...about an archaeologist. There've been cool Bronze Age archaeology discoveries here." My cheeks heat with the lie.

He studies my face, his eyes smiling. "Interesting. You must tell me more."

Yikes. Hopefully not too *much more.*

The corner suite is stunning. My steps halt as I'm greeted by a wall of windows overlooking the marina, across an opulent living

COMING IN HOT

room with a bar. An archway leads to a bedroom with a kingly barge of a bed, mounded with gold pillows.

"Hell of a view," I breathe.

"Make yourself comfortable. Bourbon again?"

"I'd take a half pour."

I watch while he assembles my drink, then casually wander away—making him chase me a bit—after he hands it to me. Peeking around the bedroom doorway, I spot a huge en suite behind a frosted glass wall. The luxurious shower is open concept: multiple heads, fancy tile, big bench.

He appears beside me and raises his glass to mine. He has such leonine grace, every movement elegant and spare, like a dance. I can smell him again, and it's making me nuts—a combination of sleep deprivation, rebelliousness, and hormones.

Taking a sip, I nod at the en suite. "I hope the one in my friend's room is as nice. I'm looking forward to a shower."

His dark-as-sin eyes shine down at me. My focus moves from his eyes to his mouth in a blatant signal I'm willing to be kissed.

Would it be so terrible to spend a few hours as the bold, uninhibited girl I've never been, rather than a Good Girl suckered by the promises of cads like Josh?

The only promise I see in Charcoal Suit's eyes is a good time.

His gaze lingers on my lips too. A shimmer of heat goes through me.

"You're welcome to use my shower," he offers in that silky baritone. "And if you don't hear from your friend, this suite has a guest room."

I don't quite rise on my toes in anticipation of a kiss, but my feet are tensed and ready. He takes a step back and saunters to the bar, his posture easy, unhurried.

JOSIE JUNIPER

Oh, just look at this lovely creature—butter wouldn't melt in his mouth. He's going to make me work for it.

I'll admit... having been genetically blessed by my beautiful (though absent) parents, I rarely have to do the heavy lifting where seduction is concerned. I'm kinda loving that this is different.

I go to my suitcase and unzip it, fishing around for loungey satin trousers and a spaghetti-strap cami.

"Invitation accepted."

~~~~~~

The hot water is divine. I want to use the massage function on my tired shoulders but can't figure it out. I twist the showerhead, then search the walls for some kind of button.

Throwing a glance toward the parallelogram of light leading to the living room, I call out, "Um... excuse me?"

I open a towel in front of myself, stepping out of the spray.

He appears to the left of the doorway, on the other side of the frosted glass.

Shirtless.

"Can I help you, kleine Hexe?"

What am I getting myself into? We both know neither the offer nor the acceptance of a shower is innocent...

"Th-the, uh, the shower massage," I stammer. "Is it controlled by an app or something?"

There's a pause. I wonder if we're both thinking the same thing.

"Would you like company?" His voice is a rich rumble.

We are indeed thinking the same thing.

Lust taps an inquiring knock in the neighborhood between my legs. For a half minute, neither of us moves.

COMING IN HOT

I don't trust myself to reply. I pull the towel off, then sidestep into the open, unwinding the scrunchie holding my hair on top of my head. It fans over my shoulders.

He steps into the doorway, the hunger in his eyes full of unexpected warmth.

"You're stunning."

"Likewise," I manage.

His torso is a feast for the eyes—elegant slopes of gym-chiseled perfection, tapering from powerful shoulders to a trim waist sketched with a magnetic V-cut.

My shameless gawking elicits a chuckle.

"There's more," he assures me in an affectionate taunt.

The way he holds my gaze as his fingers go to the button on his trousers sends a shiver through me. He unzips and steps out of his clothes.

His legs are long and sculpted with the defined muscles of an athlete. My eyes slide over him and my nipples tighten as I zero in on a fantasy-worthy cock. He isn't erect—there's just enough blood flow to give it a lift—but already delectably big.

Phae, you're officially forgiven for not texting back.

I'm not short at five-nine, but he towers over me. He walks me slowly backward to the mosaic-tiled wall. Steam curls around us. His huge hands skate over my hips. Our eyes are inches apart, and his smile is so cocky that I'm not sure whether I want to bite his lip in annoyance or lust. The mint-and-cognac of his breath is a magnet pulling me closer.

Dammit, why isn't he kissing me?

I press against him, my breasts meeting his chest with its light dusting of dark hair.

JOSIE JUNIPER

He holds my face, almost reverent. "You're shivering. Should I stop?"

"I'm shivering because the suspense is killing me."

One of his hands spreads across my lower back and the other rakes into my hair as his lips claim mine, leisurely tasting, slanting over my mouth again and again. I moan into his mouth in encouragement. He cradles one of my breasts and with a thumb traverses the areola. I lean into his touch, and he dips to lick my nipple.

My head drops back. A trembling sigh escapes me as he cups the mound of my pussy. He gives my nipple a pinch with his teeth, then returns to kissing my mouth. As his tongue breaches my lips, his fingers slide into me, wet and effortless.

"The verdict is in," I manage through kisses. "It's a major yes. Do you have condoms?"

"Mmm-hmm." He steers me under the shower spray and combs both hands into my hair.

I'm all but boneless in his clutches, murmuring approval as he lathers his hands and proceeds to deliver a scalp massage so luscious, it bodes damned well for what he might accomplish below my waist.

As he rinses the suds from my head and they coast down my body, he teases his slippery hands everywhere, following the snaking white paths of foam. Gathering my hair, he wrings the water from it, then wraps me in a towel and picks me up bride-style, carrying me to the double sinks.

I twist to look at our reflection in the mirror, and my breath catches.

He's so handsome, and I look natural in his arms—it's hard to believe we're strangers...

Setting me on the counter, he opens a leather shaving case. Sure

COMING IN HOT

enough, there's the bottle of Neroli Portofino. He draws a string of three condoms out and tears one off.

I wrap my hand around him, and he sucks in a gasp through his teeth. His long-lashed, smoky eyes drop closed above those perfect cheekbones. In the light over the sink, I can see him vividly—the laugh lines flanking his eyes are beautiful.

I stroke him and draw the condom from his fingers, ripping it open with my teeth and rolling it on before pulling him to kiss me.

"Right here," I whisper. "I can't wait."

He gives my lower lip a bite. "I have to taste you first."

He opens the towel and pulls me to the edge, then kneels. Caressing my legs, he parts them and sets them over his shoulders, kissing a trail up to the juncture of my thighs. I grip the edge of the counter with one hand and comb my fingers into his thick, soft waves.

His tongue glides and gently probes. Parting me with his thumbs, he licks in slow sweeps. I push against him, and he draws my clit between his lips, sucking lightly. His long, skilled fingers slide into me again. My hands tense on the counter—my breath coming in gasps, whispering encouragement—as he intuitively finds the gentle, patient rhythm I need.

"Please don't stop...*exactlythatohmygod*..."

In another minute, the rush of climax chases and overtakes me, wringing out a breathy moan as a shiver snakes through me. When he stands and kisses me, I taste myself on his lips. Golden afterglow dances down my legs.

He's poised at the gate, and the muscles inside me beckon. I wrap my legs around his waist. He breaches me in a gorgeous thrust, then pauses to watch my eyes as I get used to his girth. A wicked smile dances across his expression.

JOSIE JUNIPER

"Are you going to come for me again, kleine Hexe?" He slides his hips side to side, grinding the wetness between us. "A quiet girl," he teases between kisses. "Do you live someplace with thin walls?"

He draws back fully and thrusts into me deep. My fingernails jab the muscles flanking his spine.

"You say you're not shy, but"—another deep thrust—"such restraint when pleasure takes you. Are you such a proper girl that you won't scream?" He rocks into me steadily, defining the perfect angle with every luscious thrust. "Are you quiet when you touch yourself, biting your lip in silence when you come on those pretty fingers?"

I'm half delirious with arousal, eyes closed tight. "Yes...yes, I do..."

"You won't let them make you scream—those boys who don't deserve you. A peach with a stone inside no man will crack."

My eyes fly open, and his look is a bold smirk. He's in my head as deep as the rest of me, and it makes my heart hammer in more ways than one. He lifts me and strides through the bathroom doorway, setting me on the high bed. Still inside me, he positions his legs outside mine, then begins to move again. A helpless whimper rises from me. The spiral of climax is winding tight again, and I follow it. The way my trapped legs are clamped around his cock is like nothing I've ever felt.

"Tha-that's...o-oh God..." I falter, my breath catching.

"Yes?" He kisses my lips with surprising tenderness, and it sends a shiver through me.

"It's amazing—oh God, *more...*"

He kisses me harder; I suspect he's close too. I moan into his mouth, commanded by his body, restrained by his muscular thighs

COMING IN HOT

as the tide nears. His big hands cradle my head, fingers entwined in my hair while his hips arc him into me.

"Scream if you want to," he murmurs near my ear. "No need to drown your fire."

"Oh God, I can't..." My hand drifts up, ready to cover my cries as the window of climax opens a crack and a glittering white rush begins to pour in.

My shriek surprises me. I move to muffle it, and feel him lace his fingers with mine, drawing my wrist to his lips.

Hearing my own voice like this is hot in a way I hadn't expected; I've created the soundtrack to my own erotic movie. I go all in with a shouted "*Yessss!*" as he finds his own release with a gritty cry, driving into me high and hard before dropping his head against my shoulder, panting.

After a minute, he kisses my neck and moves off me, pulling me sideways into one brief, firm embrace before getting up and walking to the bathroom. The sink runs, and I curl into a contented ball, cheek nestled against the rumpled duvet.

As the water turns off, I hear the unmistakable sound of Phaedra's ringtone—Elton John's "The Bitch Is Back"—from the other room.

"Oh, *now* you call..." I mutter.

I swing my legs over the edge of the bed and walk to the bathroom—passing him in the wide doorway, exchanging mildly bashful post-sex smiles—then pull on the loungewear I've left on the counter.

I go to my purse in the living room and call Phae back.

"Where the fuck are you?" she snaps.

"Excuse me? I should be asking *you*."

JOSIE JUNIPER

"I came downstairs, and the bartender said you split with some rando!"

I throw a glance at the bedroom and walk toward the smaller guest room, dropping my voice. "Well, I dumped Josh, and—"

"Oh, good call," she interrupts, raising her voice over the swell of background music in the bar. "A total wanker."

"So, you could say I celebrated that decision with...a sexual 'palate cleanser.' And *don't* be judgy about it."

There's a long pause. "*What the hell?*" Her laugh is shocked. "Nat, you wildcat! What's his name, and where's he from? Are you gonna see him again?"

I wince, knowing the flak I'd get for the no-names thing.

"He's, uh, English." I struggle to make up the most English-sounding name possible. "His name's Reginald...um, Throckmorton."

"Oh my God. *Sure!*" She brays out a screech of laughter. "You got played! 'Reginald fucking *Throckmorton*'? Guess that answers the question of whether you're gonna see him again."

"Shut up."

"If he's a Brit, maybe he's with Allonby Racing. They're on floor eleven; I'm on eight. Not the big suite at the end of the hall—that one's my boss, Klaus. I'm in the last room on the left before his. What floor are you on?"

I swivel to peek back again and nearly jump out of my skin to find "Reginald" standing in the guest room doorway. I mute the phone.

"*What floor are we on?*" I whisper.

"Eight." He gives me a cool smile and walks off.

My stomach drops, and a tide of panic floods over me as I realize why he looks so familiar.

COMING IN HOT

Though already a racing fan, I've been studying F1 history, strategy, and drivers since landing the new job. But somehow I neglected to recognize the Emerald team principal, billionaire 40 percent stakeholder Klaus Franke. To be fair to myself, Emerald's TP isn't their "public face"—that role is held by Phaedra's dad, charismatic owner Edward "Mo" Morgan. Mo loves to talk, and fans love to listen to his folksy, idiomatic sass, delivered in his signature Southern drawl and punctuated with quotable catchphrases. Klaus is more a "strong, silent type," in the background.

Oh God. What the hell have I done?

Apparently I've had a one-off with one of the most important non-driver figures in the sport that's about to become my life.

Goodbye, professional credibility.

I unmute the phone. "I'm not sure what floor I'm on."

Phaedra's pause all but screams, *I didn't want to have to ask this, but...*

"So, uh, he's probably another married one, right?" she ventures.

My face goes hot. "I don't know or care."

For the record, I very much *do* care about that kind of thing. But I've been suckered enough times that at a certain point, I started pretending marital status doesn't matter. Being seen as a home-wrecker somehow feels less mortifying than being cliché gullible.

I catch sight of myself in a mirror and glare at the face that made my stupid ex Josh once joke, *You're too pretty to be wasted on print media.* Glossy dark brown hair and fine bone structure I inherited from my mother, my father's full lips and long-lashed blue eyes.

Unfortunately, I may also have my parents' irresponsibility, despite working hard my entire life to prove otherwise.

I fought their legacy when I chose the debate team rather than

JOSIE JUNIPER

cheerleading in high school. I fought it when I kept up a consistent 4.0, studying on weekends instead of dating. I fought it when I applied to Queens U Charlotte instead of party school University of Alabama, where my peers were dying to go.

And finally... I fought it when I got offers from both *Vogue* and *Auto Racing Journal*, and spite-chose *ARJ* because Josh once said I should "get established in the fashion industry before you age out and lose your looks."

I've completely messed it all up, right out of the gate. What do I do now?

I need to get the hell out of the United Arab Emirates and hit the reset button on this disaster. After all, I don't *need* to be here—I won't officially start with *ARJ* until next month. This trip is just to chill with Phae and get the lay of the land.

No pun intended...

I'll head back to the States, I resolve, *and by March when the new racing season begins, Klaus will have long forgotten me.*

"Okay, um, I'll meet you at your room soon!" I tell Phae. As she's replying, I hang up and hurry back to the bedroom to collect my travel outfit from the en suite.

Charcoal Suit—*Klaus Franke*, oh my God—is sitting on the bed, propped against the headboard, perusing something on an iPad and wearing a businesslike scowl. He glances over the tops of a pair of reading glasses as I enter.

Flashing a smile, doing my best not to look panicked, I walk into the bathroom. My purple dress is folded on the counter, and on top of it—

Tell me that's not what I'm seeing.

A stack of hundred-euro notes is perched on my dress.

COMING IN HOT   17

I strangle the money in one fist and clutch my folded clothes against myself, marching back into the bedroom.

"What the hell is this?" I demand, holding the cash up.

He pulls his reading glasses off. Before he has a chance to say anything, I throw the money. It flutters around him, half of it hitting the floor beside the bed.

"You think I'm a prostitute?" I rage. "Are you out of your mind?"

"I don't assume one way or another when I meet women in this manner." He sets his glasses aside. "Money is useful to everyone. Consider it a gift."

"No thanks. *Asshole*."

I storm to my suitcase and cram my dress and shoes inside, then haul it to the door in bare feet. I wave my hand in front of the confusing door latch, assuming it must be motion-activated, then spin around with a growl.

Klaus is standing a few yards away.

"What's with this techno BS?" I demand. "Does it need to scan my retina? Are normal human doorknobs too pedestrian for your cool luxury suite?"

He walks over with maddening leisure and slides his fingers under the matte metal flap that opens the door, pulling it wide.

"I'm sorry for offending you," he says quietly. "It was a terrible blunder."

I wish he looked sarcastic, but his eyes are the tiniest bit sad.

"This," I tell him, summoning my inner badass and donning a frosty mask of disdain, "has been both the best and most disappointing lay of my life."

I drag my enormous suitcase out and stride to the elevator.

2

MELBOURNE

THREE MONTHS LATER

NATALIA

It's the evening after the season-launching grand prix, and I'm practically effervescent. Everything for my first race as *ARJ*'s lead reporter has gone perfectly. Interviews have been great, I looked confident in the paddock and press room, and now I'm enjoying the payoff: an evening with my best friend, indulging in the jet-set pleasures of a glamorous job in Formula 1.

I just hope I don't run into *him* off the clock.

It's fine, I reassure myself. *So what if you do? You have as much right to be here as he does.*

As for Phae, she's trying to be her usual nonchalant tomboy self, but I catch her checking herself out in one mirrored wall of the elevator as we make our way down to the hotel lounge to meet Cosmin Ardelean—Emerald's new hotshot driver, for whom she's the race engineer—for a drink.

"You look gorgeous," I reassure her.

COMING IN HOT

19

"Huh?" she asks, feigning bewilderment. "Oh. Like, the shirt? Whatevs."

I bought the slinky white shirt for her when I was in Paris, because she's always dressed like a twelve-year-old boy at math camp—ripped jeans, T-shirts with sciencey puns, sneakers—but I had to pretend I'd bought it for myself and it didn't fit right. I knew if I just said, "I picked this out for you," she'd scoff. There'd be a million reasons why the shirt was all wrong and I was a half-wit for having wasted my money.

"I don't give a fuck how I look." She jams both hands into her pockets. "As if I care what that narcissistic dickbag thinks."

My smile is sly, and I maintain a taunting silence.

"Stop it or I'll punch you in the tit," she warns. "Ardelean may be 'hot' to some people, but the only thing I like about him is the ten points he bagged for Emerald. This 'Let's have one little drinkie with him' thing was *your* idea. And thank God I'm *not* trying to catch his eye—I look like shit next to you. Your legs are a light-year long and you have a rack like Jessica Rabbit. Who are *you* trying to impress? Did Formula Fuckboy's charms during the post-race interview work that well?"

There's a brittle edge of jealousy in her tone, but if I point it out, she'll slaughter me. I tug the plunging neckline of my red velvet dress an inch higher.

The truth is, ever since Klaus spotted me at the press conference days ago, I've been nervous about running into him. His eyes that afternoon went forest-animal startled as he scanned the group of journalists and snagged on me.

Guess he remembers me after all, I thought.

I was rattled too. Usually Ed Morgan does the Emerald press

conferences. But to his credit, Klaus gave me some dynamic quotes in answer to my question for the panelists. No one would ever guess we had anything but a purely professional relationship.

For the past three months—since our "carnal collision" in Abu Dhabi—I haven't been able to stop thinking about him. I can't deny that was the hottest sex of my life, even if I was disgusted by his throwing money at me afterward. (Okay, technically he set it down neatly, and *I* threw it. But whatever.)

Something about the man is a puzzle I keep turning over in my mind. When the cyberstalking I did revealed him to be a tragic widower, my heart ached for him in a way that made me frustrated with myself for being such a damned cliché.

Beside me, Phaedra scowls down at the neckline of the white shirt, fussing with it like she can't decide whether it should show off more or less of her pale, freckled skin.

The elevator bell chimes and the doors glide open on the opulent lobby. Standing there—being venerated by a blonde so hyperfocused on him that I could perform an appendectomy on her sans anesthesia—is none other than Klaus Franke.

His obsidian eyes settle on Phaedra.

"Good evening, Schatzi," he greets her. With cool courtesy, he deigns to acknowledge me. "And...your name again was...?"

So that's how we're playing this?

Squashing down my annoyance, I straighten my shoulders and "reintroduce" myself.

"Natalia Evans."

COMING IN HOT

As revenge for having given her crap in the elevator about Cosmin, Phae razzes me about the interaction with Klaus, claiming I was blushing as we walked away. I make some excuse about not liking him because he was rude to me once; then I derail Phae's teasing by pointing out Cosmin, who's flirting with some racing fan across the bar.

We order drinks and make chitchat. It's obvious that Emerald's new driver is smitten with Phae, showing off for her. His surveyal of me is appreciative, sure. But more like the abstract admiration you'd show to a lovely piece of furniture that wouldn't look right in your house.

My phone buzzes in my tiny cross-body purse. I dig it out, hoping it isn't my boss Nefeli, inquiring about a story I have due at midnight.

> Forgive my poor manners earlier, kleine Hexe, but I assume you'd prefer Phaedra not know of our degree of familiarity.

My heartbeat is suddenly as fast and arrhythmic as a clumsy tap dance.

How the hell did he get my number? And so quickly…

Phaedra leans in to peek, and I stuff the phone into my purse. A burst of laughter and conversation from Cosmin and the fangirl draws her attention away.

My phone buzzes again.

> I'd like to apologize in person for my misstep in Abu Dhabi.

JOSIE JUNIPER

"Who's that?" Phae asks, swiveling my way again.

"No one. Wrong number."

When the phone lights up a third time, she snatches it from my hand and I have to pummel her to retrieve it. As I secure it in my purse, I spy the message:

> I understand if you're committed. But if not, meet with me so we can talk.

Does he mean "in a relationship" committed or "already have plans with friends"?

Phae gets grouchy over my "sneaky" phone messages and launches some mean little digs, making me feel stupid in the way that's always come naturally to her. We're low-key bickering when a merciful distraction arises as Cosmin starts to wander off with the cute girl Phae would never admit to seeing as her rival.

I sneak my phone out and reread the messages. Throwing a glance at Phae, I type a stealthy reply.

> I'll wait out front for exactly five minutes. Your window is 9:18-9:23.

▞▚▞▚

Phae isn't thrilled when I bail, but she might be playing it up. Making each other "the bad guy" has always been part of our Old Married Couple vibe, so I'm not worried. Once she gets back into her room with snacks and pajamas, I figure she'll be glad for some alone time.

When I go out to the motor lobby, Cosmin is there with the

COMING IN HOT 23

woman from the bar. She's drunkenly falling all over him, slipping a hand into his suit jacket while he holds her up. They don't see me, and I discreetly go sit on a bench at one side of the doors. They appear to be waiting for a car.

I check the time on my phone: 9:18.

The countdown begins.

A sleek BMW sedan pulls into the circular drive, but Cosmin makes no move toward it. He checks something on his phone and pockets it. The sedan with its dark-tinted windows sits, quietly purring.

The hotel doors open. A pair of pristine black monk-strap shoes stop to my right, and I slide my eyes in that direction without looking up.

Leisurely, I check my phone. "One minute to spare."

He chuckles. "You allowed me very little time."

Damn the sorcery of that deep voice of his...

I lift my gaze, and the sight of him is like an erotic version of static shock. It all converges on me in a second: the memory of his scent, the texture of his skin, the rock-hard curves of muscle under my fingertips, the delicious sound of every sexy thing he murmured into my ear that night months ago, the subtle rumbles of approval he made when I came.

He extends a hand. "Shall we?"

"Where are we off to?" I ignore his hand and saunter to the car.

"As yet undetermined. I'm thinking on my feet."

He opens the rear door for me, and I pause to lean on it. I wait, one eyebrow raised. He gives me a look of chagrin, mouth quirking on one side.

"I owe you an apology," he delivers in a remorseful sigh.

JOSIE JUNIPER

"How much is *that* worth? More or less than a thousand euros?" I sit carefully—my dress daringly short—and pivot to swing my legs in, scooting over to make room. Klaus gets in and shuts the door.

"Would you like to dine?" he asks. "Have you been to Attica?"

I can't suppress an unladylike snort of disbelief. "*Attica*? Oh sure, every day. Unless this car is Marty McFly's time-traveling DeLorean and you're going to book a reservation six months ago, good luck."

"I have a standing reservation during the grand prix weekend," he says with amusement. "My assistant likely *did* make it six months ago."

"Thanks, but I'm not hungry. A fancy dinner would be wasted on me."

"Nothing could ever be wasted on you, kleine Hexe."

I hide the shiver that goes through me at the sound of the pet name I haven't heard out loud since we were naked. I clear my throat and turn forward, examining the motionless, precisely groomed back of a male head—the driver.

"We could go for a walk, I guess," I tell Klaus.

If we're walking, I won't have to look at him.

The thought of being across a table from this man, staring at his tumble of soft, silver-touched wavy hair, his shapely lips, his flashing eyes...I don't think I could take it.

"A stroll it is. Perhaps the beach?"

I'm about to agree—I was raised to be reflexively accommodating—when I decide to just be myself. "You know where I like to walk most? Neighborhoods with houses, so I can see in the windows. It's like...dozens of miniature reality TV shows. People are interesting."

COMING IN HOT

His dark eyebrows dart up. "I'd enjoy that very much, watching these small 'reality shows' with you."

Klaus directs the faceless man in the front seat to find us a neighborhood with walking-friendly streets. The driver spends a minute perusing a map on his phone, then takes off.

It's late enough on a Sunday night that traffic is easy, and soon the car pulls up curbside to a winding neighborhood road flanked with small homes. Klaus climbs out, then opens the door and holds it for me, politely keeping his eyes averted as I struggle to stand without my dress slithering up to my waist. The evening breeze is balmy with the scent of eucalyptus trees and pavement.

Klaus offers an elbow. After a pause to consider, I take it. Immediately I'm struck by the warmth of him radiating through the fabric—there's something so personal about it. We wander slowly, passing through two pools of streetlight before either of us speaks.

He lays a hand over mine in the crook of his elbow. "My gaffe the night we met in Abu Dhabi...it's no excuse, but I must clarify that this habit—the giving of money—has never been a reflection on the women. It's far more the case that..." He looks up at the city-light-tinged sky. "I sometimes find it difficult to trust that a woman is interested in me for non-monetary reasons."

"Oh, hush. I'm not buying that you don't recognize you're objectively hot."

"It may surprise you to hear that the money is rarely declined. You're the only person who has been offended—"

"*Hurt*," I cut in.

"Hurt, yes. It has shamed me, realizing there may have been *many* women over the years who were hurt or offended but didn't call me out as you did."

I pull my arm from his. "I wasn't insulted at being mistaken for a sex worker. I don't judge, and sex work is *work*. But you implied I might've been in it for a reward. That my enjoyment was...performative. I'd have been less upset if it hadn't been *good* with you. Like you understood more than just my body."

There's no mistaking the ripple of sorrow that crosses his expression at my words. "I felt that too. You may not believe me, given the circumstances." His left hand faintly moves toward me; then he pockets it—I'm not sure if he's trying to seem aloof or trying not to touch me. He clears his throat. "It was an amazing evening."

I want to agree, but I want to punish him even more.

He's making it really hard to keep hating him.

"I knew...why Sofia cared for me," Klaus continues, tentative. He tries for the comment to land lightly, but it can't *not* fall unruly and broken as a dropped sack of groceries. It's interesting that he doesn't specify who Sofia is, like he knows I must've looked him up. It's then I realize he's surely looked me up too.

"There was an ease in my essential self being...*remembered*," he goes on. "We were, to each other, always the people we'd known since our youth. Now so much feels like pantomime." He shakes his head. "Wealth changes everything, makes it harder to let anyone in. But I'm the person my life has made me: a businessman, head of a hundred-million-dollar racing team, a widower, a pragmatist."

I don't know him well enough yet to tell if his candor is vulnerable honesty or manipulation.

He studies me sidelong. "I don't suppose I have any chance with you?"

"Not a prayer, bub." I do my best to make it lighthearted—a

joking tone like a Prohibition-era wise guy. I need to act as if I don't recognize what's at stake. The moment feels bigger than both of us, bending time with its gravity.

We're quiet for a full block, watching lit windows as we pass. Mostly it's just illuminated curtains, walls, furniture. But in a few houses there are visible people: a standing man holding a beer and talking to some friends who sit on a nearby sofa, a woman carrying a laundry basket, a stocky man on an exercise bike watching TV.

"You won't forgive me for what happened," Klaus says, resigned.

"I *do* mostly forgive you for the...the misunderstanding. But I still wouldn't date you. We already made things weird by coming in hot like that, jumping right into bed. Plus, dating you would be unprofessional. Way too much chance for conflict of interest." I risk a glance at him. "Though I do find you very attractive." There's an unexpected ache in my chest. "And despite what you may've been led to believe by what happened in Abu Dhabi, I don't do the friends-with-benefits thing well. It's not where I am in life."

As I step off a curb in the dimness between streetlamps, my heel goes sideways. I grip Klaus's arm hard with a gasp, and he's suddenly like a mountain—the most solid thing I've ever felt, *impossibly* immobile, steadying me. Catching my breath, I have the fanciful sense that if a tornado roared past, I could hold his arm and not fly away.

His eyes in the darkness are touched by twin flares of reflected light. He watches me with a completeness, as if we're the only two people in the world. The thumping hum of music from a nearby house could be a faint radio transmission from a distant galaxy.

He brushes the backs of his fingers against my cheek, and I lean into the touch. I wonder if we're both too proud to initiate the kiss that is already there, a spectral thing between us, like a little soul waiting for life to be breathed into it.

God, his lips—I can't stop looking at them. What kind of idiot would I be if I stepped over a line I drew minutes ago? I can't kiss him. I can't...

I grab his silk necktie, holding it light but sure.

Would another kiss be so terrible? Maybe it won't be as good as I remember.

He gathers my hair and winds it around his hand once with the same cautious firmness I'm using to hold his tie. He's so close, I can see the pattern of his laugh lines, natural and beautiful as striations in marble.

"This is unwise," he murmurs with a troubled frown.

I give a small nod. "Let's do it anyway. Just one more—to say goodbye."

Heat floods me as his mouth makes contact in a glancing pass, sliding along my lower lip, tender and exploratory. I open to him, pulling on his necktie. An involuntary whimper rises in my throat. My heart hammers as he spreads his hand at the back of my head, cradling me, and his tongue sweeps mine in a welcome trespass.

We leave our hands where they are, gripping each other at only one point as our lips feast, re-angling, then closing in again. I wait for his free hand to connect, wanting it everywhere, anywhere: skimming over a breast, surfing the curve of my hip, grabbing my ass and clutching a handful, commanding. But he holds back; the only clue to his emotion is the way his fist occasionally tightens in my hair.

COMING IN HOT

Finally he rests his forehead against mine before pulling himself upright and opening his eyes. He releases my hair, smoothing it over my shoulder.

"I will miss you," he says.

I know it's what he *should* say. But that was before I remembered how everything about his touch is right, stunning, as real as the gravity pulling us together. I can't let him know how his words disappoint me.

Dammit, I don't want to punish myself for allowing the kiss, don't want to engineer a wall between us…but I have *to, or I'll change my mind…*

"Klaus?"

"Talia."

My eyes squeeze shut. The sound of the diminutive he's so naturally chosen for me hits like a wave capsizing an insignificant boat. Gradually I open my eyes.

"The woman who was with you tonight—where is she now?" I ask.

He moves a lock of hair off my shoulder, baring my neck.

"There's no answer that won't make me sound bad." Trying for a smile, he adds, "You'll recall I had a five-minute window, which a certain imperious queen granted. If I say I sent the woman off without another thought, I'm a cad. If she's waiting for me in my suite, I'm far worse."

I nibble the inside of my lip, studying him. "Maybe there's no nice answer, but there *is* one that's the truth. So which is it?"

He takes my hand, and I let him. His thumb coasts back and forth over my knuckles before he releases me. "She's still there."

I focus on a crack in the sidewalk, aligning the toe of my shoe with it as I determine how I feel. I try to work up some anger, but it seems forced.

"Is she, um..." I twist the thin strap of my purse. "You know..."

"A 'working girl'?" he supplies.

I nod.

"I don't know. We'd got no further than a bit of conversation in the lounge."

Ah. And there's my anger. Conversation in the lounge...

It feels worse than the thought of him having sex with her. I wonder if he asked her too, as he did with me: *Are you shy?* If he shared a sip from his Courvoisier and gave her the same wicked smile. If his charming patter with me in Abu Dhabi had been from a playbook of well-tested pickup lines, and once again my heart was swindled by a beautiful scoundrel.

My brain taunts me for my naivete:

Didn't he tell you as much when he confessed that he gives cash to them all? You're not special, Natalia Jane Evans. He's told you what kind of man he is, but you're not listening.

I wrap my arms around myself. "I'm getting cold. We should go."

I start down the sidewalk the way we came. Klaus has one arm half out of his jacket, ready to offer it to me, when I stop him.

"I don't need that." I lift a hand, warding him off, before knotting it into the cradle of my arms again. Manufacturing a blithe smile—because if he knows how upset I am, it'll give him an opportunity to change my mind—I tell him, "I wouldn't want to keep you from your date."

3

BAHRAIN

TWO WEEKS LATER

KLAUS

My preference has always been to watch races from the garage, but with Edward Morgan—Emerald team owner and my dearest friend—out on medical leave, and Phaedra and Cosmin practically at each other's throats, my presence is needed on the pit wall to help keep things stable. Facilitating rapport between team members is a big part of my job; at times I feel I'm half therapist.

Phaedra has been terse over the radio but grudgingly professional, and Cosmin is having a strong race. The Bahrain circuit is engineered for excitement, with more opportunity for overtaking than is typical in newer tracks. Sakhir is windy and dusty, which is always a challenge. But the track is a favorite of many racers, with long straights, tight hairpins, thrilling twists, and challenging high-speed corners.

Having started in eighth place, Cosmin has fought his way up to third. Emerald's other driver, Jakob, is holding steady in P6. A podium for Cosmin so early in the season would be quite a coup.

He roars down the straight after turn 13 with Akio Ono close behind, then brakes early into turn 14—a good strategy that will allow him to pick up speed before the quick but gentle turn 15, then pour on power for the main straight leading to the finish line.

Ono attempts an overtake at the apex of 14, but Cosmin brushes him off easily. I glance at Phaedra, her face lit in an open smile, lips parted to deliver words of encouragement, which go undelivered as Cosmin's car slows and Ono unexpectedly charges past. It happens so quickly that we are all in shock as a podium finish transforms before our eyes into a still respectable yet disappointing fourth.

"Ce pusca mea...la naiba!" Cosmin snarls over the radio. "No, no, *no!* What the shit?"

The broadcast version is surely one long bleep tone at his flurry of bilingual cursing. From the look on her face, I expect Phaedra to join in with a volley of her own blue language, but she retains a surprising equanimity.

"It was a solid drive, Cos," she reassures him a bit crisply. Her keen eyes rake over the data on the monitors as she speaks, trying to determine the car's sudden loss of power. "We'll take the points."

His anguished groan tears over the comms. "What fucking happened? That was *mine.*"

"*Looking into it,*" Phaedra snaps. "Let's focus on the positive."

There are smiles and backslapping all around on the pit wall, everyone celebrating the twenty points gained by our two drivers.

COMING IN HOT

Glancing over at Jakob's race engineer—jovial Alfie, known for his almost satiric British pleasantness—I wonder again whether I should have asked him to work with Cosmin this season and had Phaedra switch to Jakob.

Both drivers, I'm starting to suspect, need something other than what they're getting. Jakob has become cautious since his marriage and is driving so conservatively that a more energetic race engineer might be an asset. And Cosmin is feisty enough that he could benefit from working with someone who might ignore his "noise" in favor of the signal.

The worry that I've made a poor call, along with concern for Edward's health, is getting the better of me...but I cannot possibly show it.

Perception is all.

The face of Emerald must remain polished—it's imperative not only to team morale but also to the confidence of investors and sponsors.

Knowing that, ultimately, every failure of the team—from the most overarching principle to the smallest detail—begins and ends with me...it is a heavy weight. When Sofia was alive, it was a comfort to remove my armor in her presence. It's been five years since I've felt I could be myself entirely. The closest I come is in the ease of Edward's affable demeanor.

I'm committed to the team; it has become my family. But a weariness is setting in. Losing Sofia, and enduring the added misery of my grief being public, has already made me question whether I'm happy as Emerald's team principal. This year in particular, the stress of the job combined with worry for Edward has me restless, dissatisfied, and feeling trapped.

If Edward dies, I think, *it will render me an emotional island with no landing spot for visitors.*

I recently saw a series of photos in an art gallery: trees that have "swallowed" inanimate objects by growing around them—signs, fences, chairs, bicycles. I stared at them for a long time, unable to shake the sense that my life has "grown over" and absorbed essential parts of me, trapped in the grip of something organic, yet rigidly unforgiving.

▪▪▪▪▪

The Monday meetings the next day feel longer than usual. Our newest sponsor, Basilisk Tech, is already proving challenging. When my car pulls up outside the hotel, it's nearly eleven at night. I'm exhausted and haven't eaten since noon.

I'm saying good night to the driver and climbing out when my phone rings. After running a tired hand down my face, I swipe the call open and stride into the hotel lobby.

"Clara," I say grimly. "What now?"

Immediately I feel bad for my sharp tone. Emerald's commercial officer is every bit as tired as I am and wouldn't call so late if the issue weren't critical.

I add an apologetic sigh. "Forgive me. I'd sell a kidney for a proper night's sleep."

When was the last time my nomadic life afforded me truly restful sleep? I live out of hotels—different cities, beds, women. Lately, I often find myself reminiscing privately about the simplicity of a time when the word "home" still meant something.

"I don't suppose you've seen what Basilisk just posted?" Clara asks.

COMING IN HOT   35

"No." I wander toward the lobby's seating area and lean against the arm of an overstuffed chair, closing my eyes—half in concentration, half in exhaustion. "What happened?"

Spurred by the rumble of my empty stomach, I glance across the lobby at the archway leading into the lounge. I'm jolted alert as I spot Natalia Evans at a table with an auburn-haired man who has his back to me.

Clara's words pull me away from the scene.

"They just posted they want to break up with Emerald," she says, "because, quote, 'We aren't pleased with their potential or professionalism. Will explore sponsorship opportunities with more competitive team.' Hashtag 'DontMesswiththeDragon.'"

I set the phone down for a moment and scrub my face with both hands, at my wit's end. "Sohn einer Hündin! Der mist..." Picking the phone back up and stifling my frustrated groan, I shift to sit in the chair, leaning my elbows on my knees. "What the hell does he think he means with this Schwachsinn?"

It's a rhetorical outburst, but the very literal Clara answers, "It certainly *isn't* a performance concern. A 'more competitive team' means 'one willing to overlook the watchdog report, take Basilisk's thirty million, and roll out the livery with the dragon logo next month in Shanghai.' They're preemptively slagging us off to cover their arses. Which means they're hiding dirt of their own. Should we call Mo?"

"Edward doesn't need to deal with this." I nearly make the mistake of including the words *when he's ill*, but cut myself off just in time.

"Well, all right. You know what you're doing..." Clara says uncertainly.

I slide one hand to the back of my neck and massage the tension there. "Tell me your concerns, Klärchen," I invite in an easy tone.

"Bit of a triple-decker shit sandwich, isn't it?" she replies. "The biggest exporter in what may be a grand prix host country in two years' time? Basilisk would have been a feather in our cap—but obviously not if they're compromised. Still, losing them leaves a massive hole in the budget. And we've a duty to inform the FIA of what we learned, but few will thank us for damning intel that affects a race location—we all know how much everyone loves a bearer of bad news."

She audibly swallows some liquid, and the musical sound of ice clinking is Pavlovian—suddenly I'm dying for a drink. I push to my feet and head across the lobby into the lounge. My gaze glides over Natalia as I pass, but she doesn't see me. Her expression is put-upon. I can't help noticing there is an uneaten plate of food before her, but nothing in front of the man sitting in the other chair.

Not a date, then? Just someone disturbing her meal?

"Let's focus on hard facts and not borrow trouble for now," I say calmly to Clara. "Our budget will take a hit—not insignificant, but manageable. Next issue?" I briefly mute my phone to order a Courvoisier once I've stepped up to the bar.

"Next," she continues, "is figuring out who tipped off Basilisk about our meeting tonight. It had to have been someone on our team for them to find out so fast and make this post."

I hide my frown in the tulip glass the bartender sets before me. Breathing in the liquor's warmth, I take a generous sip.

"Let's meet tomorrow," I instruct Clara. "It won't benefit us to

COMING IN HOT

panic tonight. But we *will* figure this out and deal with the perpetrator accordingly."

Swiveling discreetly to look back at Natalia, I note that she's folded her arms, posture closed. The man across from her, I can see from this angle, is Alexander Laskaris, a fellow journalist from her magazine. He leans his elbows heavily on the table and Natalia grabs for her wineglass before it tips. She scowls and says something, and Laskaris attempts to touch her under the chin as if she were a pouting child.

I turn back to the bar. "Emerald will get through this, Klärchen," I tell Clara. "The repercussions of Basilisk as a sponsor would be far worse than the hit to our budget if the watchdog report is accurate. And if investigation reveals that the human rights problem is not confined to *one* company in the host country?" I rub my eyes again. "It detonates into a scandal."

Additionally, there will be far rougher waters ahead for the team if Edward Morgan is sick, which my intuition tells me he is. The look in his eyes before he flew to Switzerland to see the doctor...it was something I recall seeing in Sofia: a sense of resignation that said her body intuited that things were dire before it was confirmed.

I sign off the call and tuck my phone into a pocket, grimly nursing my drink, one eye on Natalia. Her gaze snags on mine, and she lifts one hand in acknowledgment before looking away. Finishing my cognac and tucking a ten-dinar tip under my glass, I push off the bar and head toward her table.

Laskaris rests with his chiseled chin on one hand, the picture of affected ease, as I walk up. I hear the tail end of his story, monologuing at Natalia.

"But, you know..." His wink is sly. "That's a joke people only get if they went to Saint Paul's. Or if they're just fans of John Milton. *The poet*," he adds.

"Glad you clarified," Natalia deadpans. "I thought you were talking about John Milton the plumber, who installed my aunt's garbage disposal."

I stop a meter from the table, and she looks up—lips parting to speak, shoulders straightening on an intake of breath. Laskaris delivers me a sulky glare at the interruption.

"I don't blame you for starting without me," I tell Natalia, sketching a wave at her untouched plate of what looks to be artichoke dip and sliced baguette. "Apologies for my tardiness. Meetings ran longer than expected."

It's a bluff, and a risky one—we've not spoken privately since the nighttime walk in Melbourne two weeks ago, when she parted from me cold and wounded, even after the unwise kiss we weren't able to resist. But Natalia's jewel-blue eyes shine now as she picks up the metaphoric baton I've passed.

"No worries. I haven't even taken the first bite yet." Shifting her focus to Laskaris, she says, "Sorry to give you the heave-ho."

"Oh, shit. Right." He pushes the chair back and stands, conceding the place to me. "Wasn't aware you had a date, Evans."

"It's business," I tell him coolly, taking his spot. I lift a finger at a passing server, gesturing toward the bar, silently communicating that the bartender knows my drink.

"Alex, I'm sure you know Mr. Franke?" Natalia asks. "Emerald's TP."

"Of course." Laskaris extends a hand, and we exchange a terse shake in which he applies 50 percent too much pressure.

COMING IN HOT

A mischievous part of me wants to say, *We've never met, in fact,* but I resist the urge to humble him.

"Well, then..." Laskaris shoots a stiff smile at Natalia. "Reckon I'll see you in Shanghai, Evans."

He saunters off, and Natalia rotates her plate a quarter turn, picking up a bit of baguette. She glances after him, murmuring, "Not if I see you first, bucko." Wielding a short butter knife, she scoops into the artichoke dip and places a dollop on a bite of bread. "I suppose you think you really rescued me there," she states, eyes on her task.

"Did I not?" I ask with amusement.

She lifts an arched eyebrow, placing the bread into her mouth and chewing. After dabbing each corner of her lips with a cloth napkin, she shrugs. "I was fine. But you got rid of him faster, so thanks for that."

I stretch my legs beside the small table, crossing them at the ankles. "Alexander Laskaris is a good-looking man," I gently tease. "Wealthy too."

She rolls her eyes. "Wealthy *family*. He's a nepo-baby clown, not my type, and such a shameless sex-pest that William Hill is probably offering odds on when he'll get canceled. I've only been at *ARJ* a few months and he's already asked me out twice. Annoying."

The server comes and places a new glass of Courvoisier before me. Natalia eyes it, then prepares another bite of food.

"Your usual cognac?" she inquires casually.

I'm flattered that she remembers. The image returns to me: that night in the Abu Dhabi lounge, months ago. Natalia sampling

40 **JOSIE JUNIPER**

my Courvoisier before slowly pushing it back my way. The way I deliberately rotated the glass so my mouth covered the red imprint of her lipstick before taking my own drink, our eyes locked.

"Shall we share it again?"

Her glare is chilly, brief. "No thanks."

I sip my drink, giving her time to eat without an interrogation. I can tell she's had as taxing a day as I. My stomach growls again, and though I'm sure she can't hear it over the music in the bar, she scoots the platter a few inches my way.

"We can share this, though," she offers. "Here, dig in."

"Thank you." I tear a strip of crust off a baguette slice and plunk it into the ramekin, then chew it. "How are you finding Bahrain?"

"It's not Paris," she replies, "but what is?"

I smile. "Paris."

"Smartass." Her tone is indulgent, which encourages me.

"No trouble whilst here?"

"Work troubles?"

I nod.

She takes a deep drink of her wine. "Nope. International journalist is definitely a different animal to working at a literary magazine, I'll admit. But I got some pointers from Phaedra about the travel part. Photo ID and press credentials on me at all times."

"Smart."

"Also—" She lifts her left hand, displaying a simple gold band. "From my pretend husband. Oh, and..."

She taps her phone, awakening the lock screen to display a photo of a man with a wholesome catalogue-model grin. He stands in blue jeans and a flannel shirt, an ax resting over one

COMING IN HOT

broad shoulder. On his left, a pile of firewood, on the right, a brown Labrador.

"Hubby," she says.

I twist the phone upside down to view the picture. He looks a bit like me—dark hair with some gray, over forty, tall.

The screen darkens. I slide the phone back toward Natalia. "You have a type."

"Don't flatter yourself."

"Did I say the type might be *me*, kleine Hexe?"

She frowns, her nostrils flaring, then tucks the phone into her purse. As she reaches again for her butter knife, I intercept her left hand, curling her fingers over my own and surveying the little "wedding ring."

"Hmm, your imaginary husband must be a pauper. You deserve far better."

She gives me a sardonic look. "Yeah, well. Not a ton of money in lumberjacking."

I skim a thumb across her knuckles, then release her fingers. There is the briefest pause before her hand slips from mine, as if she too is grieved to break our contact.

"Who is it—in the photo?" I can't help asking.

She chews and swallows the bite of bread in her mouth. "Some random guy I found on Google images. I've named him Ethan. He kinda looks like one, don't you think?"

"I'll trust you on that. You're the writer." I take another piece of bread and tear it in half before folding and dipping it. "I suppose you've dreamed up a full history."

"Oh, heck yeah. You know me."

After saying it, Natalia freezes momentarily with her hand

en route to the artichoke dip. She meets my eye as if to check whether I'll offer a comeback. In truth, we know each other both quite intimately at this point and...not at all.

I register the faint pink of her blush and give her an out while focusing on the food. "Tell me about Ethan. I love a good story, and after your confession in Melbourne—how you enjoy watching and imagining the lives of strangers—I have every confidence you've generated a creative narrative for your beloved husband."

She finishes the last inch of her wine. "We've been married six years. He got me Sparky—that's the dog—as a puppy for our first anniversary. He went to college for three years because he was planning to be an architect, but his father got sick and Ethan had to drop out and go back home to rural Oregon to take over the family lumber business."

Hearing Natalia's mention of the sick father, I wonder if Phaedra has told her about Edward's headaches or his trip to Switzerland to see a specialist. But Natalia's mood is so light, spinning her little fiction, that I can't imagine she's borrowed a sorrowful detail from her friend's life.

"We got married in front of the old sawmill. Super rustic. Charming."

"Indeed," I agree.

"The wedding cake was a zucchini cake, decorated with wildflowers."

I emit a surprised half-laugh and nearly choke on a bite of food. "Isn't that...it's a vegetable, yes? A courgette?" At Natalia's nod, I ask, "Do people make this into *cakes*, truly?"

"Good lord, you've never had zucchini cake?"

"Thankfully not. Though I enjoy steamed courgette with fish."

Natalia rolls her eyes. "You would. So healthy."

She plucks up the last baguette slice and surprises me by flipping it lightly at me, discus style. I catch it easily and tear it in two, offering half to her.

We each eat a final bite of bread and dip. Tired as I was an hour ago, I now feel almost radiant with energy. A thought arises: *This is what it was like to remove your armor—do you remember?* A needle of guilt over the small disloyalty to Sofia pierces me. My smile falters for a moment before I rally.

"What else?" I prompt Natalia. "Where was the honeymoon?"

"Mmm, good question," she says around her food, a hand over her mouth as she speaks, then swallows. "We didn't travel. Just spent a week at the family cabin in the mountains. Donated the honeymoon cash to charity. Ethan's a giver."

"As it's said: happy wife, happy life," I quip.

I take another sip of cognac, watching Natalia as she watches me. Sorrow plucks at my chest as a realization asserts itself: *As relaxed as I feel with this woman, I'll never risk a connection. There's too much I couldn't share with her.*

Not only the small daily details that might spell disaster for the team in the hands of a journalist—such as Edward Morgan's health or the sponsor problem—but the simple fact that I'll never stop missing my wife.

No one should have to compete with a ghost.

I swirl my tulip glass, fumbling to pick up the thread of conversation. "What charity did you and Ethan choose to enrich?"

She squints one eye in thought, and something about the gesture is so natural and charming that I wish I could kiss the small crow's-foot crinkle above her cheekbone.

44 JOSIE JUNIPER

"Um, something for children? Ethan adores kids. We're going to have three or four."

"Quite the full house." I swirl the cognac and peek at Natalia. "Is that part fiction? Do you want children?"

There's hesitance in her expression. "I don't know. Maybe."

I move the glass idly, examining the way the candlelight gilds the amber liquid. For some reason, I'm afraid to look at Natalia. "You've plenty of time to decide," I say, my brightness forced. I lift the glass in a toast. "To you and Ethan."

Her lips part, then close as she searches for what she wants to say. "How come, uh…you never had kids?" she asks.

"*Never?*" I return with a blithe smile. "I'm only forty-five, kleine Hexe."

"Oh—of course…" The abashed words tumble out.

I lift a hand to reassure her. "I'm joking. The truth is, we tried for many years."

"Ah." She nods gravely. "Fertility treatments and all that?"

"No. I wish I'd insisted upon it, because we learned later—*too late*—that our lack of success was due to a very slow-growing cancer. Endometrial. But Sofia wanted things to be 'natural.' She had many superstitions. A bowl of pine cones under the bed—silly things like that. It seemed harmless." I tip back the last of the cognac. "Until it killed her, of course."

I've flown the conversational plane into the side of a mountain with the comment and know it immediately.

Curse my bitterness. It would have been lovely to talk more, but her next sentence will surely be a comforting platitude followed by an "Oh, look at the time—I must get some sleep" exit. Dammit, I can't be trusted even with simple friendship, to say nothing of the cratered ruin of love...

My thoughts are pulled back by the touch of Natalia's hand on mine. In the half second before my eyes meet hers, I've already accepted what I'll find there: *pity*. A dart of concern between her brows, a benevolent head tilt...

God, I dread that look.

It isn't there.

Instead, her expression is fierce. "*Fuck* cancer," she says plainly.

It spreads inside me with a sensation like a long-empty well filling with pure water: the recognition that it's what a friend would say.

A stranger would feel the need for more words.

4

AUSTRIA

A FEW DAYS LATER

NATALIA

Phaedra pushes open a heavy metal door leading to Emerald's huge factory workshop, winging an arm out to usher me through. The room echoes with the excited babbling and laughter of two dozen kids between the ages of six and twelve. A quick headcount shows half boys, half girls have come to the Jump Start event the team is hosting, a STEM education program for disadvantaged kids.

Cosmin is there in his green racing suit, crouched down pointing out some features of the inside of his helmet to a group of four little ones. Three people who appear to be mechanics—two men and a woman—stand around a sturdy table, disassembled engine parts spread in front of them as they demonstrate how it all works. At a bank of monitors, Emerald's engineering director and chief strategist talk tech data with a few of the older kids.

Near them, Klaus stands by two children seated on high stools, walking them through how the radio comms work. One little girl

COMING IN HOT

47

has her hands clapped over the headset dwarfing her little blond head, nodding and grinning, eyes wide. Beside her, a wiry red-haired boy soberly listens to Klaus, who concludes his explanation with a warm smile before slipping the headset over the boy's ginger curls.

Phae and I pause to take in the scene, and I pull my phone from the outside pocket of my cross-body briefcase to snap some candid pics. The happy chaos swirling around the room is punctuated here and there with children's shrieks of delight.

Pulling herself tall with a deep, fortifying breath, Phae scowls. "Welp, guess I've gotta go chitchat with the pint-size anarchists."

"*Phae!*" I scold. "You're a hero to these little girls. You could be changing lives today."

She swivels my way, her face a mask of alarm. "Holy shitbiscuits— don't say that to me! No pressure, right? Jesus, this is hard enough. I don't know how to...like, *talk* to kids. It's not my thing."

"Don't be dramatic."

"It's easy for you because of the tutoring you do!" she counters. "Plus, y'know, you babysat as a teenager. Plenty of practice. But to me, they're—" She eyes a nearby child who's jumping up and down like a prizefighter waiting for the bell. "They're unpredictable and a little scary. You can't...*troubleshoot* them like machinery."

"Not untrue."

Sliding my phone back into the briefcase pocket, I set a reassuring hand on Phae's shoulder, which she glares at as if I've dropped a banana slug on her. Undeterred, I give an encouraging squeeze.

"Okay, well...pro tip: Talk to them like they're people. And smile. No, not like that!" I add as she tests out a weird half-grimace. "Smile like you're telling someone about a thing you love—which

48   **JOSIE JUNIPER**

you *are*. You're passionate about engineering, and your enthusiasm will be contagious. Also, *no cursing*," I conclude in a discreet hiss.

A little girl with a dark pixie cut and a T-shirt that shows a bazillion digits of pi walks up to us, staring at a visibly uncomfortable Phaedra. Clasped under one of the girl's arms is a spiral-bound sketchbook.

After several seconds of nervous silence, Phae manages, "Hey there, short stuff. What's shakin'?"

I close my eyes, pressing my lips together to hide a laugh.

"You are Phaedra Morgan," the little girl ventures in an adorable lilting accent. Her golden eyes glitter with fangirl hero worship.

"Uh, yep. Yours truly."

The girl calls over to Cosmin, rattling off a question in Romanian. He replies, standing and walking our way.

"Cosmin tells me," the little girl goes on, "that you are a great genius engineer."

Phae gives Cosmin a dubious squint as he draws up to our little group. "Hmm, I'm a *genius*, eh? Looking to score brownie points with me, Legs?"

The girl's lips part in an excited gasp. "We get brownies too?"

Cosmin laughs, ruffling her hair. "There will be lunch in an hour. And ice cream, I believe." He angles a quick look at Phaedra that's half playful, half admiring. "Liliana," he tells the girl, "why don't you show Miss Morgan your pictures?"

After a burst of giddy foot-tapping, Liliana pulls the sketchbook from beneath her arm and flops it open, revealing careful drawings of cars. Phae bends at an awkward angle, towering over the girl while examining the work.

I tug her sleeve and lean toward her ear, murmuring, "Another pro tip: Don't *loom* over children like King Kong. Squat down to her height."

She gives me a serious nod and does as instructed. I pull out my phone and hold it up wordlessly at her and Cosmin, letting them know I'm going to make the rounds and get some more material for an article.

I stop off at the mechanics' table and ask a few questions, getting quotes from the children and one of the lanyard-wearing guides accompanying them, as well as the mechanics. Next I shoot a bit of video for the new YouTube show *ARJ* has entrusted to me.

As I make my way around the room—keeping myself inconspicuous to ensure everyone will behave naturally—I can't ignore the prickle of awareness of Klaus's presence.

Cutting through all the noise, his dark, satiny baritone is unmistakable, drawing my attention again and again. Something about my reaction to it reminds me of the comforting sounds floating through the window of my aunt's house when I'd walk up the driveway, coming home at the end of a summer afternoon of playing around the neighborhood: the familiar sigh of water in the sink, the clink of dishes, our kitchen radio playing oldies tunes.

I suspect Klaus might be sneaking similar glances at me as I pretend to be focused purely on the activities in the workshop. Gradually I make my way closer, pausing for snippets of interviews, losing the fight with his gravity like a moon being pulled into orbit.

The hour we spent together a few nights ago in Bahrain— electricity crackling across the small table in the lounge, despite my efforts to look casual—has played on a loop in my head, nagging me to reexamine every word I said (*Was that comment silly? What about this other one?*) and every hypnotizing sentence of his, along with his minnow-quick smiles and lingering gazes.

He told me in parting that if I'd like to come to Austria to cover the first Jump Start event, he'd pay my airfare and put me up in one of the hospitality guest suites on the Emerald factory campus. I agreed, telling him that *ARJ* would pay my airfare, but I'd be happy to accept the room. It's a lovely little modern space, all soft white with emerald-green and chrome accents, the walls hung with artsy framed engineering diagrams and black-and-white racing shots.

Phaedra came over to stay with me there last night, both of us falling asleep on the L-shaped sofa after way too many snacks and multiple hours of *Love Island UK*. With the pretense of asking "in a general sense" about Emerald, I slyly extracted some info about Klaus.

Trivia tidbits: He owns a flat in Copenhagen and a cottage in Santorini, but spends very little time at either during racing season; he loves animals and wishes he had dogs and cats, but travels too much for that; he has a weakness for wristwatches, shoes, and stupidly expensive sunglasses, but also a rule that for every "self-indulgent" purchase, he sends the same amount to a charity.

He looks natural with his rapt little charges as I covertly watch him from across the garage. I wonder if he has siblings or if he's an only child like me. He seems like the type who might be the responsible eldest brother.

As he turns his attention to a mechanic who's come up to talk to him, a little boy—maybe seven years old—sidles up to the stool where the blond girl sits. He reaches up for the headset she's wearing, and when she leans away to avoid his grasping hands, he takes

COMING IN HOT

two fistfuls of her shirt and angrily tries to pull her off her high perch.

Anticipating an injury on the workshop's concrete floor, I dash their way, flinging one arm up with an intake of breath to shout at the little aggressor. Before I make it halfway, Klaus swivels around and takes the matter in hand with perfect ease. My steps slow, and I watch the scene unfold.

Klaus tends to the upset little girl, talking to her earnestly, turned away from the other child. *Okay, smart*, I think. *I like how he's checking on her first, rather than rewarding the bully with immediate attention...*

Then, dropping to one knee on the floor, Klaus addresses the boy, whose chest heaves with thwarted aggression, eyes shining with tears of frustration.

"But...it is *my turn*," the boy says indignantly, his voice cracking. "It's not fair!"

After a pause, Klaus tells the boy, "Show me your hands."

The boy tentatively complies.

Gently cradling the boy's hands, Klaus says, "There are so many things you can do with these. Think of it—you can make art, play music, build things, write a story. Our hands are powerful tools. Of all the things we make with them, fear and hurt must not be included. Never use these to express anger."

A wave of emotion shifts in my chest with a feeling like one of those liquid-filled chocolate cherries cracking—sweet and slow and just a little messy.

"Now," Klaus goes on, his tone lighter, instinctively lifting the mood for both children. "Denis, what would you like to ask Crina—after you apologize?"

JOSIE JUNIPER

With a private smile, I watch them as I wander over to the group one slow step at a time as Klaus mediates a truce. Soon the little girl has taken on a teaching role with her would-be bully, caught up in explaining the headset's functions.

With a subtle double take, Klaus notes my approach and offers a tired smile. "Talia, welcome. Are you enjoying yourself? How are the accommodations?"

"The suite is fantastic. Thank you again for inviting me." I tip a sideways nod at Crina and Denis. "I think my favorite part has been that. You're really good with kids."

One corner of those tempting lips rises. "Conflict negotiation is a large part of my job." He leans closer as if divulging a secret. "The battles between Phaedra and Cosmin have been far more challenging to referee."

I give a soft laugh, and as Klaus straightens, I catch the faint wake of his cologne, which makes my pulse jump.

"And children are just people," he adds.

It's so much like what I said to Phae minutes ago that a warm echo resounds through me. When Klaus adjusts the strap of his watch, I can't help stealing a peek at his hands—large and strong, but with a tender skill I remember vividly.

Feeling sheepish for the way my mind creeps toward memories of the night we met, I mentally shake myself, and with a wholesome smile, look over at the two children again. They're chattering in Romanian, sharing with perfect cooperation as if Klaus's words have been a magic spell. "Well, your conflict negotiation appears to be top-notch, so it'll probably work on Phae and Cosmin too. Just look at these two."

Klaus follows my gaze to the now-peaceful kids. "I only reminded them of something they already knew: People think what they want most is to have their will, to triumph in life's every small battle, but... what we truly desire is connection."

I tip my head, studying Klaus. "That's a funny thing for the boss of a racing team to say. I'd have assumed you think winning is everything."

His impossibly dark eyes return to mine. "As Emerald's team principal, I agree. But as a man, kleine Hexe, I want what everyone does."

5

SHANGHAI, CHINA

TWO WEEKS LATER

NATALIA

When I first met Phaedra in college—I was twenty and she was eighteen—I didn't like her. I thought she was mean. A poorly socialized, tutor-educated rich kid who didn't understand how friendship worked. She was what might diplomatically be called "challenging."

I spotted her diamond-in-the-rough charm and refused to give up, and once she let her guard down, we became inseparable. Fourteen years later, I'm still not only her best friend but also one of the few people who understand her.

Loving Phaedra Morgan is hard work, but a job I'm skilled at. I have to admit, though…as jobs go, I've had to take a sabbatical at times. That was easy when I lived in New York and wrote for a literary journal. Phae travels most of the year, so we saw each other in person only in the F1 offseason. But working at this new job—only three races in with *ARJ*—Phae and I are at a boiling point with each other.

I thought following the grands prix would be "an endless globe-trotting slumber party" for my best friend and me. But this week in Shanghai, our bridge of connection has collapsed.

When I got the *ARJ* job, Phae and I set ground rules about what we can discuss. Her first loyalty is to her team, so certain topics are off-limits. But Phae being her bossy self, she isn't always affording *me* the same privacy and is currently up in my business about whether I'm "allowed" to be friends with Klaus. Low-key bickering turned into the kind of gloves-off battle where everyone says things they can't take back.

I feel so isolated. "Lonely in a crowd," despite being in constant motion, spinning through a world of high-stakes action and high-octane personalities.

The thought intrudes from time to time: *Is this really worth it? Do I love this job, or just the idea of it? What if the price I pay is more than I can afford to lose?*

The fear of abandonment that's dogged me since childhood tends to make every loss, even minor ones, feel destabilizing and permanent. In my own way, I'm as guarded as Phaedra.

Like most children with absent parents, I've spent my life trying to make myself lovable. Worthy of *not* being abandoned. The rift with Phae is hitting me in my worst vulnerabilities. Half of me wants to back down just to keep the peace, and the other half says, *Maybe you've outgrown this friendship. Why should you always be the one to fold?*

It echoes in my head as I make my way, with a stubborn,

unapologetic confidence, to Klaus's suite this morning. Since our impromptu chat in the lounge in Bahrain two weeks ago, and the Jump Start event, I've thawed toward him a little. I've seen a new side to the man—a vulnerability I didn't previously realize existed.

It's advantageous to be friendly with such a powerful TP, so when he invited me for coffee in Shanghai, it felt like a smart move to jump at the chance.

Surely I'll be able to wrangle it into a little interview. Just good business, right?

Good business, yes. But...I have to confess, the sexual tension is fun too. There's no denying the attraction, even if we can't act on it. The ground rules have to be the same with him as they've been with Phaedra. So many details need to remain unshared that the path to a true friendship is littered with obstacles.

Klaus opens the door and, dammit, the guy is the embodiment of uncontrived hotness. His suit is a dark slate blue, subtly plaid.

Does he work at that perfect hair as hard as I do with mine? Gorgeous. Argh...

"Come in," he says, sweeping an arm to invite me inside.

There's a room service table near the windows with a three-tier dragon-pattern plate covered in tiny pastries. A thermal carafe—not the diner kind, but cloisonné that matches the dessert tower—stands near it, with china teacups so delicate they must weigh no more than feathers.

He holds out a chair for me. "You look lovely, kleine Hexe."

"Thank you."

I sit, then pour coffee for each of us, suddenly nervous and needing to busy my hands. Klaus settles across from me as I select

COMING IN HOT

a pink petit four and move it to my plate with a pair of silver tongs. "And how is the sphinxlike Klaus Franke this morning?"

He stirs cream into his coffee, surveying me with a playful twinkle. "*Sphinxlike*? I have nothing to hide, Miss Evans. I'm an open book."

"Wow, no. There's a lot you won't talk about, I've noticed. You can be surprisingly cagey during Thursday press meetings."

He chuckles. "Surely not. It's just a new duty, and I've not yet settled into it."

I consider using his statement as a jumping-off point to ask why Edward Morgan has been absent from press conferences lately—I tried gently inquiring with Phae, and she just about took my head off—but I don't want to spook him by barreling straight into reporter mode.

"Are you sure that's all? Let's test it with a question or two."

He pauses to sip his coffee. "Hmm, sticking to the professional? If you insist. Be my guest."

His smile, I think, is meant to look amiable-condescending—as if he's being indulgent. I can't deny I have a weakness for a guy who's a little superior, at least when it's backed up by actual power. But I spot a hint of anxiety too. He's bracing himself, and I feel clumsy for having herded us into interview territory with little preamble.

I fold my hands. "Word on the street says Emerald's budget cratered when you lost Basilisk's sponsorship. Everyone wonders why it happened. And the murmurs say the sudden retirement of your technical director has something to do with it."

Klaus's poker face is textbook. "'Cratered' is dramatic. I could cover the budget deficit with my own checkbook."

"*Ooh, nice flex*," I tease in a stage whisper.

"Basilisk wasn't a major player. Sponsorship relationships come and go." After moving a kiwi-mango tart onto a plate, Klaus sucks a bit of glaze off his thumb. I'm pretty sure it's a deliberate distraction. "But enough about that."

"Too rich for your blood?" I taunt. "Fine, I'll go with a different question: Why's Edward Morgan suddenly MIA?"

Klaus picks up a small spoon and stirs his coffee again, despite not having put anything more into it. *Definitely nervous.*

"You've not asked Phaedra?" he returns with studied lightness. "Your best friend?"

My stomach drops at the knowing tilt to his mouth. When he lifts his eyes to meet mine, he's back in control, and I think we both feel it.

"I, uh…" Trailing off, I prod my petit four.

"Don't think I've not noticed a coolness between you two this week."

I remain silent, jabbing the pastry with a scowl. *How do I both hate and love the fact that Klaus can see right through me?*

"Do you prefer we not discuss it?" he prompts. Watching me with his inky eyes narrowed, he takes a sip of coffee. "Perhaps we *both* have off-limits topics."

I give him a bland look and a conspicuous beat of silence. "Okay, tit for tat: You want to know about Phae and me. I want to know if there's a link between Basilisk and your technical director."

"Is this friendship a series of negotiations?"

"Don't kid yourself—every relationship is."

"Yet information is not typically the currency." He cuts a bite of tart and chews thoughtfully.

"Maybe you just don't trust me."

"Should I? Come now, kleine Hexe…those lovely blue eyes are not a master key to gain you entrance to any room you fancy."

It's a reach, my asking—obviously he shouldn't tell me anything that might hurt Emerald. Still, I feel sulky. And part of me *does* want to talk about Phae, preferably with someone who knows her as well as I do.

"Friends can outgrow each other," I state simply. "Phae is a bossy know-it-all. So *belittling*." I don't intend for the next part of my confession to slip out, but it leaps the fence. "I've spent my life fighting to prove myself. I can't waste energy on it in a friendship. Phae's brilliant, but I won't be an unequal partner in any relationship. Whenever she starts to lose an argument, she makes it personal and defaults to name-calling. It's immature. And I deserve better."

Anger rises from some hidden and neglected place in me as I recall cruel taunts and nicknames I heard in childhood. The words tumble out.

"She makes me feel *small*," I rage on. "Like she thinks being friends with me is charity. It reminds me of all those years getting hand-me-downs from my aunt's church—clothes, toys, donated school supplies. And I'm not trying to play some 'Boo-hoo, I grew up poor' card here. I'm incredibly proud of my aunt and the stable childhood she gave me. I'm just tired of not feeling worthy."

Klaus's face is serious. "Talia, no one could fail to see your worth. You're a talented journalist. I saw your latest episode of *ARJ Buzz* on YouTube. You're…making quite the impression."

"Well, thank you."

"Knowledgeable, erudite." There's a long pause. Something

unreadable crosses his face. "Though I—" He seems to weigh his next words, then shakes his head.

"Though you *what*?"

He gives his fork a careless wave. "Just one of the comments you closed with. It made Emerald look a bit foolish, wouldn't you agree?"

I dab my lips primly with a napkin. "Huh. Well, I feel a little ambushed now. Is this why you invited me for coffee? To scold me?"

"Certainly not. I hadn't planned to bring it up at all."

"I don't tell you how to run a racing team, so you shouldn't tell me how to report racing news."

"*Is* the YouTube show news, or is it gossip?" His tone is deceptively mild.

I set my fork down with a clink. "One point, and then—if you want to be friends—we're done talking about this. *Gossip is part of sporting news.* What people are talking about is relevant."

"Thank you for that insight," he replies. I'm not sure if it's sarcastic.

"*ARJ Buzz* isn't just 'gossip.' In the last episode, I also did a comparative analysis on the beam wings on each team's car, how they impact aerodynamic balance and cornering stability. I'm hardly going"—I wave my arms around and adopt a Valley Girl accent—"'*Like, ohmigawwwd…did Owen Byrne from Team Easton dump reality TV empire heiress Brooklyn Katz for Taylor Swift?*'"

The rumble of Klaus's laughter is contagious, and my irritation cools slightly.

"You're absolutely correct," he tells me. "Your reporting thus far has been beautifully informative. My apologies for implying otherwise."

COMING IN HOT 61

I reach for the coffee to pour myself a bit more, and Klaus moves to do it for me.

"It's fine. I guess I'm defensive too sometimes," I admit.

"Everyone has their triggers. I'm perhaps overly sensitive about journalists. Rumor-mongering specifically."

"That...exposé a couple years back?" Immediately I know I shouldn't have said anything.

"A hundred thousand Swiss francs for defamation was a slap on the wrist," he says tersely.

I read about the libel suit when I googled Klaus after Abu Dhabi. A few years ago, a European culture magazine made some shocking claims in an article detailing Klaus's personal life and the loss of his wife.

He went to work at nineteen for Sofia's father, who owned a successful tech company. Klaus married Sofia and proceeded to work his way up the ladder at the business, SindeZmos, until he ended up in auto racing through a combination of contacts he had in the tech business and in the world of superbike racing, which he did competitively in his youth. Sofia inherited her family's business just after Klaus joined Emerald. Only a few years later she died, leaving everything to Klaus.

A passage in the article mentioned that "sources close to the family" believed Klaus had only married the rather plain-looking and shy Sofia to get ahead in SindeZmos—a damned tacky line to take, saying a dead woman hadn't been hot enough to have authentically earned the love of a dashing husband.

But far worse had been a mention—which ended up being pivotal in the lawsuit—of how "according to some," Klaus may have had a hand in Sofia's death, speeding her illness along due to a concern that she might change her will to leave SindeZmos to a nephew.

The nephew turned out to be the source, no surprise. Klaus donated the lawsuit's award amount to a charity Sofia had loved, the International Rescue Committee.

His continued suspicion toward journalists certainly makes sense. We're both coming to our cautious friendship with a lot of baggage.

Dammit, though I'm pretty sure I've historically never been given equivalent grace by the men in my life, in this moment I study Klaus's face and see the vulnerable child in him. The young man who didn't expect to end up where he is.

Recognizing that I'm doing it doesn't stop me. In my mind, the decision takes root, even while I try to weed it out: *From now on, I probably won't touch on anything that reflects unflatteringly on him during* ARJ Buzz *episodes.*

Maybe I've been primed for the thought by the pain of the rift with Phae, exacerbating my habitual fear of abandonment.

Maybe it's the powerful, undeniable attraction.

Maybe it's the lost little girl in me who'll always be desperate to please.

But...I choose my corner, thinking:

I might need Klaus on my *side as much as he needs me on his.*

6

AZERBAIJAN

TWO WEEKS LATER

NATALIA

The Merchant Baku hotel is definitely giving me a strong *This is why I took the job* feeling. Everything is perfect tonight as I sit in dreamy luxury on my private balcony at a tiny mosaic table with a glass of wine and a light dinner—fruit, pickles, flatbread stuffed with cheese and squash.

Purring traffic glides below in the neon-streaked dusk, and the air somehow smells *colorful*—green and gold, a bright warmth like...expectation? How does everything feel so right in this moment, so aligned and welcoming and exciting?

Twirling the stem of my glass, I smile.

Maybe it's just me.

By which I mean...maybe it's him.

Despite recognizing the risks, I'm unquestionably falling "in crush" with Klaus. It's now obvious he's courting me with the aim of more than friendship. Before I left Shanghai, he sent me two things "for your flight"—a one-player storytelling card game with gorgeous art nouveau illustrations and a newly published novel by an author I mentioned liking.

When I arrived in Baku yesterday morning and was checking into my hotel, I received a message from him saying things are unusually demanding this race week and he can't see me in person until the press conference, but "knowing you're in the same city makes every light sparkle a little brighter."

Swoon.

Last night as I was fighting jet-lag insomnia and getting some writing done in bed around midnight, a text from Klaus popped up.

Charcoal Suit: Are you awake?

Me: Hmm, nope. Completely asleep.

Charcoal Suit: Dreaming of me, I hope

Me: Sir! So bold. I'm shocked.

Charcoal Suit: May I call?

Before I could reply, my phone rang with a video call. Thank God I wasn't wearing one of the hydrating facial sheet masks that make me look like a serial killer. I dragged both hands through my hair and smeared on a little lip balm from the bedside table before opening the call.

"I couldn't wait until Thursday to speak with you," he told me

COMING IN HOT

with a wan, apologetic smile. "Something about you, kleine Hexe, makes me feel intemperate."

"Ooh, *intemperate*," I teased. "That's an adorably prim way of putting it. But the way you talk brings strong Jane Austen, so I won't complain." I snuggled deeper into my stack of pillows.

He lifted an amused eyebrow. "You find me stuffy?"

"Okay, 'stuffy' is too much. Maybe...straitlaced? You're not a lighthearted guy. I don't recommend a career pivot to stand-up comedy."

He twisted to reach for something and held up a book—David Sedaris's *Dress Your Family in Corduroy and Denim*. "I do appreciate humor," he asserted with a playful scowl.

"And yet you phrase it so formally: 'I do appreciate humor.' I think you've made my point." I reached over my shoulder and adjusted a pillow, acknowledging to myself that I was doing it so I could give Klaus an "accidental" flash of my braless chest in a thin pink tank top. "If you're such a funny guy, tell me a joke."

"A joke?"

"Mmm-hmm. Impress me."

His attractive lips scrunched in thought, and those inky eyes shifted to one side. He was holding the phone closer than I generally stand to him, so I could really see his little details, like the geometric fringe of long, spiky lashes. The memory of kissing him rose.

"All right," he said. "A joke: Two nuns are sitting on a bench in the park. A gentleman in a trench coat runs up and flashes them. The first nun has a stroke. The second nun tries, but she can't reach him."

66   **JOSIE JUNIPER**

There was a pause as the punchline caught up to me. When I burst out laughing, Klaus winked.

"You see? I'm enormously funny, you dreadful girl. 'Straitlaced' indeed..."

We talked for over an hour, and for the first time in my life, I did something that never happened to me even as a lovestruck teen: I fell asleep with someone during a middle-of-the-night phone call.

Our voices got lighter and dreamier, our pauses longer... and the next thing I knew, it was after two o'clock, and my phone was beside me on the bed, still open to the call. Rising on an elbow, I took in the sight of Klaus, who'd drifted off too, lying sideways with his phone on a pillow facing him. The view had shifted, but I could see one closed eye, an angular cheekbone, and the sleep-disheveled hair at his temple—a fan of combined silver and espresso-brown strands.

I switched off my bedside light, and the deep, steady rhythm of Klaus's breathing escorted me back to sleep.

All day today as I've tried to get work done, awareness of him has danced near me, dark yet flashing, like seafoam on a midnight beach, visible only when it breaks and catches the moonlight, swirling around your bare ankles with a delicious shock.

I can't stop thinking about him.

Sitting on the balcony tonight, picking at my dinner, I stretch my legs and flex my feet, watching my silk chiffon robe (chosen in case he calls—not gonna lie) flutter away from my calves. I wiggle my toes, considering the chipped golden-peach polish on them and wondering if I should get a pedicure.

The image drifts into my head: Klaus moving my legs over his

COMING IN HOT

shoulders...both of us still speckled in shower water...the cool marble countertop beneath me...the anticipation of his mouth as those beautiful lips advanced up my inner thigh...

I pull in a startled gasp through my nose as my phone rings with the FaceTime tone. I glance at the incoming call, but it's not Klaus—it's Auntie Min.

It's early afternoon in my hometown, eight hours later here. Usually our weekly "catch-up" calls are Mondays at seven a.m. her time, so a prickle of panic goes through me.

I tap the call open. "What's wrong?" I ask in greeting, clambering to sit up straight. "Are you okay?"

"Good grief, Natty," she replies with a mild chuckle. "Nothing—I'm fine."

Pressing one hand over my heart, I let out a relieved sigh. "Oh, okay. Just wasn't sure why you're calling now."

"I'm calling because I miss you." She gives me a significant half-smile. "Do I need a reason?"

I recognize immediately what she's referring to. For at least a year after my parents left me, if the house got especially quiet, I'd be overcome with anxiety that I'd been abandoned again, and race from room to room looking for Auntie Min.

When I'd skid to a halt, having located her, I'd always self-consciously manufacture some excuse for needing to talk to her. *Um...is...is it supposed to rain today?* I'd stammer, thinking on my feet. Or, *Can we have chicken stew for dinner?* Or maybe, *Do you need me to do any chores right now?*

She'd pull me into her arms, answer my made-up question, then tell me, *You don't ever need a reason to be near me, Natty. I'll always be here for you.*

68 **JOSIE JUNIPER**

My aunt hadn't expected, all those years ago, to take in a seven-year-old grandniece when she was in her midforties, but she was an amazing "mom" to me after my parents flitted off to California and forgot I existed. My father—whom I've referred to as "Jason" since I was about twelve (Mom became "Sherri" the same year)—is Minnie's nephew.

A sigh of embarrassed laughter escapes me. "Of course you don't need a reason, Auntie Min." I scooch down into the chair. "I worry, being so far away now, that's all. In New York I was only a two-and-a-half-hour flight away. Now it'd take me a full day from some of these grand prix spots."

"Well, lucky for you I'm healthy as a danged plow mule," she assures me. "I've got a new walking route with Naomi—three miles. Volunteering on Tuesdays and Fridays...oh, and there's square dancing now at church!" With a wry smile, she adds, "Naomi's tickled to have an excuse to hold hands with that retired veterinarian who moved to town. She's set her cap for him."

Hearing news from home brings on a twinge of pain, and I'm not sure if that's how everyone feels about their hometown. Is that ache just part of the human condition, or does it imply that I'm not meant for the new life I've worked so hard to create?

As much as I adored New York while living there, and as fun as it is to fly all over the world and see things most people will only ever read about...I'm most relaxed, most *myself*, after I drive past the big blue barn at the Marshall farm, on the two-lane highway leading into the town where I grew up.

Passing that landmark—the location of one of my happy (and rare) memories of my father, how he'd take me there to feed apples

COMING IN HOT

to the horses—is when I know I'm about to settle into the comfort of home, like a deep, warm bath.

"Well, best of luck to Naomi in bagging the veterinarian," I say with a laugh. A moment later, stumbling into the hollow of my homesickness, I look into my lap and blurt out, "Speaking of crushes...I think I've met someone I like too, Auntie Min."

There's a silence, and I glance at the screen to make sure the call is still connected.

"Well, all right...tell me more," she says in the tone she uses when she's trying to be fair—a stiff pleasantness that telegraphs, *I won't hurt your feelings by saying this is probably going to be a disaster.*

I fight the urge to backpedal. Why should I be apologetic?

Maybe because I've come home crying, again and again, about various complete jerks...

"It's just a friendship," I amend quickly. "Early, *early* stages."

"That's wise," Minnie says, her brow relaxing. "Give it enough time to make sure you know, uh...everything you need to."

I stop myself before I can blurt out, *This one isn't married!*

"Oh, definitely," I assure her. "No rushing into things."

Aside from the one-nighter in Abu Dhabi nearly five months ago, but who's counting?

Minnie gently clears her throat. "Not to make this awkward," she ventures, "but please try not to, uh..." Her hands drop audibly to her lap. "To jump into bed with this one. The part of you that yearns for approval might, um...sometimes be awful quick to offer men more than they deserve."

I make a face. "Auntie Min, that's so—"

"And I'm not being some Goody Two-shoes," she goes on. "In

JOSIE JUNIPER

my younger days, I was as close to a seventies feminist as gals got in this town. I'm not saying you have to get married to...do *that*. Hell, I never got married myself. I just want you to spare yourself heartache."

"I know." I keep my face sober, giving nothing away.

"Getting tangled up with someone while you're in a job that hauls you from pillar to post...it might not be fertile ground for a stable relationship. That requires trust, and a deeper connection. Time to take firm root and grow."

My gaze drops. "I knowIknowIknow—I've messed up a million times jumping in too fast, and I'm sorry."

"Oh, Natty." She sighs. "Don't apologize. Everyone makes mistakes! We're so proud of you, but we just worry sometimes, and—"

As her words cut off and I look up, her free hand goes to her braid end, combing it with her fingers in a stress-tell I know well. My mind rewinds her last few sentences.

"Hold on. 'We' who?" I ask.

"Oh, just...everyone. Me and Naomi, the whole town! Everyone knows how well you've done." Her fingers comb faster and she pours out more words. "Liza at the post office told me yesterday how much she loves those YouChannel videos you do—"

"You*Tube*." My eyes narrow. "Are you hiding something?"

"Well, listen to you," Minnie drawls in the deadpan delivery that means I'm trying her patience. "Got your reporter hat on, thinking everything's a secret to bust open." Her focus darts up to the chicken-shaped clock I know is on the kitchen wall. "I've gotta go, Natty. I'll run late for quilting with the gals if I dillydally."

It doesn't escape my notice, as we sign off, that she hasn't

COMING IN HOT

answered my question. In the back of my mind, a warning beacon thrusts one beam through the fog:

Does the "we" she's talking about include Jason and Sherri?

In the absence of information, I've made up multiple explanations for their disappearance over the past twenty-seven years—everything from a child's fairy-tale whimsy to a teen's Shakespearean tragedy. With the sometimes-morbid perspective of adulthood, I occasionally wonder if they died, under circumstances owing to the same reckless decision-making that propelled them out of my life in the first place.

I've never let myself look them up online, though I've been tempted many times. The idea of doing so feels like letting them win. I refuse to care about them more than they ever cared about me. They walked away and didn't look back.

Or... did *they look back?*

7

SPAIN

TWO WEEKS LATER

NATALIA

Crappy non-apologies—the kind that pretend to be hat-in-hand but hide a hatpin that sinks into my knuckles when I reach to accept it—are Phaedra's MO. And I've always let her get away with it, not wanting to embarrass her.

Well, this time I refuse to laugh it off and sweep it under the rug, I tell myself.

Six days after the blowup in Shanghai, I got a text:

> I shouldn't have said the things I did, but I don't know if it's fair of you to say I'm "judgmental" when I'm trying to be helpful. Can we hang out in Baku? Snacks and trash TV?

Not an apology.

Then, nine days later:

COMING IN HOT   73

> If I say you win, does this go away? The silent treatment
> is silly. I'll do the bullshit "talking about our feelings" if it's
> what you're holding out for, Princess, haha. Call me.

This Monday morning in Barcelona, four weeks after our argument, I got the most annoying text yet from her—the maddening
??? universally understood to signify Why are you being a stubborn jerk and not replying?

How can she fail to take a clue? All I want is a non-qualified,
non-backhanded "I'm sorry." Part of me is tempted to tell her that,
but it doesn't count if I have to spell it out. Do I need to write a
script?

Once again, I wonder about the unexpected sacrifices I've had
to make for this "dream" job with *ARJ*. Has proximity dealt a
death blow to my friendship with Phae? One minute I miss her
horribly...but then she'll go and send me another clueless text
and I think, *No, it's not the job—it's us. We're incompatible, and
it's time to accept it.*

I'm ranting under my breath about her stupid passive-aggres-
sive question marks, reassuring myself again that I'm right and
she's wrong, one finger hovering over *Contacts > Phaedra > Edit >
Delete* when a message comes through.

> **Charcoal Suit:** Are you still in Barcelona?

> **Me:** I'm here. Why?

> **Charcoal Suit:** I've canceled plans for lunch on Jakob's
> boat because I'd rather see you.

Charcoal Suit: I oughtn't assume you're available. But if you are, I have something I'd like to show you.

Me: I'm intrigued.

Charcoal Suit: Lobby, 30 minutes? Trousers, sensible shoes.

▀▚▀▚▀▚▀

Klaus looks one part mischief, one part trepidation as I walk over from the elevators. I loop an arm through his offered elbow and follow him out the door. In the pickup area is a silver-and-black Triumph motorcycle with two helmets sitting on it.

"You should wear my jacket," Klaus tells me, shrugging his off as we emerge. He drapes his green flight jacket over my shoulders. Since I'm not in heels, he seems even taller. The scent of his cologne sends a shiver of familiar longing through me.

"Thank you," I manage, inserting my arms into the sleeves. "But, um..." I glance at the motorcycle.

He inspects my expression, and his inky eyes go serious. "I should have asked. Have you ever been on a motorbike? Are you nervous about it?"

"No, no. It's not that. I've...been on them plenty."

He gives my shoulders an amiable squeeze. "You're in good hands. I used to do this professionally."

"Oh, I know. I read about that." I anxiously twist the zipper pull on the jacket. Memories of my dad flutter through my head like moths diving at a light source: silent and harmless, but with an erratic insistence.

COMING IN HOT

Klaus touches my chin. "You're troubled—this was a poor idea. We can certainly take a car to our destination."

I draw a bracing breath and force a smile. "It's fine. Let's go for it."

He hands me a helmet and mounts the bike, and *wow*...it thrills me in some "swooning medieval maiden" way, watching the ease and command of him swinging one long leg over and settling into place, natural and confident as a knight astride a war horse. I slide behind him, affixing my helmet and wrapping my arms around his waist.

Everything about it plunges me into a vivid, body-deep recognition—the oily motor smell, the engine's feral growl, the vibration wicking up my backbone, the muscled wall of the human to whom I cling. When we launch and curve out of the driveway onto the road, the wild caress of the wind as it increases brings both elation and sorrow.

Within a mile, the physicality of the ride strips everything else away. I'm nowhere else, doing nothing else. Freed from distraction in a world where usually there's *noise noise noise*, inside and out. I'm just *here*, and it's luscious.

Every detail looms large, alive and immediate. The contrast of cool, rushing air and the warmth of Klaus's torso beneath my arms. The scent of trees and Mediterranean sunshine. The weaving pattern of a flock of birds dipping on the wind, rising and falling as if they're playing with us.

After about fifteen minutes, we approach a sign: PARC DEL LABERINT D'HORTA. We park in a shady spot and I dismount, removing the helmet and shaking out my hair. Klaus watches me, a tiny smile quirking his lips.

JOSIE JUNIPER

"Your cheeks are pink and those bright blue eyes are shining." He takes the jacket I hand to him and slings it over one broad shoulder, then scoops me under his left arm and points us toward a gravel path. His shirt smells like crisp spring air and his own musky-yet-citrusy warmth. I fight the urge to burrow against him shamelessly.

"This place is incredible," I marvel, scanning around as we wander past a marble bas-relief of Ariadne and Theseus. There are stone neoclassical buildings and staircases, elegant statues, topiary arches, and a giant hedge maze straight out of a fantasy movie.

"I thought we could get a little lost with each other," Klaus tells me.

Looking up into his beautiful eyes, I think I already *am* lost. For weeks now we've been texting and sneaking video calls into our mad schedules. The tension between us is ramping up as we've gone from cautious flirting to bold declarations of interest. Multiple times, late into the night, we've exchanged anecdotes about our lives, often surprised by unusual "favorites" we have in common (cheese toasties eaten with pickles, the classic film *The Shop Around the Corner*, "weed flowers" like dandelions and buttercups, the book *Lonesome Dove*).

Admittedly, we both have topics we avoid. I haven't revealed the truth about my parents, for one. And anything touching on Emerald turns Klaus crisp and businesslike, with short, studied replies. I'm doing my best to take Auntie Min's advice and get to know him better before I'll consent to spend time alone with him in private.

The physical chemistry is intense, and I know my limits.

This courtship has me walking on air. Klaus seems in no rush,

COMING IN HOT

never pressuring me to visit behind closed doors (even if our work duties weren't too all-consuming to make that easy). I love how he notices little details of things that please me, like how he's remembered that the romantic in me has always wanted to explore a labyrinth, ever since seeing the movie as a young teen.

It's gorgeous here. There are only a few other people around, couples holding hands or taking photos. Klaus and I fall into relaxed conversation as we stroll, chatting about the race weekend results, Spain, the upcoming Monaco Grand Prix.

After a minute's easy silence, he asks, "What you mentioned earlier, about the motorbike. Did you date someone who rode one?"

I shake my head. "My dad had an old Honda Gold Wing. I probably shouldn't have been riding around on the back when I was little, but...I loved it." Daring to offer a more personal detail of my history, I add, "I only, uh...have a few clear memories of him, but that's one of the best."

A look of concern darkens Klaus's face.

I rush on. "No, no, he didn't die or anything tragic. He and my mom skipped town and gave me to my great-aunt to raise when I was seven. I haven't seen them since."

He seems to weigh his reply carefully. "One might argue that *is* a tragedy. Perhaps more so than a death."

"Maybe. But they had me too young, and my aunt was awesome. No big deal."

Maybe the most haunting big deal of my life, but who's counting?

Anxious about having said too much, I point left at a fork in the path to change the subject. "I have a good feeling about that way."

"Onward, trailblazer."

We reach the labyrinth's center and stand before a statue of Eros. Klaus takes my hand, fingers dovetailing firmly with mine, and the weight of the moment settles around us. There's a thin, far-off whine from an airplane, the reedy intermittent calls of insects and birds, laughter and chatter in Italian from a couple in the next row.

Klaus releases my hand and unslings the jacket from his shoulder, digging in an inside zipper pocket. "A small gift for you," he says lightly, holding out a velvet box.

I suspect he's prefaced it this way because the offering of little jewelry boxes typically has the context of a proposal, and he doesn't want me to panic. I'm expecting something casual...charm bracelets are having a moment right now with driver wives and girlfriends, who sport charms from each grand prix location—a dragon from China, a kangaroo from Australia, that sort of thing.

I tip open the lid and my breath catches. Nestled in the velvet is a heart-shaped emerald as big as my pinky-nail...easily two full carats or more. The simple, unadorned beauty of the massive stone, suspended on a white gold box chain, is breathtaking.

I look up, eyes wide. "Klaus, this is"—I inspect it again, stunned—"not a 'small gift.'"

"Since you mentioned the hand-me-downs of your childhood, I've been wanting to give you something lovely that will forever be yours alone."

He gently takes the box from me and removes the pendant. The chain is long enough that he slips it over my head without having to undo the clasp. He positions the stone at the center of my chest,

COMING IN HOT

the backs of his knuckles skimming one breast, sending electric heat down my arms and legs.

I grab the placket of his shirt and pull him toward me. We pause a centimeter apart. A smile tilts one corner of my mouth at how earnest he looks. The unexpected power is heady, knowing this is a man who sails effortlessly through a world of prestige, speed, high-stakes business, and iron control...yet his dark eyes search mine with the trepidation of someone who's walked to the open door of a skydiving plane and isn't sure he can jump.

"And for months, I've been wanting to give you *this*," I whisper, rising on my toes to brush my lips against his.

We tease and slide, our mouths connecting in heartbeat-quick touches. One of his hands delves into the front of my blazer and spreads at the juncture of my shoulder and neck, and I can't suppress a breathy moan.

"Talia," he murmurs as we come together again and again. "Lioness...witch...*conqueror*."

It's a good thing we're in public, or I'd knock him to the ground and jump on him with the same confidence he showed getting on that motorcycle. Gravity pulls at the core of me—my heart, my spine, and everything below that, aching for his touch. I fall into this man with an inevitability, like displaced water flooding an empty vessel tugged beneath the surface in a cascading surrender to physics.

He pulls back first, cradling my face and combing my bangs aside to kiss my forehead. An airy whimper of disappointment escapes me, and he laughs, encircling me with one arm and pocketing the empty velvet box.

"Hot-blooded woman," he teases, setting us in motion down another gravel path. "You'll get us in trouble."

I snake an arm around his waist. Looking up at the cartoonishly perfect mounds of white cloud against the cerulean sky, I rest a hand over the pendant, wondering if I'm imagining that it's unusually warm from having been trapped between us as we kissed.

"Thank you for this incredible necklace," I tell him. "I don't even want to imagine what it must have cost you." It's easily a five-figure stone. I know he can afford it, but the extravagance still shocks me, having been raised so frugally.

"Compared to the value of your friendship, it's a trinket."

We amble along leisurely on the gravel. A prickle of worry intrudes as something occurs to me: I've accepted a gift that probably cost what most people would spend on a car, so…has my journalistic loyalty been bought and insured?

And worse yet, is that exactly why he's given it to me?

8

MONTRÉAL

ONE MONTH LATER

NATALIA

The Parc del Laberint d'Horta was one of the most romantic moments of my life, and since then, my brain has been warning my heart to be cautious. I mostly listen...but not so assiduously that Klaus and I haven't been sneaking off on little dates during stolen moments of freedom from our respective career demands.

In Monaco, we went for a midnight picnic in a retro-looking speedboat Klaus owns, a Riva Aquarama. We sipped champagne and had "picnic" items that were insanely luxurious. Around the boat were blue glass jars filled with tangles of fairy lights. We curled up together under a silvery faux-fur blanket and watched the stars.

At one point that night, noticing I was wearing the emerald necklace, Klaus traced a fingertip from the hollow of my throat down my cleavage, then followed with his lips in a scorching path to the heart-shaped stone. He moved it aside with his tongue and kissed me beneath it. I don't know if I've ever been that turned on from such a simple act.

I held back from anything more intimate, as much as it tormented us both, alone out on the water, the warm Mediterranean breeze caressing the hints of skin we exposed in the few minutes of heated petting we couldn't help falling into.

But I won't forget what my aunt said. I need to be able to trust Klaus fully, and for him to trust *me*. I can't let myself blunder into the same kind of unthinking, lust-fueled, immature relationship my reckless parents had, by all reports.

A few weeks later, in Montréal now for the Canadian Grand Prix...I've decided I'm going to bed with him. It's been six months since our "one-hour fling" in Abu Dhabi, and I can't take much more of this slow-burn, months-long foreplay.

He's been tense this week, distracted even when we're together, interrupted by endless messages when we're on late-night calls. I've assumed it's all work-related, but since we avoid those topics, I can only guess the specifics. I suspect it has to do with Edward Morgan's continued absence, but I can't ask Klaus and *won't* ask Phaedra.

She and I are still on the outs. After I ignored her "Let's sweep this argument under the rug as usual" texts, she went radio silent, clearly punishing me for not having backed down. I've violated our unspoken rule by sticking up for myself, I guess.

I can't help wondering if she's formed a secret amorous alliance with Cosmin Ardelean. She loathed him when they first met, but after they were sent on a "bonding" trip together, things shifted somehow. It was obvious to me that she was attracted to him, even when she wouldn't admit it.

COMING IN HOT

If they've cooked up a sneaky romance, I really *have* been replaced; Phaedra has never required more than one friend. She developed social competence because it's useful in business. But she still doesn't have a high need for companionship.

After the press conference on Thursday of race week—always a hectic day for everyone—I send Klaus a text:

> **Me:** Do you still want to hang out tonight?

> **Charcoal Suit:** Please come up. It will be the highlight of my day. Is ten o'clock too late?

Not for what I have in mind, nope...

I put on a strappy orange dress I know he loves and take the elevator up to his suite. My heart is doing a wild jazz drum solo in anticipation of what's to come, and my hands are shaking.

When he opens the door, he's on a call with someone who has a French accent (Emerald's chief aerodynamicist?) and quickly taps the phone to switch from speaker to private.

I don't know why, but it bugs me. *What the heck does he think I'm going to do, dash off a stealthy article about Emerald's latest wind tunnel tests?*

For that matter, part of me is annoyed that after I've spent all day building up this big event in my head, I didn't even get an appreciative once-over for the dress before Klaus wandered away. I know it's vain, but...I'd hoped he'd maybe have the same sense I do that tonight is a turning point to the next stage. A big development. Instead, I feel like I've blundered into a meeting room at the paddock.

Would a smile have killed him? A moment of eye contact?

I walk stiffly to the living room and lower myself into a chair, feeling embarrassed and trying to shake off the indignation. Making a show of how thoroughly I'm *not* paying attention to his stupid call, I swipe open the email I've neglected all day and scan it.

Whoa. A message from Phaedra.

I glance up at Klaus—who's leaning diagonally in the bedroom doorway with his back to me, immersed in his phone call—then open the email, which was sent this morning, fifteen hours ago.

> You win the bet, Nat. I fucked Cosmin before Silverstone. I'm sorry I hurt your feelings. There's no excuse. I miss my best friend. I promise I'm not saying this to be manipulative, but my dad is sick, and I'm scared. Please call me. I want to apologize in person.

My stomach drops.

Mo *is* sick?

Having it confirmed feels very different from suspecting it in an abstract sense. I recall Phae telling me in December, six months ago, that her father was having weird headaches. My wide, burning eyes drop again to her words on my phone screen: I'm scared.

She never admits to being scared. It hits me hard, knowing what it must have cost her emotionally to say that. What was the breaking point? How bad is this?

Worry for Mo spreads through me like a dark oil spill, and also genuine shock that Phaedra is apologizing. She's acknowledged that she hurt my feelings.

I have to go to her!

COMING IN HOT

I turn my phone sideways to type, then freeze. A realization smacks into me, following close and treading painfully on the heels of my reflexive compassion:

Phaedra only apologizes when she wants something from me.

I've always assumed she does that *not* because she's selfish and calculating, but because it feels safer. Like, she wants to apologize but needs to sneak it in attached to something else, like a rider on a bill in legislation.

Is Mo actually that sick? Or is this some demented Hail Mary play by Phaedra?

Maybe that's why Klaus hasn't mentioned it?

How much does he know about Mo's health problem? If it's serious, maybe that's why he's seemed "off" this week. But...with all we've shared as we've opened our hearts, he couldn't have confided in me about such a huge struggle?

The feeling of being shut out overwhelms me.

I'm so confused and torn.

I shoot another glance at him and note with a fresh wave of insult that *he's switched to speaking French*, which I mentioned to him in Monaco that I don't understand beyond tourist phrases and cognates.

A storm rises, fast and savage, inside of me. It's a kneecap-kicking, knife-in-the-teeth brawl between parts of myself. There's the compassionate person who wants to *run* to Phaedra and take care of her if Mo is sick. But there's also a skeptic, sitting back and watching, *judging*.

And in the very, *very* darkest corner of me? There's a vengeful, wounded monster who wants to make her wait...even if it's true that she's scared.

JOSIE JUNIPER

Let her deal with her own problem, like all the times I've had to when she's been too clueless and selfish to be a supportive friend…

And Klaus. How am I to interpret his saying nothing? We've talked a lot about trust and opening up. He's admitted to the scars left by his widowerhood. He's made me feel special, burrowing straight to the heart of my people-pleasing self, assuring me he hasn't felt this close to anyone in years.

Has it all been bullshit? Did he track my craving for approval and deliver the right lines in hopes of luring me back into bed? Was he saying what I wanted to hear, that day at the Emerald factory when he claimed that rather than craving "a win," he wants connection?

I wonder if he could do his job so well if winning weren't integral to his nature.

I look down at the dress I've worn with the specific aim of seduction tonight and feel like a fool. An insecure woman who's perpetually searching for—and forgiving—the sad little boy in every man. A rejected girl who's always, *always* put everyone's feelings before her own, just hoping to belong.

Across the room, Klaus hangs up his call, taking off his damned sexy-librarian reading glasses as he wanders into the living room. He sets his phone and glasses on the bar.

The words escape before I can hold back. "Edward Morgan is sick?"

His steps freeze. "How do you know such a thing?" he asks, his smooth baritone carrying unexpected coldness. "Is there a press leak?" He continues to the sofa, sitting and resting one ankle on the opposite knee, the picture of ease.

I hold up my phone. "No. I got an email from Phae. No

COMING IN HOT

specifics—just that Mo is sick. Is this why you've been moody all week?"

Klaus shakes his head, opening his hands. "I really can't discuss that."

A coal of sorrow ignites in my chest. "Why won't you talk with me about it? Obviously not as a journalist, but...just as your friend? You told me in Monaco, that night on the boat, that you feel like you can tell me anything. Like you've been 'let out of a cage,' you claimed."

"Certainly we're friends," he replies evenly. "I care for you greatly. But you're also press. I must be cautious about what I share." His expression is shuttered, controlled, and it hurts to see it. "I'd appreciate your discretion on this matter," he goes on. "It's a private issue for family. Leaking it would serve only to alarm Emerald's sponsors."

A chill runs across my skin. The distance between us suddenly feels like it's stretching into light-years.

How could I have been so naïve?

Why do I never listen to my gut instinct about men? It isn't that I fail to see the warning signs. I see them, then pirouette onto the minefield anyway...

"Are you kidding me right now?" I say slowly. "It's 'a private issue for family'? Has it occurred to you, Klaus, that *I am* like family to the Morgans? I'm not 'the press.' I've known them longer than you have. How many summer vacations have *you* spent in their North Carolina beach house? How many middle-of-the-night phone calls from Phae have you fielded?"

"From Phaedra?" he echoes with dismissive amusement. "Too many. There's friendship, and then there's business. I'm sure I get *more* of Phaedra's midnight rants." Noting the anger on my face, he adjusts his approach. "Talia, please. I didn't intend for that to sound as it did. And now you're upset." He extends an arm. "Come here and sit with me."

"Your condescension is the last thing I need," I snap. "I won't be made to feel small, or unworthy of someone's confidence— either Phaedra's or yours." After a withering pause, I throw my next words out, hoping to hurt him right back. "I don't need the grief, and...I don't even need *you*."

Ouch—oh God...

It's not inaccurate. I don't "need" *any* man to complete me. But it's also one of the biggest lies ever to pass my lips. I've fallen for Klaus Franke hard. But he obviously doesn't trust me, and I'm unsure in this moment if that means he doesn't respect me either.

Seeing him sitting across from me with that cool, unflappable stare, it occurs to me that what he shares of himself feels *curated*.

His outstretched hand withdraws. He rakes his fingers through his hair with a sigh. "I see. Is that how you feel, after all? I'm surprised."

His alleged "surprise" sounds more like an intimidation strategy to make me walk back what I've said, and his lofty expression is pure Emerald Team Principal.

The hot tears hanging at my lower lashes get heavy enough to fall. I swipe them away, heart racing, mind scrambling for how to soften my assertion without yielding fully.

"I don't *need* you," I amend, "but I do want you, Klaus...and I want to know where this could go. But only if you'll let me in. Like I said about Phae: I won't be in unbalanced relationships anymore. I deserve better."

COMING IN HOT

"I don't dispute it." His tone is heartbreakingly impassive. Why is he suddenly retreating like this?

"What do you actually want from me?" I force the question out. I know it's a dramatic move, but I'm feeling stung and—to be honest—not particularly emotionally safe. I'm not a big wielder of ultimatums, but my phrasing now feels perilously close. "Something real? Just a repeat of that night in Abu Dhabi? Or maybe a 'friend in the press'?"

I expect him to look at me—to be shocked, offended, to deny it. To soften and usher us back onto the path I thought we were on when I knocked at the door of his suite, just minutes ago. But his gaze remains anchored to the coffee table. I allow an extra few seconds, waiting for him to say something.

Spurred by a heartache colored with embarrassment, I manage, "I think maybe this—you, me, all of it—was a bad idea. I do want you. But I want a lot of things that aren't good for me. I want to eat ice cream instead of broccoli. I want to sleep in instead of working out. With those things, I exert the discipline. But I don't have self-control around you."

He meets my eyes, and he looks ruined. I suppress the impulse to walk it all back, to feel sorrier for him than I do for myself right now.

"Truth to tell," he murmurs wearily, "the power you have over me is daunting as well. The way it erodes my will is disturbing."

Realization crystalizes in me before melting into a slurry of despair: *This is not going to work. Attraction has blinded us both.*

For months, I've taken our red flags and folded them into swans, like those cloth napkins at fancy restaurants.

"There's nothing about us being together that makes sense," I state with finality, hoping it might rattle him and spur some kind of declaration.

A long silence follows.

Where are the comforting magic words to pull this breakup back from the edge of the cliff and make me believe in something that, deep down, maybe I shouldn't?

Klaus considers what I've said for a long time, and my stomach flip-flops. I want him to refute my harsh verdict, but...no such luck. Instead, he nods.

Why are you nodding? Fight me on this, dammit!

The way he leans back against the sofa cushions with a sigh, rubbing his face with both hands, tells me everything. It's all in what he *can't* say.

"Fine, then." My voice is little more than a ragged whisper, and I clear my throat. "Let's cut our losses. This dance we've been doing is the emotional equivalent of"—I flash a bitter smile, remembering the moment in Abu Dhabi when I flung those crumpled euros at him—"throwing good money after bad."

I stand and pick up my phone and purse. On my way to the door, I both fear and hope he'll speak up. I pull the door shut slowly, quietly, so I'll hear him if he calls me back at the last second. But it doesn't happen.

By the time I'm in my own room and stepping into a searingly hot shower—still wearing the dress Klaus once said he loved; the silk wilting, sodden, ruined—I've committed myself to the task of picking out the stitches that man has set into my heart.

9

ABU DHABI

SIX MONTHS LATER

KLAUS

The banquet room is so long, it may as well be a battlefield. In a sense, it is. Metaphoric ruins are strewn across it between Natalia and me—wreckage and churned earth where we fought for connection this year and failed.

I can't take my eyes off her tonight. She's in a red dress that hugs her curves and flares out to dance around her thighs in taunting challenge like a matador's cape. The dress's plunging neckline frames a gold necklace shaped like delicate tree branches studded with tiny red stones. I can't help wondering if it was a gift from someone—I've never seen it before.

The emerald heart pendant would have been lovely with her outfit, echoing the sweetheart curve of the bodice, but it was delivered back to me months ago by Phaedra, after the Austrian Grand Prix. She and Talia had mended their fences, and Phaedra wasn't shy about partially blaming me for their months-long rift.

I don't want this back, I tried telling Phaedra. *Please tell her to keep it.*

She narrowed her flashing green eyes at me and lifted the little velvet box to drop it from a great height, making me scramble to catch it.

Yeah, I'm not playing some high school bullshit game with you two, she told me. *You fucked up, and that's your problem. Getting in the middle of this shit was what made Nat and me not talk for months. So suck it up and hand it back to her yourself if you want. I'm done.*

I've ferried the cursed necklace on and off a dozen flights since then, both reluctant to go to Natalia and urge her to keep it—and pleading for her to forgive me for my stubbornness and cowardice that night in Montréal—and reluctant to let the matter die entirely by leaving the necklace at home. I suppose I've continued to carry it like some talisman that might bring her back to me.

But tonight I see clearly that she's moved on. One of her hands balances a plate of food, the other wields a fork. Her focus is all on her conversational partner, an F1 commentator near my age who seems to be putting every ounce of his Scots charm into their tête-à-tête.

The banquet celebrating the end of the nine-month racing season was already set: food and wine, music and décor sorted. But when Cosmin secured his first win in the final race, the bar was raised.

Constructors' championship winners Allonby Racing sent over a case of 2008 Dom Pérignon, and second place Team Coraggio gifted us a case of Sassicaia. To celebrate Cosmin's win—which lifted Emerald F1 into third place, at last a force to be reckoned with on the grid—I called in pastry chefs to set up a table making fresh-to-order papanași, a traditional Romanian dessert, to surprise Cosmin.

COMING IN HOT

Crossing to a table bearing flutes of champagne—admittedly as an excuse to move closer to Natalia—I swap out my empty glass for a fresh one. I study her while affecting "gracious host" observation of the party. Hundreds of Emerald team members laugh and chat. A few are merrily tipsy enough to dance near the band at one end of the room.

Phaedra sidles up to me and takes the slender flute from my hand, tipping back a sip. "Really tearing it up tonight, eh, Klausy?" she teases. "You never have a second glass." She throws a look at Natalia and one corner of her mouth twitches with mirth. "Ahh, I see. It's a prop so you could get close enough to draw a bead on Nat."

Natalia's laughter spills out and she touches the commentator's arm. The fork drops off her plate, and he gallantly stoops to retrieve it.

"You don't miss much," I confess. My gaze flicks to Cosmin, and Phaedra's attention follows mine, taking in the driver's handsome form with all the acquisitive bliss of the newly in love. "You share Cosmin's observant eye," I tell her. "You're well matched."

Her shrug is aloof, but she hides a private smile behind a sip of champagne.

"You gonna talk with Nat," she asks, "or let Shrek over there scoop her up?"

"There's too much blood under the bridge with Talia." I manage a stiff smile. "Still, thank you for your concern." Hunting for a change of subject, I scan the room, settling on Cosmin's trophy on a table. "I wish Edward could have seen this. It was his dream. A tragedy that he missed it by only months."

Phaedra's chin tightens with the emotion my words incite, and I feel like a brute for having mentioned her father to avoid talk of Natalia. Bringing him up hurts me too, though I can't show it.

I've felt adrift without my closest friend. It's further sapped my enthusiasm for my job, to be honest.

Phaedra clears her throat. "Yeah, true. We'll see how it goes with my nerdy introvert ass at the helm now." She drains the champagne in three gulps and presses the empty flute to the center of my chest. "Thanks for the bubbly. I'm gonna find a corner to hide in."

I place a hand over hers to take the glass. "I'll see you at the morning meeting."

She raises an eyebrow. "You bailing? It isn't even midnight, Cinderella."

I consciously avoid angling toward the sound of Natalia's nearby laughter. "I'm quite tired. You have things well in hand."

"Copy. But—just sayin'—if you don't stake your claim on Nat, someone else is going to have her 'well in hand.'"

I scoff, and she holds up a finger, continuing. "Hear me out. I wasn't nuts about the idea of you two dating at first, but it was mostly insecurity driving the bus on my feelings. And for real, dude... you're adults. You can work through it. I mean, hey, Cos and I did!" she adds with a smile. "I think you and Nat should give it another go." Before I can protest, she winks and glides into the crowd.

Spoken with the untainted confidence of someone whose own relationship is, at least at the moment, cradled by untroubled waters.

With Phaedra's assertion echoing in my mind, I flee the sound of Natalia's nearby voice and make my way to the bandstand, then wait for the current song to conclude. I chat with the leader and thank the musicians for the continued evening's entertainment. Along with handshakes all around, I slip each person a pair of thousand-dirham notes as a tip.

I take a step backward off the bandstand and jostle into

someone behind me. Hands clutch me just above the elbows, and my half-formed apology dies as I turn. Natalia stands, bracing her forearms with both hands as if holding herself back.

"Good evening, Miss Evans," I greet. "Did you have a request for the band? What's your wish?"

"*Wish?* Hmm, I'm supposed to ask for world peace," she replies, sardonic. "But Auntie Min always says, 'Wish for something possible, or prepare to be disappointed.' Which is—y'know—accurate in this case. With you."

Pretending not to register the barb, I hold an elbow out, inviting her to walk with me. She eyes it critically before draping a hand into the bend of my arm, her fingers not quite settling on the fabric of my jacket. I catch a wave of the warm amaretto scent of her hair, and my heart twists.

Peace between us has been challenging. We've barely spoken since June, aside from when required for business.

"Your tolerance for me is conspicuously slim," I note lightly.

Her arm withdraws. "Are you surprised?" she snaps. "It is what it is."

The bitterness in her tone spurs my own. "'*It is what it is*'? That's tautology at its finest, Miss Evans."

"Don't be snide. I only came over to talk because I have a professional request: I'd like to do a deep-dive article on Cosmin. I haven't pitched it to Nefeli at *ARJ* yet—I figured since I'm here anyway, I'd feel you out first." Apparently abashed at the phrasing she's chosen, she blushes, scowling. "Don't be gross," she adds, as if I've exploited the dual meaning.

I allow a mild, oblivious lift of my eyebrows. "I'm not sure what you mean. I said nothing."

96   **JOSIE JUNIPER**

"But I'll bet you thought it."

In our periphery, the commentator to whom Natalia was speaking earlier asserts his presence, signaling to her and pointing at the door. She gifts him with a nod and smile, and a cloud of jealousy blooms in me like ink dropped in water.

"I'm unclear as to why you'd bring this question to me," I tell her, my tone detached. "This is a matter for Emerald's head of communications." I take a step back and sketch out an inch-deep bow. "If you'll excuse me. *I wouldn't want to keep you from your date.*"

Her eyes go wide for a moment, surely remembering our walk that night in Melbourne when she said the same words, nine months ago. "*Wow*, nice little potshot," she breathes with sarcasm. "I'm glad I came to my senses about you."

Our eye contact is electric with challenge.

Natalia's gaze skates away and focuses beside me. A warm, bare arm interlocks with mine. Team Harrier's Sage Sikora—the sole woman on the grid, a reserve driver who stood in for the last eight races of the year when their lead driver was out with an injury—peers up at me from her diminutive height, wearing a kittenish smirk and a fantastical dress. The fabric is metallic silver, fashioned to look like medieval armor from the waist up, with a neon-pink tulle skirt erupting below.

"Ritzy bash, Franke," she says in her lazy, US West Coast accent. "The music would put my granny to sleep, but the food and booze are better here than at Harrier's shindig."

"Pleased you chose to defect to our gathering." I openly survey the aqua-haired spitfire on my arm, not above the vengeful pleasure of knowing Natalia is watching me do it. "Your outfit is unprecedented, as ever."

COMING IN HOT

Sage raises her liberally tattooed arms. "*All* of me is unprecedented, babes." A glance of acknowledgment to Natalia. "Natalie Everett, right? From *Auto Racing*?"

"Evans. Natalia," she corrects with a stiff smile.

"Right, right—sorry 'bout that, honeybee." Sage's attention shifts back to me. "Got your grafting boots on, Franky-boy? I believe"—her voice stretches into something with a twang of the American South—"y'all said somethin' about sweet-talkin' me."

I'm dismayed that Sage is alluding to possible negotiations in front of a reporter. At this stage, such deliberations should be scrupulously discreet. Even within the Emerald team, no one is aware I've made overtures to Miss Sikora about taking our second seat when Jakob Hahn's contract is up. Jakob himself doesn't know, and it would be a disastrous blow to his morale if he found out. His confidence has already incurred damage from finishing so far behind Cosmin in the points.

I know my response to Sage may present as petulant return fire to Natalia; my jealousy regarding her evening plans couldn't be more embarrassingly clear. Still, the flirtatious misdirection serves the interest of camouflaging business negotiations.

"Shall we seek out a quieter spot?" I lay a hand over Sage's on my arm.

"Hell yeah. I only crashed the party to see you."

My smile mirrors hers. I look up, offering a curt nod to Natalia in parting. "Reece will be in contact about the article. Enjoy your evening."

"Oh, always," she replies airily.

Sage tugs my arm, turning with a small hop and pulling me toward the doors, energetic as a child. As we exit the banquet room,

JOSIE JUNIPER

she gives my forearm a hearty pat before releasing me. "They say 'If all you have is a hammer, everything's a nail,' but I know you're better than that, Franke," she scolds with amusement. "Jealousy's an unsubtle tool. Using me to get under that woman's skin? Not cool."

"Was it so obvious?" I ask as we make our way into the hotel's lobby.

"Painfully so. And you guys'd make a cute couple. But don't be a dipshit."

I sigh. "Phaedra essentially gave me the same advice, in different words. You both appear to know what I want more than I do myself and aren't afraid to tell me so."

"Yeah, duh. First of all, can I just say Natalia is supernaturally gorgeous? *I'd* be trying to pull her if I didn't think it'd break your stony little heart. Megan Fox would look like 'the homely cousin' next to that woman. And second? Phaedra Morgan's not only hilarious as fuck, but whip-smart. You should listen to her."

"She *is* smart. All the more reason you should join the Emerald family."

"At ease, soldier. You're not *actually* gonna win me with sweet talk in a pretty accent. I want hard numbers. You think I don't know my worth?"

I push the front door open for her, and we walk out into the balmy night air. "Surely you recognize Emerald's worth as well."

Sage directs our course toward the water, the silver of her gown reflecting the cool purple external lights of the hotel. She walks backward, grinning at me and shaking a finger.

"We're evenly matched and you know it. Emerald's had a baller year with Cosmin Ardelean, but you're still number three." She twirls forward again, bouncing on her feet as she goes to the

COMING IN HOT

nearby railing and leans on it. "Jake Hahn's a nice guy—*too* nice, if you ask me—but he's a paper tiger. An empty racing suit."

I lean beside her with a shocked laugh. "Your little dagger is so sharp I didn't feel it until the twist."

"C'mon, let's be real. I've heard the gossip: Jake's wifey is expecting, and she's deep in his head, wringing her hands about his 'dangerous job' ever since his Peraltada-corner crash at the Mexican Grand Prix. As a result, *poof!*" She makes a magician's sleight-of-hand gesture. "His mojo's disappeared. Auf wiedersehen, baby."

I only lift my eyebrows, gazing at the water, allowing no clue of my concern over such murmurs making the rounds.

"You need another hotshot," Sage goes on. "Twin star attractions to make it *rain* sponsor dollars on Emerald. Can you imagine it? All eyes on Cosmin with his savage skill and pretty face, and—" She blows a kiss toward the light-spangled marina as if it's an adoring crowd. "Yours truly, the girl everyone's mother warned them about. Soon to be the first female grand prix winner."

There have been some people—the more sexist fans of the sport—who criticize Sage's arrogance, but I love the fact that she's like *all* drivers in that respect. She sees no reason to demure due to gender. She's boastful, fiery, larger than life.

My side-eye glance is coy. "It would be interesting to see what you might do with the E-19. It's certainly a different animal to Harrier's HR77."

"Tell me about it—the 77's a fuckin' tractor. And yet..." She bumps me with her shoulder. "I squeezed sooooo many points outta that thing. Wanna see me shine with a better car under my ass? Grab your checkbook and let's talk." She stands, taming her wild skirts with a swipe of one hand.

I straighten as well. "Bold words."

"*Psh!* Why waste breath on anything else?"

I adjust my cuffs. "You know Allonby, as constructors' champions three years running, are unlikely ever to take a chance on a woman driver."

Sage shrugs. "Probably not, sure. Their loss."

"And Team Coraggio?" I rub my jaw with a pensive half-smile. "Well, Miss Sikora...you aren't the only one who's heard gossip."

"Aw, ain't I?"

"No indeed. I know Bruno hosted you at his villa after Monza, hoping to get a jump on everyone else, taking your temperature. I have to assume he proposed 'taking your temperature' another way, because rumor has it you told a friend you'd 'drive a diaper truck' before you'd accept an offer from them."

Her eyes narrow for a moment. She slides a hand down her face, laughing.

"Me and my big mouth. Coraggio's boss is kind of an old lecher, true fact. But everyone's got a price. I may not be a fan of Bruno, but come on...such history! Who *wouldn't* drive for 'em? I'd be a moron to pass it up if they came knocking."

I chuckle. "At the risk of sounding like another 'old lecher,' I'd like to invite you to my Santorini home for a weekend during winter break. I'll assemble a more concrete offer for you to peruse."

"Oh my. *Saucy.*"

"You're welcome to bring a companion," I add, wanting to reassure her that my interest is purely business.

"Might take you up on that. Here, lemme see your phone."

I pass it to her, and she enters the contact—complete with a selfie, winking comically into the camera—then hands it back.

COMING IN HOT

"All righty, Franke. Guess we're BFFs now." She starts a slow, wandering gait toward the hotel, and I follow. "But this invitation had better not be because you wanna let that heartbreaker journo think we're up to no good on your Greek isle, just to get a reaction."

"Certainly not. I've no interest in playing games."

Sage laughs. "*Liar.* Our sport is one big game with mad stakes. It's only less fun when you're not winning."

I managed a fitful sleep between 2:00 and 5:00 a.m., then went downstairs to the gym, assaulting the treadmill at high speed while doing my best not to wonder where—and with whom— Natalia might wake this morning.

Like a song stuck in my head, my mind returns to the necklace. It might as well be the Hope Diamond, for its feeling of having cursed me. I've ferried it on and off airplanes in my carry-on a dozen times since Phaedra gave it back after Austria.

While finishing my workout, I make a decision: The necklace must return to Natalia. I need it out of my possession and scrubbed from my thoughts. If she doesn't wish to keep it, she can dispose of it how she sees fit.

I shower and dress, tuck the velvet box into the pocket of my suit jacket, and take the elevator to Natalia's floor, striding with purpose to the door of her room. My knock goes unanswered for a full minute. I extend one arm with a snap to draw back my sleeve and peer at my Bell & Ross wristwatch: 6:41.

Not here. She spent the night elsewhere.

I'm about to return to the elevator when the door flies open.

JOSIE JUNIPER

"Phae, what the—"

Natalia falls silent, and her eyes go wide under a pushed-up satin sleep mask. Her dark fringe sprouts over the top like unruly weeds. Sooty smears of cosmetics ring her vivid blue eyes, and she's wearing a massive pink T-shirt that hangs to her knees and reads THIS BITCH SNORES.

"Um, hi." She moves her bare legs behind the door. "Are you lost?"

My gaze darts past her into the darkness of the room, blackout curtains drawn tight. "Am I disturbing you?"

She sweeps the mask up and off, tossing it over her shoulder and combing her fringe into place with her fingers. "Don't get cute about it—we both know what you're really asking. Am I *alone*, right?"

"Not at all. I've simply realized it's quite early."

"Oh, bullshit." She lifts the neck of the T-shirt and wipes beneath her eyes, inspecting the gray smudges left on the fabric. "Cut to the chase. I'm tired. Not all of us look like a wealthy father of the bride at nothing o'clock in the morning."

My hand dives into the pocket where the velvet box is stowed, but I hesitate, struck with a case of nerves.

How does she do this to me? All week long I speak to powerful people without a ripple of anxiety: FIA officials, sponsor CEOs, heads of state in host countries. Yet this woman—barefoot and sleepy, dressed in an absurd novelty shirt—affects me as if she were a planetary empress holding my fate in her palm.

I withdraw the box. "I'd like for you to keep this. I…can't have it anymore."

She frowns, moving to sandwich herself between the entryway wall and the door, arms crossed tightly. "If that's the necklace, *I* can't have it either, and you know it."

COMING IN HOT
103

"Consider it a gift of... friendship."

"We're not friends anymore. And if I wanted to wear something worth tens of thousands, I'd hang a first-edition copy of *Catcher in the Rye* around my neck." She folds my fingers over the box and pushes my hand away.

"You needn't keep it," I insist. "You once spoke of helping the library in your hometown. This could go far in that goal. I won't be hurt if you sell it." I meet her eyes. "Please, kleine Hexe."

Her trembling hand moves to the hollow of her throat as if the necklace hangs there still, and her eyes brighten with tears. "Don't call me that," she almost whispers.

"Es tut mir leid," I automatically apologize. In truth, it was a relief to say the former pet name aloud, inadvertent as it may have been.

With one hand, she picks at her opposite sleeve hem. The little nails of her toes are painted a shimmering bronze color, and she flexes them on the herringbone-tiled floor.

"*No.*" She shakes her head. "It's too valuable. You can give it to someone else."

"Do you think I could give another woman the same gift?"

Hostility flashes in her eyes. "You once offered me *cash*, Klaus, and in almost the same breath made it clear that was your standard operating procedure. We all got your little stack of euros. Why not necklaces too?"

"It *was* my 'standard operating procedure.'" I touch her chin and tip her head to meet my gaze. "You once made me hope for more."

I graze a knuckle along her jaw, then trail it down her neck. By the time I've reached the shoulder, her eyes have closed. She sways a little. I cup her hand, placing the box on her palm.

"I won't trouble you further," I tell her soberly. "This finishes it."

Her lips part as if to say something, but then she presses them together.

"Thank you," she manages after a pause, rubbing the box's velvet with her thumb. "For your generosity. And for understanding why it can't mean more. Not at this point." She shrugs, but I can tell she doesn't truly feel the casualness implied by the gesture. "We blew it. Not meant to be."

I look down at our feet—hers bare and soft, mine armored in Berluti loafers. "It's fine."

It's not fine. It will never be fine.

"Goodbye, Miss Evans."

She steps back, swallowed by darkness, and closes the door.

When I get to my room, I sit on the edge of the bed for a long time, studying the sunrise out the window.

I should never have apologized back in Melbourne. Had she continued hating me after the night we met, it might have healed faster for us both. But I couldn't let well enough alone, and the scars are much worse for having prolonged it...

Taking my phone from a breast pocket, I look up the town in which Natalia was raised, then send a donation of thirty thousand dollars—the value of the necklace—to the library there, in case Natalia decides to keep my gift.

10

LONDON

TWO WEEKS LATER

NATALIA

When I walk through the door of The Black Penny in Covent Garden, my boss is already there. I'm ten minutes early but still look late compared to Nefeli. She's got a bowl of fancy porridge and an Aperol spritz, because hey, it's 10:30 in the morning, so why not? Surrounding her at the slab table is an open laptop, *two* mobile phones, and a legal pad crammed with notes in her all-caps script.

She slants a look at me over her square-framed glasses while simultaneously taking a bite of fruit-topped porridge and typing one-handed on the laptop. She's always reminded me of a gray-haired version of costume designer Edna from *The Incredibles*: short, acerbic, intense. Her scratchy, rapid-fire voice sounds like a malfunctioning kitchen appliance.

Just to look at her, it'd be easy to discount her as an eccentric sixtysomething who probably has a house full of weird art and jazz

LPs. But this is *the* Nefeli Laskaris, the pioneering Athens-born British journalist who broke dozens of nineties scandals wide— political, corporate, art world—with ruthless determination and searing wit. She's a legend.

She and her husband, Konstantin Laskaris, own a bunch of publications. Their only child, Alexander, is a gorgeous insufferable jerk who's my coworker at *ARJ*. We went on a sorta-kinda date earlier this year when I was trying to stop perseverating on Klaus, and suffice it to say the evening was a disaster. Fortunately, Nefeli has no clue it happened.

I pull out a chair and sit, unslinging my Kate Spade briefcase.

One of Nefeli's phones rings. She peers at it and sends the call to voicemail. "*Eeuugghh*, that little weasel," she mutters under her breath. Never one to waste energy on small talk, she fixes me with a look and adds, "Congratulations on your first successful season with the magazine. I'm giving you a raise, love. Twelve and a half percent."

"Holy shi— I, uh…wow! Really? That's incredibly generous. Are you sure?"

"Trying to talk me out of it?" she asks, amused. "Of course I'm bloody sure. Kon tried to wrangle me down to a more modest figure, but *you* certainly shouldn't."

"Of course not," I say with a laugh. "I'm just surprised."

"Know your worth, love. I don't think it's inaccurate to say you're in part responsible for the growth of F1's popularity with women this year. Your voice is spot-on. You bring the sexy and the fun, whilst making technical details approachable to new fans. Your program on our YouTube channel has massive views. Men

COMING IN HOT

want to look at you, and women want to *be* you." She takes a sip of her cocktail.

"Oh my God—thank you. I'll do my best to make you proud." I root in my bag for my legal pad and lay it on the table, rotating it Nefeli's way. "I've been wanting to talk with you about a story idea that I think will knock everyone's socks off. I'd like to do a deep dive on Emerald's Cosmin Ardelean. Not only is he—"

"Nonono," Nefeli says, planting a fingertip on the pad and scooting it away. "That's too obvious. *Autosport* and *Racer* both have splashy features on him in the works."

"But I might have a unique angle to explore."

One of her phones vibrates, and she silences it again while shaking her head. "No. I have something better. I'd like you to show the world what an F1 team principal really does. They're practically celebrities these days, but who the bloody hell knows what they *do*?" She picks up her spoon and waves it grandly like a scepter. "Sit on their thrones and bark orders, when they're not spouting something quippy for that TV show everyone's addicted to?"

There's a tugging in my chest, a prickle of dread at where this could be headed. I slide the legal pad back into my briefcase. "Might be a hard sell. Making the businessy part of the sport, uh...exciting."

"Bollocks." Nefeli sinks her spoon into the porridge. "Business can be hot. Do you have any clue how popular those 'billionaire romances' are? The glamour, the power...of course most real billionaires look like fairy-tale goblins with expensive watches, but"—she holds my eye with a twinkle of mischief—"not *all* of them."

At this point I'm praying she's not going where I think she is. I force a patient smile and wait for her to continue.

"Allonby's boss is rather a prick," she states. "And Bruno at Coraggio could talk the legs off a chair, but he's not 'eye candy.' And we want scads of good photos."

Nonono, don't say it...

"The obvious choice is Klaus Franke at Emerald. He's handsome, rich as Croesus, and a bit tragic—dead wife and that."

I try not to let my shoulders visibly sag. "True, but...maybe that's exactly why he won't love the idea of a big feature. I get the sense he's weird about journalists."

Yeah, I "got that sense" six months ago when my heart was breaking in a hotel room in Montréal...

"Rubbish. That sneaky little bitch from *Chalk Talk* did him dirty a few years ago, but I'm sure he's over it by now. Emerald's star is ascending. He'll cooperate to keep the momentum up. And I know you're close with the team owner. Morgan could insist he comply if the old boy is a beast about it."

My mouth is suddenly so dry, I have to excuse myself to get a glass of water. On my way back, I think of a possible out.

"What if Alexander took this one?" I ask my boss.

She lifts a pencil-thin eyebrow. "I love my Alekos, but thée mou, no. His writing doesn't have the proper touch for this. He thinks he's the second coming of Hunter S. Thompson. What we need is your warmth, your realness. The Natalia Evans sense of fun."

"That's flattering, don't get me wrong. But—"

"I want female fans to swoon, love. You can make readers *fall for* Klaus Franke. After winter break, you'll do a series of interviews from the first race in March until silly season. Think of the photo ops! Women will go mad for it."

It'd put me in far from a good light, but for a moment I consider spilling everything about Klaus's and my history. I allowed myself to be swayed by our attraction, and the results were unprofessional. I have to own it, at least to myself. Giving him a second chance after that first night together was bad enough—there can't be a third.

This assignment will be work only. *I'm not letting down my guard.*

Resigned, I do my best to inject enthusiasm into my smile before Nefeli clocks my resistance. "I'm sure that'd make a terrific article. Thank you for the opportunity."

I'm screwed.

KENTUCKY

TWO WEEKS LATER

Auntie Min has always been a believer in Mary Poppins's "A Spoonful of Sugar" philosophy, which is why she plied me with my favorite Christmas eggnog muffins before we had to redecorate the guest room.

We've been at it for hours. I'm sitting on the floor, screwing together a bed frame. A new queen-size mattress leans against the wall, plastic stripped off, airing out. Minnie's on the glider rocker near the window, supervising.

I check the directions again and fish another bit of hardware out of the bag. "This big bed isn't necessary. I don't mind the twin when I'm here for the holidays."

"Who says I won't have other guests?" She combs the end of her thick silver braid with her fingers.

I narrow my eyes. "Why do you seem nervous?"

A memory comes back: her odd tone over the phone when I was in my little London flat, packing my suitcase after meeting with Nefeli, preparing to fly here to Kentucky. Auntie Min told me she has "special news for Christmas," but isn't sure if I'll like it.

Could it be...Oh my God, maybe she's getting married? What if the veterinarian fell for Minnie instead of Naomi?

A grin spreads across my face. "Auntie Min, 'other guests'? Do you have a beau who occasionally stays the night? Because I suspect you'd make him sleep in the guest room until he buys you a ring." I stand and flop the mattress sideways onto the bed platform, sliding it into place with my knees.

"Child, *no*." She chuckles, flapping a hand at me. "Focus on your task and hush. I'll fetch the linens so I don't feel useless."

"*Useless*?" I give her a hug. "Before I was even up, you spent hours packing sack lunches for the shelter. Give yourself a rest on Christmas Eve."

"A rest feels better after you've *done things*," she asserts.

I follow her into the hall. "After the guest room is tidied, can we have cocoa and watch movies? I wanna do the first presents."

It's our tradition to open just one the night before, then watch holiday films. Minnie has always spoiled me, despite her image as a practical woman. A dozen perfectly wrapped gifts await me beneath the tree, which is loaded with ornaments I made in childhood or bought on my travels.

COMING IN HOT 111

"Get a fire going," she says. "I'll pop these sheets on and heat up cocoa."

I make a fire in the woodstove, then curl up on the floral sofa with my laptop. One of Minnie's crochet blankets is tucked around me, lights twinkle on the tree, the scent of white pine and spices hangs in the air. From the kitchen comes the comforting sound of Minnie fussing about, talking to herself.

This is the house I grew up in. I can't recall a ton about the apartments where I lived with my parents until I was seven—there were several. I remember I had an orange cat named Gingersnap at one, and my parents left it behind when we moved again.

It should've been a warning to me, that cat.

I pull my focus back to the document on my laptop screen:

Within the high-stakes world of Formula 1, a team principal holds the critical role, guiding the team to victory both on and off the track. This "superboss" oversees everything from strategy to hiring to budgets, but perhaps the most important role is ensuring effective communication between experts who are all part of a precisely functioning machine of over a thousand "parts." This complex, demanding position requires extensive knowledge and skill...

Ugh, my writing here is undeniably boring. It might as well be a ninth-grade essay. Lacking in clarity, full of facts and padding, but no damned soul.

So much for the alleged "Natalia Evans sense of fun" Nefeli lauded...

I clap the cover shut and set the laptop aside, snuggling into the sofa cushions with a sigh. I don't know why I'm bothering with this before the season has even started. Whether I type five words or five thousand before things kick off in Bahrain, I'll be stuck with that maddening, haunted, gorgeous man for *months*. Reminded, practically every time I look at him or catch his tempting scent, of how close we came to making it work...

Auntie Min comes into the den and sets a tray on the coffee table—cocoa and spritz cookies—before flopping onto the sofa with a soft groan. "It's so good to have you here." She combs her braid end. "Nothing feels quite as nice as...coming home, does it?"

Driving past the blue barn at the Marshall farm was as wonderful this week as it always is—that relief, the simple joy of homecoming. Part of me longs to stay, I have to admit. Everything is moving so fast now in my life. I'm *supposed* to love the *ARJ* job, the travel, the prestige. And mostly I do. But...a slower pace—a quiet home office with a bird feeder outside the window, maybe working on one of the many book ideas I outline as they come to me—it sounds pretty damned good some days.

Minnie's expression does a sudden U-turn, as if she's afraid she's said too much. She gives a soft laugh. "But enough of that corny claptrap. Let's do our gifts."

I jump up and beeline for the tree like I'm thirty-five going on seven, playing it up and shaking presents. "Hmm, this feels like...a sweater? Ooh! And this is rattly."

"Mind you don't break it," she scolds good-naturedly.

I grab the gift I want her to open first—a new ornament—and hand it over before returning to the tree and digging around toward the back. "What's this one?" I hold up a small, flat box that's wrapped in red paper with *HO HO HO* printed in white, not the Disney paper Minnie has used for all her gifts. "No tag."

COMING IN HOT   113

Minnie frowns. "Bring that here."

I pass it to her. "Who's it for?"

"It's for you. But choose something else tonight." She sets the little box aside and unwraps her own gift, a felted Highland cow with a Santa hat. "Could that be any more adorable?" she breathes, getting up to put it on the tree. "I absolutely love it."

I stretch to grab the mystery box. "I wanna know what this is," I tell her. "And who sent it." *Could it be Klaus? Is that possible?*

She turns to face me, and the smile wilts from her face. She perches on the edge of the sofa, hands tangled in her lap. "I wanted to have a talk before giving that to you, but..." She shrugs, eyes troubled. "Maybe this is better."

I remove the paper the same way Minnie does—gingerly, so it can be reused—and lift the lid. Beneath a layer of white tissue, a photograph stares up at me.

I'm seven years old, sitting on the hood of a dented and rusted Honda Accord, wearing lavender OshKosh overalls with a flowery thermal shirt, hair in two braids. My parents are on each side, leaning on the car.

Dad looks smirky, his arms folded. Hair rockstar long, grunge-era flannel, ripped jeans. He's like Kurt Cobain's more handsome brother. My mom is so similar to me it's spooky. She's biting her lower lip, flirting with the camera. They both look like they're in a fashion shoot and a random kid happened to show up—there's no sense they're aware of my presence.

Unsurprising.

"I remember that car," I say evenly, betraying nothing of my storm of emotions. "But not the people." I put the top on the box. "I've never seen that one. Did they send it? They're... *alive*?"

"Natty!" Auntie Min bursts out. "Good gracious, of course they're alive. Why would you say such a morbid thing?"

I shrug as if I couldn't care less, then attempt to hand the box to Minnie.

"There should be another picture in there." She gently pushes my hand back.

My heart hammers. The news is flying at me like branches smacking me in the face during an out-of-control horseback ride with no reins.

They're finally contacting me. Oh God...

I tip the lid off the box again, whipping the top photo aside to view the one beneath.

Whoa.

They're in their fifties now, but unmistakable. Mom's hair is in a bob and has a little silver, her makeup is subtle rather than kohl-eyed nineties drama, but...it's her. Dad has some middle-aged spread and his hair is grayer than Mom's, but he hasn't changed it—still long, in a messy ponytail—and his face is the same.

His smile shows a peek of his teeth, and with a shock, I remember something I'd absolutely forgotten: He has a diagonal chip in the top left incisor. I don't know why this affects me so much, but it's more jolting than anything else—like a song you haven't heard for decades, which ushers in the exact feeling of being a certain age.

My hands shake as I replace the lid and hand it back. Minnie sets it on the table.

"They're, uh...still together, huh?" I ask.

"Yes. But that's a long story—the circumstances."

What the heck is that supposed to mean?

COMING IN HOT

I reach for my cocoa, then set it back down. My stomach tumbles like a runaway barrel down a hill as I fight to integrate all this new information. "Did they have..." *Oh God, I can barely get the words out.* "Um, other kids?"

"Lord *no*, child," Minnie says, a little shocked.

I keep my face impassive. "Well, the 'Ho Ho Ho' paper is fitting, because I'm waiting for the punchline. *Why* did they send this?" I swallow hard. "I mean, now?"

Auntie Min scoots closer. "That's why I got the new bed. Your daddy and mama are coming home. They'll be living with me for a while to get on their feet."

The barrel rolling inside me hits a wall and explodes into splinters.

"They're in town, staying with friends," she goes on. "Coming over here tomorrow."

I jump up, my knee hitting the coffee table and sloshing cocoa onto the tray. "*No.* I'm not doing this."

"Sit down, honey. *Stop.* Let's talk."

"I'll go right to the airport and back to London," I threaten. "You can't make me do this!"

"Please. Sit. *Down*," she orders, more sternly than I'm used to.

I lower to the sofa, eyes burning with suppressed tears.

"I'm going to let them explain to you where they've been, and why," Minnie says soberly. "It's not my story to tell—they always made me promise not to talk about it. And believe me, Natty...*it wasn't easy on me*. When you stopped asking, a few years after they left, well...I didn't know if that was a relief or just plain tragic. I didn't agree with their reasoning for hiding what happened, but I kept my word. It was a joy to raise you, so..." She stares into her lap for a moment. "Maybe my selfishness was part of it." Her eyes are intense when she looks up. "Their foolishness was my gain. I got *you*."

The emotion I see on her face is intimidating, so I can't help making a dismissive joke about my parents, holding on to my resentment like a point of reference in a dark room. "Yeah, okay, what was it?" I ask with a sneer. "Is this some cheesy movie where 'mommy and daddy went on the run to escape the mob'?"

"They made big mistakes, and they know it. There isn't going to be a heroic plot twist. But you have some changes coming—"

"Forget it," I interrupt. "No thanks. They can't pop up twenty-eight years later and expect to be a family." I lean in, emphasizing. "*They...are...strangers.* I don't know them, and I don't want to."

Minnie's icy-blue gaze sears into mine. "You know I rarely insist on things, but *I'm insisting*. Hear them out. I raised you with manners. If I can be strong, so can you."

I sag back with both hands over my face, suffocating under a combination of guilt and fear and fury.

Minnie pulls me into a hug. "Oh, Natty," she sighs, rocking me. "Do you think I want to give up my status after all these years and say, 'There ya go—I raised your little girl. Now you can have her back'? I'm scared shitless. And I know you're angry. It's justified."

"I hate them so much right now," I mutter savagely, "and I don't think I've *ever* actually hated them. I was sad and confused for years; then I just didn't feel anything, but...this is the first time I've hated them, and it's *so much*. I don't know where to put it."

"It's time you stopped putting your anger someplace and started letting yourself look at it. You've got some unresolved stuff, kiddo.

COMING IN HOT

It's not an accident that you always lose your heart to unavailable older men. You gravitate toward people who are bound to disappoint you, and men are just...well, the handiest candidates in that department."

I can see that my aunt is really upset. She's desperate for me to be okay with all this. I have to look like I'm swimming, smiling and waving to her as she watches from the shore while I'm actually drowning. Making people feel okay, putting their needs before my own, it's what I do. But inside, I'm furious.

I was such an easy child, because I started my life with Minnie as a respectful guest, and even when it became apparent that the arrangement was permanent, I worked hard to be no trouble: clean room, good grades, no high school summer keggers by the river, no messing with boys in back seats.

I was the only witness to my quiet heartache, which leaked privately out of the well-hidden cracks in my sense of control. I could exert the discipline never to talk with Minnie about my grief over my parents' absence—it would have felt ungrateful, so I was careful to prove at all times that I was a responsible and sunshiny Good Girl—but I couldn't choose what I dreamt...and I *did* dream of my parents often.

What do you do when you find out that the characters who inhabit your dream world are about to "come to life"?

My smile is stiff. I rise to my feet and grab the cocoa tray with the excuse of mopping it off—I need to hurry to the kitchen before my tears betray me.

"Fine, all right." I take a bracing breath and inject warmth into my expression, turning away and saying over my shoulder, "It's going to be fine. This won't ruin Christmas."

118   **JOSIE JUNIPER**

▚▚▚▚▚

The morning after Auntie Min drops the parent-bomb, I hear a car pull up while I'm in the bathroom getting ready. Instinctively I shut the door and lock it, then hold the edge of the sink, listening to the ambient sounds of their arrival. Strange voices. Minnie's familiar tones, gone high with emotion—she's crying. A bit of laughter. Kitchen chairs barking against the linoleum. The clang of a kettle hitting the sink as it's filled.

If I wait much longer, Minnie will come get me, and I don't want to be dragged in like a cowering child. I'm eight years older now than they were when they dumped me with Minnie to take off on a one-way trip to Los Angeles. *I'm the grown-up here, dammit. Not them.*

I open the door and stride down the hall.

Jason looks up as I pause in the doorway. Sherri swivels, white-knuckling the chair back. No one speaks. My legs feel like water, but I stand rigid.

Minnie comes toward me, hand out as one might coax a bird to eat from their palm. "They're here, honey."

I lift my chin. "So I see."

Jason stands and pulls out a chair between himself and Sherri, across from where Minnie's favorite coffee mug marks her place. I go to Minnie's spot and claim it, sliding her mug across the table to the place where Jason grips the finials of the rejected chair.

I look at each of them with the *What do you have to say for yourself?* energy of a school principal.

"Merry Christmas, baby," Sherri ventures in a hopeful voice.

Jesus, I'd forgotten it's Christmas Day. Minnie and I had our

COMING IN HOT   119

festivities last night—I think she suggested opening the rest of the presents to jolly me out of my bad mood after the parental-return revelation—and since waking, there's been nothing but the horrible countdown to this moment.

Both of them stare. Jason's eyes—blue as Minnie's and mine—glisten with emotion.

He looks at Sherri, his expression between joy and panic. "My God, Pinkie...she looks just like you."

"She has your eyes, though," she responds immediately.

A quarter-century on the West Coast hasn't scrubbed away Jason's rural Kentucky twang, but Sherri—who was a "city gal" from Lexington when she met my father—sounds flatter, more like me. I expected their voices to give me a shock of recognition, but... *nothing*.

"I'm sitting right here," I say coldly, "so please don't talk about me like I'm a piece of furniture."

"*Natty...*" Auntie Min whispers.

"I have things I need to get back to today," I lie. "Let's...uh"—I lift my hands, then drop them to my lap, a conductor who's forgotten the music—"do the catching up and get on with our lives."

"We're real proud of you," Jason says. "Been reading everything you write."

"Cool," I respond, blasé.

"*Natty!*" Minnie whispers with more urgency. She fixes Jason with a pleading look. "For pity's sake, Jace. Quit dragging this out. Tell her, so she'll understand."

Sherri plants both hands over her eyes like a child in a game of hide-and-seek. The words spill out of her in a rush, tense with held-back tears.

"We didn't plan to leave you here forever—we were just going on ahead to get settled. Everything in L.A. was expensive and the apartment was in a bad neighborhood, and we knew you were better off here until we could afford something safer. We were so broke it started to seem like that'd never happen, so we started doing some...delivery work." Her hands slide down to her cheeks. "For a...a drug dealer. It was stupid, but we figured as long as we weren't selling it or using it—"

"You weren't using *your damned heads*," Minnie inserts under her breath.

"—it didn't seem as bad, but..." Sherri trails off, lowering to rest her head on the table.

After a pause, I speak up. "Lemme guess, you guys got caught and went to prison." I'm surprised at how impassive I sound. It's like a story that has no connection to me. I'm just a reader, spying the plot twist in a disappointing book.

"*I* did, yes," Sherri confesses, deflated. "But it wasn't like you probably think."

▚▚▚▚▚

It's seven hours ahead in Romania, where Phaedra is spending the holidays with Cosmin. Two o'clock in the morning here, and I can't sleep. I send Phae a text.

Me: You awake?

Phae: Duh of course. When do I evr sleep in? The question is what are YOU doing up

COMING IN HOT 121

Me: I have a car question, and you can build engines and stuff, so I figured you're the one to ask. Can a car really be "hot-wired" with a screwdriver, or is that just in movies?

Phae: Okay that's random AF. Many cars up til the mid 90s could be hot-wired with a flathead screwdriver, yeah. Why?

I flop back onto the pillows with a sigh, thinking over the conversation with my parents this afternoon. I pick up the phone again.

Me: Bc my mother apparently killed someone with a screwdriver, and I guess I was trying to find a lie in her story. She said she had it in her bag bc she and my dad had this janky old car and that was how they started it.

Phae: HOLY SHITMONKEYS. What??? Your mom is a screwdriver killer? This sounds like the plot to a 90s dark comedy

Phae: Sorry, not funny

I laugh a little, despite myself, at the absurdity of it all, and it's actually such a relief—I don't think I've smiled all day.

Me: She's been in prison for 25 yrs, Phae. Jason stayed in Cali to be near her. They never wanted me to know but had a change of heart after Sherri got out.

Phae: Did she tell you why she did it?

Me: She was working for a drug dealer and someone tried to rape her. Prosecution said the guy could've lived if she'd called an ambulance. Her public defender was crap. Also she wouldn't inform on the dealer, bc she was afraid Jason would get killed for it.

Phae: I'm so sorry, Nat. WOW. Fuck. I wish I could hug you, and you know I hate hugging

Me: Second question: Auntie Min said I date older unavailable guys bc of my parents. That seems too obvious, too cliché. She's wrong, isn't she?

There's a very long pause before the reply comes through.

Phae: Everyone's a cliché sometimes

11

SANTORINI, GREECE

SIX WEEKS LATER

KLAUS

There's little point in ruminating on everything I did wrong last year. I've no clue why I torture myself still. For several months after the catastrophe of our initial meeting, I briefly succeeded in winning Natalia's cautious affection. But having made a mess of it again last summer in Montréal, I'd be mad to expect a third chance.

I've not seen her since the end-of-season party eight weeks ago in December, when I turned my back on her and strolled away with Sage Sikora. Our only contact has been a recent exchange of brief emails in which we set up this visit to launch the interview series.

Her flight is going to be late, which means when it arrives precisely on time, *I'm* the one who looks late. She's waiting outside—fingertips drumming on the tow handle of her suit-case—as I swoop into a stretch of free kerb.

She offers a terse nod when I wave. I pop the boot and pull the safety brake, moving to climb out of the convertible Alfa Romeo to help stow her luggage.

"Please don't," she insists, her voice flat.

I lower myself into the seat again, and the car shifts as she slings her suitcase in. She strides to the passenger door, which I stretch to open before she can instruct me not to. Her huge octagonal sun-glasses obscure half her face, and I push my Bulgari Le Gemmes up onto my head, hoping she'll do the same when she climbs into the car so we can make proper eye contact. She doesn't.

"How was your flight?"

"Mercifully uneventful," she says simply, smoothing her travel-wrinkled skirt, then placing her handbag into the footwell.

I flick a glance over my shoulder and ease onto the road. For a few minutes, we say nothing. Natalia's glossy hair roils like a dark storm cloud, and she digs a tatter-edged pink chiffon scarf from her bag, folding it diagonally and tying it beneath her chin like an elderly woman.

"I can put the top up, if you prefer," I offer.

"I'm fine."

After a pause, I venture a smile. "Hermès?" I ask cheekily.

She tips her head my way with a flat expression, lips in a severe line. "It used to belong to my aunt, and she probably bought it at the Woolworth in Lexington decades before I was born."

"An orange Hermès scarf would look lovely against your hair and complement the blue of your eyes."

"Thanks for the fashion tip, Tim Gunn. I'll be sure to add that

COMING IN HOT   125

to my list of 'how to waste a thousand bucks on ninety centimeters of silk.'" She turns her attention to the scenery zipping past.

I'm stung by her rebuff, though I have little right to be. A dozen replies cycle through my mind over the next few miles. My frustration wins out and I cut a hard-jawed look at her. "Is this how we are going to be with each other? Because if so, it will make for a long and miserable season."

"Oh, you are *priceless*. I love how you assume I can flip a switch and be smooth and impartial with the jerk who toyed with my feelings for half of last year." She whips the sunglasses off her face. "I didn't want this assignment, Klaus. And—"

"Nor did I!" I shoot back. "Reece spent three days convincing me of the value in speaking with you at all before I assented."

Natalia looks stung, to my surprise. After a beat, her eyes narrow and her expression reverts to indignation. "*Sure.* I'd bet my bottom dollar it was *your* suggestion to do the first interview in Santorini. Coaxing me into your...sexy little spider lair."

My lips quirk. "Sexy spider lair?"

"We could've met up *anywhere*," she goes on, "because you're a damned billionaire. The first interview could be at McMurdo Station in Antarctica if you'd wanted, but...nooooo!" She flips her hands with a sarcastic laugh. "It's a sultry shag pad in Greece. *Show-off.*"

I have to bite my lip to hold back laughter. She jams her sunglasses back on and swipes a tendril of escaped hair under the kerchief.

"What wicked images dance in that dazzling mind of yours, hmm? You're showing your hand, kleine Hexe, using words like 'sexy' and 'sultry.'"

"And you're showing your egotism by assuming my bad mood is because I'm pining away over your pompous self. Or do you think everyone just ceases to exist outside the boundary of your shadow?"

I give her an affronted look. "You're trying to bait me."

"Okay, perfect. Let's definitely keep it all about *you*."

Another mile passes in stiff silence.

"Fine," I say coolly. "We will be professional. Cordial."

"Works for me."

Another mile.

"How was your Christmas holiday?" I ask, trying for something neutral.

"Dandy. Santa brought me a new pair of roller skates, and the news that my long-lost mother is a screwdriver murderess."

I glance at Natalia, who's retying the scarf.

"Is this a joke I'm failing to get?"

She sighs with enough drama that I can hear it over the engine, then cradles both hands on her face and slides them off.

"It's... Forget it. Sure, a joke. Let's stick to the professional stuff—I agree. Lemme get a bath and an hour of downtime, and we can start the first interview before dinner."

While Natalia bathes and rests, I go over the menu with my cook and housekeeper, Elena, for tonight's dinner. Next, I go outside to pick some fresh oranges. I set one in front of the statue of Aphrodite in the garden, then bring the rest to Elena so she can make portokalopita—an orange cake that is one of my favorites.

Going to my bedroom with the intention of getting a book to read on the patio, I round a corner and find Natalia leaning

COMING IN HOT 127

half into my room. She's changed into a gauzy maroon dress that brushes her calves and leaves her shoulders bare.

I walk up quietly. One of her hands is gripping the doorway, and her fingers caress the wood, restless.

"Can I help you find something?" I ask.

She chirps out a tiny shriek, hopping back with a hand braced over her chest. The dress has abalone-shell buttons down the front, from the low neck to the hem.

"Holy crap, you startled me," she says with a flare of anger. "I was just curious." She points at my doorway. "The, uh, architecture is interesting."

"Is it?" I pass her into the room, then sweep an arm out in invitation.

She wanders inside after me, clasping her hands behind her back and scanning the surroundings—tile floors, white stucco walls, beamed ceilings, stained-glass windows. Going to one of the two bookshelves flanking the hearth, she trails a finger along the spines, then tips free an old hardbound copy of *Don Quixote*.

"Hmm. These actually look read," she murmurs, almost to herself.

"If they were for display, they'd be in the living room where people could admire my excellent taste." I give a tight smile. "Isn't that what a 'pompous' man would do?"

She replaces the book. "I'm sure you entertain plenty of admirers in here. I know your reputation."

"I don't 'entertain' in *this* room," I retort.

Natalia drifts to the other bookcase, and the urge to call her away is strong. Instead I watch her, with a sense not unlike peering beneath a bandage: I don't want to look, but I can't resist—it's sore, fragile, too soon, naked. I'm testing myself.

128   **JOSIE JUNIPER**

"Not alphabetized," she says lightly.

"No."

"Or divided by subject." She pulls down Margaret Atwood's *Cat's Eye*. "And not sorted by color, like on those silly home remodeling shows." She replaces the book a few inches from where it originated.

I cross to where she stands. We're so close I can smell the shampoo scent of the still-damp hair she's pushed behind her ears. A visceral memory intrudes: washing her hair the night we met. My pulse jumps. Her wide, black pupils are like dangerous holes in a blue sky. She drags her gaze from mine and looks at the bookshelf again.

"This one...is Sofia's," she says.

"What of it?" My defensive grief is so obvious I can hear it myself.

Natalia lays one hand flat at the center of my chest—a lightning-quick touch, and no less shocking. "Don't take it like a criticism, Klaus. It's just a thing I noticed."

Could she feel my heartbeat against her palm in that moment? I'm not sure if its pounding is more like the promising kick of a growing infant or that of an unbroken horse warning away those who venture too close.

Suddenly we're farther apart. I assume she's taken a step backward before I realize it was me—the woundedness on her face clues me in.

"Isn't it time we got this thing started?" she asks crisply.

My eyebrows lift. "*This...?*" I echo, the word more a shape than a sound.

"The interview." She takes a step back and points a thumb. "It, uh, smells like the food's almost ready. Let's work during dinner. No need for phony small talk." She pivots and nearly collides

COMING IN HOT 129

with the wall before redirecting her path and disappearing into the dark corridor.

I watch the empty doorway as the warmth of Natalia's touch on my chest fades like a handprint on cold glass. Before following her out, I turn to the shelf and put *Cat's Eye* in its proper place— exactly where Sofia chose.

✶✶✶✶✶

The food is so good that conversation is impossible until we've razed the appetizers—marinated eggplant, goat cheese spread with thyme and lemon, rosemary pita, tomatokeftedes.

"Damn," Natalia sighs, mopping up a puddle of seasoned olive oil with her flatbread, "I'm almost scared of Elena. How's she such an amazing cook?" She folds the bit of bread into her mouth. Her tongue darts to catch a drop of olive oil sliding down her thumb, and I try not to stare.

She dabs her mouth with a napkin and leans back. "I'm not going to have room for the main course if I don't control myself."

She flips back a fresh page on her legal pad and uncaps a fountain pen—lapis blue with mother-of-pearl. Something about the way she holds it tells me it's new and unfamiliar. I assume it's a gift, but it seems too luxurious to have been bought by the aunt whom Natalia has described as frugal and practical.

"Did he gift you that for Christmas?" I ask, nodding at the pen.

The "he" in question isn't a specific person, though an image springs to mind of the Scotsman who was Natalia's date at the party two months ago. I'm purely cold reading, hoping she will fill in the blanks.

"He *who*? Nice try. It's from Nefeli. Lots of writers at the magazine got one." She scribbles a spiral in the margin of the page to set the ink flowing. "Okay, let's cover basics: your thoughts on last season, hopes for the upcoming one, blah blah blah."

As the interview unfolds, I glance at the legal pad and pause midsentence, surprised by the collection of curls and swoops there.

"You know shorthand? Quite skilled."

"It's just Teeline, not Pitman or Gregg," she says with an airy wave, as if this is somehow less of an accomplishment.

"I've always seen you use your phone recorder on race weekends." I give her a mischievous smile. "Are you trying to impress me?"

"Wow, absolutely," she deadpans. "Again, it's all about you. What time are you getting up tomorrow so you can crow and make the sun rise?" She sweeps her heavy curtain of dark hair around to one side of her neck. "Okay, back at it. What would you say was your biggest challenge last season?"

Trying not to fall in love with you...

From inside the house, I hear the front door open and close. Then a woman's voice calls out: "Yo, Franky-boy! You here?"

Natalia's eyes are cold when they light on mine. Moments later, Sage Sikora appears in the open patio doorway, gripping the frame with drama like she's a fashion photograph.

"Theeeere you are," she announces brightly. "Think fast!"

She underhand-tosses a ring of keys to me, and I catch them against my chest.

Sage's attention shifts to Natalia. "Oh hey, it's you! Natalia. *Evans*," she adds with a self-deprecating smile. "I remember this time. Got Klaus in the hot seat, eh? Or..." She angles a sly look at me. "Is this more recreational?"

I'm about to reply, but Sage goes on without waiting for an

COMING IN HOT   131

answer. Her mind is as energetic as her driving, and she's off chattering again after an interval shorter than the quickest pit stop.

"Thanks for letting me use your new Jag while I was here. Awesome ride."

I check Natalia's expression, trying to decrypt it, but she gives no more than the Aphrodite statue in the garden. "I thought you flew out this morning and left the car at the airport," I tell Sage.

"Wellllll…" she drawls, coming to lean against the arm of my chair, tiptoeing one hand up my shoulder with her natural, playful physicality, "that was the original plan, yeah. Then I met these cool cats who'd just flown in—locals. They recognized me and we got to talking, and I waved off on my flight and hung out with 'em all day. Ooh, and guess what?"

Her feet tap the flagstones in a little dance, and her grip digs into my bicep.

"I bought a sweet-ass twenty-one-foot Sea Ray this afternoon, and Nic and Theo and Penny and Kass—those are the new friends—are gonna boat with me back to Athens. There's a shitload of cool islands to visit en route. *Waaaay* more fun than flying." She tips her head toward the driveway. "Penny's waiting out front to take me to the marina."

When I throw a glance at Natalia, she's examining Sage's hand resting on my shoulder. Her stony glare moves to my face, and there's a flicker of a sarcastic smile at one corner of her lips.

She jots something on the legal pad. I'm in a quandary, well aware it could be damaging gossip if she determines that I'm in negotiations with a driver from a rival team.

If I confess the offer Emerald has made, can Natalia keep it a secret? Do I owe her an explanation?

132   **JOSIE JUNIPER**

I place my hand over Sage's and hold her gaze with just enough ambiguity in my expression. "It was a delight having you."

After a pause, catching on to my intention, Sage rolls her eyes with the tolerant smirk you'd give a child who's hiding a stolen cookie behind their back. "Oh, Franke," she says, her voice low but still loud enough, "don't do that. It's weak sauce to taunt her." She tips a sideways nod, indicating Natalia. "Put on your big-boy pants and just tell the woman how you feel. Do everyone a favor."

I'm mortified that she's said this aloud, but I suppose it's always a risk with a rebel like Sage. Feeling a contrite blush creep up my neck, I hand the ring of keys back to her. "Will you set these by the door?"

"Of course." She twirls them around one finger and saunters toward Natalia. "Love your YouTube show, bee-tee-dubs."

"Thank you," Natalia replies. "I'd like to have you on as a guest sometime."

"Little ol' me?" Sage breathes, once again falling into the American Southern accent. "I'd be pleased as punch, y'all." She lifts her aqua-dyed hair and piles it on her head, clicking her tongue in a thinking way. "Umm, talk to Robin Mackey at Harrier. Let's make that shit happen." She leans toward Natalia, offering a closed fist.

Natalia stares at it for a beat, then realizes what's expected and bumps her own against Sage's.

"Toodles, Franky-boy," Sage calls over her shoulder as she heads into the house. "It's been a blast." Her high-heeled sandals click away across the tile. She drops the keys into a ceramic bowl in the entryway with a jingle, then goes out the door.

COMING IN HOT

Natalia and I watch each other in challenge for a minute. Sage's friend's car starts up and drives away, gravel popping, leaving us with only the sound of the sea.

"Interesting," Natalia finally says.

"Oh?"

She rolls her eyes, then picks up her pen. "Next question: What do you have to say about the criticism that Emerald's new E-20 car looks like, um...how was it put?" She taps the pen cap against her lips in mock contemplation. "I believe the quote was 'last year's Allonby, in green drag.' Thoughts on that?"

I shoot a squint of disbelief at her. "You can't be serious."

"There are a lot of people," she continues, attention trained on the notepad, "who think it's not just an 'imitation is the sincerest form of flattery' thing, but Emerald engineers blatantly ripping off the constructors' champions' car design."

I wave her comment away like a gnat. "People always talk, every year when the new cars are revealed. It only takes on an air of scandal when *unscrupulous journalists* bang on about it."

Her mouth pulls a quick, sarcastic downturn. "Oh dear. 'Unscrupulous'? You sound touchy about the subject for some reason."

I release a rueful laugh, shaking my head. "The tone of this interview, Miss Evans, turned on a dime. I wonder why?"

"So, that's a 'No comment' from you?" she says with a smirk.

I lose any pretense of indulgence. "Dammit, Talia," I grit out, gripping the arms of my chair and leaning forward. "I know what you're doing."

She sets her pen aside with a flip of her fingers and mirrors my posture. "No, I know what *you're* doing."

"Let me ask you: Will the satisfaction of punishing me outweigh the pain of punishing your best friend? Because if you behave like a petty tabloid shit-stirrer, you're harming Phaedra far more than me."

I'm taken aback by Natalia's look of cold fury.

In the patio doorway, there's a small throat-clearing noise as Elena attempts to announce her presence. Natalia and I both sit back and feign ease, murmuring polite thanks to Elena as she sets the next course on the table. The cook takes her silent leave, pulling the patio doors shut as she goes inside.

Natalia lays into me again immediately.

"*My God*, what an absurd narcissist you are. Sage may be free-spirited, but she's a professional. There's no way she'd tank her credibility or her chance at a drive with a top-three team just for a roll in the hay with *you*, and it was disgusting of you to imply that's what happened, just to make me jealous." Her words hit with venom like a snakebite. "Grow the hell up, Klaus. Quit jerking people around, tormenting everyone just because you can't make up your damned mind."

She stands, chair stuttering back on the rough flagstones. I leap to my feet as well.

"*My* mind?" I growl. "You're playing the same fucking game. Your attitude toward me changes like the wind! Since you arrived this morning...back and forth, endlessly. One minute a hint of tenderness, then cold and snappish. A touch, then a retreat—"

"You're the one who backed away from *me* like I was toxic waste!"

Her eyes are bright with a sheen of angry tears. We glare at each other in stunned silence for the space of several breaths. With an exasperated sigh that's almost a snarl, she snatches up her pen and legal pad, pivoting toward the patio door.

"Talia, please..." My voice is a rasp.

COMING IN HOT

She freezes, half looking back, shoulders high and tight.

"Don't walk away," I urge. "Let's start over."

I study her profile as if I'll never see it again—expressive lips, elegant bone structure, eyelashes clustered into dark, wet daggers with tears that shame me.

"We should…there's…there's food," I manage, knowing I sound like a fool. I sweep a wave toward the table as if it will help.

The pen fumbles from her hand, smacking to the stone. Retrieving it, she rolls the barrel between her fingers.

"Perfect," she sighs. "It's cracked." Stepping back to the table, she sets the pen beside her plate. "Another broken thing of mine I can leave with you. Enjoy."

She slips into the house without another word. I sit, leaning my forehead on one hand for a long time, trying to decide whether I'm meant to go after her or leave her alone.

Sunset deepens around me. I rest my fingers on the side of the cloche over dinner—unglazed red clay with a delicate pattern—and feeling the warmth, think of Natalia's hand over my heart earlier today.

Why did I step back?

I'm pulled from my musing by the sound of the Jaguar starting in the drive. I get up and walk to the front door to look out the narrow leaded pane, watching the taillights retreat. On the table beside the door is a note.

Took your car to the airport. I figured you wouldn't mind—Sage was going to leave it there anyway. I'll talk with Reece to reschedule if I can't get Nefeli to reassign me.
Tell Elena the food was wonderful.

I fold the note and tuck it into my pocket, then walk to the guest room. There's not a wrinkle on the bedspread or a dark hair in the en suite sink to suggest she was ever here.

But on the carved olive-wood dresser is the velvet box with the emerald necklace.

12

SANTORINI, GREECE

KLAUS

Hours later, I've shut down the house, caught up on some business correspondence, and am undressing for bed—chinos, bare feet, white linen shirt unbuttoned. I stand before the tall mirror near the window, staring impassively at myself as I undo my cuffs.

My right side is illuminated by the standing lamp nearest the bookshelves, and the effect—half golden, half shadow—seems fitting. My left eye is a hollow of darkness.

The trill of nighttime insects outside the open window is usually comforting, but tonight nothing soothes. The scent of orange trees drifts in, and the only thing it makes me think of is the fact that Natalia was gone before dessert was served.

Lovely house... empty, I taunt myself silently. *Lovely life... empty.*

I open the cuffs and slide the shirt off my shoulders when there's movement behind me in the mirror's reflection. Elena never comes into this part of the house at night, so my assumption is that something is wrong. I turn, intaking a breath to ask what's happened, and find Natalia framed in the doorway.

Flustered, she lifts one hand. "So, um...*hi*."

My heart lifts. "Hello," I manage, barely above a whisper.

She steps across the threshold into my room, and the floor lamp's glow creeps up her like a spotlight, searching.

"How are you here again?" I ask, taking a single step toward her. "I didn't hear the car."

Her hands twist together. "I guess Sage is used to having other people take care of whatever she drives, because the Jaguar's tank was near empty. I made it to the airport fine, but there weren't any open flights. I drove to the marina to see if I could find Sage and ask for a ride—I mean, this is pretty much her fault—but she wasn't there. So...I came back. The car ran out of gas at the bottom of the road."

We each take a step closer. Half a room apart now. I track the path of her gaze, which roams over my bare torso. Her hands stop their twisting as she clasps them hard, an upside-down prayer.

"I'm glad you've returned," I confess.

She nods faintly, eyes wide and trained on mine.

"Are *you* glad you did?" I add.

Another nod, which morphs into a shrug, then concludes as a headshake in the negative. "I don't know yet. That depends."

A silent half-minute passes as we study each other.

I cross the room to stand before her. "I'm going to do two things. First, I'll apologize." I cup one side of her face, barely making contact. My thumb traverses her lower lip, which is dry as if she's been nibbling at it. "I'm sorry, Talia. You're absolutely right—it was childish of me to pretend such nonsense. Insulting to you, insulting to Sage. Will you forgive me?"

COMING IN HOT

She takes a slow breath but doesn't offer absolution. "What's the second thing you're going to do?"

My gaze moves from one of her eyes to the other. "I'm going to *make you say it.*"

"Make me say what?"

"Your truth. No more of these games. Tell me what you want. Stop forcing me to guess, then punishing me when I get it wrong"—I move my hand to the back of her neck and take a handful of her silken hair—"and punishing me even *more* when I get it right."

She steps back and I open my hand. Her hair trickles free of my fingers, and for a moment I'm certain I've offended or frightened her, or both.

She goes to the bedroom door and shuts it, then returns. "You know what I want. You knew it even when we were nameless strangers."

I lift my chin, looking down at her with a touch of imperiousness, a part of me vexed that she isn't asking for more than that.

Have I gone mad?

My left hand spreads at her lower back and I pull her close. The other hand rakes into her hair again, holding her firmly.

"No more than a tumble, delicious witch?" I ask, closing in, inches from her lips now. *"Just a repeat of our night in Abu Dhabi?"*

I can't resist echoing the words she threw at me in Montréal— their barbs dug into me like foxtail seeds, though she couldn't have known it at the time. I wanted so much more from her then but didn't know how to admit it. Letting her walk out that evening was a mistake. Tonight, there's no way I'll be so careless.

She angles her hips to fit seamlessly against me. The cautious deference in her face evaporates as she narrows her eyes, blue and alive as burning copper.

"Maybe *a bit* more," she counters. "Because I've never had you in my mouth...and I want to."

The phrasing may be demure, but her expression is all heat and knowing. Without hesitation, I pick her up and carry her to the mirror where I was undressing. I place her on the cool tile floor and rotate her to face the reflection with me. My cock, straining against my trousers, settles into the valley of Natalia's curvaceous ass, and I brace her hips with both hands, pulling her against me.

She watches me in the mirror as I slide one hand up her body. I trail a fingertip along the line of her buttons, caress the generous breasts beneath the filmy fabric, and spread my fingers between her collarbones to gently manacle her throat in the V of my hand.

"Why are you looking at me?" I ask. "Look at *yourself*. What a fucking masterpiece you are." My thumb and forefinger trace the column of her neck. "Kings would once have launched ships to war to see this face lost in pleasure."

Her eyes drift closed, head falling back. The fingers of my other hand dig into her hip. She gasps, and her eyes fly open again.

"Pay attention, kleine Hexe," I say near her ear. "You love to play the little spy, yes? Peeking into windows, prying into souls, spinning your stories." I undo the top button on her dress. "So watch yourself now. Enjoy the sight of that angel face pained with rapture as you come."

Her focus darts back to my eyes, startled.

"Have you watched yourself?" I ask, flicking more buttons free. A slight headshake.

COMING IN HOT

"Tonight, you will. I can tell you want to very much, now that I've put the idea into your mind." I graze my lips along her ear. "I've seen you like that—in the throes of climax, your little scowl, trying to be quiet when you're aching to scream."

The dress gapes open, buttons undone as far down as I can reach. The swell of her full breasts rises and falls in quick waves. I push the dress off her shoulders and over her hips. It puddles around her high-heeled feet, leaving her in a matching bra and panties—the barest lace, pale peach.

I unclasp the bra, and she twists her arms to drop it on the floor. The warm weight of her generous tits fills my palms. I stroke her nipples, featherlight. Her attention follows the movement of my hands, rapt. Even at the mirror's distance I can see her pupils have spread into pools of desire.

"*Voyeur. Shadow. Wicked thief,*" I whisper.

The cascade of her hair is like satin against my skin as my cheek presses to the side of her head, keeping her gaze aligned with mine. Together we're riveted to the mirror's reflection as I tease her body.

She parts her legs a few inches in unspoken invitation, and my right hand drifts down the plane of her belly in a tantalizingly slow migration.

"Thief?" she asks. "What have I stolen?"

I give her left nipple a pinch, and she rises on her toes with a squeak.

"My sleep, my peace—"

My heart . . .

"—my sanity." I cup a hand over her mound, and through the lace I feel the humid heat of her need. With a fingertip I trace a circle, and she moans.

JOSIE JUNIPER

"Touch me," she begs in a ragged murmur. "More, please...oh God..."

When I move the fabric aside, advancing through one leg of the delicate undergarment, Natalia arches into the path of my fingertips, widening her legs further.

"That's it," she breathes. "Yes, your hands are perfect..."

I run two fingers along either side of her clit, diving to converge at her slick entrance, pausing, luxuriating in the feel of her wetness. She bucks against me.

"Put them inside me," she pleads. "Do you know how much I've thought about this?"

I dip in just to a knuckle, then retreat, flirting with her tight pussy, which twitches with longing. The nipple I stroke with my thumb is rigid and flushed with arousal. I drag Natalia's hot nectar up to her clit and massage, slow and slick, studying her reaction, captivated by her open pleasure.

"My God—*look at us*," I say in wonder. "We're spellbinding together. Luscious witch...feel what you do to me."

My cock is like marble and my heart drums against the smooth slope of Natalia's back. My fingers work her in lazy, steady strokes, and she pants and whimpers. Against the support of my legs, her own tremble as she gets closer.

"So powerful," I tell her, my voice rough with lust. "Right now, armies would kneel before you to share this moment. Your eyes, Talia...don't hide. See the sweetness spill through you as you reach the peak. Take everything you deserve."

Her breathing comes in short, musical gasps and her head nods ever so slightly in welcome as—with a faint, lascivious smile—she

COMING IN HOT 143

cries out quietly, jabbing her nails into my thighs. She squints but keeps her eyes open, locked on the spectacle of her own bliss.

"You're radiant," I say soothingly as she sags backward into my embrace. I wind my arms around her and kiss her damp temple. "Like a comet, tearing the night sky in half."

She rotates in my arms and lays her head against my collarbone, her quick breathing slowing. I comb both hands into her hair and coax her to look at me.

"Do you want more, kleine Hexe?"

"Yes. *Yes.*"

I angle her head to the side and place my lips near her ear. "The necklace."

She goes stiff with startlement, eyes snapping to meet mine, and I nod.

"You have a naughty habit of misplacing your belongings," I chide. "I want you wearing that necklace when I fuck you."

She scrutinizes my face for long enough that I'm afraid I've made a misstep, but finally she speaks.

"Make me."

For a moment, I assume it's meant as a form of *no*. She must sense my confusion, and she clarifies.

"I want you to *make me do it.*" Her tone is near breathless. One of her hands slides up my chest, and she tenses her fingers.

I try not to look surprised at the turn of events. "And just how might I enforce the behavior of such an unruly woman, hmm?"

She licks her lower lip nervously. A worried crease appears between her dark brows. "You might have to…do something…that makes me think about my behavior."

144   **JOSIE JUNIPER**

An erotic slideshow of possibility flickers through my mind. Natalia is tense, waiting. My gaze pans the room, landing on a span of clothesline with black-and-white photographs affixed to it by wooden spring clothespins. It's out of fashion now, but Sofia liked it, so I've never changed it.

I go to the wall and remove two clothespins from a photo of a bare tree on a cliff overlooking the sea. I set the photo aside and return, circling Natalia, eyes roaming her in stern inspection.

"After I put these on you," I instruct quietly, "you'll go to the guest bedroom and retrieve that necklace." I stop, feet planted, arms crossed in feigned disapproval. "You will not dress first. You will not dally. And you will not defy me. Understood?"

She nods, eyes wide.

"That's not a proper answer."

"Yes," she says, just above a whisper. "Understood."

"Good girl."

I cradle one of her lush breasts in my left hand and carefully trap the nipple in the shallow divot of the clamp, closing it slowly, mindful of Natalia's reaction. When it's firmly in place, she releases a discreet sigh, closing her eyes as if focusing on the sensation. I position the other clothespin, then take a small step back to survey the effect.

"Almost perfect..."

I ease her panties down her legs, and they slide to the floor. Giving her inner thigh a tap, I wordlessly direct her to open her legs more. Her luminous blue eyes are riveted on me, lower lip trapped between her teeth. I deliver a flick to both clothespins, and she moans.

I lift one eyebrow as if in censure. "Surely you can't love that,

COMING IN HOT 145

do you? You'd have to be quite willful to stand there chastened and enjoy it."

I trail one knuckle down her belly and place a hand over her pussy, sliding my fingers back and forth at the opening.

"My God—*incorrigible*," I reproach. "So wet."

She can barely hide her smile. "I can't help it."

I turn her shoulders so she's facing the door, then give her a mild smack on the ass to propel her forward. "Bring the necklace, impudent thing."

She's gone long enough that I wonder if she hasn't gotten cold feet with her game, but in a few minutes she glides in again. In one hand is the velvet box. In the other, a wooden-handled hairbrush. She comes to where I'm sitting at the foot of the big bed, handing me the jewelry case.

Recalling how much she enjoyed it when I washed her hair the night we met, I ask, "You'd like me to brush your hair?"

She presses her lips together hard, and as they go nearly white with the pressure, a desperate blush colors her cheeks. Suddenly it connects, what she wants but is afraid to ask for. I correct my course, taking the brush from her and tapping it against my palm.

"Maybe I will, as a reward...after you're a bit pink."

Her nod is tiny, but energetic.

I open the jewelry box and withdraw the heart-shaped emerald on its weighty gold chain, then slip it over her head to drape around her neck.

"There now. Let me see you, kleine Hexe."

She gathers her hair, piling it on top of her head and holding it to display the necklace. Her heavy breasts lift, the clothespins

146 JOSIE JUNIPER

cocking outward. I give them another flick, and Natalia emits a lusty whimper.

"But I think," I tell her with a slow smile, "you're in want of correction for your carelessness, yes? Does that seem fair?"

"Yes," she whispers.

I ease her hands off her head. A tumble of glossy coffee-dark hair spills over her shoulders, parting around the deliciously indecent display of those tits. I turn her to face the bed, guiding her hands flat on the mattress so she's bent at a slight angle.

She peeks at me over her shoulder as I position myself behind her, to the left.

"It's just a small transgression," I tell her. "So perhaps only a small consequence is necessary."

Again, she nods. Her gorgeous tits sway a bit, and she tilts her round ass in invitation. I deliver a light smack, and she tenses with a squeak, then looks back at me.

"I can't imagine," she tells me with a saucy smirk, "learning much of anything from such...*hesitant* instruction."

"Really now?" I say with a chuckle.

Placing one arm in front of her hips for leverage, I land two sharp swats. She lets out a surprised "*Ah!*" and lifts a high-heeled foot off the floor.

Her bottom cheeks have two oblong patches of color, and she reaches back to smooth a hand over the area.

"Ooh, it's warm," she says. "But maybe...not warm enough."

I move her hand aside and deliver another smack, a tiny bit harder.

"Ah! One," she breathes.

"Counting your strokes, wicked girl? How many do you think you should take?"

COMING IN HOT

She pauses. "Six. But fast. I want it to feel like...a little more than I expect."

I wrap one hand around her wrist and firmly lock it at her lower back, then arc my arm down in five more quick, stinging blows. When I stop, she exhales with a trembling sound that's half relief, half lust. I tenderly caress her ass, which now feels lightly toasted.

"I've never seen you wear pink before," I tease. "It looks stunning on you."

She straightens and turns to me with an expression of exhausted pleasure, and I gingerly remove the clothespins before pulling her into my embrace.

Finally I kiss her, just a brush of our lips. "I confess, I didn't know I might have a taste for such a thing." Another kiss, longer. "But everything is pleasure with you."

Her hand works between us as we kiss more deeply. She opens my trousers and starts to push them off impatiently. I help, stepping out of the rest of my clothes. Natalia moves the bundle of fabric into position with her foot, creating a landing spot on the tile floor before dropping to her knees. Without hesitation she wraps my cock in her hand and plunges her mouth over me.

Her hunger is overwhelming—this is no cautious exploration but has the urgency of someone long denied an irresistible delight. It takes me a few moments to regain command of my wits; then I sweep her hair back—relishing the feeling of her head moving eagerly beneath my hands—and gather it to keep the disheveled tresses from her face.

"So sehe ich Dich gerne," I growl, falling helplessly into my native tongue, enraptured by the sight of her, the feeling, the depth of her passion. "Du hast immer noch nicht genug. Such a greedy woman..."

After a few minutes of her enthusiastic labors, a warning tension creeps through me, bright and potent as glowing coals.

My fist tightens on her hair. "Stop, Talia...wait."

She pulls back and gazes up at me, lips parted and flushed, glimmering wet like her eyes. I draw her to her feet.

"You're not crying, are you?" I ask, cupping her chin in concern.

"Hardly," she says with a small laugh. "I just, um...choked a little, and it made my eyes water."

Her words inspire a visceral stab of need, and I lift her into my arms. She kicks her shoes off and wraps her legs around my hips, my cock trapped between us. As I stride toward the en suite where my shaving bag has condoms, she grinds against me. The flexing of her ass in my hands, the warm patches that bring back the memory of her sighs and whimpers as I applied the hairbrush to her bottom...it almost conspires to unman me, as if I were half my age.

I stop at the marble counter, leaning her on it so I can free one hand and riffle through the shaving kit to snag a string of condoms. Devouring her lips, I make my way all but blind to the bed and lay her half propped against the bank of pillows before sinking between her legs, kissing my way down her body.

Her heavenly tits still retain the pink imprints of where the clothespins were, and I pause to lovingly soothe the marks, bathing her nipples with my tongue, sweeping and swirling, tugging gently with a suction that makes her hips shoot toward me.

Humming a low, taunting laugh against her skin, I continue my path downward, my mouth and hands everywhere, insatiable. I move one of her knees and slide down, eager to kiss her firm, slick clit.

COMING IN HOT

She digs her fingernails into my shoulder. "Please," she gasps. "I need your—" She breaks off, shy even in this moment. "I...need you. I'm so close already, and I want you inside me when I come."

I rise on my knees and she tears open a condom packet, hurrying to sheath me before she launches herself and topples me back with my head at the foot of the bed. She throws a leg over me. The lamplight gilds her hourglass curves, shimmering with patches of faint sweat. She rocks her hips, sliding along my length tauntingly for several passes before aligning with me and sinking slowly to the hilt, head thrown back.

I settle my hands on her hips, fighting the impulse to grip her hard and pound her against me, compelled by primal need. My fingers almost tremble as I coast over the path of her waist and hips, transfixed by the sight of Natalia riding me. Her arms are rigid behind herself, braced on my thighs, and her tits quiver mesmerizingly on each impact as she drives herself against me, eyes squeezed shut, hair churning.

"That's it, my siren," I urge. "You've placed the tools you wanted right into my hands and demanded the service of my cock. Can you let yourself cry out in victory as you take everything you deserve?"

"I want that," she replies in a tight groan, moving faster. "I need everything..."

"It's yours, sorceress. No door is barred to you. No lock can keep you out."

After I say it, I realize the implications. Talia has infiltrated my soul, and at this point, I'd incur far more damage in resisting. My eyes settle on the green stone, stuck unmoving to her damp chest despite her vigorous thrusting against me.

Something shifts in me as I feel—for the first time in many

JOSIE JUNIPER

years—truly *with* the woman I'm inside. All points seem connected at once: past, present, future. I surrender to it with a simple elation. Unable to hold back, I'm overtaken by climax, perplexed by my own words as the tipping point is ushered in by my crying out, "*I am!*"

"Yes!" Natalia gasps, her expression triumphant. I'm not sure if she's replying to what I've rather cryptically shouted, or welcoming her own moment, but her single word rises into a wail of joy as she slows her movement, undulating her hips to rub against me, wringing out every lingering second of her orgasm's assault.

She collapses into my arms, and our fevered pulses ricochet against each other, sending wordless dispatches.

After a few minutes' recovery, Natalia sighs out a tired laugh. "You are... *what*?" she prompts. "Leave it to you to get all existential during sex. '*I am*'?"

I echo her drowsy laughter and roll us sideways, knitted together in a muddle of spent limbs. "I don't know," I admit, kissing her. "It came from somewhere, I suppose, but is a puzzle to me as well."

When my distracted gaze lights on the clothesline across the room—missing one photograph—it occurs to me that this is the first time I've made love in this room since Sofia died. I expect the realization to drag pain in on its wake, but to my shock, it doesn't. Instead, the room feels almost sanctified. I let my eyes drift closed, joining Natalia in tranquil repose, unsure but accepting of whatever comes next.

Though I didn't fully recognize it at the time, this moment with Talia is what I dreamed of nine months ago, when our hearts opened to each other in Spain.

13

SANTORINI, GREECE

THE NEXT MORNING

NATALIA

Whoever came up with the phrase "My cup runneth over" must've had servants to clean the mess. Wouldn't it make more sense for one's cup to runneth just shy of the top? Full, but not *so* full that the slightest false move threatens disaster?

I can't help thinking this in the shower this morning after having tumbled into bed with Klaus last night...more than a year after our first time. It's been fourteen long months of anger, forgiveness, flirting, struggling, longing, and resentment. What a journey.

Is this really the destination, or...just a detour on the way to somewhere else?

The sex was epic and creative. We barely slept. I wonder if he was thinking the same thing I was when we'd roll together—sleepy

JOSIE JUNIPER

and eager, if a little sore—again and again: *If we stay in this bed, it only counts as once, and we don't have to think about whether this is a terrible idea.*

Everything was perfect. Weirdly so. Klaus and I were easy, tender, and effortlessly communicative, in everything from the (did I mention *amazing*?) sex to how we casually arranged our bodies in sleep, curled together as naturally as if we'd been doing it forever. My happiness when I opened my eyes was "runneth over" full.

Followed by panic by the time my feet touched the cool tile floor beside the bed.

I've retreated to the guest room rather than showering in his en suite, because I need time to think. As I gingerly glide basil-peach scented soap over my aching girl bits, I outline my morning.

First, I need to reply to what will certainly be a stern email from Nefeli, responding to the angry one I jabbed out on my phone in the airport parking lot last night. Then I have to tell Klaus this either has to be completely discreet or...can't happen again. No way can we "date" openly. Nefeli would be appalled at my lack of professionalism.

Anxiety drums in the back of my mind like approaching hoofbeats, warning, *This will tank your journalistic objectivity, just like last year. How did you not learn your lesson?*

I can't let myself ignore the murmurs about the E-20's startling design similarities to Allonby's car—it has to be addressed. Other publications absolutely *will* talk about it. There's also the matter of having seen with my own eyes that Emerald is courting Sage Sikora. That's big news.

I'm worried that Elena, the housekeeper, might know what Klaus and I got up to last night. I twist my hair into a

COMING IN HOT

professional-looking, severe chignon and choose my most sensible skirt-suit before heading into the main part of the house, as if looking faultlessly prim will somehow make up for any lusty caterwauling she might have heard.

Klaus isn't in the living room or on the patio, so I brave the kitchen—Elena's domain. She's cleaning the oven, her bony behind wagging side to side in a slate-gray pinafore dress as she vigorously scrubs.

Clearing my throat seems bossy, but I don't want to startle her, so instead I try a kind of sighing yawn. Apparently this is the wrong thing, based on the critical look she delivers when she stands and rotates. Her gaze rakes me as if to say, *I'll just* bet *you're tired after the night you had, tramp.*

"Have you seen...um, Mr. Franke?" I ask with false brightness.

"He is in the garden. Talking to Sofia." There's malicious mirth, maybe even a hint of victory, in her eyes.

Sofia his dead wife? No, it must be a common name here. The gardener?

Stepping toward the counter, I open a hand at the coffee maker. "May I?"

"Certainly. There are breakfast selections on the dining room table. Help yourself."

It sounded like there was a double meaning in the way she said, *Help yourself.* As in, *You clearly need professional help, you walking disaster area...*

She inserts her upper half into the huge oven again, and I flash on the part in *Hansel and Gretel* when the children shove the witch into the stove and slam it shut.

I pour a cup of coffee and splash in some almond milk, then

154 JOSIE JUNIPER

go to the table to peruse the offerings: fresh fruit, squares of thick flatbread studded with vegetables, something that looks like doughnut holes glazed with lemony syrup. I peek toward the kitchen before plucking up a fried dough ball and popping it into my mouth whole, then walking outside.

The angle of light in the garden touches me with a blend of chill shadow and golden warmth as I stroll the path, inspecting the flowers and trees. Behind the cottage I spot Klaus on the other side of a fountain, sitting on a brick semicircle abutting a natural rock cliff, where a statue of Aphrodite is featured.

I quiet my steps in my high heels, reading his posture, worried what I'll see when he turns. With a pang of sorrow, I acknowledge to myself that I should be relieved if he's regretful about last night. Because really, has anything changed? Of course not. What happened owed only to proximity—a powder keg of hormones and a spark of heartache detonated and propelled us into each other's arms.

The obstacles that were there last summer haven't gone away, I remind myself.

As I draw closer, I notice items at the base of the statue—an orange, a lemon, a few figs, a long gray feather, a cluster of pink bougainvillea.

Ah. So this is what Elena meant by "talking to Sofia"—it *is* his wife.

What's he telling her? *I apologize for taking another woman to our bed? I miss you? She'll never replace what we had?*

It's not my finest moment, the surge of competitiveness that rises in me. Twenty feet ago I half hoped Klaus would suggest we

COMING IN HOT

155

forget last night; it's the sensible thing to do. But seeing the way his hand lies open on the sunlit brick, fingers fanned out as if he's grasping its warmth...part of me wants him to need me as much as he seems to still need *her*.

I stop, fingers curling hard on the coffee mug as I chastise myself. *Stop it this instant, Nat. You know what you're doing—this is well-trod ground.*

My "Smart Girl Achilles Heel": angsty men. The only thing saving me in this case is that Klaus hasn't sniffed out my weakness to exploit it deliberately.

Plenty of them have. In grad school I had a boyfriend named Chris who clocked my susceptibility in this respect and manufactured an entire "tragic childhood" with a monstrous stepfather. Any time it seemed I might slip through his fingers, he doled out fresh details, like someone feeding quarters into a Laundromat dryer. My tender heart had wept for the terrified child he'd been...right up until I discovered he'd never *had* a stepfather.

After that, I got more skilled with fact-checking—a talent that's helped enormously in journalism. Unfortunately, it hasn't made me less emotionally vulnerable to a sob story.

I'm poised to pivot and walk back to the cottage and give Klaus his space when he turns and catches me staring. Forcing a smile, I head his way, lifting a hand in greeting and settling on the brick ledge. I place my mug between us so he can't scoot closer...but I'm still disappointed when he doesn't try.

I peruse the collection of objects around the statue. "I wouldn't have guessed you're superstitious," I tease. "Offerings to the goddess for a successful race season?"

JOSIE JUNIPER

He gives one of her stony sandaled feet a pat. "She's impartial. Bestowing neither blessing nor censure for any of my mortal deeds."

And there we have it. The look on his face says it all.

The statue isn't Aphrodite to him. I know it's Sofia who gets fruit and flowers, Sofia he turns to in moments of struggle, Sofia who will reign over the garden of Klaus Franke's heart. Like this sculpted white marble, her presence will endure, silent and cool, unchanging, unquestioned.

I've been so focused on the possible danger to my career that I've conveniently forgotten the *other* critical reason I shouldn't touch Klaus with a bargepole: He'll never stop grieving. He's all but integrated it as part of his identity.

I flick a fingernail against the side of my coffee mug, tapping out a bell-like rhythm, unable to meet his eyes. "So, we should consider last night to have been an 'oopsie,' right? A one-off. Back to business now?"

"*No.*"

I look up, startled. "What?"

"I hoped we might at last be on the right path with each other." He draws aside the high neck of my blouse. One eyebrow lifts. "Though I see you've retired the necklace again."

"It was—" I put one hand against my neck. "Y-yes," I falter.

He stands, sinking both hands into his trouser pockets and glaring down at me. "Merely a useful toy for the fantasy?"

"Klaus." I hold out a hand for him to take, which he does after enough of a pause to make me feel it. "Don't be like that. We needed last night. And I'm not actually saying that it can't…happen again. Casually. But I won't *date* you."

COMING IN HOT 157

His hand drops away. Our silence stretches, punctuated by the ocean's susurration and the intermittent questioning tweeps of birds.

"Last summer," he says, "you seemed willing to take a chance on us."

"I wanted very much to try. I won't deny it."

I'm dying to blurt it out: *Part of me still wants to try, more than anything...* but I force the words down. They move through me with a crawling, painful heaviness, like a bite of bread swallowed too quickly. I wait until the feeling is bearable.

He scowls at the ground. One dark lock falls from his widow's peak hairline in a mussed arc. "I damaged your trust. I offer this not as an *excuse* for my clumsy words and coldness that night in Montréal, but as an explanation: It was the day after Edward Morgan told me his illness was terminal."

I place a shaky hand over my mouth, then pull it away. "Oh God."

"The helplessness, knowing I would go through it once more, after"—his eyes flick to the statue—"after Sofia...I was feeling all but cursed. The thought of being that vulnerable ever again, of life being just a series of painful goodbyes..." With a sigh, he sits back down. "It was bad timing when you asked what I wanted from you. There was no way I could express it, with a war raging inside me. When you walked out, I told myself it was for the best." His eyes lock with mine. "I was wrong. And I've regretted it every day since."

My erratic heart drums in my ears, and I look away first. I'm relieved, elated...but also terrified. *Aren't these the words you've been waiting for?* I ask myself. *You're both scarred by loss, afraid of people leaving. But Klaus is willing to try. Why are you hesitating?*

I take a steadying breath, staring into my lap. "You weren't ready last year. To be honest, I probably wasn't either. And...I'm not confident anything is different now, aside from what happened last night. Which was wonderful, but..." I clear my throat. "Casual."

There's a hard glint in his eye when I look up. "Interesting. You once told me you wouldn't do 'friends with benefits.'"

"The irony, right?" I say, trying for a lighthearted tone.

The joke falls flat. I always forget about men's need to have their pain taken terribly seriously.

I rush in with more words. "Please try to understand. After the day in Shanghai last season, when you mentioned my *ARJ Buzz* content 'making Emerald look foolish,' I put on kid gloves. I can't make that mistake again. I have to remain impartial. It's not just about—"

Somehow it feels rude to refer to his mourning here in front of "her." Sofia's shadow falls over us, figuratively *and* literally. But part of me wonders if I'm being fair. Is it *me* who has the problem? People believe they understand grief if they've had losses of their own. But I think maybe we understand only our *own* grief.

"Last night," Klaus asserts, moving the coffee cup and shifting nearer, taking my hand, "something crystallized for me. I don't want to be *casual*, Talia. I'm not an adolescent, finding thrill in the clandestine. I want all of you."

A vibration resonates through me: desire, hope, a familiarity almost like nostalgia. I think of the "secret chord" in Leonard Cohen's "Hallelujah." *What is this music inside me?* For a moment as Klaus and I watch each other, I think I'll never feel anything else.

COMING IN HOT 159

Call it what it is: *love.*

Would it break the spell to speak its name aloud, like in a fairy tale?

He pulls me into his arms. "I was shortsighted and cowardly last year, keeping you at arm's length. I should have trusted you. I will never again complain about what you report. Free rein—say what you will, ask what you wish. On my honor."

"Are you sure? What about problems with the location for the new race that's in the works? You were prickly yesterday when I asked about the rumors I'm hearing. Like...the political stuff."

He tenses slightly; then his arms soften. "There's nothing to discuss on that subject. If I was terse when you asked, it's only because we were at odds." He drops a light kiss on my hair. "I've nothing to hide."

I relax against his chest. "If we...y'know, let ourselves *be close*...I'd have to be sure it won't impact my writing. I've worked hard to get where I am, and I have big goals." I smile at a memory of myself in grade school. "I was the kid who said I wanted a Pulitzer Prize when other girls in my little town wanted to be champion horseback riders or beauty pageant winners or Nashville singers. Don't get me wrong—those are big goals too. I hope we *all* achieve our dreams. I'm very hesitant to risk mine."

He pulls back, tucking my hair behind my ear. His expression is slightly worried, then smooths into a gentle reverence. "I've every confidence you'll get your Pulitzer. And everything else you deserve." He brushes my bangs aside. "Though I confess to being terribly jealous of your lumberjack, Ethan. That's one dream I hope I can replace with something else."

My eyes go wide. "I can't believe you remember that."

"A wedding at the old sawmill. Sparky the dog. Three or four children." He lifts my hand and brushes the knuckles in a whisper-light kiss. "I remember your dreams as if they were my own, kleine Hexe. Please give me a chance to make them all come true."

14

SAUDI ARABIA

ONE MONTH LATER

NATALIA

Despite Nefeli's annoyance with my tantrum in Santorini, *ARJ* has been putting me up in great hotels. For the first race of the year, I was booked at Sofitel Bahrain Zallaq Thalassa Sea & Spa, where, as a "season kickoff bonus" (because, in the words of Nefeli, "You're a nervous wreck, love"), I got an amazing massage. This week I'm looking out at a gorgeous palm-tree-silhouetted nighttime land-scape from the windows of my suite at Shangri-La Jeddah.

It's Saturday night and the grand prix is tomorrow. I'm madly typing, fingers flying across the keyboard, cross-legged on my bed with a bottle of mango juice and bag of Mr. Chips falafel-flavored snacks on the bedside table in arm's reach.

There was plenty of drama in qualifying today, and I'm putting together a mini-article for the ARJ Pit Lane Pulse column on our website, trying to get it proofed and posted by the top of the hour. Cosmin Ardelean from Emerald is on pole, with Allonby's world champ Drew Powell in second. Row 2 has Team Easton's Owen Byrne, and in quite the shake-up, Sage Sikora is in fourth. Harrier's second driver was stricken with appendicitis, so Sage is standing in again and has risen to the challenge impressively.

It's remarkable not only for being the highest quali position *ever* for a woman driver in F1, but also because it's odd for a Harrier car to be that close to the front. Historically, they possess all the speed and cornering finesse of a Zamboni resurfacing the ice on a mall skating rink. But the HR78 is looking surprisingly racy this season, and there were a couple of helpful grid penalties for other drivers that bumped Sage up.

Also she's just pure magic on track. The combination of a quicker car this year and a driver whose style is balls-to-the-wall gutsy ("ovaries-to-the-wall"?) rather than cautiously analytic... it seems to be working beautifully for them.

I'm already a huge fan of women in sport, but since the day at Klaus's cottage when Sage gave him a metaphoric smack on the nose with a rolled-up newspaper for trying to incite my jealousy, I'm especially a Sage Sikora superfan. She may be an "agent of chaos" on track for Team Harrier, but personally she's Team Sisters-Before-Misters, and I love her to death for it.

My fingers hover, frozen above the keyboard while I strategize how to phrase the concluding paragraph. Klaus and I haven't had, um, a "sleepover" again since Santorini—the beginning of the season has been crazy for us both. But despite the in-person cooldown, which I've hoped would help me to maintain my journalistic objectivity, there's still an internal censor popping up as I write.

Since the issue of trust was the iceberg that sank us last year,

COMING IN HOT 163

we've discussed, this time, the fact that honest communication will be imperative to the development of... whatever this could become. Klaus doesn't treat me "like the press," but I also don't get any *special* access that could imply favoritism.

Our still-nebulous "relationship status" isn't public—I can't risk having my boss see me as unprofessional, right after she gave me a generous raise and entrusted me with this deep-dive piece, which is commanding major resources.

The biggest change for Klaus and me is that instead of making assumptions or hiding things, we *ask each other*. There's a refreshing maturity in it. I feel like the "third Little Pig" who finally got smart enough to make a house out of bricks.

I refocus on my laptop screen, trying to finesse the last sentences of this article. I'd love to conclude with a great quote. There's been a lot of chatter already this season about Emerald's car bearing such overt similarity to last year's winner from Allonby. Drew Powell—a driver who's normally quite stoic—even commented on the issue. I can hardly *not* talk about it. Fans are referring to it on social media as the "EmerAllon." There's even an *#emerallon* hashtag. I can't ignore the controversy.

I stretch to grab my phone, considering the late hour before swiping it open to my message thread with Klaus. It's nearly midnight, and he's either still at the paddock and exhausted, or mercifully asleep. Either way, I probably shouldn't bother him.

I scroll back through the exchange from this morning, when we "had breakfast together" via text. Pics of our food (me: cappuccino and some of the best house-made date granola I've ever eaten; him: salmon Benedict) and reminiscences of our favorite childhood breakfasts. I told him about the smiley-face pancakes

JOSIE JUNIPER

my aunt would decorate with raisins and how my favorite topping was aerosol whipped cream. He told me about the deep-fried apple rings his mother made with beer batter (!) and topped with powdered sugar.

I asked if he had any childhood photos on hand, and he sent a picture of one he carries in his wallet—he and his mother in a little green rowboat on a lake when he was around four years old.

I saved it to my photo file, and . . . yeah, I've looked at it a few times today—not gonna lie. He was an adorable kid, all big dark eyes and mussed curls.

I go ahead and send a quick message:

> **Me:** Hope this doesn't wake you if you're asleep, but if not, I'd love a quote for the piece I'm wrapping up.

> **Charcoal Suit:** I'm in the car, riding back from the paddock. I'd have messaged you but thought you might be asleep. Such a treat to see your name on this screen. Thinking of you today, even amidst the pre-race pandemonium.

Warmth spreads in my chest. With a shaky little delighted sigh, I type back.

> **Me:** You just might have crossed my mind one or two (hundred) times too. :)

> **Me:** Can you address what Drew Powell said after quali today?

COMING IN HOT

There's a long pause, and I'm worried I shouldn't have said anything. But I'm taking Klaus at his word—the reassurance in Santorini that I don't have to be gloves-off. I send him a screenshot of the piece from Sky Sports, showing the brash Powell quote: "If Emerald had pinched one of our sponsors rather than our car design, maybe they wouldn't be in financial trouble."

Moments later, Klaus's reply:

> **Charcoal Suit:** The heat from having Cosmin in his mirrors must be getting to him, to lash out with such an absurd accusation. The next thing Cosmin will "pinch" is the WDC title—that is Allonby's real fear.

> **Me:** Ooh, nice one. Aggressive, yet artful. I think I'm a little turned on.

> **Charcoal Suit:** My god, I wish I could go to your hotel rather than my own. If I didn't have to wake up in four hours to return to the paddock, I'd love to indulge in some "aggressive yet artful" acts.

I'm about to send a cheeky reply when a new email chimes on my laptop, popping into the corner of the screen. Before it slides away, I note the sender:

Pinkie_evans.

My father's nickname for my mother, "Pinkie."

My heart thuds so hard I can feel it in my throat. I reach for my tepid juice and choke down a sip before dashing off a goodbye to Klaus.

Me: Oh shit—message from my editor. Must get the article in before midnight! Sleep well. I'll dream of you.

I sink back on the pillows and try to calm my pounding heart. *This is it. The email I've been dreading for months...*

Our Christmas morning "family reunion" didn't end much better than it started. I was stiff and formal when I thanked my parents for coming and wished them the best of luck in their post-incarceration life.

Basically, I looked like a jerk. Especially since Sherri cried and I didn't.

For a few minutes, I watch the city-light-studded shadows outside my hotel, steeling my nerve, then sit up and jab open the email.

From: pinkie_evans@gmail.com
To: njevans@arjmag.net
Subject: It's your mom

Hi baby, hope you won't mind your aunt gave me your email. I've done a lot of thinking since Xmas trying to figure out a way to talk that you wouldn't reject. Jace said maybe it's not in the cards for us to be a family, but I have to try.

So I'm going to give you my stories, and I hope you'll take it for what it is—me trying to make a connection and fill in 28 years of blanks, not being manipulative. If you're at all like me, you might have a weakness for what my granny called "a two-hankie tale of woe," so I want to make it clear this isn't an appeal to your pity.

COMING IN HOT

167

At that I stop cold, breath stalled in my throat.

My mom is a sucker for a sob story...just like me? I guess in my selective memory, I've imagined my parents to have been hard people. Unsentimental. Lacking empathy.

Settling my tensed hand over the center of my chest, I go back to reading.

> I didn't tell you on Xmas why I didn't want you to know when you were little that I was in prison. First I hoped to get out on an appeal, which I lost. After that, I was afraid I might die there—the medical care was awful. After I almost died from an abscessed tooth, I figured there was a chance something would take me out before I'd served my time. If I *didn't* ever come home, it'd be years of you counting down for nothing. It seemed kinder to go away.

> I'm taking online classes and got this laptop for that, so I figure I'll write out stories for you about what happened in California. I attached the first one, about how Jace and I got the idea to move to California, and what happened when we ran out of money. Please don't delete it.

> You may not want to hear it, but I love you, my baby girl.

The feeling in my chest is something worse than crying. It would be a comfort to cry, but my eyes won't do it. I'm not one of those stubbornly dry-eyed people who stare impassively at a movie when everyone else is blubbering. I'm more the type who gets misty over a stupid ad for arthritis medication featuring an elderly couple dancing.

Maybe the attached document will bring on the waterworks and give me some relief...

No. I can't look yet.

I start a new folder, just titled "Sherri," and move the doc there.

She waited to speak.

I can wait to cry.

15

ONE MONTH LATER

NATALIA

My coworker Alexander Laskaris—Nefeli's nepo-twerp son—is the last person I want to see. But here he is with his signature smirk, leaning nonchalantly in the doorway of my hotel room, which I only opened without checking because I hoped it might be Klaus making a surprise appearance.

"Happy birthday," he says. On his outstretched palm is a USB flash drive, black plastic with a brand name in small red lettering and a key-fob hole at one end.

"It's not my birthday, and whatever that is, I probably don't want to see it."

"Aww, go ahead—*touch it*," he teases in a mock-sultry whisper. "It's not loaded with dick pics, if that's what you're worried about." He waits while my skeptical gaze moves from the flash drive to his face. "Not even curious?" he goes on. "Want an explanation?"

"Is it worth it? I'm kinda busy."

"Too busy for the scoop of the season?"

I pluck the USB stick off his hand. "Are you angling for me to invite you in? I might be, uh...busy soon."

I'm waiting for a call from Klaus, though we haven't had time to see each other since arriving in Imola, aside from in a business capacity. The rare times *he's* been free in the past month, I've been bouncing around the globe, splitting time between F1 grands prix and World Rally Championship races—Sweden to Saudi Arabia to Australia to Croatia to Italy. The schedule obstacles have created something like slow-motion extended foreplay, and the tension is almost unbearable.

Let's just say I'm keeping my legs shaved.

Following Alexander to the sofa, I rewrap my silky robe to cover more of my chest and tie the belt tight. He pats a cushion beside himself in invitation, but I opt for the perpendicular wing-chair, shielding my neckline with one hand as I set the flash drive on the glass coffee table.

"Okay, start talking." I arrange my robe to cover my calves. "It's rude that you showed up unannounced, and at this hour. Why didn't you just send an email?"

"Because *this*, pet, is sensitive information. I offer it in hopes of resetting that pretty little nose you've stubbornly kept out of joint since the quarrel during our date last year."

"It wasn't a date," I retort. "You tricked me into coming to your family's art gallery and ambushed me with a dinner I was too embarrassed to decline."

"Tricked? Ambushed? *Tsk*, such drama." He reclines against the cushions, arms stretched across the sofa back. "I think we remember the night differently, sulky puss. No sense of fun, you."

COMING IN HOT 171

With a slow smile, he lazily rubs the side of his neck as if scratching an itch, but I can tell it's actually to open his shirt a little more—already two buttons too low—so I can see his chest. His good looks—floppy auburn hair, beautiful bone structure, full lips, mischievous eyes...why has nature wasted it on this douche?

He's such a chameleon. It's by turns fascinating and annoying. His accent is fluid, tailored for the person to whom he's speaking. When he's trying to be intimidating, he's all posh Oxford RP. When he's going for badass, a hint of New York creeps in (a type of accent even people *from there* rarely have anymore—he lived in the Williamsburg neighborhood briefly and thinks it's a good excuse). And occasionally his voice reveals a generous splash of the Lake District in Northern England, where he grew up.

"Look, it's late," I tell him, "and I don't much like you even when it's early. Tell me what's going on."

He perches on the edge of the sofa and stretches toward the open bag of Pan di Stelle chocolate biscuits on the table, helping himself. "It was mailed to me at the *ARJ* London office." He takes a bite of cookie and continues to talk around it. "No return address. Postmark is Merton—southwest London—so that tells us precisely bugger-all."

I stand and hold out a hand for the cookie bag, and he claims one more before surrendering it.

I fold the top down and set it aside as I sit. "Pick up the pace."

"That, pet..." he tells me, pointing grandly at the flash drive, "is evidence that a disgruntled individual at Allonby shared engineering blueprints with someone at Emerald." He spreads his hands. "The 'EmerAllon' smoking gun."

A jet of adrenaline zaps through me. "Wait, *what?*"

172 **JOSIE JUNIPER**

"Mmm-hmm." He leans back and crunches on the cookie, looking smug.

"Who are they—the Allonby employee and the person at Emerald?"

"Doesn't include names."

I give an indelicate snort. "Well, it's hardly 'evidence,' then. Did you fish your journalism degree out of a claw machine?"

He rolls his eyes, sighing. "Read it. I trust you'll find the information credible."

"Sure. No names, anonymous informant, but... 'credible.' You'll forgive me if I don't dance with glee."

Another reason I'm not exactly dancing? A sensational story like this would destroy people I care for... even if it could be huge for my career.

Alexander pops the last bite of cookie between his lips and brushes a crumb off his shirt. "Reserve your judgment until you see it."

"Why are you giving this to me? You're too selfish to let a scoop like this slip through your fingers, and we both know it."

He sighs. "Fine. My mother told me to give it to you. For the deep-dive Klaus Franke piece you're working on."

"Nefeli weighed in? She saw it?"

"Not specifics. But I told her the gist of it. She said she trusts you to investigate and determine what to do."

Nefeli Laskaris, queen of the '90s exposé, thinks it's worth looking into. Whatever's on that flash drive must be potentially explosive...

Pausing to think, I rub and pinch my lips with fidgety fingers, until I notice Alexander watching me do it.

I jerk my hand away. "Okay, but why did they send this to *you?*"

COMING IN HOT

"I'm a hard-hitting reporter. You're the decorative one. The new kid in town, with mile-long legs and a supermodel face—"

"Excuse me?" I cut in. "Why would that be—"

"Calm down. I'm trying to give you a compliment. I was going to say, I've developed a theory about you. Despite your reputation for 'fun' low-stakes writing—"

"*How's this a compliment?*" I protest.

He gives a huffy sigh at the interruption, then goes on after a corrective pause. "Natalia, pet...you may write about millionaire pretty boys driving in a circle, but your aggressive approach to research says you're a secret journalism assassin. You want to be writing things that *change lives*. Punchy pieces that shine light into dark places. You can't fool me."

"I don't need to," I reply automatically. "You're already a fool." My tone is grumpy, but I'm gratified that he's noticed I'm a serious journalist. *Dammit.*

"And since I know one should always include a card with a gift, here it is."

He pulls a business card from his shirt pocket and extends it toward me. I take it, and I'm about to put him on blast for giving me his *own* card, like he expects I'd want his personal phone number. But he sketches a circle with one finger, prompting me to turn it over. I look at the back.

Tidily handwritten in black ink: *I apologize for being an arse that night at the gallery.*

I slant a look his way, and he offers a shrug that's as close to remorseful as I think I'm going to get.

"Fine," I mutter. "I'll take a look at the stupid flash drive."

"Stunning." As he gets to his feet, he says blandly, "You don't

174   **JOSIE JUNIPER**

sound all that excited for a scoop that could make your career."
He saunters toward the door. "What's the matter? Is the torch
you're carrying for Herr Franke blinding your view?"

It was Alexander giving me shit about Klaus last summer that
caused our not-quite-a-date to end in disaster, and it appears he
still wants to have the last word on the subject.

"Really, thirty seconds after the apology?" I snap. "Don't start
with me again."

Alexander peeks back with amusement. "Oh my. Like a little
fish she takes the bait—*snap snap snap*. I'll see myself out. Enjoy
the gift."

I shove the door shut behind him hard, then stand with my
palm splayed on the wood until I hear the ding of the elevator.
With trepidation, I walk back to the coffee table. Planting my
hands on my hips, I glower at the flash drive.

Depending on how bad this is, it could damage Klaus, Phaedra,
Emerald—a thousand people on that team. Who knows where it
could go? It might be anything from silly gossip to a malicious
rumor to the kind of corporate espionage for which people are
prosecuted...not just handed a fine by the FIA or stripped of
championship points.

I pick it up, turning the device between my fingers. So small,
but it could devastate people's lives.

I could destroy it.

But has it been sent to other journalists too? Burying this won't
stop the story from coming out if the intel is legitimate—it'd just
be someone else whose name is attached to breaking the news.

Or it could be *me*.

I shouldn't have excitement mixed with my dread, but...not

COMING IN HOT

gonna lie, I *do*. The golden shimmer of ambition rolls through me, and I hate myself for it a little.

We all know how well "ambition" worked out for Julius Caesar.

A sigh of apprehension trembles out of me. I go to the bedroom and open my laptop and plug in the flash drive, feeling sick as I realize that, although it hurt me at the time, Klaus just may have been right not to trust me last summer in Montréal.

16

BARCELONA

ONE MONTH LATER

KLAUS

I'm not superstitious, but I confess to being sentimental. When Sofia and I were young and not yet involved—she was still just my boss's shy daughter, with whom I couldn't resist flirting—the first time she ever touched me was the day she dropped a little glass good luck token into my shirt pocket. I had a bike race later that day, and when she stepped up close to me and placed something in my pocket, whispering, *For luck...* I captured her hand against my chest, smiled down at her, and asked, *Isn't a kiss even better luck?*

I didn't get one that day, but I won the race anyway. The kiss I won months later.

I've carried the little blue-and-white mati "eye charm" ever since, in my briefcase. When Sofia was alive and I'd be having a particularly frustrating race week, she'd say, *You're downwind of the storm, my darling.* That's certainly been the case this week. It's late on Monday, the day after the Spanish Grand Prix, and I'm still in my

COMING IN HOT

office at the paddock, checking my watch as I lose hope for either the desired result of this phone call with the race director, or making it to my date with Natalia on time.

The glass mati rests in the hand not pressing the phone to my face. My thumb skids restlessly over the smooth surface. I have no illusions that this will keep the relentless shitstorm at bay. Still, it's comforting.

"Lorenzo," I tell the race director, my voice level, "I'm merely asking you to consider the possibility that your data is flawed. Our telemetry didn't show the same result, and we—"

"The stewards reviewed the evidence more than once," he cuts in, "and the ruling stands. Jakob Hahn has been disqualified, Klaus, and it will *stay that way*. He exceeded the fuel flow limit on his opening lap. End of."

I flick the mati toward my open briefcase like a bottlecap, watching it land and skate across a thick manila envelope in which yet *another* disaster rests. The documents inside are copies of sensitive information that was the focus of an earlier remote meeting.

Sixteen people were in attendance: every team principal, the CEO of the FIA and two of its lawyers, a PR specialist in damage control, and heads of state from two countries, who exchanged barbs with careful obliqueness, never directly addressing each other.

I can't think about that right now...

Jakob's disqualification is comparatively "small change," but still a serious matter. In a season where he's struggling, he managed his best showing yesterday with fifth place. But being stripped of the 10 points he earned puts him in a position—after only six races—where the gap between his total and Cosmin's becomes greater than the acceptable 100-point difference outlined in the performance clause in his contract.

Cosmin is at 116 points, and the disqualification drops Jakob to a dismal 12. With so much else falling apart, the last thing I need is pressure both from the social media hordes and from within the team—Phaedra especially—on the question of subbing in our reserve driver Kalle, long before our agreed-upon reassessment deadline of summer break.

The decision has already been made that this is Jakob's last season, after which he plans to work as a trainer at the academy. His wife, Inge, is overjoyed at this, but Jakob doesn't share her view. He came to me weeks ago—before we concluded the deal to bring Sage Sikora to Emerald next year—and asked if the door might still be open to negotiation. It wasn't a comfortable conversation.

You know the cause of your lack of mettle as well as I do, I told him. *Please understand I'm not disparaging your new role as a father, but...since Noah was born, you've been driving as if he were strapped to the front wing.*

At times like this, I miss Edward even more. His folksy sensibility could de-escalate even the most tense situations; he had the perfect combination of pragmatism and jocular warmth. Phaedra is settling in well as team owner, but the transition would have been smoother if there hadn't immediately been a half-dozen catastrophes to manage this season.

It doesn't help my state of mind that while embarking on a new attempt at closeness with Natalia, many of the metaphoric plates I'm spinning must be hidden from her. Despite my claim in Santorini that she could ask me anything, one issue in particular is dangerous enough to remain off-limits.

COMING IN HOT

I've made a terrible error and am not sure how to fix it.

The vivid blue button of glass stares up at me from the shadows of my briefcase.

Nothing can protect me from the bad luck that's coming, for I cast this evil eye upon myself the moment I lied to her...

Lorenzo's words over the phone pull me back from my grim musings.

"I understand this puts you in a tricky place with your driver," he says. "You have some hard choices to make. But surely you recognize that this cannot impact my decision."

"Of course," I say automatically.

"We're friends, Klaus." Lorenzo's voice is lighter, with an edge of humor. "But my hands are tied. Maybe the DSQ is doing you a favor, eh? Jakob has one foot out of the car. I know Reece has to force-feed you the socials, but you can see which way the wind is blowing. It's time to put Jake Hahn out of *everyone's* misery."

I rumble out a small courtesy laugh, conceding. "I think this is a mistake, but if I can't convince you to—"

"You *can't*," he interjects amiably. "Enough on the matter, eh? After the GP, stay with us for a few days in Monaco. Ines would love to have you. You know you can't resist her fideuà."

"Hmm, I know it too well. Last summer I gained two kilos after a week of her cooking." Behind me, there's a tap at the door frame. I twist around and Cosmin lifts a hand in greeting. "We'll talk next week, Renzo. Hasta luego—chao."

Cosmin ambles in, and as he sinks into a chair, I glance again at my watch, hoping to let him know I don't have much time to spare.

"Lorenzo?" he asks, pointing toward my phone as he rests one ankle on the opposite knee. "I'm sure it did not a bit of good."

180 JOSIE JUNIPER

"None. But I had to try." I lean on the desk, closing my brief-case in further indication of my intent to leave.

Cosmin rakes both hands through his unruly dark-blond hair and blows out a dramatic breath. "You know Kalle is unlikely to secure any more points for Emerald than Jake. Possibly fewer."

"Agreed. It's a risk."

Throwing a glance at the door, Cosmin drops his voice and notes, "Phaedra wants to cut Jake loose and has not been shy about it."

My nod is tight. "Yes. She and I spoke earlier. *If* we make the switch—and it's not yet decided—Jakob stays for Monaco, then Kalle comes in for Baku. He has experience there. Montréal, I suppose, is a sacrifice, since—"

"I'm giving you a win in Canada," Cosmin says with a gleam in his eye. "I can feel it."

"I'll take it," I say with amusement. "At any rate, we get Kalle up to speed by Silverstone." With a sigh of laughter, I smooth one tired hand down my face. "Though if he does *too* well, fans won't let Sage forget it next year."

Cosmin smiles. "She can handle it—she's a bloody ace, that woman."

Conversation falls into a brief lull, and as I'm shouldering my briefcase to make my departure, Cosmin speaks up. "I have a concern, if you've another minute." He stands and shuts the door. "I...It's something I overheard two days ago. Phaedra was in the bath and took a call from Natalia on speaker, and—" He shrugs. "The echo made it almost unavoidable to hear the exchange from the adjacent bedroom."

"Yes?" I lower my bag, leaning again on the desk.

"She asked Phaedra if either she or...*you*...might have any 'enemies' within Emerald. Disgruntled employees at an executive level. Those with access to privileged information."

I'm careful to keep my smile light and unconcerned. "*Enemies*? My, how theatrical."

Cosmin mirrors my smile, but the set of his brow belies his worry. "I thought the same. But you know Phaedra can be hot tempered, and she demanded to know if Natalia had heard rumors in the press. The exchange became rather heated, and both of them seemed to be withholding information. I tried to ask Phaedra about it, and she pretended to have no idea what I was talking about. Then after the race yesterday, she avoided Natalia. Whatever this is, it's contentious."

I lift my eyebrows, attempting a blithe expression. "I wouldn't be alarmed. Those two are like bickering sisters. They will—"

"It's not the friendship that gives me concern," he says quickly, angling his sober blue eyes my way. "I'm shocked you don't appear to be disturbed by this yourself. Almost indicates that it comes as no surprise."

My foothold seems to sink deeper into the mire. I try the distraction of turning the question around. "Does it ring true to you? Do you have suspicions about someone on the team?"

He takes a long, slow breath, as if weighing what to say. "I wouldn't go that far, no. Though Jakob's statements at the Thursday press conference were a bit salty. I have to wonder if he's spouted off to the wrong people privately, and Natalia caught wind of it."

My shoulders relax as Cosmin's assumption shoots wide of the truth. Standing again, I shoulder my bag definitively. I don't know if I imagine the shifting weight of the packed manila envelope inside, like a hibernating bear with the potential for deadly chaos if awakened.

"I'll talk to Jake," I reassure Cosmin. "And it so happens that I'm meeting with Natalia shortly. I can mention the coolness between her and Phaedra yesterday and see if it throws light on the issue."

I take my leave with all the appropriate pleasantries, but inside I'm in turmoil. For the past two months, I've been caught between two equally horrible choices: watch helplessly as Natalia dances closer to danger, possibly chasing a story so volatile that some people might kill to keep it from the press; or lie to keep her safe and risk destroying the trust we've fought so hard to build.

This can't go on. I must confess tonight, no matter the consequences.

The sun is low as I cruise into the labyrinth's deserted parking area. Only one other vehicle is here—a blue SUV with lightly tinted windows. As I'm removing my helmet and setting it on the back of the motorbike, the door of the SUV opens and Natalia's unmistakable shapely legs become visible as she pivots out of her seat.

She's wearing a skirt of tiered pearl-gray ruffles that stop just above the knees, like a cross between a cheerleader and a CEO, a pink cap-sleeve blouse, and strapless low heels.

I dismount the bike and meet her at the halfway point, both of us eager for the greeting. Sliding one hand lightly into her hair, I attempt to deliver a restrained double-cheek kiss when she intercepts me in transit and lands on my mouth. Her warmth

COMING IN HOT

183

intensifies as I respond, and she leans in, snaking her arms around me and clutching the back of my jacket.

"*Talia*," I whisper as we re-angle before colliding again.

Her fists tighten on my jacket, and her lips part. Her tongue skims mine and I groan, one hand coasting down her back and splaying on the generous curve of her bottom, pressing her closer. I pull my head back for an instant, glancing at our surroundings.

Natalia smiles and rises on her toes to reclaim our kiss, murmuring against me, "There's no one here. They're closed—we got here too late. Plenty of privacy." She nips my lower lip with a hum of laughter. "Now give me more of this."

Every problem, every other person, even the world around us dims, eclipsed by the presence of this woman. The aroma of Spanish cedar and mastic trees, their mingled piquancy and musk, serves as a setting for the gem of Natalia's own scent—her skin, her hair, the heat of her mouth on mine. We feast on each other, hands roaming. Time sags away, elastic, measured in kisses and the breaths to sustain them.

At last Natalia closes the interlude with a quick peck to my lips, tauntingly pulling back when I try to lean in again.

"What a welcome," I say, cradling her face and brushing a light kiss on each of her soft eyebrows.

"You don't seem to be complaining from the waist down," she teases, grazing her hips side to side against mine.

"No complaints." I trail my thumb below her ear and down the side of her neck. She closes her eyes, tipping her head to encourage my touch.

"I ha—" She breaks off with a happy little whimper. "Mmm. Oh God, that's lovely."

The tips of my knuckles define a path from her shoulder back up to her hairline. I comb my fingers into the back of her hair and slowly squeeze a handful of the tresses, watching the convergent dip of Natalia's brows, which betrays her pleasure.

Blue eyes open, misty as a daydream. "I have something for you."

"More than this?" I stroke her lower lip with the thumb of my free hand. "You'll spoil me, kleine Hexe."

She laughs and takes a step back, catching my hand in hers and pulling me toward the car. "It needs privacy."

"You have my full attention," I say playfully. "Lead on."

We get into the car and she reaches behind my seat, retrieving her handbag and setting it on her lap. She unzips the top, then leans toward the windscreen to peer up and around, as if searching for CCTV cameras. Biting her lip, she zips her bag closed again and starts the car.

"What are you up to, little spy?" I ask. "Quite cloak-and-dagger."

"With caution, condoms, and umbrellas," she states, holding a finger aloft as if quoting someone, "it's better to have it and not need it than the other way around." She stops at the car park exit, then takes a right onto the road. "So sayeth my auntie Min."

"Wise woman. I regret to inform you I've forgotten my umbrella."

Natalia lets out a giddy cackle of laughter. "Impeccable comic timing, sir." She angles a side-eye at me. "Are you saying you *do* have condoms?"

"Your asking makes me wish I did."

For the next ten minutes, she explores various roads, settling on a dead end with a large ginkgo tree and no buildings or footpaths nearby. She parks beneath the tree and shuts off the car. It's

COMING IN HOT   185

sunset, the skies faded to the lavender gray-blue of alpine sea holly, blotched with patches of cloud.

For a long moment, Natalia studies me with concern, until I lift my eyebrows, mouthing a helpless, *What?*

She digs in her handbag and produces a USB thumb drive. "I've held on to this for a month," she explains in a rush, "torn about what to do. It contains confidential information that's . . . well, it doesn't look good, Klaus. You said I have no obligation to go easy on you, and—" The look on my face must be telling, because she stops, mirroring my stricken expression. "Wait . . . do you . . . know what's on here? You look like you already know."

I can't hold her gaze, seeing the woundedness there. My eyes drop. "Yes. And it was my intention to speak with you about this tonight. I've made a terrible mistake."

She sits back, one hand over her mouth, watching me. Above her eyes—glistening in the dusky light—her feathery arched brows are crumpled with emotion.

Her hand falls away. "Under other circumstances," she says carefully, "I might've taken this ball and run with it. But something about it seemed off."

She sets the USB drive on my palm and folds my fingers closed.

"It has emails, blueprints, aero testing results. But I don't know who the source is. On the screenshots, names and email addresses are redacted. The mention of money seems too clumsy. It couldn't be you. I mean . . . you don't even need the money. So you'd have to be protecting someone." As I open my mouth to speak, she hurriedly says, "And I don't want to know who— seriously."

"That's not it at all. You've misunderstood."

186 JOSIE JUNIPER

"No, I really don't think I have. I know very well how devastating this could be. And I wasn't willing to risk Emerald's reputation on it without being a hundred percent sure." She swallows hard. "But if I'm understanding you right, you're saying...it's all true?"

I caress down her arms and clasp both her hands in my own. "Let me explain. It's not what you assume. I sent—"

"Stop. *Don't* say it. Please? I need to think." She pulls away from my touch, then pivots to look out the window for a long, quiet minute. "Shit, I didn't expect this," she murmurs under her breath.

I know what I have to say. Now is the time. The *only* time. But in this moment, I'm not sure what's worse—the mistake she thinks I've made, or the real one that's much worse...and potentially dangerous to reveal. The fact that I thought I was protecting her wouldn't garner much sympathy.

It's all or nothing. I'd rather look like a scoundrel than risk her safety.

"Talia. I know you'll be disappointed in what I must tell you, but I can't hide this from you if we're to make things between us work. It's a serious issue. Big news, with devastating repercussions. I didn't want you to know about it because I thought you'd—"

"Are you sorry?" She turns back to me from the window and interrupts my preamble to the truth as if she's heard none of it.

My breath stalls in my throat, then releases in a gasp of rueful laughter. "My God, Talia. *Yes.* If I had it all to do over..." I shake my head, and my eyes burn with reluctant tears. I take one of her hands in mine and cover my forehead briefly with the other. "I knew immediately it was wrong. But the die had been cast. Please—" I squeeze her cold fingers. "Let me explain what really happened. You have the wrong idea."

She puts a finger to my lips, a quick touch. "But you've learned from your mistake? Nothing like it will ever happen again?" Before I can reply, she rushes on, speaking in an avalanche of words directed into her lap. "Because one of the most useful things I learned from Phae, back when she was helping me with math in college, is that errors are good information. You learn *more* by screwing up and reflecting on it." She scoots closer.

"Talia, wait," I manage, barely audible.

I know she's not going to let me say it, and...yes, I know I could blurt out the full story, but part of me is whispering, *This is still salvageable if you say no more. She's writing you a blank check on forgiveness, even thinking you've potentially committed corporate espionage. Accept that check and spend it elsewhere. It's true that you've learned your lesson, isn't it? That's all she really wants...*

"So, you know what?" she continues, eyes bright, her face so close to mine. "We've made a *lot* of mistakes, you and I." She interjects a tiny, tired laugh. "Maybe we got them all out of the way. And..." She leans in and kisses me, just a brush against my lower lip. "This time we have a better chance. Possibly *because* of how hard we've struggled to get here."

My shoulders sag, and I know she's confused and hurt by the response, so I force a weak smile. "I believe that too. *I do.* But only if I tell you everything."

She sits up straight. "No one can legally ask me about what I *haven't* been told. I'm rejecting the intel on that USB stick because I don't know the source. Let's keep it that way."

"The source," I murmur, staring down at where our hands are entwined in Natalia's lap. "The fucking source..." Guilt wells up around me like water trapping a passenger on a sinking ship. I pull her close and linger on a kiss to her forehead, choosing my words carefully. "Did you happen to show the contents of the flash drive to your publisher?"

She shakes her head. "When Nefeli asked to look, I panicked. I didn't want her to force me to move on it. So, uh...I claimed it was 'clearly a prank' and said I'd thrown away the flash drive." She winces. "Because Alexander Laskaris *did* see it first. Me saying it was a hoax bought some time."

My stomach sinks. I cradle one side of her face. "You oughtn't have risked your job like that. She'll think you're biased, or at the very least, terribly careless."

"I know." She leans into my palm, then takes my hand between both of hers. "Clean slate, okay? The past is the past—whatever was done or said by either of us. I don't want to haul our old screwups around anymore like a sack of wet laundry."

I nod. "You're certain you could forgive me if I gave you details?"

A look of wry humor flits over her lips. "Wow, you're making it sound pretty bad. Am I going to be sorry I said yes when I find skeletons buried under your rosebushes?"

Relieved laughter stutters out of me. "Nothing of the sort, that much I can swear. My crime is...of an ethical nature. And more personal than professional."

Her fingers comb through the hair over my left ear. "You look so sheepish. Like a guilty little boy. And I love—" She sucks in a breath, then bites her lower lip.

In the fading light, Natalia and I study each other.

Leaning in for a delicate kiss, I ask, "Were you going to say you love me?"

COMING IN HOT

189

"Maybe," she whispers against my lips. "*Possibly.*" She pushes my jacket off and begins unbuttoning my shirt. I slide a hand up her thigh, and she opens her legs to give me access. "It's been too long—all the waiting is torture..."

A lingering cloud of guilt over what hasn't been said hovers near, but the momentum of lust propels us forward nonetheless. I want to give her more pleasure than she's ever known, more connection than I've ever dared. Perhaps it's naïve to think we can fix everything with our bodies, but tonight—after a month of self-recrimination—I finally feel hope again.

Everything in me needs to honor her, worship her.

My fingers reach the warm satin stretched taut over her pussy as she angles toward me. I caress slowly front to back, then settle my thumb over her clit, pressing down lightly and then stopping. Her tightly shut eyes open with a longing look. She arches a few inches to take the tension out of the fabric from the way she's twisted in the seat. I hook a fingertip into the gusset and draw the damp fabric aside, zeroing in on her swollen bud and stroking.

Her head drops back against the seat. For a few minutes, she breathes in a fractured pattern of sighs, punctuated with silence as she holds her breath, chasing her pleasure.

"Let's get in the back," she manages, just above a whisper. "I want more."

"You forget, kleine Hexe, that I've neglected to bring my... *umbrella.*"

Her laugh is a groan, and her thighs tighten around my hand. "We can do other things. Come on."

We straighten our disarrayed clothes enough to exit and relocate into the back. Natalia adjusts the bench-style seat, creating maximal room. Wrestling out of her blouse, she sits perpendicular to me, legs draped sideways over mine. A mosaic of sunset-pinked light and ginkgo tree shadow paints her bare calves. I smooth a hand from her ankles up to the eager heat at the apex of her thighs.

"I'm so glad it's too hot for tights," she breathes.

I slip my other hand under the skirt and pinch one side of her silky panties, giving a little tug. "Shall we remove these?"

Her look is wicked. "*No.* Touch me through them. It makes me feel like I'm doing something I'm not supposed to."

My fingers glide over the satin in lazy passes, circling and teasing until the fabric is soaked and Natalia is sprawled against the door, one foot planted on the floor, the other shoeless and flexing, toes curled as she cocks her hips in time with my caresses.

"What an indecent girl you are," I taunt, slipping my hand beneath the fabric.

She's so wet that my cock jolts. I slowly push two fingers into her and she moans, high and trembling. My thumb returns to her clit, finding the rhythm that draws from her a whispered chain of "Yes...*yes*..." slow and soft and steady as water droplets.

She clenches around my fingers and I push in deeper, sensing what she needs. A dappling of sweat is on her upper lip, one glistening bead at her temple like a lustful diamond.

"Don't stop, don't...*oh please* don't stop..."

"Never," I murmur back.

She grips the shoulder of my unbuttoned shirt, and I see and feel the storm overtake her—head tossing to one side, throwing her dark hair across her face as her hips jerk upward and she pulses on my fingers, a startled cry trailing off to a panting whimper. I lighten my touch, skimming her clit gingerly, and she locks her thighs on my hand hard, covering the area with both of hers as if trying to hold the pleasure there forever.

Scooping her into my free arm, I gather her against my chest. She sags on my shoulder, raking hair away from her face. Gradually catching her breath, she gropes for my cheek and lays a hand on it. Her thumb passes once back and forth over my lips.

"Thank you," she says in a dreamy voice.

"I may never get used to how beautiful that looks." I embrace her closer, kissing the dewiness of her forehead. "So thank *you*."

She sits up and repositions herself and her skirt to straddle my lap. With one hand she glides a path down my chest and stomach, settling over my cock, which asserts itself in an aching black-denim-encased bulge.

"I've inspired you," she teases, yanking the button and easing the zipper down.

"In countless ways."

She falls against my lips with an eager sigh, and soon she has my bare cock in her grip. She strokes me, long and slow, as we kiss.

"*Klaus*," she whispers. "Can we...? I mean, are you, um..."

"Mmm?" I manage a rumbled questioning, but she doesn't continue.

More kissing as she scoots closer, trapping me between her hand and the damp silkiness of her panties. Her hips undulate, augmenting the movement of her hand, driving me half mad with need. I groan into her mouth, digging my fingers into the smooth, warm curve of her bottom cheeks.

She rises higher on her knees and presses herself against the head of my cock, rolling her hips. Her head drops back, and I unclasp her lacy pink bra and slide my hands into the cups from beneath, gently squeezing, thumbing the nipples. She sucks in a sharp gasp.

Suddenly I can feel there's no fabric between us—she's pulled her panties aside. She's hot and wet, bracing my cock hard in her fist and dragging it through her engorged labia, tormenting us both by flirting with penetration, pressing her entrance against me over and over, a few times enveloping me just a centimeter or two.

"I want..." she begins, her voice a cracked whimper. "Would it be bad? Are you clean? Like, have you, uh...Do you know if..."

"I've only been with you since February on Santorini," I tell her through a volley of kisses. I know it's not a perfect answer, but it's the best I can do, driven to the edge by her slick heat, the weight behind the way she's balanced at the tip of my cock, ready to plunge down. "But there are other concerns, yes?" I force myself to ask. "Pregnancy?"

I lightly pinch her nipples, and she cries out. I feel her opening clench against me. In this moment, no force of physics seems stronger than the need to fill her—it's a boulder of arousal thundering downhill, obliterating every sensible concern in its path.

"It's a safe time of the month," she says.

The words are barely out when she sheaths me entirely, stopping at the base and dancing her hips side to side to emphasize how thoroughly we're joined. Her eyes flutter open, and she fixes me with those soul-deep blue pools as she begins to move on me.

"Is it okay to not finish inside me?" she asks. "Just give me a warning."

"Anything you like. God...Talia..."

She rides me, slowly at first, then more energetically. Her hands roam, fingernails scraping my chest, pinching my nipples in reply

COMING IN HOT

when I squeeze hers. I flip up the lace of her bra and pull her to my mouth, sucking and flicking until she loses herself entirely. Breathy praise and pleading spills from her kiss-abraded pink lips as she bounces in my lap shamelessly. The car is a symphony of wantonness—the sound of our flesh colliding, her wetness, and my gulping breaths as I try to hold back, sensing she's near her peak.

"Talia," I grit out, "it's too good. I can't..."

"Yesyesyes...I...I need it," she says between gasps.

"Come for me again, kleine Hexe. Let go and give me everything."

Her arms shoot behind herself, bracing both hands on my knees. She stops moving up and down, tilting her hips to drag her clit against me, her throat opening in an uncharacteristic wail of surrender as her tight pussy tremors almost violently with her bliss.

I don't want to diminish her moment, but the intensity of her response spurs my own, and I feel molten energy gather, ready to overtake me.

"You should move—oh God, it's now or never, Talia." My jaw clenches and my hands drop to her waist, encouraging her to lift up and off.

Instead she throws her arms around my neck and grinds down hard in my lap. "All of it, please," she pants against my neck. "I want to keep you. Fill me up..."

My teeth grit hard as I'm dashed by the wave, crying out in shock as much as ecstasy.

This is right, this is right...it's perfect. Exactly where I need to be, tumbles through my barely coherent brain. The flood of heat seems endless, my cock an earthquake of tribute to my desire for this woman.

"*Yes*," she murmurs against my neck, fingers combing into the damp hair at the nape of my neck. "All for me. You're mine...I'm keeping you."

When she pulls back, we study each other with mingled seriousness and joy. I draw a stray lock of hair away from her lips, then kiss her.

"I hope we won't regret that," I confess.

"Sorry I didn't exactly consult you about the changeup," she says with a wince. "At first I just didn't want to get the rental car messy. But..." She hides against the crook of my shoulder again. "I think also I just *needed* that."

"Technically, the 'please' made it a question," I say with an indulgent smile. "I could have said no, but I wanted it too. Welcomed the moment." I smooth a hand down her back in desultory strokes.

She squeezes my cock, almost like a reassuring hug, and I'm so happy to still be inside her. I never want to leave.

"There's nothing to worry about," she assures me. "I'm regular as clockwork, and two days from my next period. We're good."

I hold back my lovesick reply, only thinking it: *We* are *good. Together.*

But trailing in on the tail of the thought, I worry how long I have until this sandcastle is dashed away.

17

MONTRÉAL

ONE MONTH LATER

NATALIA

It's the third call today from an unknown number in Corbin, Kentucky, and again I tap Ignore.

Phaedra steps over the back of the bench near the water where we're sitting at Parc Jean-Drapeau and plonks down with a grunt, glancing at my phone as she shoves a small paper sack—splotched with translucent butter stains—toward me.

"They were out of the pain au chocolat, so I got you a Kouign-amann," Phae tells me. She digs into her own bag and tears a piece of the pastry inside, folding its golden flakiness into her mouth. "This is my *second* one," she confesses, mouth full. "I won't need to eat for a week—like a python that's swallowed a capybara. But holy shit these are incredible."

I peer into my pastry bag, then peel off a bite of Kouign-amann, admiring the decadent lamination before popping it into my mouth.

Phae points at my phone when it dings with a voicemail. "Her again?"

I shrug, chewing.

"Just letting her dangle, huh?"

My eyes narrow and I swallow too quickly. "Let's see... it's been six months since Sherri and Jason elbowed their way back into my life, so I figure in another, hmm"—I pretend to calculate, tapping at my temple—"twenty-seven and a half years, I can reassure them I'm alive and got the message. Sound fair?"

Phae rolls her eyes, twisting another chunk of pastry free. She surprisingly doesn't have a snarky comeback and instead nibbles at a sugar-encrusted edge of dough, gazing across the water to the adjoining island where the Circuit Gilles Villeneuve is located. Her dark auburn hair blows across her cheek and she swipes it aside, leaving a pastry flake on her eyebrow, which I brush away.

I go back to dismantling my own breakfast, but it's hard to enjoy it, distracted by everything Phae *isn't* saying. "Okay, just... out with it," I mutter. "I know you're brimming with opinions, so let's get it over with."

She swallows, rolling the crumpled top of her bag and setting it aside. "I try not to be too up in your business, ever since the falling-out last year, because... y'know, I'm"—she makes air quotes—"*bossy and judgmental*. Last year, here in Montréal, we weren't even speaking."

"Yeah." The rift lasted three months and was a miserably lonely time for both of us. I set down my bag and reach for Phae's hand to squeeze it. "I can never apologize enough for not being there for you sooner with... *that*." I'm afraid to mention her father's death.

"That isn't why I'm bringing it up. Hear me out. Look, I know

COMING IN HOT

you're pissed at your parents for being fuckwits when you were a kid. But, Nat... you might be sorry when they're the *dead* kind of gone if you don't have a relationship with them now. They're trying. All those emails your mom sends, telling you her story... How many are there so far?"

"She sends one about every other week. Six now."

"And you still haven't read them?"

I shake my head, more of a toss, like a stubborn horse. "I don't delete them—that's as much commitment as Sherri deserves." I point at my phone. "She wants to ambush me, calling like that. Who just *calls*, without texting first? I know she's Gen X, but seriously."

Phaedra grits her teeth in frustration. "*Rrrrraaaahhh!* You're so annoying. A reputation for being a softie, but you're really like that bunny in the Monty Python *Holy Grail* movie—cute and fluffy, but looks are deceiving. And you're going to regret it, being a hard-ass and not accepting the olive branch."

"You're not a relationship expert, Phae. Last year you thought I was an idiot to take a chance on Klaus, and then you changed your tune. You're wrong now too. I don't need my parents, and I doubt I'll regret it."

"Whatever. Last comment, then I'll drop it: I have an Edward Morgan–shaped void in my life that says you *will* regret it. 'Nuff said."

I glare but remain silent, chewing slowly.

"And I think you should read the stuff your mom sent."

"You said 'last comment'!" I snap.

She falls silent. For a minute there's only the crinkling of paper bags as we go back to our breakfast, scored by the sounds of kids and dogs and ducks around us in the park.

"So...how are things with Klausy?" she finally asks, mercifully changing the subject.

"It's good." I feel heat creeping up my neck and across my cheeks. "Thanks again for covering for us in Monaco. The dinner at L'Escale was amazing."

Phae grins. "It was kinda fun, helping you sneak around with your boyfriend."

I dig in my pastry bag. "I don't think Klaus is my 'boyfriend.' It's basically just hooking up." My tone is more angsty than I intended.

The truth is, I'm feeling...*a lot.* Impulsively throwing caution to the wind on birth control in Barcelona was a bad sign, and I'm lucky my period arrived right on time, as expected. The fact that I took such a risk has made me examine my emotions more sternly since that night. I really need to keep a cooler head as much as possible.

Phae almost touches my knee in some attempt at comfort, then pulls back. After a pause, she asks, "But you do want it to be more, right? Because I'm pretty sure he does."

That metaphoric skydiving feeling floods through me again: definitely scary, but a euphoria so fast and so free...revealing an open view that was never done justice by other people's descriptions of it. I can influence the direction, but the fall itself is subject to gravity, irrevocable.

The sweetness on my lips as I lick away a bit of sugar glaze makes me think of his kiss. I glance at my phone on the bench, noting the hours until I'll see him again.

"Maybe I do want more," I confess to Phaedra. "But *wanting* doesn't make it happen. Everything rides on how well we've packed our parachutes for the jump."

COMING IN HOT

This is my second time seeing a race at the Circuit Gilles Villeneuve. Opinions are divided about this track: Some people say it's sorta predictable, simple, and old-fashioned, "not very technical," while others glow about its high-speed straights and heavy braking, with cars running thrillingly close to the walls.

I'm watching the race from the grandstand outside of the Senna corner. Most often I'm in the media center during the race, but occasionally I opt to watch in the grandstands with fans, enjoying the energy and mingling with the crowd to get material for *ARJ Buzz*.

Cosmin qualified on the front row in second, and Jakob Hahn is in seventh. Despite the rumors after the Spanish GP that he'd be replaced with Emerald's reserve driver, Klaus and Phae chose to give Jakob until summer break and see where he stands points-wise.

The grand prix gets off to a dynamic start. Emerald must be using a two-stop strategy, because they begin the race on soft-compound tyres. Cosmin overtakes current world champion Drew Powell and starts building up distance.

Cosmin boxes at lap 19 of 70 and the Emerald pit crew sends him on his way outfitted with hard tyres. He emerges behind Powell but has a good chance of reclaiming first place by race end after changing again to fresh softs.

There's drama on lap 45 when Jakob tries to overtake Mateo Ortiz and gets into a tangle that sends him smashing into the Wall of Champions. When the safety car comes out, Powell has just passed the pit entrance, but Cosmin is a few turns behind.

Emerald makes a quick decision to box for new soft tyres, capital izing on the yellow-flag time savings.

The battles between Cosmin and Drew Powell have become legendary this year. Four laps before the end, they're going at it hammer and tongs, Cosmin attacking at every opportunity. They scream into the Pont de la Concorde corner and Cosmin gets the upper hand just before the hairpin, overtaking for first place. He holds off Powell for the last few laps and bags his third career win.

Heading back to the paddock, I pass by a family with a little girl who's wearing lavender overalls like the ones I had on in the photo my parents sent. On one cheek she has Cosmin's number painted, 19, and on the other, three stripes in the colors of the Romanian flag. Her father lifts her onto his shoulders. The mother gathers their things and tucks under the arm of the father, and my eyes follow the three of them as they move with the crowd toward the exit. For just a moment, watching the family, I remember with a pang of loss a happy time before I knew my parents were irresponsible.

I miss the girl I was. And I miss who Sherri and Jason were... when they were still Mom and Dad.

There's a celebration for Cosmin at a hip tiki bar, and I can't resist showing up for a little of it, even though I should be in my hotel room right now preparing for a video call related to a story I'm pursuing. I feel guilty that I've deliberately not mentioned it to Klaus, but... it has to do with murmurs of a human rights issue in the country that may be hosting a new grand prix. As a team principal, he has "a dog in this fight," and I don't want him to influence how I do my job.

I'm finishing the last of a cocktail with a plastic flamingo in it when Klaus draws up behind me and runs a fingertip along my shoulder. I give a ticklish squeak and rotate to face him. He's had a few cognacs, and the scent of it on him, mingled with his cologne, instantly makes my pulse race with the memory of our first meeting.

He leans in as if to kiss me and I bob to one side, scanning the crowd for any nearby Emerald figures other than Phae or Cosmin, who know to keep our secret.

"Watch it, mister," I tease. "Can't have anything about us get back to my boss until I turn in the article. Six more weeks," I add when Klaus's brow pinches in a mock-sulky way.

"I was hoping you might dance with me," he says, nodding toward the small space where a few couples sway to the crooning of Dean Martin.

"Oh dear." I put a hand on his shirt and bring my lips just beside his ear. The warmth of his skin is more intoxicating than the rum I just drank. I can feel the feathery softness of his hair against my cheek as I murmur, "That would be very indiscreet."

"One friendly dance," he coaxes. "I'll be the soul of discretion."

I'm honestly dying to—we've never danced together—so it doesn't take any more convincing than that. I offer a hand and he takes it, leading me to a patch of hardwood splashed with marbled blue light meant to look like ocean waves.

We position our arms, and for a minute maintain a proper distance. But when the song changes to Etta James's "At Last," I melt against the muscular wall of his chest and let him hold me close.

202   **JOSIE JUNIPER**

He drags one thumb down my spine, and the sensation is too delicious.

Putting a foot of space between us, I clear my throat. "That's hardly fair."

"I have to make love to you tonight."

"You know I can't—I have a deadline." I draw a circle around one of his shirt buttons with a fingertip. "But in a few weeks we'll stay together during the British GP, at the house Phae's lending us in Towcester. A whole week, just you and me." I flash a winning smile.

"Come to my room, Talia." His gaze is heat and hunger.

With a frustrated groan, I say, "Do *not* tempt me. I have an important call at midnight. It's eight hours ahead where the—" I break off, not wanting to reveal too much. "Where the person is calling from, and I was lucky to get their time at all."

A pensive shadow darkens his expression, as if he's going down a list of the countries that are eight hours ahead of Montréal. Something about it pokes at my guilt over hiding this, when we're supposed to be committed to honesty now. It must be obvious that I'm leaving out details—I have no poker face.

I sigh. "It's someone from Amnesty International. A lead I'm working on again."

He scowls. "About the new race location?"

"Wow." My eyebrows lift. "Quick line you drew between Amnesty International and the new grand prix. So...guess I don't have to tell you why it's important that I don't miss this call."

His feet come to a halt and his hands smooth over my upper arms before he grips me lightly. The look on his face is one I've come to know—tight intensity beneath a mask of calm. "To whom will you be speaking?"

People move around us as we stand, conspicuously still, no longer dancing. I open and close my mouth, deciding whether I want to tell him. Finally I shrug. "A woman I got in touch with through that watchdog organization—the group that gave Emerald the report on your old sponsor, Basilisk."

Taking my hand, Klaus leads me off the floor and to a hallway near the restrooms. "You shouldn't be poking the hornet's nest on this issue, Talia. When journalists ask the wrong questions, it can be dangerous."

"Uh, you just described the whole point of journalism," I deadpan. "And if you're referring to the reporter from Al Jazeera who fell off that balcony a couple weeks ago, it was an accident. She was trying to get social media pics or something, they said."

"Oh? You know this for certain—an *accident*? I wasn't aware you witnessed it."

I fold my arms, waiting for it to catch up to Klaus how condescending he sounds.

He has the grace to look annoyed with himself. "My apologies. But…" He rubs his face. "I thought you'd set this aside, after Santorini."

"Huh," I say with a squint. "And why after Santorini, specifically?"

He seems about to reply, then sighs and rubs his face again.

Quietly, I add, "*You claimed the sex wouldn't change things.* That I'm free to write what I want. So your alleged concern for my safety sounds a little disingenuous right now."

"I don't want you to pursue it further," he insists, his tone almost a growl. "*Please.*"

I take a step back, glaring. "I abandoned a story for you once"—I drop my voice—"*with what was on the USB drive.* You already used your one veto. It's not fair of you to ask me to let this one go too. A big exposé like this could make my career."

At the dismay on his face, it occurs to me that the last time we mentioned an "exposé" was when we discussed the libel case over the article about Sofia's death. I must've hit a nerve—he looks so stricken.

Softening my expression, I take his phone from his jacket pocket and check the time. "I don't want to fight about this, okay? I have to get back to my room. The call's in ninety minutes, and I need time to prep."

We manage to make up before I leave the bar, but I can tell there's something he's not saying. It nags at me like heartburn during the cab ride back to my hotel.

Ten minutes before the scheduled call, I get a one-sentence email from my contact:

> I am so sorry, but circumstances have changed, and I must unfortunately withdraw from the interview and cannot reschedule.
>
> All best,
> Beshira

This feels like too much of a coincidence. Did Klaus do something to make her cancel? I'm so mad that I jab out an accusing text to him, but then delete it unsent. I need to calm down first. It's past midnight, and I have a ten o'clock flight in the morning.

I get in bed, but of course I'm not relaxed enough to sleep. I open and then reject a dozen books on my e-reader.

Tap, swipe away.

Tap, swipe away.

Phae's comment echoes: *You should read the stuff your mom sent.*

With reluctance, I climb out of bed and get my laptop, then tuck under the covers again. Opening the desktop folder, I peruse the file names:

Trip_to_California.docx

Money_Runs_Out.docx

Meeting_Bux_and_Shockley.docx

Job_Gone_Wrong.docx

Hiding_Out_in_Barstow.docx

The_Arrest.docx

I fiddle around with the cursor arrow, gliding it over the words, pointing it at different letters like a tiny, inky accusation.

I close the laptop.

I reopen it.

I click on the first document.

For almost a year while Jace and I saved up the money, a name hung in my mind bigger and brighter than the Holly-wood sign: Venice Beach. How could it be anything other than a paradise?

Venice: the romantic City of Canals in Italy. I'd never

be rich or lucky enough to go there, but I could have the American version.

For a girl who'd never laid eyes on a body of water bigger than the Ohio River hugging Louisville, any beach sounded magical.

Everyone told us we were fools to go. But the sweet call of that blue Pacific was louder than the sensible warnings of people Jace and I saw as boring adults—those who would live and die working the soybean fields and mopping Kentucky sweat-dust off their faces, never to experience the joys awaiting us in California.

My friend Lila Knox worked at the Merry-Go-Round clothing store in Lexington, had pink streaks in her hair, and had once gone to bed with a man who had a genuine Australian accent, so I thought her mighty worldly.

She told me she was moving to California, and I should go too. Said with my looks, there was a good chance I could model or even end up in the movies. It took a year of pinching pennies to save the $2,000 Jace and I thought would be enough to get us started out west. Sometimes he'd look at that thick roll of twenty-dollar bills as it grew and talk about everything else we might do with it.

"Those are small-town things," I'd tell him, disgusted.

I wanted California. For the beach named after a city in Italy, for the thought of seeing myself on the cover of *Mademoiselle* (my favorite magazine because it had a French name), but most of all, for my little girl. I wanted her to grow up someplace sunny and glamorous.

COMING IN HOT

When we left her with Jace's aunt Minnie and drove off that morning, Natalia didn't wave goodbye. She'd found a moth on the screen door and was cupping it in her hands. She just smiled at me—that bright, beautiful smile that was my world—as I waved. Our plan was to come back for Natty in a few months after we'd gotten settled.

I was already in tears by the time we hit the main road. I told Jace I'd changed my mind. He was never one to get sore with me, not even when he'd had a few, so I was surprised when he looked at me fierce and said, "Dammit, Pinkie...I already quit my job. We're going."

I cried all the way to St. Louis.

I'm only a page in, and already I'm crying too. I pick up my phone, both grateful and mad at Phaedra for making me read this and not caring that the message might wake her.

> **Me:** Oh God, Phae. My mother's writing sounds a lot like mine.

> **Me:** SHE SOUNDS LIKE ME. I don't know how it's even possible. She's a stranger.

Immediately, there's a reply.

> **Phae:** Maybe she's not as much of a stranger as you thought.

18

ENGLAND

ONE WEEK LATER

NATALIA

"I hope you've enjoyed this 'Tech Talk' segment, *Buzz* fans," I conclude with a bright smile, setting the F1 braking system's master cylinder on the table beside the calipers, disc, and brake pads. "Don't forget to vote on the funniest radio message from the Canadian Grand Prix"—I lift an arm and point to the area where the link will appear in the video—"and of course, like and subscribe. See you next week when we'll check out some of the most dramatic Silverstone moments in history in preparation for the next race."

Olivia stops the camera and straightens, giving me a thumbs-up. "Nice one. It's a wrap." Moving to the softbox light and switching it off, she says over her shoulder, "I'll get this to Ajay and let him know the second intro of those three is the one you like best."

"Thanks, Liv." I head for the door of the small room we use for shooting *ARJ Buzz* episodes.

COMING IN HOT

"Oh, Nefeli told me to have you stop by her office after we're done," Olivia adds, fussing with the camera to remove the SD card.

I almost ask what type of mood it seemed she was in. With Nefeli Laskaris, you never know, and I've been "on her list" since I claimed I tossed that USB stick into the bin.

I walk across the expansive main room of the *ARJ* offices, taking a mint from the bowl on editor Riley's desk, high-fiving photographer Lachlan, and trying not to roll my eyes at Alexander, who's perched on the edge of an intern's desk, shamelessly flirting.

Nefeli hates the sound of knocking but also doesn't want anyone to walk in unannounced. Her door is glass, fortunately, so the accepted procedure is to stand there until you're noticed. She's on the phone when I walk up, so I crunch the mint and wait.

After about two minutes, she twirls toward the door and flicks her fingers to invite me in. She concludes her call and sets the phone down while taking her seat and waving at one of the tufted slipper chairs opposite the desk. On it is a laptop, a fountain pen laid diagonally across a legal pad, a teacup on a saucer, and a succulent in a ceramic pot.

"You wanted to talk to me?" I ask.

She angles her head to peer through the bifocal part of her glasses and taps the keyboard of her laptop, then rotates it and scoots it my way. "Tell me what you see, love."

I move to the edge of my chair. The smile on my face wilts as I'm faced with a page from a French Formula 1 gossip website. The headline reads, *"Un Repas Romantique pour Deux... Qui Est Cette Femme?"*

The photo: Klaus and me at L'Escale in Monaco, holding hands

JOSIE JUNIPER

across the table. The smoldering expression on Klaus's face says this is definitely a date.

I sit back, ruler-straight in my chair. "It's not what it looks like."

"Don't insult me, please. It may have been a while since I inspired that degree of lovesickness, but I can still *identify* it—the man is dead gone on you."

"Just let me explai—"

"Enough," she interrupts, flapping one hand as if repelling a cloud of mosquitos. "I don't care if you're fucking Klaus Franke, for God's sake."

My eyebrows dart up. "You don't?"

"Is it unprofessional? Probably. Will it influence how you write about Emerald? Definitely. Can we use it to our advantage...?" She winks. "Possibly."

I twist my fingers together, lowering them to my lap. "I'm not sure what you mean, but I don't like how that sounds."

She chuckles. "Oh, don't be such a little puritan. The man is putty in your hands. Have your fun, but...don't be afraid to capitalize on the perks inherent to this level of intimacy. It's an all-access pass."

She may not realize it, but pretty much since middle school, it's been one of my biggest pet peeves to be called some version of "little puritan."

Prude. Goody Two-shoes. Miss Priss. Wet blanket. Killjoy.

My nostrils flare. "The award-winning articles and books you've written didn't come from sleeping with the right people."

She leans her chin on one hand with a droll look. "No, but you'd better believe I once spent two grueling hours flirting up a storm with Henry Kissinger to get some useful tidbits about

COMING IN HOT

Kosovo. And that, darling, ended up being the basis of my book *Dancing with Milošević*. Pulitzer Prize winner."

The mention of my lifelong fantasy goal gives me pause before indignation prods me onward. "If I use my relationships to manipulate people for story details, my life would be littered with very short friendships. I think we're done here." I get up to leave.

"First of all," she says coolly, "writers of every type—journalism, novels, screenplays, songs—mine details from the people in their lives. I wasn't suggesting you shag the dear boy into exhaustion and go through his pockets for secrets, like some Mata Hari. Now sit down."

I reluctantly lower into the chair.

"When I gave you this assignment," she continues, "you mentioned Klaus Franke being resistant to interviews. An 'all-access pass' means he's comfortable with you. He trusts you, so getting a good story will be easier."

"He *does* trust me," I retort. "And I'd never abuse that trust."

"Well, kudos. Very ethical—*rah rah*." She lifts her pencil-line brows in amusement. "You look impatient. I'm sorry, have I become tedious? Should I and my nearly fifty years' experience in journalism go crawl into my box until one of you plucky know-it-all youngsters feels like dusting me off to ask a question?"

I feel bad for getting snippy with her and look into my lap.

"I called you in," she continues, "so we could circle back to the evidence you were sent on the flash drive. 'Blueprintgate,' as Alexander termed it."

Oh God…did the story break somewhere, and I threw away the scoop? My panicked brain hunts for a defense. I grip the chair's edge. "Nothing in those files seemed—"

"Don't go to pieces," Nefeli interjects. "Your intuition was correct. Even if you were just protecting your beau." Her phone rings. She glares at it, then flicks the side button. "It's been three months, and no other news outlet has broken the story. Even if the source had initially sent the material only to *ARJ*, after a few weeks of seeing nothing done with it they'd have tried someone else. But that didn't happen...ergo, we were the sole recipient. The question," she poses in a stage whisper, "is why did someone want *you* to have it?"

"They didn't. They sent it to Alexander."

Nefeli leans back with a reluctant-sounding sigh. "About that, love. I don't want to start a war, but...the thumb drive was addressed to you. Alexander had a wee case of professional jealousy and took it out of your inbox."

"Wait, *what*?"

"Try not to hold it against him; the child has no impulse control."

That miserable creep! Pretending it was a peace offering...

"You're not doing him any favors by babying him," I bite out. "He's *not* a child."

"Fifty pence for your unsolicited parenting advice," Nefeli says dryly. "The question remains: Who sent it, and what was their agenda?"

"To make Emerald look bad. And because they noticed I'm doing interviews with Klaus."

"But if the information is a load of bollocks, to what end?"

I don't have the luxury of thinking it *is* "a load of bollocks" anymore. Clearly some sort of malfeasance occurred. Klaus is

COMING IN HOT

such an honorable person...I have to believe he was protecting an Emerald employee.

"So here's a thought..." Nefeli goes on, tapping a nail against the edge of her teacup's saucer. "Is it a red herring? Or as they call it on your side of the pond, a 'snipe hunt'?"

She looks so smug, I want to scoff. Has she been reading too many suspense thrillers? In real life, there isn't always a plot twist. Most answers are boringly straightforward.

"I can see the protestations on those lips," she tells me. "But I didn't get where I am by having poor instincts. I suspect this phony intel relates to the kerfuffle surrounding that new race location. Blueprintgate might be nothing more than a cover for the *real* story. I'd start beating the bushes, were I you."

I cross my arms, eyes narrowed. "So why don't *you* investigate?" A slightly petty and mean impulse spurs me to add, "You used to love that stuff, in your day."

She smiles slowly, not taking the bait. "Can't be arsed, love. I already earned my stripes. Also?" She drops her voice wickedly. "*I'm not the one dating Klaus Franke.*"

▗▞▚▞▚▖

When I take my leave of Nefeli and walk out into the main office, Alexander is still sitting on the intern's desk. I have the urge to blast this genteel fuckboy in the face with a squirt bottle as if he were a misbehaving house cat. That's a little impractical, so instead I catch him by the sleeve of his tailored sage-green suit and haul him upright.

"A chat in private, please?" I grit out.

JOSIE JUNIPER

"Ooh, someone's keen for it," he jokes, giving Gilly a rakish wink. "I'll catch up with you later, pet."

I pause to look back and warn the wide-eyed intern. "Don't let *this* moron," I tell her, jabbing a finger toward Alexander, "be your least rewarding experience at this job."

As I plow toward Alexander's office with him in tow, he extracts his crumpled sleeve from my grip. "Do you quite mind? This is Thom Sweeney."

His office is modest—Nefeli has at least made a nod to not playing favorites—but has a much larger window than mine, with a better view. I shove him through the door like a mall security guard herding a shoplifter, then shut it behind us.

"You're nothing if not true to form," I begin, eyes raking over him with disgust.

He relaxes, smoothing a hand down his jacket and shooting his cuffs. "Been eyeing my 'form,' Evans? I'm flattered." His gaze angles to the door. "Flip that lock, and—"

My growl of frustration is practically an animal's snarl. "*Rrrggghhh!* Turn that flirting shit off, can you? *Like, ever?* For one minute?"

He leans on his desk and tilts his head in feigned remorse. "My apologies."

"The memory stick you gave me in Italy. *You stole it from my inbox.* I can't believe I fell for your stupid compliments saying you think I'm a terrific journalist! As much—"

"Natalia," he cuts in softly.

His usual smug glamour has been replaced with an expression that for once doesn't seem engineered to showcase his charming smile. It's almost...vulnerable?

COMING IN HOT   215

I fold my arms. "What."

He rakes one hand through his auburn hair, then blows out a breath, upward to adjust the picturesque lock falling over his brow.

"The compliments I gave you when I handed over the USB stick were sincere. And the dig I took at your professional qualifications last year during our date were...*not*." He picks up a paperweight made of magnetic spheres and digs into it with a fingertip. "I was embarrassed by your rejection and still wanted to hurt your feelings. It was immature and sullen, and I'm genuinely sorry."

I'm pretty sure he's not manufacturing his candor right now, because I catch the faint change to his speech that I notice only when he's at his most unguarded. The childhood Northern accent tugs at his vowels—I hear it on "sullen."

I let the silence hang. My aunt says it's unforgivably rude not to accept an apology, but then again, she's never met Alexander Laskaris.

"You know you're awful, right?"

He peeks up at me through dark lashes. "I'm sure you'll be shocked to learn you're not the first person to say so."

I'm not letting him off that easily.

He offers a sad smile that's mostly confined to his dark gray eyes. "I took the USB stick from your inbox in a fit of pique. I'd just heard that you got *ARJ Buzz*, and...I'd already told several people the job was mine."

"Ah. *Female* people," I surmise with some amusement.

His lips scrunch into a sulky frown. "You're enjoying this too much, but *yes*. And surely you know how much men love to be laughed at by women."

216   **JOSIE JUNIPER**

I give him a pitying, big-sisterly look. "Oh, for God's sake, Alex. Why do you care what people think of you? You're too rich and pretty to be this insecure."

He smirks. "You think I'm pretty?"

"You know you are, idiot," I say, rolling my eyes. "But seriously...what's with the disguises, the chameleon thing you do? Trying to carve out the perfect key for every lock. Even the posh accent you wear like armor—you think I haven't noticed your real one? With all your obvious gifts and privilege, it's like you think it still isn't enough."

His helpless chuckle is like a long-held breath finally released. "I don't think I have a *real* accent. Even as a boy, it changed for my father, my tutors, the kids around our village. But you're no different, Evans. I scrub Northern England from my voice; you've scrubbed the Southern US from yours—proper Broadcast American, that. So who are *you*?" His eyes narrow with mirth. "Don't pretend you have it all sorted. Has Herr Franke ever met the real Natalia Evans, or are you still figuring out who she is?"

His question tumbles into an empty space inside me, bumping around in the darkness. "I'm...I'm a fundamentally honest person, Alexander."

"That," he counters, pointing at me, "answers a question altogether different to the one I asked."

Getting to my feet with a sigh, I move toward the door. "I have nothing to hide. And thanks for the apology, but I still don't trust you."

"But you *like* me just a little bit," he teases. "I'm not all bad. Give me a chance to prove it."

With one hand on the doorknob, I pin him with a look over my shoulder. "Wanna prove it? Leave Gilly alone. Oliver in graphic design has a crush on her, and I think she likes him back. But you're confusing her, and you only about ten percent mean it."

He takes a slow breath. "All right. But for my valiant sacrifice, I get upgraded to 'acquaintance-plus' in your eyes, if friendship is right out."

"Oh, Jesus—*fine*. As long as you never ask me for a date again, ever." I turn the doorknob, then pause. "Also, if you hear any credible intel about the human rights issue with that new grand prix location, let me know, okay? I'm looking into it."

"Deal."

As I exit, I can't help thinking that it feels odd to have an alliance with Alexander. But his mild sleaziness might come in handy.

Because unfortunately, I can't ask Klaus about any of this.

19

AUSTRIA

TWO WEEKS LATER

KLAUS

Natalia and I flew in separately to Vienna, coming respectively from London and Paris, where I attended an FIA meeting with major partners and several team principals. She and I hired a car with the aim of driving to my hometown—about an hour south of Vienna near Lake Neusiedl—before we proceed to Spielberg for race week.

I haven't been "home" in nearly twenty years. But I've felt guilty and sad about having to hide some things from Natalia lately, so the trip was a sort of offering, to satiate the curiosity she rightly has about my past.

She's been asking a lot of questions as we wend down the A3. I find myself slow to reply, turning each question over in my mind, examining for pitfalls and being somewhat vague.

"I'm not *interviewing* you right now, Klaus," she says dryly. "Fascinating as you are, I doubt I can get a story out of your favorite sport as a boy or the name of a girl you kissed when you were twelve. Quit being so uptight. I just like knowing more about you."

"Forgive me," I say with a tired smile. "I need to switch gears into holiday mode."

"Seriously," she teases. "Lighten up, pal."

"I did save a joke for you, come to think of it..."

She chuckles. "Still practicing for that career in stand-up? Okay, lay it on me."

I glide through a patch of slower-moving cars, then send an expectant grin Natalia's way. "What is a zombie's favorite part of the newspaper?"

She lifts an eyebrow.

After a pause, I deliver the punchline. "The *head*lines."

I'm gratified at her helpless burst of laughter.

"Wow, *no*. Points for trying, but that is...honestly terrible. Dad jokes, without even being a dad."

She lays a hand on my leg fondly, and I entwine my fingers with hers.

"Someday, perhaps," I say lightly.

We're still holding hands when we get to my hometown.

Natalia gawks out the window as we cruise along the narrow main road. "This is insanely cute. Look at these colors! I feel like I'm in a Wes Anderson film."

Though I was an adult the last time I was here, everything looks smaller. Maybe it's only that my life has grown in scale. We pass bicyclists, people sitting at umbrella-covered tables outside a restaurant, an elderly couple walking, each carrying cloth market bags.

JOSIE JUNIPER

"I wonder if you knew it was this special when you lived here," Natalia muses, gazing at an old church as we pass. "It's so easy to miss what's right in front of you."

I'm unsure how to reply. In my youth, I noticed the town's appeal chiefly through the eyes of others. I wonder if there's a subtext to her observation.

Two weeks ago she forwarded me a link to a website with a photo of us in Monaco. She seemed concerned about the online reveal, but really, who is interested in the romantic life of the third-place Formula 1 team's principal? I'm hardly "news."

What *is* news is the troubling situation I've hidden from her about the new grand prix location. It's still brewing and has expanded to nothing short of a crisis for the sport.

My phone buzzes in my breast pocket and I slide it out to look when we come to a four-way stop. As if summoned by the worry simmering at the back of my mind, a message from Phaedra is there, the preview on the screen reading, This is a fucking shit-show. Another follows close on its heels, then a third.

"Ooh," Natalia says, gazing out the passenger side at a shop on the opposite corner. "Local glassware. Look at that decanter in the window! Gorgeous."

I take advantage of her admiration for the object and pull the car over once I've cleared the intersection. "Go ahead and look— I'll catch up with you." I lift my phone, its back toward her. "I must reply to this."

"Okay, perfect." She leans to give me a peck, then wipes a smudge of lipstick off me. "See you in a few."

She climbs out and I open Phaedra's messages.

COMING IN HOT 221

Phaedra: This is a fucking shitshow. Ben from Allonby threw a fit in the lobby after you left for the airport, leaned on the other teams to take his side, saying they "shouldn't have to suffer bc of Emerald."

Phaedra: What if this blows open before we get it under control? Terrible timing for you to be dating a journalist, haha.

Phaedra: Anyway, hate to rain on your parade. Enjoy the getaway with Nat. But an announcement needs to be made soon, either denouncing or reassuring. PlatiNumeric say they won't have their name on our fucking car if this goes forward, so I'm not feeling great (though I agree with them in principle)

I scrub a hand over my face with a groan. The passenger door opening startles me as Natalia gets back in. I shove my phone into my pocket, and her eyes follow the movement with a glint of suspicion.

"Back so soon?" I ask lightly.

"They were closed. That is, the door was locked, and the old woman inside was way too into eating a sandwich to acknowledge my knock."

I glance at my watch before starting the car up. "Ah. It's the lunch hour." We ease back onto the road, headed for the end of town where my childhood home is.

"Everything okay?" Natalia asks.

"I'm fine. Just a bit tired. It's odd to be here, perhaps, after so long."

She's quiet for another minute. "Did you ever…come here with Sofia?"

"Once, a few years after we married." I give Natalia a weak smile. "There was scant reason. My mother was long gone, and my father…he wasn't an easy man. He was unkind to her. Called her 'das Bücherwurmmädchen'—the bookworm girl."

Natalia runs her finger along the windowsill. "I wonder what he would've thought of me," she says, her voice tentative.

"He'd have been glad you're beautiful. You're more spirited than he preferred in a woman, however."

"Was your mother pretty and deferential?"

"Pretty, yes. But not deferential enough for them to be happy together."

Natalia puts a hand gingerly on my leg. "You've never told me how, um…how your parents died. Or when."

"My father had a stroke when I was in my thirties. My mother was only twenty-nine when she died. I was six."

In Natalia's long silence, I can feel her shock at this revelation, her uncertainty in how to proceed. "What happened?" she finally manages.

"She drowned."

"Oh, Klaus." Natalia lifts my hand and kisses it. "I didn't realize you had so many tragedies."

"Life is a house constructed of tragedy. We decorate it with our fragile joys to make a suitable home."

Hugging my hand against her heart, she laughs. "I don't think you've ever said anything more Austrian. We should start a social media account where you offer grim quotes every day. Like gloomy poetry."

I stop the car in front of the house that was once mine.

"Here it is," I say quietly.

It's a different color now. A cat is curled on the stoop. In one window a plant hangs, in another—the kitchen, I remember—a dangling prism. It comes back to me, the scent of my mother's baking. Linzer plätzchen. Icing sugar dusted across the table, and my fingerprints walking through it.

These small details before me now—the cat, the plant, the winking crystal teardrop—are the fingerprints of someone else's life. The seeds of their future memories.

Natalia and I watch the house in a close silence. Her hand repositions, dovetailing more firmly with mine, and the connection seems to align like a battery I've been installing incorrectly for many years. An intense wave of complex feeling lights up and moves through me.

I've left so many things behind in life and been left behind by so many. This cocktail of emotions I'm experiencing is overwhelming: tenderness, communion, fear, expectation, hope, a passion somehow both physical and spiritual.

It's soon, maybe too *soon... but I can't risk leaving this behind.*

"Not all my poetry is dark," I say. Turning in my seat, I pull her toward me for a lingering kiss. "The loveliest poem, perhaps, is one of the simplest." Her eyes are bright with earnestness and desire as we realign and kiss again. "Three words—short and sweet, but certain as sunlight."

Her hand on my face is warm. She smiles against my lips. "It's not always sunny."

"Sunlight is always there, even when obscured by clouds, or on the opposite side of the globe."

She ducks her head on my shoulder as if shy. "And just what *is* this mysterious three-word poem?"

I sweep her hair around her neck and put my lips against her ear. "*I love you, Natalia Jane Evans,*" I whisper.

"Oh my God." She combs one hand into the hair at the back of my head, and the other grasps the fabric of my trouser leg. "I love you too…"

Where I'm touching her back, I feel her heart pounding. My own drums in echo.

It's been years since I said these words to anyone, even in a casual sense. And nothing about this is casual. It's a full commitment. I've been standing at a cliff's edge, and a prescient gust of wind has toppled me into the void, knowing I will fall only long enough to remember my wings.

20

HUNGARY

THREE WEEKS LATER

NATALIA

During the week of the French Grand Prix, Klaus and I stayed in a beach cottage twenty minutes from the track, at Saint-Cyr-sur-Mer. Despite the overwhelming busyness of the GP lead-up, we were, in those precious hours together on the French coast, like the only two people in the world. He cooked for me, read to me, and we made love with abandon.

It would've been paradise if not for the fact that he's hiding something. There were a lot of furtive texts, or him wandering off to "take a quick call" alone, pacing the beach in front of the cottage. I'd watch his body language, his agitated gesturing, and wish I could overhear what was being said.

I confess, one of the times he was outside ranting into his phone about something that had him more emotional than I typically see him, I crept to his laptop and tapped the track pad, hoping some clue might pop up. It was, of course, passworded.

226 JOSIE JUNIPER

I do feel emotionally safe with him, but as far as business stuff goes, we're both *so* cautious. More than once I've idly fantasized about another life we could have where he's not a team principal and I write books in that cozy home office of my dreams. Lazy days with coffee and conversation and long walks, no pressure...no secrets. I've even pictured it as being at the old Marshall farm in my hometown, which has been for sale for the past year. But the idea of a jet-set billionaire setting aside his glamorous life and moving to some tiny Kentucky town is pretty silly.

On Nefeli's not-quite-an-order, I've kept my ear to the ground about the issues with the new GP location, but there's nothing solid. On fan forums, people discuss the rumors of political instability in the host country. Once I'm done with this deep-dive article about Klaus, I plan to focus more energy on the topic. I gained a few new contacts since losing the one from Amnesty International, but I haven't secured anything concrete enough to be useful. A trip to the country in question will be necessary, and...yeah, that's not a conversation I'm looking forward to having with Klaus.

I didn't tell him about it last week when I got an anonymous, semi-menacing email telling me to keep my nose out of things. I turned it over to the IT department at *ARJ* to see if they could determine whether it was a credible threat. But I won't allow myself to feel intimidated when this could be such an important— and career-making—story.

Formula 1 is no stranger to controversy. The ultra-high stakes aren't only on track. It's a billions-per-year business. As a journalist,

COMING IN HOT   227

I know the rules aren't the same for me in every race location. There are questions that would land me firmly on the "persona non grata" list if I dared to ask them during Thursday press days.

The few times I've tried to extract info from Klaus on anything hard-hitting rather than merely "entertaining," I've quickly discovered the limit of my alleged "all-access pass."

Why are you asking me this? he'll challenge.

Phaedra isn't any help either. I tiptoed into the new-GP-venue topic once, and she not only got aggressive and mocked me for "having delusions of some Harriet the Spy investigative reporter bullshit," but minutes later she sent someone a text, and Klaus replied—his text alert noise is the shriek of a 1990s naturally aspirated F1 engine, unmistakable. So they're in cahoots, on the same page about leaving me in the dark.

This race week in Hungary, for the first time, Klaus and I are openly rooming together, staying in a suite at the Four Seasons. We have a balcony with a view of the Danube, and I should be a euphoric puddle of relaxation sitting out here right now—gazing at the sunset, colors melting over the cityscape and reflecting onto the river. A bottle of Tokaji Aszú is open, and we have a light meal laid out: gorgeous bread, local cheeses, fruit, squares of dark chocolate.

So yeah...I *should* be relaxed. But the phone calls from Sherri—which stopped for a while after the Canadian Grand Prix—have started up again. She's pushing me, dammit, and I'm not ready. It's got me on edge and defensive.

Then a half hour ago, Klaus took a call and hustled off to close himself in the suite's bedroom. When I tried to go in to get my bathrobe, *the door was locked.* I eavesdropped a little, because I had a paranoid thought: *What if it's Sherri, and she's trying to enlist Klaus's help on badgering me into a mother-daughter relationship?* But what I overheard instead was no better—more furtive business stuff, confirming his lack of trust in me where work is concerned.

So I've been sitting out here picking at the food and shivering slightly from the breeze off the river in my short silk chemise, arms and legs bare. As the last of the sunset's reflection is fading from the Danube, Klaus comes out. I ignore him, stabbing a bit of melon with a bite of walnut-studded Gomolya cheese and popping it into my mouth.

He stands beside my chair. "I brought this out in case you're chilly."

He's holding the bathrobe I wanted to get from the bedroom, and instead of being touched that he thought of it, I'm irritated that he's in my head.

I shrug one shoulder. "Thanks, but I'm fine."

First draping the robe along the back of my chair, he goes to the other side of the table and sits. "The gooseflesh on your arms says otherwise, but suit yourself."

His mildly amused tone says he knows I'm being stubborn. I'm hoping he'll ask me what's wrong, so I can have the satisfaction of saying *It's nothing,* but he's better at this game than I am. He pours himself a glass of the Tokaji Aszú and takes a strawberry from the tray and eats it before sipping the wine, gazing off the balcony.

"Lovely night," he tries.

COMING IN HOT

"Mmm-hmm." I fork up a segment of apricot, and before I get it to my mouth, my phone buzzes again. *Sherri*. With a sharp sigh, I turn the phone face down.

"Talia."

I look up, one eyebrow lifted, expression bland.

"Either block the number or let the woman speak," Klaus counsels soberly. "If the message you're trying to convey to her with this obstinate silence is that you don't care, you're achieving quite the opposite." He chooses another strawberry. "It's childish."

I set my fork down. "Wow, you almost had a point there, until you decided to make it into an insult."

"I had no—"

"As for what's 'childish'? That'd be *you*, skulking off and locking the door for a phone call. Once again demonstrating that you don't trust me."

He sits back and folds his arms—*dammit, why does he have the sleeves rolled up, torturing me with his stupid sexy forearms?*—and gives a maddeningly cool smile, his shapely lips quirking up on one side. "I wonder why you are trying to start a quarrel."

"You tell me! I'm sure you have an opinion about it, right?" I jump to my feet and grab my phone. In the other hand I scoop up a chunk of pear and a square of chocolate, putting them into my mouth and chewing as I stalk inside.

I pace a full circuit around the sofa, both wanting Klaus to follow and hoping he'll leave me the hell alone. As I make another furious loop around the living room, I see through the windows that he hasn't moved, sitting pretty as you please with one ankle resting on the opposite knee, leisurely drinking his wine. Irrational

230 **JOSIE JUNIPER**

fury goes from a simmer to a boil, and when my phone buzzes again in my hand, I spin away from the windows and throw it hard with a snarl of frustration.

While the phone is mid-flight, my hand claps over my mouth as I spot its inevitable trajectory and know I'm helpless to undo it. It smacks into the mirror behind the bar and bounces into the sink. Somehow I managed to avoid breaking any of the liquor bottles, but the mirror is cracked.

"Dammit...no!" I trot over and fish my phone out of the sink. It's intact, but the mirror hasn't fared as well. I lean in to survey the damage. The small starburst of broken glass is obvious—the whole thing will have to be replaced.

Perfect. Could my night get any better?

I straighten, chirping out a yelp as the full reflection of Klaus looms behind me.

"Are you hurt?" he asks. He tries to gather my hands in his to inspect them for injury, and I tear myself away from his grasp.

"I'm fine! Jesus, do I have to lock myself in a room like you to get a minute's peace?"

He retreats a step, leaning back against the counter. *Are his feelings hurt?* I don't want him to be hurt...not because I care about his feelings right now, but because it would make me the bad guy, and that is very unsatisfying.

He studies me seriously. "I'm sorry if you were upset by the locked door," he says evenly. "I needed freedom from distraction, so I could focus. My Portuguese isn't strong, and I was speaking to Armando at Harrier."

My stomach sinks at the casual untruth. I'd love to call him out on what he's claiming, but it's better strategy to keep it to myself for now.

"Whatever. But you need to stay out of my business about Sherri. I can't handle a guilt trip on top of how complicated my feelings already are."

He pushes off the counter and comes toward me, cupping the elbows of my tightly folded arms in his palms, smoothing his hands up my bare arms. "Understood." He presses a kiss to my forehead. "You're in a sour mood tonight, kleine Hexe."

"I'm allowed," I grumble, responding to his cautious smile with a faint, reluctant one of my own.

"Certainly." Another kiss, this time at my temple. "And I hope *I'm* allowed to sweeten it." His knuckle curls beneath my chin and he tips my face up, studying my eyes for the invitation before closing in on my mouth for a deep kiss.

As we part, I say, "I'll bet I know what kind of sugar you're offering."

"Two kinds." He delivers another kiss. "Because I was also going to say, I'm happy to give you the first interview about Sage's move to Emerald after we make the announcement. Would that please you?"

It would, but something in his manner tells me he was going to offer that anyway and is framing it as a "gift" to distract me from what's really going on.

I didn't say so a few minutes ago—playing ignorant is an advantage with overheard secrets—but he wasn't speaking Portuguese on that call. It was French, and I recognized three things: *les droits de l'homme*, human rights; *scandale international*, international scandal; and *Aristide*, the first name of the CEO of Emerald's biggest sponsor, PlatiNumeric.

He's trailing hot kisses down my neck and across my shoulder, and when he pauses to look at my face again, some hint of my frustration that he's lying must show, despite how turned on I'm getting.

His smile is full of mischief. "You want to remain cross with me, hmm?" He caresses me from waist to hip, catching the hem of my short nightie at the bottom and sweeping it up, his touch whispering along my skin. "Because..." One finger hooks into the strap of my panties. "That day in Santorini you were *quite* angry. And that anger..." He drags the lacy strap down. "Was a dash of salt to your palate. Something you can't wait to taste again."

I shiver deliciously as the fabric of my underwear glides over the curve of my bottom, stopping halfway down. My nipples are tight and tingling, and it demands all my will to remain still as a statue, eyes cool, imperious, letting him try to thaw me.

"You asked me to tame you that night," he says an inch from my lips, flicking the straps of my chemise off my shoulders. "Do you enjoy behaving like an ill-tempered little wildcat sometimes so you can be subdued?"

"Maybe. *Ohhh...*"

As Klaus strips the bodice of my nightie down and cups my breasts, taking a nipple into his mouth and rolling it with his tongue, my animosity burns away like a flash of steam from ice thrown onto a griddle.

He releases the nipple and kisses his way back up to my mouth, claiming my lips with intensity, stroking my tongue, impressing a bold bite to my lower lip that makes me whimper with both the sting and the knee-weakening hunger. As he pulls away, I lean toward him, following his mouth.

"It's a lot of work, being such a good girl," he murmurs, hypnotic. "How many times have you called *me* an enigma, reproached me for being evasive? Yet you"—he turns me around to face the counter, and I lean on my forearms with a gasp—"hide your deepest nature from the world. So polite, forgiving, accommodating." Drawing my hair aside, he kisses the nape of my neck. "*So biddable*," he whispers.

He pushes my panties down with torturous slowness, and I'm already so wet that I can feel how the fabric peels away. I moan, and an eager twitch shivers inside me. I'm aching to feel him, and madder at myself for needing him like this than I am at him for lying about the phone call. Why can't I resist his touch, his scent, the timbre of his voice?

"Biddable? Me?" I ask as his hands glide over my bottom, dipping between my legs to tease me from behind. I duck my knees and move my hips to one side, playfully dodging his caress.

He gives me a little swat, then braces my hips in his big hands. "Wicked tease."

"Do that again," I urge, my tone a longing sigh. He delivers another two, and the intimacy of his warm hand against my skin lights me up inside. "A little harder…"

"I know what you need," he growls. His leg moves between mine, and he nudges my thighs apart. "Wider," he directs. "Open for me."

I comply, waiting to hear the rasp of his zipper lowering, and am shocked pleasantly breathless when he lands a sharp smack

234   **JOSIE JUNIPER**

against my pussy. A burst of lustful electricity shoots down my thighs. "Oh God!"

"Yes?"

His voice borders on smug, and I want to be annoyed about it. But I'm eager to feel his hand again. My clit is wide awake, throbbing with need.

"Please, more—"

I barely have the words out when his flattened hand smacks again, twice, three times. I'm taut with anticipation, breathing hard, my hips angling to give him better access.

"*Fuck...*" I moan. Surprised at myself for cursing, I open my eyes wide, then squeeze them shut again.

Klaus chuckles, and finally I hear the welcome sound of his zipper. "There's my lewd girl. Such *unchaste* words."

He moves my legs together so I'm not as low to the floor, then slides his cock between them, his hands stealing around me, holding my breasts, warm and firm. He churns his hips, rocking back and forth against me between my legs, outside of me. I try tilting my hips to angle him for entry, and he pinches my nipples.

"No," he says firmly. "You'll come for me like this before I fill you. You keep asking to be tamed, kleine Hexe. I'll oblige and make you so weak you can't stand."

Waves of pleasure rise as he plows against me. The wetness as we move together is so abundant, my thighs are getting soaked. One of his hands digs into my left hip as the other teases my nipple, herding me toward climax.

Through the pre-orgasmic haze, I insist, "I'm not as weak as you think..."

"I'll only make your knees weak—never your spirit, my little

COMING IN HOT

conqueror," he says. His jaw is tight; I can hear it in his voice as he tries to hold back.

I undulate my hips and let myself moan, knowing how it inflames him. I want to make him finish first...deny him, control him, *break him.*

The memory flickers up, the Mata Hari quip Nefeli made: *Shag the dear boy into exhaustion and go through his pockets for secrets.*

Admittedly, she claimed that *wasn't* what she meant...but right now it sounds like a great idea. *He lied to me.* Maybe I'll wear him out and put this mystery to rest once and for all, sneak out of the bedroom while he's sleeping and go through his briefcase.

Nefeli referred to him as "putty in my hands," but Klaus has always been more like a fistful of sand: conforming to the shape I want for a moment, but as soon as I remove the pressure, slipping through my fingers. My vexation at his power over me is nearly as intense as my arousal.

Why shouldn't I try fighting fire with fire, if deception is his game?

Despite the vengeful thoughts in my mind, my traitorous body is lost in a delirium of desire. I've instinctively hit a rhythm, moaning, panting, thrusting back against him as his slick, steely heat rubs me just right.

Like a river tide lapping at the shore, he pushes me onward, until the warning glimmer shows through the cracks in my will, breaking deep in me. Sudden, blinding fireworks of orgasm follow. I'm leaning nearly face down against the counter, and as I come hard, one arm shoots out sideways, and I dimly hear the clatter of a container of bar tools as I launch it to the floor.

He slows his movement and stops, gripping my hips like he's at the edge of his limit. A sound comes from his throat, a helpless groan mixed with a laugh of triumph. "Ich möchte Dich betteln hören," he grits out. "Beg me for what you need."

I straighten, swiping back the piles of hair tangled over my face, and turn around. My legs are, as promised, trembling. "Beg you?" I shoot back with a haughty smile. "Am I your servant?"

He captures my face in both hands and kisses me hard. "No, Talia. I'm *yours*. I've belonged to you since the moment you took a drink of my cognac. You left your bloodred imprint on my glass, my heart, my life."

He lifts me, and I wrap my legs around him. Digging my fingers into his shoulders, I work my hips into position. The head of his cock is pressed against my entrance, and I move against him in a sinuous, taunting dance before I sink down, gradually taking every magnificent inch, watching his face.

The silver-flecked dark hair at his temples is dewy with the sweat of our urgency. His lips are parted, and as he tips his head back for a moment as if overwhelmed, the white ridge of his teeth captures my attention. There's something so vulnerable and *real* about every part of our bodies as we're entwined like this.

My worries and resistance evaporate. I'm viscerally *here*, watching the tenderness of his mouth, connected to him, wrapped in him. Clamping his shoulder with one hand and wringing his hair with the other, I kiss him like I'm feral, like my heart is breaking, like I want to live inside him the way he's in me.

The sound in his throat is a plea. He takes a dozen steps, heading for the bedroom, before he stops and presses me to the wall of the passageway from the living room. The wood paneling at my back is cool and hard, but somehow I welcome the rhythmic jolt against my spine as he pounds into me.

COMING IN HOT

Our feverish mouths take and take, both of us selfish, starved. The wooden floor creaks in staccato protest as Klaus surges against me hard. His panting is almost a growl—stern, combative—as if every sharp exhale is commanding me to reveal more of myself, to let him in deeper.

My body in a place of striving that's beyond the dictate of pleasure, I hear myself gasping out, "I know you, *I know you*," as we buck against each other.

"*My Talia*—you know me better than anyone," he returns in a harsh whisper.

I can feel how close he is. In a fever of greed, I cling to him, begging, "Fill me…don't leave…"

With a throaty cry he lets go, crushing me against the wood paneling, his body tense. His release shudders inside me, and I dig my heels into him, murmuring nothing and everything, a nonsense of comfort, my half sighs, half kisses gusting against his shoulder.

After a pause to catch his breath, he straightens, lifting me reverently and carrying me to the bed. His left forearm supports my weight, and his free hand caresses my back.

"My God—I don't know what came over me," he says. "Did I hurt you?"

Not in the way you think.

I administer a reassuring kiss to his lips. "I'm fine."

He's still inside me and carefully withdraws before setting me on the bed. "It was careless lovemaking on my part," he says, a dart of worry between his brows.

"It was exactly what I wanted too. Don't be upset."

He kneels beside the bed, studying my expression, then parts my legs to move closer before guiding me onto my back. "Let me take you where I'd intended to go." He strokes his hands up the insides of my thighs, then follows the path with his lips. "Are you sore?"

I rise onto my elbows, looking at him kneeling between my legs. "Do you mean my legs? Or...*there*?"

"Shy girl." More kisses on my inner thighs. Grasping me carefully behind the knees, he scoots me closer, and I realize his intention.

"Klaus, *wait*. Do you want to do, um...*that*? Right now, after, y'know..."

He chuckles. "I may be a disciplined person in many ways, but this isn't one of them." He presses another kiss to me, closer. "I'm not fastidious."

With his thumbs, he glides up to the apex of my thighs, strokes my labia, then passes a thumb over my clit, featherlight. I suck in a tiny gasp but angle myself to encourage him.

He swirls two fingers of his other hand in a circuit around my entrance. "You're the most stunning shade of well-fucked pink."

A wave of heat goes through me—both bashful and turned on—at his words. His fingers slip inside me. I'm extravagantly wet, humming with the pleasant ache of energetic sex. Pushing past my shyness, I ask, "Can you keep your fingers in me but don't move them while you...do that? I want to feel you inside me, but I'm a little tender."

He smiles. "You can't imagine how happy I am that you've asked."

He moves my legs over his shoulders and I cock one knee outward to give him better access. His tongue sweeps over my

COMING IN HOT

vigorously worked flesh, testing my reaction. He gingerly strokes and explores, finding the ideal rhythm and pressure. My hands drift to my nipples, toying with them as he licks and kisses, mixing in an occasional careful hint of suction on my clit.

I've never had anyone go down on me right *after* sex before, and the sensation is surprising—very different from foreplay. The fullness of his fingers and the careful ministrations of his lips and tongue quickly conspire to bring on an orgasm so new feeling and unexpected that when the peak hits, I'm sobbing with the intensity.

My thighs tremor, and he strokes up my legs and torso as he climbs onto the bed by my side and pulls me into an all-encompassing embrace. We're both wordless, exhausted, communicating only through trailing fingertips, snowfall-light kisses, contented sighs.

Just before I drift off, I hear him murmur, "The door will never be locked to you again, Talia."

The moment is so perfect, I clutch it to myself and carry it with me like a confident traveler as I fall into a catnap.

But when I wake alone sometime later to the sound of a text—shower water hissing in the en suite—a message from Alexander startles me upright.

> **Alexander:** Call me. Big news about prospective GP. They're pulling out, and my sources say return of payment withheld due to concern it could fund an arms deal. Protests, and a fire at the headquarters of the sponsor Emerald jettisoned. This is massive, Evans.

Alexander: Engineering blueprint intel was definitely a smokescreen. I'm trying to determine who sent it to you, but don't be afraid to get dirty turning over a few stones yourself in the meantime.

Just then, Klaus's phone on the bedside table buzzes. I scramble across the big mattress, one eye on the open en suite door, and tap the screen to read the previews of two messages from Phaedra.

21

HUNGARY

THE SAME NIGHT

KLAUS

Natalia isn't in bed when I walk out of the bathroom. When I go to the night table to look at my wristwatch, my phone isn't there, and I'm certain it was when I got up. Securing the thick white bath towel around my waist, I stride into the suite's living room.

On the balcony, her dark hair crowned with moonlight, Natalia stands, looking toward the river, her posture stiff. I pause in the open doorway.

My phone is on the outside table with the half-empty bottle of wine, a hurricane lantern with a lit candle inside, and the forgotten food. A fork shifts on one of the plates as I collect my phone, and Natalia flinches at the sound but doesn't turn. When I tap the screen, the text previews from Phaedra—which Natalia has clearly seen—make my breath catch in my throat.

242

JOSIE JUNIPER

Schatzi: Shit has hit the fan. Protests. Arson (here's a
link). Journalist from Reuters injured or possibly killed.
Thank fuck we severed ties when we did. This is a
disaster.

Schatzi: UN sending a special envoy. We made the right
call but still may not come out with our noses clean—
Ben and Jack are so far up that president's ass they look
like Cerberus.

I set the phone down and go to the railing, leaving several feet
between Natalia and me, and lean on the ledge with my hands
steepled. "I know you must have questions. I'll be as forthcoming as I can. But you must understand why I couldn't talk to you
about this."

"Sure. You didn't trust me—I get it."

"Talia—"

"That's not why I'm the most upset," she cuts in. "It's…what I
found in your briefcase. I'm trying to figure out if it means what
I think."

I turn slowly to face her. "*In my briefcase?* Well. Be my guest," I
say acidly. "What's mine is yours, apparently."

She turns to me with a hard look. "*Nothing* that's yours has ever
been mine, Klaus. And I don't think it ever will be. I'm exhausted,
trying to climb the walls of your fortress."

"I've only held back when I had no choice."

"Oh, bullshit."

I look at her seriously. "It's true. I *love* you, Talia."

She covers her eyes. "*Stop.* You're making it so much worse…"

COMING IN HOT   243

I sink my face into my hands. The thin sound of post-midnight traffic drifts up from below.

"Tonight," Natalia begins, her voice shaky. "Earlier, with the locked door…you were talking to Aristide Bridoux at PlatiNumeric, right?"

"I'm not happy you eavesdropped." The words come out feebly—it's a poor defense.

Her jaw is hard, the line of her mouth pitiless. "Answer me."

"You know I was speaking with him, clearly. The things I've concealed…it's so politically volatile, I've had to be careful while the matter is investigated. Intel reached Emerald over a year ago about human rights abuses in the new GP's host country. We went to the FIA with evidence of slave labor, torture. A massive government cover-up ensued. We heard rumors that one journalist went missing while chasing the story. Then recently, the reporter falling off the balcony. No one really believes it was an accident—don't be disingenuous and claim *you* do." I point toward my phone. "And now? Possibly another death. I cannot stress enough how dangerous this is."

"Dangerous to Emerald's reputation?" Natalia counters, cynical. "To the sport? To the all-important bottom line?"

I rise from the chair and cross to her, but when I try to touch her shoulders, she steps back. My hands drop uselessly. "To *you*, Talia. My God. And potentially to every citizen in that country."

Silence follows, and Natalia's head drops. My arms ache to hold her, but I don't dare try. "What is this about my briefcase?" I ask quietly. "What did you find?"

A gray spot blooms on the sleeve of her dressing gown, and I realize it's a tear. With a helpless sound, I move closer, but she sidesteps me. She reaches into the pocket of her dressing gown, then extends and opens it to reveal a handful of USB thumb drives.

"A whole bag of these. Exactly the same as the one I gave to you in Barcelona," she tells me, her voice a rasp. "Something I *risked my job* to do."

I shake my head, mouth opening but freezing on the shape of a denial I know is useless. *Why didn't I confess months ago, that evening in Barcelona?*

"You sent me the 'stolen engineering blueprints' evidence, didn't you?" she continues with a chilling calm. "All fake. A snipe hunt, like Nefeli suspected—a stupid trick to distract me, like a mother giving her phone to her toddler so they won't climb out of the grocery cart." Her fists clench. "You made a fool of me."

There's a musical *tink!* as a moth hits the chimney of the hurricane lantern on the table, clumsily trying to find its way inside, then a faintly audible hiss as it succeeds in the goal and drops, scorched, beside the candle.

"Yes, I sent it."

Natalia stares at me, absorbing my grim confession. She focuses on the lantern with tired eyes, her shoulders lowering as if she's deflating. Her gaze roams across the remains of our meal, then rakes over me in detail before tilting upward to focus on the moon.

A cramp of panic seizes my chest as I realize what she's doing: saying goodbye to it all, studying the scene as if painting a picture that will have to last a lifetime.

"*Wait,*" I breathe. "I did it, but you must let me explain."

She pushes herself into motion, veering around me and dropping the handful of USB sticks on the table before going inside. I

COMING IN HOT

follow, trailing her like a stray dog with the hope of offered scraps. She hauls out her suitcase and flops it open at the foot of the bed, immediately returning to the closet and yanking clothes off the wooden hangers.

I pull on some cotton pajama bottoms and sag to the side of the bed. "Please," I ask gently. "I know you're angry. And it's justified. But will you talk with me?"

She folds a blouse in her efficient way and rolls up a skirt, placing them into the suitcase with right-angle accuracy, then marching back to the closet.

"My phone call with the woman from Amnesty International, that night in Montréal," she throws over her shoulder. "Did you do something to kill it? Because I'll bet it wouldn't have been hard. You got your hands on *my* phone number in like five minutes when we ran into each other in Melbourne last year. Such a big shot. Everyone falls all over themselves to do your bidding. No one else's will matters, I guess, when Klaus Franke decides what's best, right?"

The ache in my chest is horrible. I force myself to speak through the maelstrom of awareness that I may have irreparably fucked up.

"I...I wanted...to protect you," I stammer, opening my hands, then dropping them to my lap. "After we made love during your visit to Santorini, you spoke so passionately about your lifelong desire to write and publish earthshaking work—something that would earn awards and change lives. I knew if you dug deeper into the rumors of what was occurring with the new grand prix location, you wouldn't let go. Danger be damned."

She sits back on her heels with a furious look. "And you'd be *right*, Klaus. I'm a journalist, and it's my job." With a disgusted scoff, she turns away again. "You could've *helped me*. Just think what a very different conversation we'd be having right now if instead of being a patronizing asshole, you'd seen me as a partner."

The truth of what she's said sinks through me and shimmers away, like a key dropped into deep waters, unrecoverable.

"My heart was in the right place," I assert. "I couldn't risk you! Please try to understand. Some mistakes…" My heart wrings in my chest. "Some you cannot come back from if you make a poor call."

"It's not *your* choice what I risk, Klaus!"

"I panicked and was buying myself time—please understand," I all but beg. "You'd asked, that same weekend, about the rumors of Emerald stealing engineering designs from Allonby, so I thought, 'If she gets a tip about that, she'll chase it.' There was no validity to the suspicions, so it seemed safe. A dead end, but one that would take time to pursue."

"Well, thanks for being a *hero* and saving me from my assumed complete lack of self-preservation," she mutters, pushing past me in the bathroom doorway. She stomps to the suitcase and dumps the contents of her arms into it with a clatter.

"In retrospect it looks condescending—I know."

"Ya think?" she drawls, thick with sarcasm.

"I tried to tell you, that evening in Barcelona…I was in the process of confessing everything. But you stopped me, again and again."

She glares up at me. "What kind of a delusional asshole says 'My lies are *your* fault, because you didn't let me take them back later'?"

COMING IN HOT

247

I rake my hands into my hair with frustration. "That's not what I mean."

She zips her suitcase shut and it sticks halfway. Sitting on it, she completes the job, then regards me critically.

"I'm gonna tell you something, Klaus. For most of my life, my greatest fear has been abandonment, because of my parents leaving. But their sin was actually *the lying*. It turned out they didn't abandon me voluntarily! And I wouldn't have spent *eighty percent of my life* thinking they had if they'd been honest." She stands and pulls the suitcase upright. "Instead, they 'protected' me. They may not have chosen the abandonment, but what they did choose was the goddamned lie."

My horrible mistake is spread between us like a tar pit I can't possibly cross. I'm afraid to say what's in my head—it's far too naked—but if ever there were a time for complete honesty, it's now.

"I wish I'd been brave enough not to mislead you. All I could see was the danger to you, and the fallout of my past failures." I go to the bed and sit, staring at my hands, knotted together as I lean on my knees. "I wasn't able to save Sofia, because . . . I hung back and didn't insist on her seeing a doctor, *for years* when they might have caught her illness. I thought I was sparing her feelings—I didn't want her to think that having children was critically important to me. With this situation, with you . . . *yes*, I knew I was making a choice for you. I acknowledged the arrogance of that, but I fucking did it anyway, because *I can't lose you*."

I meet her eyes. A flicker of hope rises in me that what I'm saying makes some sense.

"I can't help what my life has made me," I tell her with intensity. "When I've erred, you'll certainly always get an apology. But I make no apologies for *who I am*."

One corner of her mouth lifts wryly. "Men always say that like it's a virtue."

Returning to the closet, she scoots her feet into sandals.

"You know what really stands out to me?" she goes on. "How much effort it took you to make up the phony evidence. Writing fake emails, blocking out the 'names,' hunting down a few useless blueprints to attach. Must've taken hours to get it just right. Which makes me think..." She cocks her head with a stinging smile. "*What else* would you expend that kind of energy on to deceive me down the road?" She extends the handle of her suitcase with a snap before dragging it out of the bedroom.

I leap up to follow. "Talia. *Wait*, please." I dash to stand between her and the suite's entryway. "Don't go—not like this. I'll sleep on the sofa if you don't want to share the bed. You can leave in the morning if you're still upset."

Her laugh is harsh. "*If I'm still upset?* Yeah, okay. You're right— you know how women are! Silly weaker vessels. I should take a Valium like some fifties housewife and lie down until my 'fit of hysteria' passes." She sidesteps around me.

"Where will you go? The hotel is full."

"I'll text Phaedra and take a car to the paddock and stay in her motor home." She yanks the door open and, as I see the yellow daisy sticker on her suitcase, which she uses to tell it apart from others at the airport, the memory hits me full force: The first time I noticed that sticker was twenty months ago in Abu Dhabi, the night we met.

COMING IN HOT

Weakly, I repeat my plea. "My impulse to protect you was pure. The thought of losing you—"

"This is how you lost me. *This.*" She looks back, framed in the doorway. "I'd hoped you were different."

I reach for her. "Tell me what I can do. I'm deeply sorry. I know words are inadequate, so *tell me what to do.* I'm listening."

She scrunches her lips to one side in an expression of pained regret and backs through the doorway. "Read 'The Wife of Bath's Tale' from *The Canterbury Tales.* Geoffrey Chaucer. But you won't be doing it for me. Do it for yourself, and whoever you date next." She turns and starts down the hall. "You could use some educating."

22

LONDON

ONE MONTH LATER

NATALIA

The night I walked out on Klaus and went to stay with Phaedra, she tried to pry out of me what had happened, but all I would say was, "I'm not wasting the rest of my thirties on another broken bird. Best of luck to the next girl."

I knew the breakup could throw a wrench into the deep-dive article I'd been working on for over five damned months, but I kept things professional. Most of it was written at that point, and I did my best to ensure there wasn't a shift in tone. I can't pretend my heart didn't ache every time I sat down to work on it, though, vividly bringing to life all the fantastic Klaus Franke qualities I needed to showcase.

Nefeli's required "thirst trap" pics bewitched and haunted me when I penned the article's cutlines. His intense espresso-dark stare, focused in the gym, a sexy sheen of sweat gilding his skin.

COMING IN HOT 251

That serious V of his brows as he chatted with colleagues in a meeting. The charming openness as he led a factory tour. And especially killing to me was the warm, candid snapshot of Klaus with a group of adoring children during a Jump Start event. So natural, like he was born for it.

Every sentence I wrote stung, but I knocked it out of the park. No one who reads those five thousand words will have any clue my heart is broken.

After turning in "Klaus Franke: Wizard of the Emerald F1 City," I ask for a week of personal leave. *ARJ* arranges to send Alexander to the first race after the August summer break, the Belgian Grand Prix. I hole up in my flat in West Ham, working on a new project, though I do go into the office once to shoot an episode of *ARJ Buzz*—a "Spill-the-Tea Special," focusing on silly season and all the wild rumors swirling around, driver line-ups and general gossip, murmurs of feuds, alliances, offers, and swaps.

On the weekend before my return to the office, I email Nefeli two things: the first chapter of the book I'm working on and a letter of resignation.

She calls me in twenty minutes after I arrive on Monday.

"What the bloody hell is this?" she demands, pointing at her laptop screen.

"Uh, which thing?"

"Don't be obtuse. *The resignation letter.* Am I to get our solicitors involved? I'll remind you, you're under contract."

I sit across from her desk, and I think the look on my face changes her angle of approach.

252 **JOSIE JUNIPER**

"Don't even *try* with the long puss, love. You know I have no heart," she says with an indulgent half-smile. "If you need to avoid You-Know-Who now that your fling has run its course, we can work something out temporarily. But I can't lose you."

Her closing words—the same thing Klaus said the night I walked out—spur a wave of pain, and I have to pinch my leg to keep an impassive expression.

"I don't want to sound like a jerk, playing hardball," I tell her soberly, "but my contract says if I leave early, all I have to do is return my signing bonus, which I'm willing to do."

Nefeli sighs, leaning back. "That bad, eh?"

"It's not entirely the issue you think. Things are changing for me, and...I've actually been questioning my career path all year anyway. I want to try being closer to my family, and I need to work on this book." I sit up, eager to hear her verdict on the writing sample. "Do you think it has promise?"

By way of reply, she prods her keyboard and adjusts her glasses to peer at the computer screen. "I wish I could discourage you by saying it's shite, but I fucking love it. Do you already have an arrangement with a publisher?"

I laugh. "Um, *no*. This is just a dream, currently."

"Willing to put it all on the line for a dream?" She lifts an eyebrow. "I don't know if I admire your pluck or think you're daft." She taps at her keyboard again. "But I'm chummy with someone at Abacus Books—history and memoirs and that. I'll send this over if you'd like."

"Holy sh— I mean, *wow*, thank you! Yes, please."

"But upon one condition: You merely take a leave of absence for the remainder of the season, and in January give me the chance to coax you back. *No* resigning today. I won't say you *must* return—I'm not a monster, contrary to popular belief. You'll have four months to work on your book. Then"—she lifts her hands—"we'll see if I can sweeten the pot."

We spend a long time talking things over. Nefeli, despite being a flinty old gal, has surprisingly sensitive and insightful advice about my career, my cautious beginnings of a relationship with Sherri and Jason, and even my broken heart.

I feel lighter when I leave her office. I've agreed to continue doing the *ARJ Buzz* segments remotely for the remainder of the season but make no appearances at the grands prix, letting Alexander take over for now. Next step: arrangements to move back to Kentucky.

As I walk to my office, my heart stirring with real optimism for the first time in weeks, Alexander leans out of his doorway.

"Evans! A word, please?"

When I go in, he's holding a handful of papers, which he extends toward me. Confused, I take it, looking down to see the first page of my book project—*Faded Sunlight: A Mother's Nightmare in a California Women's Prison.*

"How did you get your hands on this?" I demand. "Did Nefeli give you a copy?"

"She sent it to me last night, yes."

"Why?!"

He tips his head, sardonic, and leans casually on his desk. "Because I'm Mummy's special boy. You needn't get stroppy—I called you in here to heap praise upon you. That"—he points at the pages I'm mashing in one fist—"is fuckin' brilliant. And I know you still essentially loathe me, but I'm a solid writer, and...I'd like

254 JOSIE JUNIPER

to offer to beta read. I have a good eye with critiques. My comments could be useful."

I'm about to deliver a *Hell, no* when he holds up a hand and adds, "Let me rephrase that: I'm more *begging* than offering. Your writing is a delight, and I'm already invested enough in the story that if I have to wait a year or more until you publish—which you certainly will—I'll go mad."

I inspect him with a moody squint. "Hmm. Considering that 'negging' thing you always do, I can't imagine your crit comments being helpful."

"Give me a chance. I'll do the first chapter, and if you hate my style, you need never send me another word. But I promise, I'm good at this." His tentative smile is boyish. "I'd like to be friends, and make it up to you, what a pain in the arse I've been this year. Truly."

I smooth out the pages and cautiously hand them over. "Just one chapter. But you'd better not be doing this to clear the runway for asking me out again, because the answer is a permanent no."

"On my honor." He taps the little stack square and sets it aside, taking a pencil from his desk and jotting something at the top of the first page. "And condolences on things not working out with Emerald's TP. I know he's *dishy*." Alexander punctuates the assessment with a roll of his eyes. "Besides, I've ... set my sights on someone new. I'll plague you no longer with my affections."

"That poor thing, whoever she is," I tease, backing into the open doorway. "Somebody should warn her."

"Cruel woman." Alexander lobs the pencil in my direction, and I slip around the corner.

Heading to my office, I think about the book project, and where it might go. The opening paragraphs—which I've been over so many times they're all but tattooed on my brain—unfurl in my mind's eye:

When Sherri McNeil was a 1980s teenager in Kentucky, resentful of a world that felt too small to contain her big dreams, she never expected life to contract around her further, as it did over the next decade. But months after meeting Jason Evans—a rural country boy with Hollywood looks and charm—she found she'd traded her little home in Lexington for an even more suffocating one in an unincorporated South Kentucky town. The baby, unexpected but loved by the nineteen-year-old parents, made the rented clapboard house feel all the more crowded.

Seven years later, Sherri spread her wings and flew west to L.A., hoping to free her family from the limited future she envisioned for them in a map-dot hamlet with one stoplight, two fast-food restaurants, and four churches.

The moment the door of her prison cell shut behind her, she thought, *If my life gets any smaller, I may disappear entirely.*

And to her seven-year-old daughter, she did.

KENTUCKY

SIX WEEKS LATER

Opening the lines of communication started with an email while I was still in Hungary, but Sherri had to convince me before I'd pick up for a phone call. The next hurdle was video calls. I almost put the kibosh on that after the first one because it freaked me out how she kept bursting into tears and saying, "It's just so good to see your face!"

By the time I flew home in early September, I was cautiously ready to attempt in-person family stuff. I asked Auntie Min to give me a few days to acclimate and manage the jetlag, plus get my feet under myself emotionally, post-breakup. Then I agreed to muffins and coffee—a one-hour commitment. Next we did dinner, a backyard barbecue. The week after that, Minnie and I went to visit at Sherri and Jason's little rental, a half hour away.

The "excuse" for interacting has been the book project. Sherri is taking online college courses in writing, world history, and algebra. During our second phone call, I asked her if maybe we could collaborate on telling her story. She was initially skeptical that anyone would want to read "a biography about a regular person who made a lot of mistakes," until I showed her examples of some fantastic popular memoirs. I asserted that books like this incite changes in the world, expanding readers' perspectives on controversial subjects.

My boss's connections in publishing were a big help—I got a modest book deal, and Nefeli's own longtime agent has taken me on. I hope *Faded Sunlight* isn't just entertaining, but also *important*. I have an office set up in Auntie Min's guest room, under the window looking out on her garden—a perfect view of the bird feeders!—and I write and do research (and consult with Sherri on FaceTime) about ten to twelve hours a day.

Keeping myself busy has been critical, but it doesn't always work—my heart still aches for Klaus, remembering our passionate

COMING IN HOT 257

moments together, his touch, his scent, his voice in the dark, his low laugh. When you're waiting for time to heal a wound, the only thing that can make time speed up is a deadline, so I've been giving myself strict ones.

This week's challenge in "the Sherri and Jason Project" is spending time stuck in a car together. Sherri and I are going to Mammoth Cave National Park, two hours away. I only see a little of Jason. I think he's slightly afraid of me. Sometimes I catch him watching me with a nervous optimism like I'm a feral animal he's trying to befriend.

We stop at the Dairy Bar, so the first fifteen minutes of the trip are mercifully taken up by eating and listening to a nineties playlist Sherri made. She's learned how to make playlists (everything was CDs when she went to prison) and she texts them to me constantly. Sherri has a peanut butter milkshake and I'm eating onion rings because...why not? No one's going to kiss me on the mouth.

It's strange getting to know her when she's in her midfifties. My childhood memories of her are vague. As she pops the lid off her shake and stirs, trying to soften it, then gives up and pulls the straw free and licks the ice cream off, I'm struck by the fact that she seems simultaneously as awkward and unfinished as a kid and has an "old veteran with a thousand-yard stare" look in her eyes that only decades in prison can bestow.

My view of her is always snapping back and forth between recognizing her young essential nature and seeing the fine lines around her eyes, the threads of silver in her hair, and the way she's baffled by things like streaming services and hashtags.

She scoops out more ice cream and maneuvers it into her

mouth, dripping some on her chin and wiping it off with a self-conscious hum of laughter. "I'm a disaster." She wads up a napkin and swipes at a drop on her shirt. "Food is so awesome—I'm making up for lost time. Probably gained fifteen pounds this year. This milkshake must be six hundred calories."

I crunch my last onion ring and drop the packet into the bag. "Here's the good news about another way the world has changed since the mid-nineties: body positivity. It's a whole thing now. Counting calories is neurotic."

She snorts. "Okay, tell that to the jeans I bought in August and can't zip." She pokes at the stereo to change the song or maybe turn the volume up, and scowls when she can't make it work.

I pluck my phone from the center console and hand it to her. "You do it here."

"I'll never get used to this shit."

"You will—it hasn't even been a year."

She monkeys with the music for a few minutes. "It's crazy that I can listen to...*everything in existence.* My God, the money I wasted on sixteen-dollar CDs to own just one song I loved!" She chuckles, shaking her head. A new track starts—something buzzy and gloomy with that distinctive nineties growling moan.

She stirs the milkshake, alternating between taking sips and singing along to a song. I'm about to launch into book talk so the lack of conversation doesn't feel weird when she sprints headlong into Weirdville by asking the one question I don't want to hear.

"So...you really think it's over with your boy? Finito, no hope of reconciling?"

"He's hardly a 'boy' at forty-six," I mutter.

"You know what I mean."

COMING IN HOT

"Yes, it's done. I'm moving on with life, and I'm sure he is too." After a few groveling messages the first week, Klaus stopped trying. Not a word since then. Is he as brokenhearted as I am, or relieved to go back to his billionaire bachelor lifestyle?

There's a freeway-mile-long silence, and I can tell Sherri is deliberating over saying more. It makes me feel bad that she and Jason live in fear of annoying me and having me cut them off. Taking pity on her, I offer a question of my own.

"Did you, uh, have breakups? I mean, you started dating...um, *Jason*...so young. Was he your first boyfriend?" For a second I almost said "my dad," but it felt too unnatural. I'm not sure if they'll ever be Mom and Dad. It might be like learning a language late in life, my brain "translating" every time rather than feeling the meaning.

"Ha! Oh, definitely not. Maybe it's TMI, but I was kind of a slut in my day."

I wince. "Slut-shaming also went the way of calorie-counting, just so you know."

"Even if it's about myself?" She shrugs. "Whatever. Jesus, your generation is so touchy. And not to rub salt in the wound, but you guys don't get laid enough. If these dating TV shows are to be believed, millennials and Gen Z take forever to have sex with a new person. What's the big deal? Sex was casual and friendly in my day. We were more worried about AIDS than emotions in the eighties and nineties."

"Is that...somehow better?" I ask pointedly.

"Made it easier to not get your heart broken, that's for sure." There's a squeaky suction noise as she works at pulling the thick ice cream through the straw. "What are your numbers?"

"My what?"

"Numbers. Body count. Like how many guys."

I glance at her, aghast.

"Oh," she says. "Is that one of the things people don't ask now? I'd tell *you*."

"I one hundred percent don't need to know."

Another half mile of silence.

"This isn't a diss," she continues, "but I can't tell if your generation is overall uptight, or if it's because you were raised by an old lady."

I give a sharp sigh. "Some from column A, some from column B. Can we talk about, like, *anything* but this?"

"Fine, yes. Sorry. Jeez." She fiddles with her straw. "I'm just curious to know if you have a plan about him. Klaus."

"No."

"You probably should. Because of... y'know. Maybe go to that race next week in Texas?"

"Not gonna happen, thanks."

What was I thinking, suggesting a hiking excursion that's a nearly five-hour round trip away? I'm losing a day of writing, and my goal was to hit fifty thousand words this week. As I'm doing mental calculations of adjusted daily word count and thinking about emails I've sent to some expert consultants in the US criminal justice system, Sherri pipes up again.

"You've never mentioned if you love him. It'll be my last question if you're firm on avoiding the subject, but I'm curious."

I watch the scenery roll past, waiting to reply as I battle a tightness in my throat that would make the words come out as a pathetic croak.

COMING IN HOT

"Yeah, I did love him."

She takes another sip. "Then part of you still does."

"It doesn't work like that," I retort, rolling my eyes at her "wisdom," which I can't help finding smug and simplistic. "This isn't a sappy old movie. He lied to me, and—"

"But to *protect you*, right? Not to cover his own ass, like *malignant* liars do. Don't you think it was sort of sweet and...I don't know, heroic? Manly?"

"Good lord, Sherri. 'Manly'? *Hell no.* Sorry to drag you kicking and screaming into the twenty-first century, but life isn't a Brontë sisters novel, where men get a free pass to be haunted jerks who treat women like helpless pets who need to be 'protected,' and sent off to the seaside to recover if they get the vapors."

"Okay," she mutters, defensive. "Shit almighty."

"Klaus lied to me, his 'protection' was condescending, and...he's probably not even over his sainted wife. We can't be partners if he doesn't see me as an equal. End of story."

I immediately feel bad for unloading on her, because the word "partners" reminds me of how clueless Sherri still is, and how she's trying her best. The first few times she heard people referring to their partners, she discreetly asked Minnie, "Are way more people gay now?" because in her day, that designation was only used in same-sex couples.

I let out a slow breath, struggling for patience. "I'm sorry I sound mad. It's...it's not you. I'm sensitive about this, and I took it out on you, which isn't fair."

I'm not sure if she's sulking when there's no reply for a solid three minutes, just the intermittent gurgle of a straw trying to suck up milkshake.

262 **JOSIE JUNIPER**

"I understand," she finally says quietly. She puts the lid back on her empty cup and drops it into the bag between us. "And I'm sorry if I'm being nosy or pushy or whatever. I just panic about all the lost time. I guess I'm trying to have the conversations I always imagined I'd have with you as a teenager. But obviously you're an amazing adult woman now with a whole history. I know you don't need me."

If she'd said that last bit in a self-pitying tone, I could be annoyed...but she doesn't. Her calm resignation is neutral.

I mash down the fast-food bag and take her hand, giving it a squeeze. It's the first time I've touched her voluntarily, rather than in submission to a Sherri-initiated hug. I don't say it, but in my head the response hovers:

I actually think I do *need you.*

<hr/>

The last race was Suzuka, and Circuit of the Americas in Texas is fifteen hours earlier—a rough time zone adjustment, even though the events are two weeks apart. A few days after the trip to Mammoth Caves with Sherri, I concede to inevitability (and necessity) and text Klaus.

> Any chance you can stop by here and talk with me
> before you fly to Mexico City? I know it's out of the way.
> But there are some things that will work better to discuss
> in person.

For a full ninety minutes there's no reply, and I get wounded that he's ignoring me. A lag before a return text never bothered

COMING IN HOT

me before; I always figured he was in a meeting. But since I took my sweet time replying to his texts in the days after leaving Hungary—and kept my responses under four words—I'm assuming this is payback.

While I'm poring over data about illnesses, injuries, and deaths in the prison where Sherri served her time, my phone buzzes on the little seafoam-green antique desk.

> **Klaus:** Apologies for the delay—I was in a meeting. I've already scheduled the flight. There's a small airport called McCreary just a few miles from you. Does Tuesday work? I'm happy to arrange for a hire car to be there for me if that's your preference, rather than picking me up.
>
> **Me:** It's your call.

His next reply is uncharacteristically terse, I suppose in response to mine.

> **Klaus:** I can make my own way—I have the address. Late afternoon.

For the next five days I'm a nervous wreck. My writing focus is garbage, so I let myself just do research and some editing. I go for brisk walks with Auntie Min every morning, help her with volunteering—assembling sack lunches for her church to pick up and take to the shelter—and work on my bedroom, making it feel more like my own space. In the evenings, Minnie and I cook or bake, then watch movies. She's also teaching me to crochet, which is surprisingly relaxing, despite how slow and clumsy I am at it.

Sherri comes over every other day to work on her class assignments for a few hours, sitting with her laptop in the wing chair in the corner of my room. We're getting comfortable enough with each other that we can be in the same space silently. At first I was irritated to have her nearby distracting me from full concentration. But it's nice now. If I have a question, she's here to clarify, tell me a new story, or provide a quote or detail.

We may never really feel like mother and daughter, but we're cultivating something of a friendship. Kind of like…cousins? Not the shared context of people who grew up in the same house, but a sense of family connection, and the ability to be natural—even a little cranky sometimes—with each other.

The evening before Klaus is going to arrive, Sherri asks me, "Can I meet him?"

"No!"

She holds her hands up in surrender. "All right, all right. Don't rip my head off. I just…y'know, he's a big deal in your life."

"*Was* a big deal."

"*Is*, Natty. There's no denying it at this point, considering."

She returns to typing out an essay she's writing about whether there's a "fourth wave" in feminism, or if it's a continuation of the "third wave." I recommended the topic for her midterm essay. She's catching up, culturally. It's not like she did her time in a Siberian snow cave with zero access to the larger world, but she still has plenty to learn about sexual harassment, rape culture, and body shaming.

"I need to do this alone," I tell her, doing my best to keep my

COMING IN HOT

265

tone light. "Auntie Min isn't even going to be here. She has choir practice."

There's a pause that feels very deliberate, and when I look up from my keyboard, Sherri is smirking at me.

"*Well well well*," she stage whispers. "I don't suppose you arranged for this summit to happen when the house is empty...on purpose? A little privacy for a 'happy reunion'?"

"*No.* I didn't have any control over the timing. The race was Sunday, then Mondays are always crammed with team meetings and such, and on Thursday he's back in the game with press meetings for the next GP. He doesn't have a huge window."

Sherri grins. "Does he have a huge *anything else*?"

I feign shock for a second, then grab the plush squeaky hedgehog sitting on my desk and chuck it at her. I point at her laptop. "Quit teasing me and get to work."

"That's what she said!" she crows, dissolving into giggles. She return lobs the hedgehog and it bounces off the side of my head.

I pick it up, growling to mask my amusement. "Good lord— you're relentless. Are you going to keep this up all night?"

She clamps a hand briefly over her mouth, stifling her laughter. "Okay, I don't even have to say it with *that* one. You're pretty much gift-wrapping these for me."

23

KENTUCKY

THE NEXT DAY

NATALIA

I'm typing at lightning speed, trying to get to a good stopping place, when I hear a motorcycle coming up the road. My hands freeze and my eyes go wide.

I jump up and peek around the window's edge. Into the driveway swoops a black BMW motorcycle, its rider unmistakable.

"Oh, *of course* you did," I murmur under my breath. I wish the sight of those long, black-denim-clad legs as he dismounts didn't set my heart racing, but...yeah. *Dammit.*

He removes a silver helmet and combs his hands through his hair. Setting the helmet on the bike seat, he glances up at the sky as if to check for the threat of rain, then unzips the leather jacket he's wearing. It's that vintage "café racer" style—form-fitting, standing collar, red stripes down the arms—and my knees practically go weak. He shrugs it off and drapes it beside the helmet, then unbuttons and rolls up the sleeves of his white dress shirt as he strides up the walkway. I duck, afraid to be caught gawking.

I assess my outfit as I scurry into the hallway, second-guessing my decision not to dress up. I'm in gray yoga pants and one of Auntie Min's handmade granny-square sweaters. My hair is a careless bun, and I have only a nod to makeup—just enough to look alert for the Zoom call I did earlier with a therapist specializing in post-incarceration patients, with whom I'm consulting on a chapter of the book.

The doorbell chimes, and when I open the door, Klaus is so picturesquely framed by the low, late-afternoon sun that it's like a magical aura. *Annoying.* How is he always effortlessly delicious? My body strains to fly into his embrace like scrap metal hurtling toward an electromagnet in a junkyard.

I plant one hand on my hip and the other against the door frame in a pose of alleged ease, but it's really to hide how I'm shaking. "Hey. Thanks for coming over."

I'm trying for a cool, unruffled vibe, but I don't know if it's working. As wildly as my pulse beats in my throat, I wonder if he can hear it as a flutter in my voice.

He opens his arms. "May I?"

Oh God...

"Um. Okay, yep." Next thing I know, I'm pressed against the wall of his chest.

He smells like heaven, and I can hear through his sternum that his pulse is as fast as mine. I squeeze my eyes shut. My hands open from their reluctant-fist position to lie flat against his lower back, and the simple warmth of him almost destroys me.

"*Hi,*" I manage in a breathy voice.

"Hello." He lightly kisses the top of my head.

Pulling away, I step back and twist my hands together like a shy child. I finally remember myself and wave him in, darting past to close the door, then leading him to the living room.

He looks around before sitting on the sofa, and I perceive the house through his eyes. It's clean and cozy, but very much a time warp from the eighties: knickknacks, crocheted doilies and blankets, wall art that suddenly looks to me like budget motel décor, when an hour ago it was just the familiar framed landscapes I've seen since childhood. I stifle the stupid urge to apologize for everything.

"Do you want anything?" I ask. Instantly I blush, thinking of a dozen cheeky answers, and quickly add, "Like water? Coffee or tea?"

"I'm fine, Talia." With a soft smile, he gestures at the overstuffed chair perpendicular to the sofa, prompting me to sit with him. "It's more than enough just to see you. It's been too long."

"Two and a half months," I supply, purely for something to say. The tenderness in his expression is breaking my heart all over again, and his eyes are so dark I feel like I'm drowning if I look for too long.

He smooths a hand over his face with a helpless chuckle. "Forgive me for saying so, but nothing has made me this happy in all that time. Not even Cosmin's wins at Spa and Monza. You're...a treasured sight." His smile fades, and a wrinkle of sorrow creases between his eyebrows before he looks away.

I give a comically self-deprecating glance at myself, wanting to make a joke about looking like crap, then remembering how much I've nagged Sherri about avoiding appearance-based comments.

"Thank you," I say instead. "You, uh...you're looking really well yourself."

"Tired. But I appreciate the compliment." He leans back. "There's so much on which to catch up. How is the book going? And life with the family?"

"Good and good." I chew at my lower lip. "I didn't ask you here to chitchat, though."

I can't say it. I can't say it. Maybe I should've waited until next spring to see him, so it would be obvious. But that'd be bad, right?

My hands tangle in my lap. "Sooooo...I'm pregnant." I examine a chip in my peach nail polish as I listen for a reaction. Klaus has gone absolutely still. What will I see if I dare to look up?

"Oh, Talia." There's a brokenness in his voice, and it startles me into eye contact. He takes a deep breath as if struggling to master his emotions. "How far along?"

"Uh, two and a half months. You know, Budapest. The night we broke up."

"How did this happen?" He rubs his face slowly with a long sigh.

I shoot a flat look at him. "I'm gonna assume that's a rhetorical question. *The usual way*, obviously. I went to a drugstore the next day, but they were out of the morning-after pill. And I was very busy with work."

Admit it, at least to yourself, I think. *You were heartbroken, and a tiny part of you was somewhere between uncertain and...hopeful. Dying for a reason to quit that job and come home.*

"I figured I'd deal with it back in London the next day." I focus on the ceramic flowers on the coffee table, avoiding his eyes. "But I got waylaid with an unexpected assignment, and then it'd gotten

270 **JOSIE JUNIPER**

to be too long for a pill to work, so I threw caution to the wind." I force myself to look up without seeming apologetic. "And this is what the wind blew back at me."

"At *us*." His voice is so quiet.

I sit up, spine straight, defensive and alert as a meerkat. "We were *both* careless, and often, if that's what you're getting at. And to be clear: I'm not telling you about this because I expect anything."

He studies me. "Expected or not, you'll have everything you need or want. Surely you can't think I'd do less? Talia, please... come here."

Stretching to ask for my hand, he coaxes me to my feet and scoots to make room on the sofa. His fingers shift to lace more closely with mine, but I slip out of his grasp, perching sideways, drawing my legs up and hugging my knees. "This conversation isn't an overture to get back together," I say crisply. "I'm staying in Kentucky."

A combination of confusion and...is it *grief*?...darkens his expression. "Alexander Laskaris told me you're returning to London next season."

"I said I might be open to the possibility. But I've decided I'm staying here with my family." It sounds strange, saying it aloud for the first time: *Family*. "I can tutor once I'm done with the book. Everything's remote nowadays, so I'm not limited to local students. And ninety bucks an hour is good money."

"Yes..." His tone is uncertain, and I'm not sure why.

"I have good support here," I forge on, a little defensively. "Free childcare if I need it. This is a nice place to grow up. There's—" I break off and point at one wall as if he can see the end of town. "There's a farmhouse I've loved since I was a kid, and it's for sale.

COMING IN HOT

271

Needs a lot of remodeling, but...good bones, lots of promise. And I like a challenge. A fixer-upper."

His eyes close for a beat. I know what he must be thinking: *Our relationship was a challenge, a "fixer-upper" with lots of promise.* I'm half hoping he'll say it.

Why? I ask myself. *So you can disagree? Or so he can change your mind?*

His expression when his eyes open is something I've never seen. I thought I knew all the "faces of Klaus Franke," which are as deliberate as his clothing, wristwatches, and cuff links: the serious concentration of his team principal mask, the coy "smize" of his flirting, his stony "The matter is settled and we'll say no more about it" face, the mocking amusement with his left eyebrow up and one corner of his lips quirked.

But something is different now; his armor is gone. Emotions dance across the stage of his beauty. I spot longing and tenderness, paired with bewilderment and fear. I know him well enough to recognize how he's trying to camouflage it all, like someone dashing around to secure a loose tarp in storm winds.

He gives up and cradles his face again with both hands before sliding them off. "Everything I want to say right now is a risk. I don't know what I'm allowed to feel."

"*Allowed?* What are you even talking about?"

His look is bleak, his words measured. "I'm afraid of creating more distance between us through my ignorance if I say something unwise or unwelcome."

Like Sherri and Jason, he's so cautious, searching for a way in. It's messing with my Nice Girl self-image. I've always been the person to put others at ease—the peacemaker, the self-sacrificer, reflexively accommodating. Whatever made others happy was what I convinced myself *I* wanted too. In my attempt to create boundaries, I'm digging a fire line around my life, but using new tools so sharp that I sometimes cut myself in the process.

I stare again into my lap, picking at the chipped nail polish. "Speak your truth," I invite with a sigh, remembering when he asked the same of me that night in Santorini. "I'll do the same."

He's silent for a minute. "I...I read 'The Wife of Bath's Tale.'"

Surprised, I meet his gaze, but it's frustratingly neutral. "What did you think?"

"I got the message in less than a year and a day, unlike the fool in the story."

"Tell me."

His smile is a little chilly. "Said the queen to the disgraced knight."

We study each other, and he looks away first.

"The knight learned," he says soberly, "that what women want is *sovereignty*—power over their own lives and decisions. I robbed you of that when I didn't trust you to protect *yourself* and instead made choices for you, based on what I thought was best."

My throat is tight; for a moment all I can do is offer a thumbs-up. "You got the message loud and clear," I manage, little more than a whisper.

"My patronizing actions were misguided, though inspired by a love I was far too clumsy at expressing. But...my deception was inexcusable. After long consideration, I see why this was a killing blow to your feelings for me. Nonnegotiable and irreparable."

Why does a part of me *not* want him to be phrasing it quite that strongly? Hormones must be messing with my head.

COMING IN HOT

"Thank you for accepting that," I say, not sure if I mean it.

"A painful lesson, but critical." He takes my hands in both of his, which are so comparatively warm that it highlights how cold mine are. "If I may ask: Did you feel you had 'sovereignty' in this...unexpected development? I hope you're not sidelining your journalism career due to a perceived lack of options."

Aside from the fact that he's touching me, he's gone "business-like," and I know it's a defense mechanism. Suddenly I wish I could take back my *Thank you for accepting that*, words I scattered between us because I thought they'd make me sound strong, brave, equipped for what's ahead.

I could have said, *Not irreparable...*

I could have said, *A stunning blow, not a killing one...*

But I'm too afraid.

I watch our joined hands, remembering the feeling of his arms around me while we slept. The rightness of it. Memories bleed through the cracks in my heart, and for a long minute, I can't manage a word—I'm waiting for him to somehow hear what I can't say.

I was so angry in Budapest when I found out he'd made a choice for me. How can I possibly be wishing he would right now?

What would be weaker? Forgiving him and trying again, or letting this go?

When I realize he's not going to save me from my own uncertainty—I told him not to rescue me, after all—I collect the pieces of myself and force a confident expression, even while the sorrow is killing me.

"I did have options," I state firmly. "Plenty of women *don't* have as much freedom, and I recognize how lucky I am. There were

274 **JOSIE JUNIPER**

many things I could've chosen to do, and I considered several of them. I didn't take this path because the others were wrong."

His thumbs move back and forth over my knuckles, and I feel it all the way up my arms. "I respect that. Still, if you wish to live in London and work at *ARJ*, but you've stricken that from your list due to a lack of support, you have that support in me. Whatever resources you need, should you prefer to return to work at the magazine next season, I will make it happen. A bigger flat. Three bedrooms—one for a nanny. I will pay for it all."

My eyebrows go up. "I get that you're trying to be nice. But offering to pay for everything is presumptuous."

I've seen a lot of unfamiliar vulnerability in Klaus tonight, but the expression that overtakes him now is startling. He's like Scrooge glimpsing his grave, terrified of a future he feels powerless to avoid.

"I don't mean to sound controlling," he rushes to assure me. "It wasn't my intention. But...you do want me to be involved in the child's life, I hope?"

I sink my head into the cradle of my arms on my bent knees. *This wasn't how I imagined the conversation, dammit.* I've been fretting for a month, my mind rehearsing the possible exchanges, but it was strangely academic, two-dimensional, like a table read. But this—the cold sorrow clinging to me, the awful distance, words spilling out small and frail and inadequate—no, *this* I wasn't prepared for.

"We weren't the best for each other as, uh, whatever we were," I say flatly, still hiding in my folded arms. I lift my head, and Klaus's anxiety is strange and terrible to see. I want so much to reach for him. "But I do trust you'll be an amazing father."

COMING IN HOT 275

He unwinds my arms, pulling my hands to his lips and kissing them. A shiver goes through me, both at the fearful sense of unwelcome power I have in the face of his desperate gratitude and at the very-much-welcome feeling of his touch.

"You've seen a doctor?" he asks. "Are you well?"

"It's...I'm fine. It's called a 'geriatric pregnancy' at thirty-five, which is kind of insulting," I say with a wry look. "Things are great so far, but caution isn't a bad idea. By the halfway point, I'll breathe easier. I'm getting some tests just before the end of the F1 season. Hopefully we'll have lots to celebrate—Emerald might bag second in the constructors' championship."

When he pulls me into an embrace, I stiffen momentarily before melting against him.

He exhales into my hair. "Nothing work related seems to matter right now, I confess. Only *this*."

I wonder how long I can get away with staying in his arms. Is it just a relieved hug, or...are we holding each other? If I looked at him from this close, our lips would be inches apart. It's the thought of my heart betraying me, of making that move to invite a kiss, that prompts me to push him gently away and sit back.

I clear my throat. "Just so we can put the subject to bed," I say, immediately feeling heat rush to my face at the thought of something being *put to bed*, "I don't want a flat in London and a nanny. I'm staying here. When the baby is older—like a traveling-age child—we can arrange visits."

"Perhaps he or she can stay with me during the offseason," he ventures, "and summer break in August?"

"The offseason is right in the middle of the school year."

He rakes his hands through his hair and turns away. Resting

his elbows on his knees, he steeples his hands, and the posture reminds me of prayer. He scowls in thought, then quietly asks, "What if you lived in Santorini full-time...at the cottage?"

My heart trips. I'm afraid to reply, unsure what he's suggesting. "I...uh, I don't—"

"There are enough rooms for everyone," he hurries to add. "Please don't say no until you've thought about it. Elena can help, and...you could write books. Or work part-time with the magazine, freelancing."

When he mentions freelancing, a shimmer of euphoria goes through me. I examine the feeling. I've been so focused on the book project and the family stuff, I've ignored the things I love about my job: the travel, the excitement, hanging out with Phae, seeing everyone around the paddock, chatting with drivers and TPs and engineers.

I thought I was just missing Klaus, but in this moment, I know I've also missed a part of myself these past few months.

As quickly as I light up inside with the temptation of what he's offering, I accept that it wouldn't work. I'd be away on assignments, Klaus would be gone most of the time, and our child would wander a Greek island with the world's grouchiest housekeeper as their chief companion.

My current plan may not be perfect, but it's still the best fit.

"I don't need to think about it," I say, hoping he can't detect the ambivalence in my voice. "It's just not possible. We'll visit when school is out."

He's so clearly crestfallen that I reach to touch his leg, but he doesn't take my hand as I expect—only glances down at my fingers, like I'm an insect that's landed on him.

COMING IN HOT

277

"August in Greece?" I go on with a winning smile. "It'll be *lovely*. And there are the US races—you can come here then and visit."

We're both silent for a long time. Klaus finally drops his hand over mine, but it feels obligatory.

"You'll come to Santorini too?" he asks.

I can't read his tone; I'm not sure if he's implying I'm not invited, or hoping I'll be there. It occurs to me how much will change in our lives in the next few years. At the point when we have a child old enough for transatlantic flights, Klaus and I might both be with other partners. Maybe his girlfriend—*wife?*—won't be comfortable with me at the cottage.

An image jumps into my mind of his hypothetical future partner. She's intense, gorgeous. A French artist. I see her in a black beret, smoking, her flashing eyes narrowed. *That 'orrible American woman expects to come to* my *house?* she rants at Klaus, erupting into a noir-film-dramatic tantrum and throwing things at him.

Her name is something like Celeste or Sabine, and she's amazing in bed . . .

I shake off the image and reply, hoping I don't sound timid. "I mean, yeah, I guess I'd come too? It's a long flight for a kid of any age. And you work so much, even in the offseason. I'd need to be there."

"I wish my damned job weren't so all-consuming," he muses. "I would of course try to take time off and prioritize family. Work remotely whenever possible during visits."

"Team principal of a hundred-twenty-million-dollar racing team isn't exactly a 'work-from-home' gig. Emerald could surpass

Allonby and become number one in a few years. But they'll need a firm hand on the rudder to get them there."

There's a resigned pause before his crisp "Yes."

As I study his grim expression, I realize the one question I never asked him during those months of interviews: *Do you love your job?* I just assumed he did.

I hear Auntie Min's car pull up and leap guiltily to my feet, like a teenager who's "studying" with her crush. Klaus stands as well. As the door opens, we glance at each other, as if there's something we were both waiting to say, but the opportunity is gone.

Minnie comes in with two bags, one from the grocery store and another from a craft store. She sets the latter on the coffee table and extends a hand to shake with Klaus.

"Well, here he is," she states in a tolerant deadpan. "Pleased to meet you."

"You as well."

She looks him up and down. "Tall drink of water." Shifting her focus to me, she gestures at the craft store bag. "Naomi picked up that extra yarn for you so you can finish the baby blanket." She fixes Klaus with a look. "Congratulations. Don't screw it up."

His eyebrows jump. "I'll do my best."

"I'll let you say your goodbyes," she throws over her shoulder, heading for the kitchen. It's a clear dismissal. In the kitchen doorway, she pauses, telling Klaus, "Natty's got a doctor visit in a few weeks. Getting a sonogram. I'm sure you'll want to be here for it." She turns away, flicking the kitchen light on with her elbow, and disappears around the corner.

Klaus gives me a cautious side-eye as we walk toward the front door. "Am I welcome to attend this appointment?"

COMING IN HOT

"Oh. Um, I figured you'd be busy."

We linger in the entryway, watching each other. Minnie bangs pots and pans in the kitchen. It's very telling that she hasn't invited him to stay for supper. That woman will invite *anyone* for a meal, from the drunk guy sitting outside the Quick Stop to the gas company man who reads our meter.

Still, she all but commanded him to attend my doctor visit. Maybe she's as conflicted as I am. I'm about to add something along the lines of *But if you'd like to be there, that's wonderful*, offering an opening, when he speaks up first.

"Yes, quite busy. There's a crucial FIA meeting before São Paulo. Team principals and owners will all be there. We're debating two alternates for the new race location and dealing with the fallout from the one that was pulled." He blows out a weary breath. "I just want to go racing, but we've been dragged into politics."

"You're doing the right thing," I assure him with a half-hearted smile, pulling the front door open.

He looks at me like he's not sure if I mean the grand prix location change or attending the meeting instead of coming to my appointment. I want to say so many things, but it all seems wrong.

I track his eyes moving to the side of my neck. He lifts a hand—slowly enough that I could stop him—and reaches for the chain of the emerald necklace. I wondered if he would notice. My eyes close as his touch connects. He slips a finger beneath the chain but lifts it only an inch out of my sweater before letting it fall. Countless times he's drawn the necklace free of my shirt and positioned it over my heart, but today he doesn't.

He steps back, and I open my eyes. With a small incline like a bow, he says, "Send me a picture of the sonogram, if you're willing. Good night."

He's out the door and across the yard before I can muster a reply. I put a hand over the emerald beneath my sweater. It hits me, with a cold rush of finality, that in asking Klaus to read that *Canterbury Tales* story, I may have taught him his lesson too well.

24

SANTORINI

TWO WEEKS LATER

KLAUS

Between Mexico City and São Paulo, after the meeting in France, I stop for a few days in Santorini. For years after Sofia died, it was difficult to be at the cottage, but I find now I'm at my most relaxed here.

Returning from a walk up to Oia, I pass through the kitchen, setting a cloth bag on the counter. Elena is digging in the refrigerator, and when she turns, she hands me a bottle of Pellegrino.

I try to hand it back. "Thank you—it's not necessary."

"Take it," she grumbles. "You're thirsty. And you've got too much sun again. You're so vain about that head of hair, you won't wear a hat?"

I suppress a smile at her motherly nagging and twist the cap off the bottle. "What would I do without you, eh?"

"Live in squalor with an empty belly." She riffles through the cloth bag, removing a block of cheese wrapped in paper and a bundle of asparagus. She peels back the tape on the cheese paper and opens the package, sniffing it. "Did you get this from that little idiot at the deli? It smells old. Why you don't insist on a fresh round, I'll never know."

"It's fine," I return with amusement. "I had a sample first."

Elena emits an impatient grunt, holding the asparagus to the light, determined to detect some flaw. "Get out of my kitchen and find something to do with yourself."

I offer a small salute and head for my office, checking my watch en route. I have a call scheduled with Phaedra in ten minutes. I sit at the desk and open my laptop, clicking on the meeting link early before leaning back and gazing out the glass doors, across the patio to the glittering blue sea.

Every day since arriving home, I've tried to picture the child here. That little person, eating lunch at an outside table. Running along the garden paths. Napping in the nodding shadows of one of the bedrooms. Being carried to the orange tree and held up to pick one. Playing on the living room rug, pushing a toy car around and under the furniture.

Will it ever happen? So much will change in the years before he or she is old enough to come here. And before then, there will be long months between the North American grands prix around which I could fit in visits to Kentucky.

Would an infant even remember me? Perhaps it's easier if they don't. I'll just be a tall stranger who periodically shows up with gifts. A face on a computer screen, like so many others, trying to hold a baby's attention during a fussy video call.

When Natalia gave me the news, I wanted to fall at her feet like the knight in the tale. Hearing how adamant she was about staying in the US, observing the stiff courtesy it required of her to have me in the same room when she so definitively will never forgive me...I couldn't humiliate myself by asking—once again—for her to reconsider.

My pleas after Budapest had no effect. I told her, when she broke the news of the pregnancy, that I would supply her with every resource for comfort. The most valuable of those resources, I now see, will be my lack of interference in her life.

The child will want for nothing, but I dare not make again the same mistake that spoiled Natalia's love for me—I cannot assert my will over hers.

Phaedra's face pops up in my peripheral vision, and I tap the keyboard to unmute the call. She waves while taking a sip of what looks to be a fruit smoothie, then sets it aside.

"What's shakin', Klausy?"

"I'm well, thank you. How was the trip to Switzerland?"

She shrugs. "Twenty-four hours of sticking my metaphoric tongue down the back of Leon's trousers. I pretended to believe his pharma company is doing important research into various 'lady problems,' as he so quaintly puts it, and he pretended they don't make most of their money off boner pills and lip fillers. Downside: I wanted to take a fuckin' shower after every convo with him. Upside: He went with us instead of Team Easton, and I walked outta his place with twenty mil from our newest sponsor."

"You clearly charmed him."

A bray of laughter escapes Phaedra. "Oh, you know it. He was so enchanted that he said he'd be happy to provide a free appointment for what he called 'the works' at one of their clinics. Said I wouldn't look 'so tired' if I got a little Botox and collagen." She gives a sarcastic eyelash-flutter. "I smiled and curtsied; then me and my troublesome uterus got the fuck outta Dodge."

I chuckle. "Your legendary temper has been mellowed this past year with a dash of your father's diplomacy."

"Right? I was channeling Mo for sure. Otherwise I'da told Leon to go Botox his dick."

I take a drink of my Pellegrino as Phaedra pauses to drink her smoothie.

"What did you think of those new numbers from aero?" I ask. "Noel was optimistic."

"Already chatted with him, yep." She ticks off things on her fingers. "Met with Noel, ironed out that confusion with Anika's and Quinn's departments, talked Charlie off the ledge about the ERS fuckery. After this I should probably get on the horn with Jakob's physio. He thinks Jake might have rotator cuff tendinopathy, for fuck's sake."

"You can cross that off your list. I spoke to them both a few hours ago, with Dr. Bartosz, who recommends against a cortisone shot."

"Okay, cool."

I'm torn on whether to compliment Phaedra for how masterfully she's done this year with the team after her father's death. On one hand, it seems like the type of condescension for which Natalia took me to task. On the other, Edward specifically asked me to step in as a surrogate father figure, and I'm sure the acknowledgment would be valued if she'd heard it from him. I try to find the right phrasing.

"Emerald is flourishing in your capable hands," I say. "Your attention to detail and your intuition are impressive."

COMING IN HOT

She rolls her eyes, dismissive, but I can see her pride bloom under the sunshine of praise. "Yeah, whatever. Thanks. So, you gonna see Nat again before São Paulo?"

I don a cool expression at the sudden change of subject, taking a slow drink of my water, eyes fixed on her.

"Oh, stop it," she says, flipping one hand. "Don't do your icy psych-out look and expect me to cower. I know you too well. We're not going to tiptoe around the fact that *y'all are in the family way*, as my mom would put it. 'KlauTalia' is expecting a mini-KlauTalia, so let's put that shit on the table." She strokes her chin in a parody of contemplation. "Is that a good celebrity couple nickname for you guys? It doesn't exactly roll off the tongue, but neither does 'Nataus.' They both kinda suck."

"You seem to have forgotten, Schatzi, that she and I are not a couple."

"Ooh, '*she* and I.' Can't even say her name? And yeah, not currently. But owing to the existence of the pea in the pod, you'll always have a connection. Could've been something more if you hadn't been such a dumbass with those fake plans you sent her."

A sore spot of shame flares in me, knowing Phaedra knows. "She told you about that?"

"Duh. Best friends tell each other everything. Though I had to wait as long as you did to hear you knocked her up. She held that one close to the vest. But quit brushing off my question: Are you going to Kentucky for the doctor thing on Monday?"

"I wasn't invited. She prefers to—"

"The fuck you weren't," Phaedra cuts in. "Nat said her aunt left the door wide open." She looks down at her phone, thumbs flying over the keyboard. My own buzzes in my pocket. "There

JOSIE JUNIPER

ya go—contact info for Nat's aunt. Why don't you ask *her* if you should show up?"

My nostrils flare. "Talia's reaction made it clear my presence would be unwelcome."

With a flat look of impatience, Phaedra blows her fringe out of her eyes. "Y'know, most guys are such dipshits that it's like their brains are just a support system for a penis, but I've always thought you were smarter."

"We're done with this conversation." I reach for the laptop's keyboard.

"Hold up there, K-Dog," she drawls.

It's enough like hearing Edward—right down to the nickname—that I pause and drop my hand.

"After Mo died," she goes on, "you gave me great advice on how to do my job better when a thousand new things were being thrown at me. You taught me to ignore the noise and see the essential content so I could problem-solve better. As an engineer, I thought I was already a total badass at problem-solving, but you showed me the human mechanics, the skill of dealing with a large team of people who all want different things, many not expressing it in a clear way."

"I'm glad my guidance was helpful," I manage stiffly.

"So I want you to mentally go back to the last conversation with Nat and look at it again. Cut out the noise of all the fear bullshit you were both feeling, and focus on the reality...not the story your anxieties and assumptions were writing." She leans closer to the camera. "Who's driving here?"

"Talia is," I say automatically.

COMING IN HOT

"That's not what I mean. Okay, so you got a crash course on how not to be a patronizing douche-canoe. Huzzah. Believe me, it'll make everyone's life easier, especially yours. I mean, are you going to let your past mistakes dictate what happens next...what happens *forever*?"

I have at the ready a half-dozen retorts to what she's saying, but they all drop away. A taunting view of what's possible stops me in my tracks.

Phaedra sits back, folding her arms. "But don't let *me* tell you what to do—this isn't my life, it's yours. And Nat's and that kid's."

▰▰▰▰

Long shadows are stretched across the garden as I wander toward the statue of Aphrodite. My fingers are loose around the contents of my hand. As I sit on the brick ledge, my gaze falls to the small tributes at the goddess's feet, in various states of age. A flower from a month ago, now brown and flat. A fig that has split and been partially hollowed by wasps. A lemon still so perfect it might as well be made of wax.

I collect the flower and fig and toss them onto the grass, then set down three items: a long pin with a teardrop-shaped plastic pearl head, a one-koruna coin, and the glass mati charm. Minutes ago, I stared at the pin and coin inside my dresser drawer for a long time. Now I place them at the base of the statue quickly, before I can change my mind about letting them go.

I'm not particularly spiritual, so I don't imagine that Sofia sees me. I can see and hear *her* in my mind's eye, and that's enough. Part of me wishes I could put more into this moment, a ritual in which the right words might be a spell to free me. But that wouldn't be accurate. I don't feel trapped. Sofia simply is, and will always be, a part of who I am.

She's now a beloved memory of something that shaped me. So many joys along the path of my youth: my mother's cooking, rowing on Lake Neusiedl, being able to climb a tree with the same speed it took to jump down, hearing a new song on the radio as a teenager and falling in love with it, racing motorbikes, making Sofia blush for the first time, flirting behind her father's back.

I study the pearl-tipped silver pin, which affixed a white calla lily to my lapel on our wedding day, and remember how Sofia's hands shook when she took it off me that night. The way she laughed with joy and covered her face when she came, looking at me with shock and saying, *My friends told me it would take years of practice!* and then shyly asking how long we'd have to wait before doing it again.

And the Czech koruna she found on the street the last day of our honeymoon in Prague. It was crown-side up, and she claimed it was a good luck sign. *See?* she said, displaying it between her fingers. *My grandmother says if you find a coin on the ground on your honeymoon, the denomination tells you how many children you will have.* As she tucked the little silver coin into my pocket, she asked, *Are you disappointed we will only have one?* I pulled her close and kissed her, teasing, *I'm delighted with one, and even* more *delighted you didn't find fifty koruna!*

I turn it over now so the side with the lion is showing, hiding the numeral.

I imagined, before Natalia told me of the pregnancy, that I

COMING IN HOT

wouldn't be able to father children. This likely contributed to my lack of caution.

The first time I took someone to bed, a year or so after Sofia died, I wondered how I might feel if I ever did have a child—whether there would be guilt that this joy found me in Sofia's absence. There is, admittedly, a small pang. But in the mingled warmth and coolness of the statue's shadow, draped half across me, there's also the open happiness Sofia would feel for me if she could know.

Part of me may always grieve for the fact that she never had something she dearly wished for—one of the few things I was unable to give her. But it doesn't pain me in the way I feared it might, because this is a different time and place. *I* am different. Natalia is Natalia. This experience is not fungible. *Apologies to me are inappropriate*, I know Sofia would say. *You have taken nothing away from us. Now go be the father I always knew you could be.*

This child is real and right, and *now*. A sovereign small person who is owed to no one, belongs to no one other than themself, and for a time that may seem too short in retrospect, will gift us with the treasure of raising them.

I'm going to be there for it.

I head back into the cottage, steeling myself for the conversation with Natalia's formidable aunt.

25

KENTUCKY

TWO DAYS LATER

KLAUS

I booked my own flight since the trip wasn't work-related, and with foolish optimism assumed six hours extra would be enough. But my connection from New York to Lexington was delayed, then trouble with my last-minute reservation consumed another hour at the hotel. As I rushed south, staying a safe five miles over the speed limit so as not to risk a ticket, I came upon a traffic snarl after a truck spilled its cargo across the highway. It seems everything is conspiring to make me late.

At the time of Natalia's appointment, I'm still thirty miles north of the birthing center. My only hope is that she will be delayed too, with the doctor running behind. But as I turn into the car park, Natalia is walking out the double doors, heading down the stairs as she gazes at a small square of paper in her hand, a coat slung over her left arm.

COMING IN HOT

My heart tumbles in a tug-of-war, both lifting to see her and falling when I realize the appointment is already over. I swoop into a parking slot and climb out, jogging a half-dozen spaces down, where she's standing beside an older Jeep with wood-paneled sides.

"Talia," I call out, lifting an arm.

She looks like she's seen a ghost when she wheels around, and my spirits drop. The surprise was a bad move—I've blundered again. Her aunt sold me on the idea that it would be "romantic" if I showed up to the clinic unexpectedly, with a winning smile and an armful of roses. In my haste, I've even neglected to get the flowers.

Colossal failure . . .

I pause as I round the car. Her fingers tighten on the door handle, and she slips the square of paper into a pocket of the handbag slung across her body.

"How are you . . . here?" she asks.

I take a few steps nearer. "I wasn't sure whether you wanted me to come to the appointment, but I spoke to your aunt and she suggested I surprise you. Claimed it would be 'like something from a movie.' Flowers, and . . ." I trail off hopelessly and give a general sweeping wave, as if gesturing at the world. "But there were countless delays."

"A *movie*?" Natalia echoes with a wry look. "Maybe Auntie Min and I like different movies. Because I would've preferred a phone call to warn me. But instead?" She shrugs. "Radio silence from you. Which didn't feel too great."

A ruffle of wind musses her hair. She rakes it impatiently out of her face, then folds her arms against the chilly air. I go to her and draw the coat from her arm, holding it open. She pauses only a moment before removing her handbag and slipping into the coat's sleeves. When she turns, I fasten the two center buttons.

"Guess it didn't occur to either of you," she goes on, "that if you just show up and I'm not thrilled to see you, I look like a jerk after you've flown a gazillion miles. No pressure, right?"

"I'm doing this very badly, aren't I?" I rub my face, sighing. "May we talk?"

"We are talking."

"Let's not spar with semantics, Talia. You know what I mean." I glance up at the dark-streaked sky, which threatens rain. "Can we go somewhere? Even sitting in a car is fine."

She scrunches her lips to the side in the peevish thinking way I know so well. I can't help wanting to kiss her every time she does it. She catches me looking at her lips and takes a step back.

"I...Yeah, sure. We should sit in whatever you rented, because Auntie Min's Jeep is forty years old and drafty as a barn."

I offer an elbow. She snakes her arm through it and walks with me to my hire car, a black Audi sedan. I open the passenger door for her, and when she sits and I bend to lift the hem of her long coat, she reaches for it at the same time and our hands collide. She snatches her hand away, then leans to grab the door and pull it shut before I can.

The rain begins just as I take my seat on the driver's side. Natalia watches raindrops blotch the windscreen and twists the strap of the handbag in her lap. I can smell her hair, and the familiar amaretto scent causes a tug of sorrow in my chest, knowing I don't dare to pull her close.

"Are you well?" I ask her. "What did the doctor say?"

COMING IN HOT

"It's a midwife. And she said it looks great so far. Everything's as expected. I won't know more for a few weeks, when I have the tests." She finally turns to look in my eyes, and the wild blue of them takes my breath away. "Do you want to know what the baby is—girl or boy?"

Adrenaline floods me; that simple question has suddenly made things startlingly real. "They could tell?"

She nods, pulling a thin paper photograph from the pocket of her bag and handing it to me. "Not super picturesque yet. Babies look like space aliens at this point."

I'm a little embarrassed at how my hands shake. My heart thuds in my ears and joy melts the sharp edges of my anxiety as I greedily take in the strange-yet-unmistakable curled shape.

I smile, my eyes burning. "Hello, small traveler," I manage, just above a whisper. "I look forward to meeting you."

Natalia thankfully allows a long pause for me to study the sonogram—if she asked me a question now, my reply would be choked and raspy. She delivers a pat to my thigh.

"You can keep that one," she tells me, her voice husky with repressed tears of her own. "They gave me a bunch."

I look down at the square of paper. "Beautiful."

Natalia closes in to look too, leaning on my shoulder. "Isn't she?"

The words catch up to me a beat late, like an echo in close quarters. I look at Natalia, then back at the photo. "A girl?"

Her eyes narrow. "You're not one of those sexist jerks who's all, 'I must have a son! An heir for my kingdom!' are you?"

"She's perfect." Natalia's hand is still on my leg, so I take a chance on twisting in my seat to embrace her. "Thank you," I say into her hair.

294   **JOSIE JUNIPER**

"You, uh...It's...I mean, 'thanks' aren't called for. A person isn't a favor or a gift."

"Very true." I hold her tighter, knowing any second now we will reach the limit on a celebratory hug. "I'm at a loss for how to express my feelings—gratitude is the closest to what I'm experiencing. I've no context for this."

She grabs a fistful of the back of my shirt and presses her forehead against my shoulder hard. Her breath catches, then releases in a stifled whimper.

I disengage to look at her, cupping her cheek in one palm. "Talia...what's—"

Before I complete the question, she kisses me. I'm too shocked to respond for a moment, and she withdraws an inch, eyes troubled, before I pull her close again, plunging one hand into her hair, combing up from the nape of her neck and squeezing a handful of the warm silk.

I'm not sure if this is a last kiss or a first, but either way it *must* be something we both remember, something to last a lifetime. Three months of longing seem to pour out of us, disintegrating the wall between us. Our mouths are hot and demanding, mapping the landscape of each other, exploring every curve. She feeds on me as if famished, and when she pulls back to reconnect and we both close in too quickly, hitting our teeth, we smile against each other, comforted in the recognition of the hunger we share.

Our mouths soften with the reassurance that the kiss isn't over. Here in the insulated hush of the car with rain drumming on the roof, our eager breath saying more than words ever could, we shape this moment so it feels both infinite and outside of time. There's nothing beyond our pleasure in each other. No yesterday,

COMING IN HOT

no tomorrow—only our lips and tongues and roaming hands and the need to be here together, steeped in the beautiful ache of simple need.

When Natalia finally retreats, her cheeks stained and her lips swollen and nude with kisses, she peeks at my eyes and says, "We can't really get into the back seat like we did in Barcelona. Not in a parking lot."

I tuck a lock of her tousled hair behind her left ear. "Would you suggest it, if we had privacy?"

My question isn't spurred by lust, but a need to know if this kiss means the same thing to her as it does to me. I feel like I'm staring at a door, unsure whether it leads to "the lady or the tiger," as in the fairy tale. It's either the portal out, or in.

Painful remorse comes to me as I remember how Natalia once said I felt like a locked door. The night she left me, I'd locked it quite literally. I want to dismantle every barrier that's ever stood between us, tearing apart nails and hinges and mortar and lies and silence.

She sits back, smoothing her hair. "I probably *would* suggest it, so I'm glad we can't. It'd make everything more complicated." She chews at her kiss-abraded lower lip, studying me. "Attraction can't be what holds us together. And—I can't stress this enough—*neither can a baby*. The idea of a baby 'fixing everything' is the basis for millions of unhappy childhoods, and relationships that should've laid down to die with dignity years earlier."

I force myself to breathe out slowly, dropping my gaze. "I don't agree with your estimation of our prospects. But I have to accept that the place where you are, emotionally, is the place *we* are. My hopes don't move the marker."

296　　　JOSIE JUNIPER

She wrings the strap of her bag between nervous fingers. "Auntie Min's best friend Naomi would say it's probably a bad omen that a bunch of delays prevented you from getting here on time. Like...it means this wasn't meant to be."

I give a grim half-smile. "Does this vast and impartial universe care enough to overturn a cargo truck and slow me down so we might receive a message? Bad luck for that driver, having to become the instrument."

Natalia chuckles, shaking her head. "Yeah, I guess not. It's silly, I know."

I take her hand. We hold loosely, needing the connection but wary of being any closer.

"Elena is a big believer in signs as well. Quite superstitious. And while I may not share her exact feeling on the matter, I credit her with helping me to see something recently."

"Yeah?" Natalia's eyes seem to be searching for hope, but I'm not sure if I'm only seeing the reflection of my own.

"We were on the patio and a gull's feather fell on the table in front of me. Elena said, 'A sign of change to come.' I reminded her I don't believe in portents or dispatches from the Great Unknown. She called me 'malakas'—a stupid person—and said, 'It is a lonely man who won't believe in signs. What benefit is it to choose silence?' Considering it, I realized something can be a sign if you take it as such. Whether you think it came from elsewhere, or your own subconscious, the result is the same. So you should listen if it's helpful."

Natalia brushes her thumb back and forth across my knuckles. "What are we 'hearing' today?"

I squeeze her hand. "I suppose we each have to decide if my

tardiness was merely circumstance, or if it feels relevant because in our hearts we know we oughtn't be together." I meet her eyes. "I can only speak for myself. I won't trouble you with continued entreaties, but... if there's any chance you still love me, please allow me to prove I deserve it."

She frowns. "Klaus—"

"I don't need a yes, kleine Hexe. Only the absence of a definitive no."

A mobile phone chimes. Natalia digs in her handbag, naked lower lip trapped between her teeth, and withdraws the mobile. Her eyes go wide; then she gives a wry smile. "If I didn't know better, I'd think my aunt had one of those find-your-teenager apps installed on my phone. But her built-in 'location services' are probably better than any technology."

She shows me the screen.

Auntie Min: Invite him to dinner so we can all meet properly. Jace and Sherri will be here at 7. Pick up vanilla ice cream at the market on your way home.

"Who needs 'the universe' sending subtle messages if they have Minnie Evans giving *un*subtle orders?" she says with a chuckle. "Ever had a Kentucky hot brown casserole?"

<hr/>

I follow her back to her small hometown. After we've exited the main highway and turned onto a long, picturesque two-lane road, I drink in the sights, conscious of how familiar this all is to Natalia. The memory comes back—the two of us in *my* hometown, gazing at the house in which I grew up. Her hand on my leg, our fingers weaving together, the fear and certainty when I told her I loved her. Euphoria flooding me when she spoke those treasured words back.

No, not "loved" her... *love* her. I still do, and the pain of it is like a bit of shrapnel from an old wound. Today, for the first time in months, I have hope. But hope can be a killing thing rather than a comfort.

We drive through a stretch of countryside lined on the right with walnut and willow trees. Opposite is a wide, fenced expanse that seems to have once been a pasture, overgrown with tufted grasses. A blue barn and white farmhouse are across the field.

I hit my brakes hard when Natalia's car slows dramatically in front of me.

As I park behind her on the tilted shoulder, she clambers out of the Jeep and hurries across the road to examine a sign affixed to the weather-beaten fencing. The original sign reads, FOR SALE BY OWNER—6.4 ACRES, BARN, HOUSE 2200 SQ FT. Affixed to a corner is a newer sign: SALE PENDING. COMING SOON: AMAZON DISTRIBU-TION CENTER.

I climb out and go to Natalia. Her expression is anguished.

"Talia," I breathe, scooping my arm around her. "What's the matter? Is this...?" I join her in looking at the barn in the distance.

"That *jerk* of a grandson!" she chokes out. "It's bad enough that he wouldn't give me a shot at the place, but... now they're just going to tear it down!" Her voice cracks and she buries her face against my jacket with a sob.

Holding her, I find myself instinctively murmuring comfort to her in German, words my mother used long ago. Natalia's stifled tears shudder through her, and I hold her tighter, kissing her hair.

Finally she draws back, pulling a handful of tissue from her coat pocket and mopping her face. "I offered Braeden Marshall five thousand over list—the most I could get the bank to agree to. I have some savings, but... I just quit my job, and my advance on the book isn't huge. I tried appealing to his sense of community, sent an email telling him how important this farm is to me. He said *no*. He's never even lived in this town—he's in Chicago."

She pivots to gaze miserably across the field. The wind blows a strand of her hair across her face, and I smooth it away.

"It was wrecking me enough," she continues, bleak, "losing out on the place... but knowing it'll be *gone*? Turned into a parking lot and a damned warehouse?"

I comb her hair behind her ear. "Why didn't you ask me for help?"

She shoots a bitter look up at me. "Good lord, Klaus. Obviously I wasn't going to have you lend me a hundred fifty grand." She jabs a finger at the sign. "The corporate high rollers probably came in with a bid like *two hundred* thousand so no one else had a prayer."

"Is that all?" My tone is disbelief over the modest price, but at the look on Natalia's face, I know how arrogant it sounds. "Forgive me—I'm not making light of things. But that seems very little for so much land."

She scrunches her mouth to one side. "This town's in the middle of nowhere, and the house hasn't been lived in for years. It's probably a disaster inside." Her nostrils twitch with a frustrated sigh. "And it's too late anyway."

I wrap my arm around her shoulders again, and together we stare at the house and barn. "If someone offered double the accepted sale price," I venture, "unless the ink is already dry, I suspect the owner would reconsider."

Natalia stiffens under my arm.

"With a bid of, say, a half million, the matter could be settled," I add.

She takes a step back, assessing me gravely. "I can't ask—"

"You *didn't* ask, kleine Hexe. I offer this as a gift to our child, with no strings attached." I take Natalia's hands, cold in the wind, and squeeze them gently. "If I pondered it for a hundred years, I couldn't conceive of a gift that would mean more than this...a place you love, which has history for you."

Her expression is intense, but unreadable. I drop my eyes, focusing on our enmeshed fingers.

"As you said," I continue quietly, "it may already be too late. But let me try. And know that however things turn out between us...even if we have no romantic future...my esteem for you is immeasurable, and my love for our child—"

...and for you, always...

"—is boundless."

She continues watching me, and the language of her eyes is rich with all the things I suspect she's afraid to say.

"At the very least," I add with a weak laugh, trying to make light of the offer, "let us prevent the blight of a warehouse spoiling this beautiful landscape."

When Natalia pulls her hands from mine, my heart sinks, anticipating rejection. Instead, she hops across the ditch to the fence where the sign hangs. Pushing her coat sleeves up, she grabs

COMING IN HOT

301

the edge of the SALE PENDING sign and pulls. It resists her, and she grits her teeth and leans back. I jump across to join her, adding my own hands to the effort. The sign pops free, revealing a phone number beneath.

Natalia gives me a determined smile. "*Us* sounds better. I'm in for thirty percent of the half mil. Let's do this together."

26

ABU DHABI

THREE WEEKS LATER

NATALIA

Phaedra flails a bare arm out the window of a white SUV, emitting an excited screech that makes nearby people swivel to look. I speed my steps across the walkway, wheeled suitcase purring behind.

"Look at you!" she shrieks. "Holy shitbiscuits, you have a certified bump. Wow! Get in here and— No, wait…what am I thinking?" She launches herself out of the car to wrestle the tow handle of my suitcase away. "You can't be lifting shit, right?"

"Yes, Phae," I say blandly. "I also can't step over a rope or look at any ugly animals. Did you time-travel to the 1800s to learn about pregnancy?" I pull her into a hug, and despite not being a hugger, she just about collapses my lungs. "I do technically need to breathe though…" I add, my voice thin and strangled.

"Sorry!" She disengages and moves to hoist my bag into the back of the car. Slamming it shut, she plants her hands on her hips and surveys me head to toe. "Can I touch?"

COMING IN HOT

"Um. Sure? Not very interesting yet. It just looks like I had too much pasta and garlic bread."

She extends a cautious palm and flattens it over the slight roundness of four months' pregnancy. "Weird. It's hard, not squishy."

"I'm not Santa Claus."

"Very funny. Everything's okay in there?"

"Right as rain. I just got the test results back in an email when we landed." I smack her hand away from my abdomen. "Enough fondling. Let's get outta here and stop tying up the loading lane."

She takes two manic steps toward the passenger door before skidding to a stop and whipping around. "Wait, where the fuck are Sherri and Jason?"

"Stopped in Italy. They'll be here day after tomorrow for the Thursday press conference. Mom has always wanted to see Venice."

Wow. It still feels a little strange to say "Mom," but…sometimes it sneaks in there lately, and I kinda like it.

I hop into the car when Phae holds the door for me. She jogs around and climbs in, quickly swooping into the exit lane traffic. "How'd they get passports this fast?"

"They applied December of last year—Auntie Min told them I lived in London, and they hoped to visit. Neither of them has ever been anywhere other than Kentucky, California, and the points on the map between. This is huge for them."

"Well, I can't wait to meet 'em." She glances at me with apprehension. "It's all good now, family stuff?"

"Maybe '*all* good' is ambitious. But we're getting closer. I'm working hard to *make* us a family, for obvious reasons." I lay a hand briefly on my belly in my houndstooth skirt. "We're gonna do it right this time."

"No plans to become a screwdriver murderer?" Phae teases.

"Too soon!" I deliver a mock-punch to her shoulder.

We fall into comfortable silence as Phae navigates a traffic situation. I sink deeper into my seat, sapped from the exhausting flight and looking forward to a long bath in the room Nefeli booked for me.

She didn't play her usual blasé self and make me wait and wonder when I suggested covering one last grand prix in person but rather jumped at the chance. Alexander was surprisingly gracious about my stepping into his place—next season he'll have the job to himself, so one race is no biggie.

Thinking of it—Alexander in my role next year, both at the grands prix and with *ARJ Buzz*—I can't help feeling a tiny bit bluesy, which in turn makes me scold myself for being selfish and shallow. I remind myself of all the thrilling things that'll happen over this next year instead, but I can't pretend this isn't an unexpected pivot in my life's course, to which I'm still acclimating.

The good news: The book, *Faded Sunlight*, is going amazingly. Like...sometimes-I-get-prickles-on-the-back-of-my-neck-level amazing, when I glimpse what it may become. The research has taken me to unexpected places and *whoa*, if I've ever hoped for a "big and important" topic, this is it. I don't know if it's the Pulitzer Prize winner of my fantasies, but there's little question it'll get people talking.

My publisher said I should expect making the rounds on some talk shows and podcasts. Sherri too. As exposés go, this is a barn burner. The baby will be about a year old at the time of publication, and I'm hoping it won't be too upsetting to leave her with

COMING IN HOT

my aunt during the book tour. I can hardly expect Klaus to drop everything during an F1 season and come to Kentucky for dad duty.

Sherri will be traveling with me, and...there's part of me that worries about Auntie Min going solo, being in her seventies and having a lot of arthritis. Can she keep up, and deal with all the lifting and bending and running around? Jason will be there to help when he's not working, but it isn't ideal.

I take a deep, slow breath and watch the scenery out the window, doing my best not to "borrow trouble," as Auntie Min calls it.

"Ooh, *that* was a major sigh," Phae comments. "Are you, uh... nervous about seeing Klausy?"

"No! Not in the least. We're very friendly. He met my parents that time he was in Kentucky before the São Paulo GP, so everyone's fine with everyone. We'll be good co-parents. Even if we won't be a couple."

"Okaaaaay." Her tone is that maddening half-amused know-it-all one that makes me want to mildly strangle her. "Since you're trapped in the car with me, it's a good time to get it out of you how you're feeling about that whole thing."

I flash a grumpy look at her. "You're awful."

"Ha! I know."

I wonder if Klaus told her about the kiss? I know they're close, but I can't imagine him confessing something so personal. He'd think that terribly awkward. In the past three weeks since our spontaneous (and oh my God, *so incredible*) lip-lock in the car, I can't stop thinking about it. Obviously I wish we could make it work. But there are massively complicating variables.

I'd have to feel confident he's really learned from the blowup in

Hungary. Months of lies and evasions, followed by the painstakingly engineered insult of the USB drive "intel"? It still makes my teeth grit with indignation when I think of it.

I do trust that his remorse is genuine, and I also believe he thought he was "protecting" me, in his incredibly dumb way. But part of me worries—especially with the heightened safety concerns inherent to adding a child to the equation—that he could easily fall back on that sort of crap again in the future.

Phaedra has argued in his favor. She reminded me that when her father was terminally ill and the transition of power within Emerald F1 was in question, Klaus could've pressed Mo for a buyout, taking total control rather than just his 40 percent stake in the team. Instead, he was the first person to accept—more like *embrace*—the idea of Phaedra as team owner.

All the years she's worked as a race engineer in a male-dominated field, taking flak not only on social media but also straight to her face by a few sexist idiots on the team, Klaus has staunchly defended her. He's responsible for Emerald being one of the most diverse teams in the sport.

So. Let's say I take a chance on Klaus Franke 2.0, the absolutely-not-patronizing upgrade version. That brings us to the second problem: How would it work logistically, being a couple? Long-distance romance is miserable. But if I move to Europe, I wouldn't have the consistent, daily support system of Auntie Min and Sherri and Jason.

Even imagining I'm a work-from-home mom, writing books on a Greek island, I've given up the stability of a nice little family unit in Kentucky for life with a grouchy housekeeper who hates me and Klaus traveling for nine months of every year.

Realistically, it wouldn't be much more than the time he'll spend with our daughter visiting Kentucky here and there. It's better to let him go back to being the freewheeling bachelor who used to pick up a new one-night "lady friend" at every grand prix location.

And...maybe someday I'll meet someone who'd be a great stepfather, a man who's home every night—there for Halloween trick-or-treating and parent-teacher conferences.

Rather than giving me optimism for the future, the thought of a relationship with someone else droops over me like a heavy storm cloud. But I have to be realistic.

After Klaus's visit to my hometown was over—once he was gone and I could think clearly, rather than existing in a fog of longing—I gave myself a stern talking-to about our prospects and the insurmountable obstacles.

I blow an impatient raspberry noise. "How I *feel* about Klaus is irrelevant. Am I a little mopey that I won't be jet-setting to the GPs with my bestie next year, flashing my press pass and rubbing elbows with the 'beautiful people'? Sure. Am I always gonna be kind of halfway in love with him? *Ugh, yes.* But I'm—"

"You're being deliberately vague. Dammit, be straight with me, woman!"

"I said I'm still in love with him!" I snap. "Are you trying to rub it in?"

She holds up a hand. "Jesusfuckingjones, don't go ballistic." A minute of tense silence passes. "I can't help noticing your phrasing went from 'kinda halfway in love' to 'I'm still in love with him.' Don't be a dipshit like I was with Cosmin last year." She flashes an impish grin. "As the maid of honor and best man at my wedding next week, you and Klaus will be fully expected to get frisky and make out in a coat closet."

I turn slowly, eyes wide.

"A little casual thing in Gibraltar," Phae goes on. "It's why I lobbied so hard for you to come to the last race. Cos and I are making this shit official. A year's engagement is enough for me to have concluded that Formula Fuckboy is gonna make a great husband."

"Eeeee! Oh my God, Phae...I'm so happy for you guys." I dance my feet giddily in the footwell. "Hey, maybe our kids'll be besties like you and me."

She shoots a raised eyebrow my way. "That's sweet, but hells to the nope. We don't want babies. Cos gets enough happiness from the kids at Vlasia House, and we spend a lot of time there. The Ardelean Foundation his sister runs—and the children's home—have expanded this year. Vlasia House has more than a hundred kids now. Cosmin says he's aiming for World Driver's Champion specifically so they can build a *second* children's home at another location with the sixteen mil he'd get as a bonus."

"That's very cool. And it makes sense that you guys aren't planning on kids." My mind flashes to Klaus. "This sport is so demanding with all the travel and pressure, it's probably not conducive to family life." I chew at my lower lip. "I mean, that's exactly why it's better that Klaus and I aren't going to be a thing."

Phaedra's look is sly. "Don't speak too soon, chickie. There's no telling what's around the corner. Something could happen to challenge those assumptions."

COMING IN HOT

Wednesday morning, I'm hoping to hang out with Phae all day, but before this final race of the year, her duties seem to have compounded exponentially. She's running around to meetings and taking calls right and left.

We finally manage to carve out a free hour together. Over a spread of room-service snacks, I try to make her look at white dresses online that have quick shipping and would work for a wedding, and she throws a very on-brand tantrum.

"If you don't stop insisting on some stupid floofy-ass gown," she growls, "I swear to God, I will show up at my own wedding dressed as a hot dog."

I pull a face. "I wish I could call your bluff, but you'd one hundred percent do it just to spite me."

"Damned straight I would. And Cos does *not* expect me to wear a dress. He knows me better than that."

"I nagged you into a dress for that party in Sochi, and you looked amazing." I clap my hands together in prayer. "Please don't wear a math T-shirt and jeans. For me?"

After more pleading, I get her to agree on a skirt to go with the gauzy white shirt and tuxedo jacket she already owns—she was wearing them when Cosmin proposed—and the rest of our hangout is stress-free...aside from her still teasing me about Klaus.

I ran into him this morning as I went down to the hotel's gym to speed-walk on the treadmill and do some weights. The elevator doors opened and there he was inside. I don't think it was lost on either of us that the last time we were in this exact elevator together, two years ago, we didn't know each other's names and were hustling up to his suite with the unspoken-yet-clear intention of tearing each other's clothes off.

As we made conversation on the descent this morning, the way Klaus leaned on the elevator's railing and studied me provocatively—wearing that damned sexy smirk, eyes dark as sin—must have been intentional, taunting me with the memory of how good we are together. The night we met he had that same pose, and I remember wondering why he wasn't kissing me, since we were alone in the elevator.

Part of me was wondering the same thing again this morning.

🏁🏁🏁

On Thursday, it's time for the pre-race press conference. Sherri and Jason have arrived in Abu Dhabi, looking sun-kissed and as in love as the teenagers they once were. They're staying with me in my suite and have an all-access VIP pass from Emerald, which Klaus arranged. They're watching the press conference live right now in a reception lounge at the Emerald paddock.

I take a spot near a friend, Ian, who writes for *Autosport*, and we chat for a few minutes while six of the top drivers assemble for interviews. Cosmin is one of them, and he and the rest reply to questions, amiably trash-talking each other while joking around and offering tantalizing comments engineered to create speculation through the offseason.

It's critical that fans' eyes stay on the sport even while there are no races, and throwing out teasing hints is the way to do it. Implying behind-the-scenes drama and big upcoming changes—whether

COMING IN HOT

to the driver lineup or the cars themselves—is the best way to ensure that racing fans keep following the news.

Cosmin need only finish in the points—come in at least tenth—on Sunday to give Emerald second place in the constructors' championship, which would be its highest accomplishment to date. So there are plenty of questions about the scenarios that could play out this weekend. His rivalry with current world champion Drew Powell is a big topic, as well as his feelings about losing Jakob Hahn as a teammate and having Sage Sikora at Emerald in Jakob's seat next year.

When the drivers are done, the top four team principals come in and take their spots. Ben from Allonby is typically close-lipped and prickly, saying no more than necessary and having little sense of humor. Coraggio's Bruno is a chatty, jolly old veteran of the sport, head of the team for nearly thirty years now. Team Easton's principal, Conrad, is so warm and soothing that Phae jokes he's the "marry" in everyone's "team principal fuck-marry-kill game."

As for Klaus...oh mercy. He's a gorgeous creature, half a head taller than his peers, one ankle crossed on the opposite knee as he sips from a glass bottle of water and responds to questions in that smooth rumble of his. My face is hot when I look at him, and when it's my turn to ask a question, I wonder if people can hear my voice shake. I really hope I look cool and confident and professional while my parents are watching.

I suspect everyone knows about Klaus and me. The photo in that French F1 gossip rag didn't blow up or anything, but rumors do get around in the press pool.

I don't know what's wrong with me. I didn't feel this nervous

312 JOSIE JUNIPER

even when he was the smug, infuriating smokeshow I'd had a one-nighter with, the guy who insulted me with his stupid bundle of euros. Nor was I this nervous earlier in the season when we were secretly dating behind closed doors. Why am I falling apart *now*, when things should feel settled between us?

We're friends.

Friends who are having a baby next April.

Friends who shared a panty-melting kiss three weeks ago…

As the question-and-answer session winds down, Klaus lifts a hand toward Conrad, who's holding the mic. It's passed to him, and he sits forward, resting his elbows on his knees and saying, "One last thing I'd like to share."

I exchange a look with Ian, who smooths a hand over his bald head and gives a confused shrug. We focus on Klaus, who suddenly has the silent, rapt attention of everyone in the room.

"After this race, I'm stepping down as Emerald team principal," Klaus announces, his voice so light that it doesn't seem to 'fit with the shocking revelation. "Next season, owner Phaedra Morgan will take over the role. I know this seems sudden, but Ms. Morgan and I will be working together during the offseason to ensure a smooth transition. She's a strong leader and the ideal team principal to guide Emerald F1 into a new era of dominance. Thank you."

He hands the mic back to Conrad, but the room explodes with a buzz of conversation. The press pool is a sea of waving hands, clamoring to ask questions.

With an expression of friendly resignation, Klaus retrieves the mic. He scans the crowd, and his eyes fall on me, one of the only people *not* to have a hand raised. I'm too stunned. Lips parted, I stare at him. He gives me a secretive half-smile.

COMING IN HOT

"One question only," he tells the room. "I don't want to spend much time on this—I'd prefer to keep the focus on racing."

He glances at me again; I think he's hoping I'll be the one to ask. But I can't. My brain won't assemble the words. I'm spinning on a wild current of bewildering emotions, like someone going down the rapids in a battered rowboat with no oars.

Finally, Klaus points to a woman from the Formula Fangirls website. She's sitting near the back, and I can't help loving him even more when he calls her by name, bypassing the dozen more prominent journalists in the room whom anyone else would choose first.

She stands. "I don't think I'm alone in wondering about the reason behind your sudden retirement," she says. "The last time a major figure from Emerald bowed out—Edward Morgan—it was under tragic circumstances."

"Thank you, Jamila. I can assure everyone that I'm quite well. I'm retiring to focus exclusively on my upcoming role as a father, next spring. My time in Formula 1 has been rewarding—it's a great honor to have been at Emerald's helm as it's grown. Now I'll have the even greater honor of being there for my daughter as she grows as well. Thank you."

He raises one arm in a wave before passing the mic again to a stunned-looking Conrad. Bruno is laughing heartily and leans across to give Klaus an encouraging slap on the shoulder. Conrad shakes Klaus's hand enthusiastically, and Ben does the same, with a tight smile that shows he's only doing so because it's socially required.

The room falls into chattering chaos again as reporters talk among themselves. A few stand, waving and calling out, trying to sneak in one last question.

"Klaus, Klaus! Who's the child's mother?"

"Have you married, Mr. Franke?"

"Wait—one more question, please!"

He stands and lifts a hand to the crowd, saying a silent good-bye before walking out the side door, followed by the other team principals.

As they exit the dais, I hear Bruno telling Conrad, "We're in for some entertainment next season with Phaedra Morgan as Emerald's TP. She's a tigress."

With his typical diplomacy, Conrad replies, "Yes, quite a colorful manner of expressing herself."

A few chairs down, a woman reporter from a rival magazine says to her neighbor, "Welp, that's it for 'Emerald's most eligible bachelors.' Cosmin Ardelean snapped up last year, and now Klaus Franke is off the market too…"

My hands shake as I collect my things—I can barely get my phone into my bag without dropping it. As I stand, I subtly inspect the belly area of my outfit, but the blazer covers my skirt in a way that camouflages the "bump."

I guess people *don't* know? Nobody's looking at me, aside from Ian, who—to my shock—says, "That wasn't *entirely* unexpected."

I shake my head slightly. "What? How so?"

"Your article in August. There was a bit of hauntedness to Klaus Franke in it, didn't you think? You captured it beautifully. Like…he's this battle-weary general who can't wait for the war to be over." He tips a nod toward where Klaus exited. "Looks like the general has retired."

I struggle to reply, quickly examining the article in my mind, its shape and texture and tone. "Do you really think so?"

COMING IN HOT

315

Ian chuckles. "Don't *you*? You must—you're the one who wrote it." Shouldering his bag, he gives a friendly wink. "See you at lunch, Evans."

I walk out as if in a dream...and keep walking. I can't be here right now.

In the outside pocket of my bag, my phone is buzzing insistently. I take it out and see messages from Phaedra plastered down the screen.

> **Phae:** Don't keep me in suspense. WHAT DID YOU THINK?

> **Phae:** Omfg you have no idea how hard it was not to say anything

> **Phae:** Bitch, open these messages! I'm dyyyyying to talk

> **Phae:** Looks like you're out of excuses not to be in love with him

I shut down my phone and shove it back into my bag, then head for the hotel.

▪▪▪▪▪

I'm trying to keep my expression and body language as neutral as possible, sitting here, because there's nothing that draws creeps faster in a bar than looking like the proverbial "little lost sheep." Some smarmy businessman with a comb-over will invariably conclude that you need an umbrella drink and their sparkling wit, and dammit, I want to be left alone. But I know if I go back to my room, someone will find me.

Phae's words echo:

You're out of excuses not to be in love with him.

Something could happen to challenge those assumptions...

Your phrasing went from "kinda halfway in love" to "I'm still in love with him."

Has life called my bluff? I thought I had iron-clad reasons not to take another chance on Klaus, but they've fallen away one after another. Which means...the resistance I'm still feeling must be something else. It's time to be honest with myself.

My aunt said, *You've got some unresolved stuff, kiddo. It's not an accident that you always lose your heart to unavailable older men...*

It's the last hurdle, a thing that stands between Klaus and me. Growing up, I still had a great mother figure in Auntie Min. But a dad? Somehow it felt like he'd abandoned me *more* than Sherri had, because there was no replacement for him.

My childhood didn't include "healthy male influences." There were men at church, but they were just cordial. I didn't even have any particularly great male teachers.

There's no denying it: Part of me is afraid to install Klaus as a full-time father because I'm worried our daughter will get used to him, *and then he'll leave.*

I thought it was the perfect solution, him being an ocean away most of the time. A good excuse for his lack of involvement. I've pictured it in my head a hundred times, me talking to our daughter, telling her consolingly, "Your father would love to be here for [major life event], but it's just not possible with his job. He'll visit in a few months and bring you a present."

COMING IN HOT 317

Suddenly it hits me with such force, such obviousness, that my hand jerks on the glass and sloshes the contents: Every time I picture a scene of me making comforting excuses for my daughter's absent dad, she looks around seven years old.

My age, when Sherri and Jason left.

The funny thing is, Jason *was* loyal and steadfast...to Sherri. I've learned the whole story while working on the book. He knew I was in good hands with Auntie Min, who'd half raised him too when his own parents were doing a poor job of it. After Sherri went to prison, he could've divorced her. But he moved to the town nearest the prison and made a life there.

He visited four days a week—the maximum allowed. He wrote her a postcard *every...single...day*, most of them handmade. And California is one of four states that allow conjugal visits, and once Sherri was approved for them, they spent their thirty-six hours of "trailer time" together whenever possible.

A few weeks ago, in a discussion about why he didn't come back to Kentucky even to visit me, I angrily asked him, *Didn't you think* one *parent might at least be better than zero?*

His sorrowful half-smile cut into my resentment when he said, *Yes, that's exactly what I thought. Which is why I chose Minnie. One good parent is better than a bad one. And in a lifetime of painful choices, it was the hardest thing I've ever had to do.*

That conversation helped—I've reflected on it a lot. I'm still a little uneasy around him. It's slow going but progressing. He's actually really warm and funny and a big reader, so there's every reason to like him. I guess I just have more work to do in the "relationships with men" department.

Klaus has been collateral damage.

318   **JOSIE JUNIPER**

Where do I go with this revelation about my subconscious fears? And how do I feel about the epic career sacrifice Klaus is making? Can I trust it?

When I first sat down here tonight, I opened my phone and read through the article I published in August, trying to detach myself from it and see it as a reader. And dammit, Ian was right: All the signs of Klaus's discontentment with his job were there. How did I miss it?

Since meeting him, I've been so focused on the things that impacted *me*—like his grief over Sofia—that I missed a lot.

We both got plenty of things wrong.

I'm so confused…

I reach for a bowl of pistachios on the bar and crack one, spinning an empty shell half beside my glass, lost in thought. Then, exactly as it happened two years ago, charcoal gray moves into my periphery, and I smell Neroli Portofino. I close my eyes for a moment, steeling myself for the conversation.

"This is the last place I expected to find you," Klaus says with amusement. "Under the circumstances."

I flick a fingertip at the tall glass in front of me, which is still nearly full of the magenta sludge I'm having trouble getting down. "This time I got the beet juice on purpose. I thought it'd be healthy, but…yeah, it's super gross." I glance at Klaus, admiring, as I did that first night, his charming one-side dimple. "You're free to order a Courvoisier though."

"It's not the same if we can't share it. I don't plan to have *any* drinks until the day you do again, should you choose to."

"Ah. Out of pity?"

"Solidarity."

COMING IN HOT

"Enjoy the flavor of solidarity." I slide my glass toward him.

He takes a sip, and his brow crumples. "That is admittedly vile."

"Right?"

We sit silently for a minute. They're playing French pop music over the lounge's speakers again, and around us there's conversation in several languages: I recognize Italian, Arabic, Russian.

"I'd like to talk about my announcement today," Klaus finally says.

"I'm still processing."

"I assumed as much. I'm not trying to compel you into a decision about our future. I'd like to tell you more about my choice to retire, and what my long-term intentions are."

I wave a vague hand his way. "Have at it."

"Talia." He brushes back the curtain of hair I'm hiding behind as I look down at my steepled hands. His simple touch on my ear sets my heart racing. "Please look at me."

With a sharp sigh, I twist on the barstool. "A 'grand gesture' like that is...You claim you're not railroading me into a decision, but how else am I supposed to see this? You're walking away from a five-million-a-year job."

"Not to sound insufferable, but you know I don't need the money. My stake in Emerald and my wealth from SindeZmos amount to more than I'll ever need, frankly. Half my income goes to charitable giving each year."

I wish I had a good comeback, but the last part ensured I'd look like a jerk for snarking about his wealth. Everyone knows Klaus is generous.

He puts a hand on one side of my knees, very lightly. "I will *never* coerce you. I wouldn't dare try to tell you what's best, because"—he lifts both hands with a boyish look of vulnerability—"I have no clue what that might be. But I'm following my heart." He gently braces my knees between his own. "I'm in love with you, Talia. I have been since before I was sure I *could* love again. And I'll do whatever it takes, for as long as you need, to become worthy of your love in return. If in the end you don't share my feelings, I will accept that. But irrespective of the nature of our relationship, I'll be a good father to our daughter. Nothing else on earth is more important."

Dammit, now I wish we'd had this conversation in my room and not the lounge, because my vision is shimmering with tears, and I don't want to cry in public. Partially it's happiness, because...what person doesn't long for a swoony declaration? But it's also fear. I'm a wobbling Jenga tower before the last piece is pulled, threatening a rain of messy, noisy chaos.

"I want to believe in this—believe in *us*—so much," I confess. "But just wanting it doesn't make it magically work, even if I'm in love with you—"

The inadvertent admission stops me, and my face heats unbearably. Klaus lifts my hands and kisses them. I'm expecting him to latch on to the confession, but he surprises me by letting the words just exist between us.

"I must show you something," he tells me, sliding his hands from mine with reluctance and taking his phone from a pocket. "An email I received this morning."

He looks so serious that I'm expecting the worst. We've been waiting to see if our joint offer for the Marshall farm has been accepted. His thumbs dance across the screen and he sets the phone down, rotating it my way.

> We hereby accept your offer to purchase the property
> located at 41 Poplar Drive for the price of $500,000 USD,
> subject to the terms and conditions outlined in the attached
> purchase agreement.

My head is spinning, and I put a hand over my eyes. The thudding of my heart dulls the music in the lounge.

I peek at Klaus from between two fingers. "Is this real?"

"It is." He stands and gently draws me into his arms.

"Oh my God…we did it!" My face is pressed against his chest—so warm and solid—and my voice is an overwhelmed sob of laughter as I manage to squeak, "Looks like I'm the thirty percent shareholder of my dream house."

Klaus pulls back a few inches to look down at me. "The other seventy percent will be held in trust for our daughter for the next few months, with you as trustee, and legally hers when she's born." He bends to kiss my forehead. "The two of you, together, are the *one hundred* percent shareholders of my heart."

The dark espresso heat of his gaze dissolves the last of my misgiving, and I take a steadying breath. "Seeing that you're retired," I manage in an emotion-raspy whisper, "I don't suppose you've ever wanted to live on a fixer-upper farm in Kentucky?"

His lips near mine. "Nothing could possibly make me happier."

I push up on my toes to meet him, throwing myself into a kiss as inevitable as the fall of that Jenga tower. My hands are on his cheeks, as if I'm afraid he'll disintegrate like a dream. I don't even open my mouth; I'm just so happy to be pressed against him, feeling his arms holding me firm and sure, smelling the spicy and

322   **JOSIE JUNIPER**

familiar scent of his skin, feeling the vibration of his small, helpless groan of happiness.

When we finally part, staring at each other from a foot away, there's a timid throat-clearing noise from nearby. I find Sherri and Jason looking on, awkward and apologetic.

Sherri waggles her fingertips hello. "I wasn't sure if interrupting or eavesdropping was worse," she explains with a wince. "Sorry for the bad timing."

I turn in Klaus's arms and step toward them to hold out both hands. Sherri grabs on right away, but Jason hangs back, staring at my left hand as if unsure what it signifies before gingerly clasping with mine.

"We got the Marshall farm!" I tell them.

Sherri yanks me into a strangling hug, bouncing on the balls of her feet like a kid, then thrusting me out at arm's length, her delighted gaze going from me to Klaus, then over to Jason. She tips her head my way, encouraging him to say something to me.

He smiles, then glances to one side as if too bashful to meet my eyes. "Congratulations. I always remembered how you loved to go and feed apples to the horses when you were little. We'd ride over there on that old Gold Wing of mine. Not sure if you recollect that."

My heart twists, but not in a bad way—more like a clock being wound up so it can move again. "I do," I manage.

Sherri gathers me back into a one-arm hug and pulls me aside. Jason sits on the stool by Klaus's, and they start chatting about the old farmhouse.

Leaning close to my ear, Sherri says, "Klaus is pretty great. We love him already."

COMING IN HOT 323

"You really do?"

"Oh, hell yes. He's a peach—even Minnie's warming up to him. Do you know how much fun it'll be, *all* of us sprucing up that old farm together? Your dad's real handy. There's nothing he can't build or fix." She takes my hands in hers. "Fixing our family is the project he wants most of all, if you'll let him."

I look over at Jason and Klaus talking easily, and the clock of my heart ticks faster.

"You know," Sherri goes on, "if you end up living half in Kentucky and half on that gorgeous Greek island of his...it'd be a pretty amazing life. When I was planning for us all to move to California—picturing a glamorous and happy future for my daughter, full of possibility—it's exactly the kind of thing I was wishing for." Her mouth tips in a bittersweet smile. "It was a long detour, but we made it."

I glance at Klaus and my dad again, now both looking at what appears to be a website with horses on Jason's phone. The last door opens inside me. The old scene in my mind fades away—the one where I'm telling my daughter why her father is gone—and is replaced by a new one.

All of us are in this picture.

Don't miss Sage's story,
coming in Winter 2026

ACKNOWLEDGMENTS

I should probably start by acknowledging all the friends who offered encouragement by saying, "Writing and editing book two will be SO much easier!" You were kind, optimistic, and completely full of shit to have said so, and I adore you for it.

I'm unfathomably grateful to my parents, who have always been readers, thinkers, iconoclasts, and risk-takers. It fueled my imagination growing up and has made my life as an author possible. I love you, Mom and Dad.

To my husband's family, the wonderful people I've been lucky enough to call *my* family for the past thirty years; Linda and Beau and Aunt Taddy: You are all amazing. I can't thank you enough for your love and support. Infinity-plus-one hugs.

To my great friends from my journalism days, back in ye olden times of the 1990s: Bill Redden, DK Holm, Ben Munat, and Jim Redden. Things are pretty different now from when we were all standing over a light table or typing on those beat-up beige Macs, but my experience at *PDXS* still inspired the character of Natalia. Love you guys.

Carman Webb, you are the best-kept secret in angsty women's fiction, and this is your year, babe. Bring on the quiet, masterful suburban despair! Can't wait to see you in print, my stunning friend.

ACKNOWLEDGMENTS

Massive thanks to Elin Corva, rock star romance authoress extraordinaire and dear friend, for encouragement, smart critiques, and Pittsburgh Parking Chairs stickers. You rule!

To Amanda, for forty-four years of mischief and adventures. Here's to forty-four more, bestie. You are the model for every "patient and good-natured friend of an asshole MC" I've written.

For Sean, the swoony MMC of my life, eternal love. (Let's hope neither of us is secretly a mop and a tin can.)

To all the people who have helped midwife this book-baby, and who continue to inspire and support me: my wonderful agent, Melissa Edwards at Stonesong; my brilliantly skilled editor, Leah Hultenschmidt at Forever; my tireless ray-of-sunshine publicist Caroline Green; production editor Mari C. Okuda; interior designer Taylor Navis; production coordinator Xian Lee; devoted and insightful beta readers Heather McPeake, Lisa Larkins, and Kate Cole; and artist Fernanda Suarez, who gave *Coming in Hot* this deliciously sexy cover.

And, of course, my wonderful readers. Thank you all for reviews that melted my heart, excited comments and questions via DM, and for loving Formula 1 as much as I do.

ABOUT THE AUTHOR

Josie Juniper is a Pacific Northwest native who has worked chiefly in mathematics and journalism. She writes romance featuring STEM, sass, spice, smart women, and angsty, wicked-talking men. She lives in Portland, Oregon, with her artist husband and a flock of rescue turkeys. In addition to weird, loud birds, she's a fan of Formula 1 racing, prime numbers, tattoos, rain, crochet, and lost causes.

Find out more at:
josiejuniper.com
Instagram @JosieJuniperAuthor
TikTok @JosieJuniperAuthor